The Lost City of Ithos

John Bierce

To KRP- I can't think of a better revenge than dedicating this book to you.

ISBN: 9798675092659

The Continent of
ITHOS
N
Shattered Isles
Skyreach Range
The Endless Erg
Stoneknife River
Havath Dominion
Havath City
Greywise River
Ylosa River
Zophor
Themesere
Alto Forest
Helkote Ruins
Ctesia
Highvale
Skyhold
Theras Tel
Ras Andis

CHAPTER ONE

Boundary Zone

Hugh of Emblin, sometimes known as Hugh Stormward, was staring off into the distance, across the dunes of the Endless Erg. He wasn't really focusing on anything in particular, just staring.

"Hugh," Kanderon Crux asked. **"Are you listening to me?"**

Hugh glanced up at the crystal-winged sphinx— who dwarfed most barns several times over, who had lived for centuries, who had helped bring down the greatest empire to ever exist, and who could destroy him without more than the slightest effort— and grunted.

Kanderon glared down at him, pursed her lips, and blew. Hugh was sent tumbling backwards into the sand.

"You could have just knocked him down with a paw, you didn't need to cover us all in sand," Talia complained.

Kanderon glared at her too, and the short red-haired girl subsided promptly, though she muttered to herself as she brushed sand off the blue geometric spellform tattoos that covered her body.

The seven of them stood atop a small sand dune in the south of the Endless Erg, a great sea of rolling dunes. To the east, the mighty Skyreach Range loomed overhead. To the west the Endless Erg stretched uninterrupted for hundreds of leagues.

Or at least five of them stood atop the dune. Kanderon stood at the dune's base and still loomed over it, while Hugh just lay in the sand moping.

"Up yeh go," Godrick said, leaning down to haul Hugh to his feet. The massive youth, seven feet if he was an inch, lifted Hugh up as though he were a child.

"Beyond here," Kanderon continued, **"you're on your own. This is the farthest southern extent of Skyhold's territory."**

"This is the farthest extent of *your* territory, you mean," Sabae said. The tall, scarred girl was spinning gusts of wind around her body to get the sand off. "We've already left the extent of the territory Skyhold could hold without you."

Kanderon arched an eyebrow at Sabae, but continued.

"Beyond this is the buffer zone between Skyhold's territory and Lothal's," Kanderon said. **"Try to behave yourselves in Lothal. Relations with Ampioc have been strained enough in recent years, and I really don't have the time to deal with a diplomatic incident if you irritate him. I have more than enough work repairing the damage Bakori did to Skyhold."**

Hugh found his attention drifting again, only to be nudged gently by Godrick's father Artur, who stood on Hugh's other side. The huge battlemage was every inch as tall as Godrick, and weighed even more, most of it muscle.

A gentle nudge from Artur was still almost enough to send Hugh stumbling.

Hugh grimaced, but he focused his attention back on the conversation. Artur and Godrick were from Lothal, so he should be able to go to them for anything he'd missed.

"...mention the increased risks from Lothal's cults at the moment," Kanderon said. **"It's best to stay out of the maneuverings of cults whenever possible. A lesson I think you all learned well enough last summer. I'll never understand why so many other great powers tolerate or encourage them."**

The great sphinx rustled her wings, and the hovering blue crystals chimed against each other musically.

"How many cults are there in Lothal at the moment?" Sabae asked.

"Too many," Artur said. "Ah wouldn't bother keepin' track— they change like clockwork."

Hugh tuned out again and stared back out over the sand, keeping watch for a familiar set of sails he knew were nowhere near here.

Eventually, the conversation wrapped up, and Hugh turned to head back to their own ship with the others.

"Wait a moment, Hugh," Kanderon said.

Hugh stopped, and slowly turned to face Kanderon, who shifted closer to him.

"You," Kanderon said, **"are sulking."**

"I'm not sulking," Hugh replied quietly.

Kanderon raised one massive eyebrow at that and stared at him for a long, uncomfortable pause, broken only by the gentle chiming of her crystalline wings.

"You miss the Radhan girl," Kanderon said.

"Her name is Avah," Hugh said, a little heat creeping into his voice.

Kanderon sighed, making Hugh's clothes and hair flutter.

"Believe it or not, Hugh" Kanderon said, **"I'm not mad at you for sulking, nor even for not paying attention. Irritated, yes, but not angry. I've been dealing with adolescent humans for centuries; this is an utterly normal part of your lives. I even factor it into my education plans for students. The only unpredictable part of it is the precise timing, and it's hardly *that* unpredictable."**

Hugh, if anything, felt even more irritated at that.

Kanderon reached out a great paw, which vanished into the air. She shifted as she rummaged around whatever extraplanar space she had reached into, her front leg disappearing farther and farther into it. Finally, she grunted in satisfaction and pulled out her leg.

Held delicately between two of her enormous claws was a book, which she tossed on the sand in front of Hugh. He immediately recognized it, though it was smaller than it should be.

"Why are you giving me an Index Node?" he asked. "And why is it so small?"

"It's a communications diary— a type of modified Index Node I give out to all Librarians Errant," Kanderon said. **"You're not a Librarian Errant just yet, but as you're pacted to me, and are prone to an**

inordinate amount of trouble, I've decided that we need a more convenient way to stay in touch with one another. This node lacks the functionality to search the Index itself, instead only possessing the communication and encryption enchantments. It's quite mana hungry, so make sure you're safe before using it. It will, circumstances allowing, enable me to advise you or even come to your rescue in an emergency."

Hugh slowly picked it up and ran his hand along the spine, feeling his irritation at Kanderon fade away.

"Thank you," he said quietly.

"I'm merely protecting my investment in you," Kanderon said. **"And we *will* be conducting lessons through the book as well, so don't expect this expedition to be a vacation."**

Hugh felt the corner of his mouth twitch a little.

"I didn't exactly expect a search for an enchanted city-killing weapon to be a particularly relaxing vacation, Master," he said.

Hugh could swear he saw a hint of a smile in response on Kanderon's face before she returned to her habitual look of irritation.

She nodded at him, and wings chiming, she launched herself into the sky.

Hugh started trudging back towards the ship, his momentary amusement already forgotten, his thoughts back on the horizon.

When Hugh reached their sandship, *The Ox of Indris,* there was a loud argument coming from the deck. Hugh sighed, then levitated himself up to the deck, lacking both the energy and inclination to climb the ladder.

The lumbering freighter from Theras Tel was nothing like Avah's family ship, *The Moonless Owl*. The *Ox* was a massive, slow, ungainly beast of a ship that had to steer around dunes of any decent size, rather than climbing them. Its sand-runners were splintered and patched, and its sails were even worse.

Hugh landed on the deck to find the ship's first mate

arguing with Alustin.

"That damn book has been fighting with the ship's cat again!" the woman shouted.

"Strapping a pair of knitted cat ears to a two-foot long spider really doesn't make it a cat," Alustin said.

"Precious likes her ears," the woman retorted, "and it's traditional to always call the ship's rat-catcher a cat, whatever it actually is."

"That's absurd," Alustin said.

Before he could continue, the first mate spotted Hugh.

"Stormward!" the woman snapped. "Call your damn book, and keep it at your side!"

Hugh sighed, then pursed his lips and whistled. He heard a clattering from above, then Hugh's spellbook leapt from the drake's nest and flapped its way down to him. The green crystal book didn't need to flap its pages and cover to fly, it had just picked up the habit from the grimoires in Skyhold's Grand Library.

The spellbook settled contentedly in Hugh's arms atop the Index Node. He sighed, plucked the knitted cat ears off the spellbook, and tossed them back to the first mate.

Hugh had no idea how the spellbook had managed to get them on in the first place, nor did he particularly care.

He was glad the first mate wasn't giving him the usual Theran deference and awkward staring, but the yelling wasn't any better. He wished it had never been made public that he'd built the ward that had saved the desert city last summer. Hugh would take being ignored over being yelled at or idolized any day of the week.

He turned and walked off before either of them could say anything else to him, and went down the steps into the hallway with the passenger cabins. He was sure Sabae would get irritated at him for not using proper terminology—everything onboard a ship had some weird nautical name—but Hugh honestly couldn't make himself care at the moment.

Hugh let himself into the cabin he shared with Godrick, crawled into the top bunk, and rolled himself into fetal position facing the wall. Or… bulkhead, maybe?

He hadn't even bothered taking his boots off, not caring that he was getting sand in his bunk.

Talia scowled at Hugh as she watched him trudge belowdecks.

"How much longer do yeh think he'll be sulkin' fer?" Godrick asked.

Talia almost jumped out of her boots, not realizing her oversized friend had snuck up on her.

"Why would I know?" Talia said, trying not to let her voice squeak. "Why are you asking me?"

"You are sort of the expert on Hugh's moods," Sabae said from her other side.

Talia actually did jump at that.

Sabae gave her a mildly surprised look. "You must really be worried about Hugh if you didn't even notice us walk up."

Talia glowered at her.

"I'm more worried about my stomach once we get moving again," she lied. "Anyhow, I thought you two were planning to ogle that pretty deckhand more."

Sabae looked vaguely offended. "We're not ogling him, we're just…"

She looked to Godrick for support.

"We're definitely oglin' 'im," Godrick said. "Especially when he decides he doesn't need a shirt."

"Traitor," Sabae said.

Talia sighed and made her escape as the two started arguing again. It was still weird seeing Sabae expressing romantic interest in others. And she was still vaguely offended that Sabae was turning to Godrick for advice on men rather than to her.

She didn't notice several deckhands very quickly jumping out of her path, or nervously eying her hand resting on one of her sheathed daggers.

Hugh would be fine. It had only been a short while since

Avah had dumped him. He just needed time was all.

She realized, with a start, that she had gone belowdecks without meaning to and was standing in front of Hugh's door. She reached out to knock, then slowly lowered her hand.

Talia scowled, but before she could make up her mind, she felt the ship lurch, and her stomach lurch with it. She quickly dashed for her room, and the chamber pot in it. Not to mention the enchanted glass sphere Hugh had loaned her that absorbed unwanted smells.

Alustin glanced at the hatch that Talia had gone into, then over at Sabae and Godrick making nuisances of themselves.

"Is it just me," he said, "or are they acting more dramatic and ridiculous than usual?"

"It's the stress," Artur said, cutting open a brightly colored fruit with a knife.

"What stress?" Alustin asked. "There's no one attacking us; nothing dangerous going on."

"Exactly," Artur said. "They spent the entirety a' last year caught up in tha' ridiculous business with the Council, not ta mention just survivin' a battle that killed a lot a' fully grown mages. With everything tha's happened ta that lot, ah'm shocked they have'na turned inta shiverin' wrecks already. They're just burnin' off the stress is all."

He took a bite of the fruit. Its insides, in sharp contrast to the outside, were pure white, dotted with pitch-black seeds.

Alustin grimaced. "I was never that bad when I was their age."

Artur swallowed, then chuckled. "Ah was one a' yer teachers, remember? Yeh most certainly were. Stones, yeh're worse than that still."

Alustin glared at the bigger man and sniffed to show what he thought of that.

Artur just smirked and took another bite.

He was still amazed that Artur had decided to join them on the ship— the stone mage almost always took the roads through the Skyreach Range when leaving Skyhold, rather than take a ship across the Endless Erg.

Alustin wouldn't complain about that— they were likely to need all the extra firepower they could get on this trip.

CHAPTER TWO

Lothal

Hugh was lying in his bunk when Sabae barged in.

"This is distressingly familiar," Sabae said. "Haven't I had to haul you out of a ship's cabin due to you sulking before?"

Hugh rolled over to face the wall. "Yeah, and last time you did that pirates attacked."

"We're already out of the boundary zone, so that's not likely this time," Sabae said. "We're almost to Lothal."

"Boundary zone?" Hugh asked, not really caring.

"Were you not listening at all when Kanderon briefed us?" Sabae asked.

Hugh didn't say anything, though he could feel the bunks shift as Sabae clambered up.

"Most of the great powers other than dragons don't bother keeping sharp borders with their neighbors," Sabae said. "They just have a sort of neutral zone between them that both powers stay out of to avoid making their neighbor suspicious. You tend to find more bandits and pirates there."

Hugh just grunted.

Sabae sighed, and Hugh felt her hands wrap around his arm just below his shoulder, followed by a sharp pull.

Before Hugh could be dragged entirely out of his bunk, he envisioned a quick spellform, and rather than fall to the floor, he fell up to the ceiling, then stuck there on his side. Sabae was still holding onto his arm, her feet just shy of touching the floor.

"Could you let go?" Hugh asked. "This is really quite

painful."

"Not until you come down from there," Sabae said.

Hugh sighed, and then Sabae fell upwards, crashing into the ceiling as well.

She still didn't let go.

"Hugh," Sabae said. "Enough."

Hugh closed his eyes and flopped his head against the ceiling.

Sabae muttered something, then Hugh felt her moving around. One of her hands moved to his torso, and then Hugh felt himself being lifted up into the air.

Or down into the air? The fact that up and down were relative to the direction of gravity was a growing linguistic concern for Hugh. Not, to be sure, a problem he had ever considered having.

Hugh opened his eyes to see that Sabae had stood up— or maybe down— on the ceiling, and had hefted him over her shoulder.

Hugh's spellbook shook itself a little, then launched itself off the bed. It fluttered curiously in the air around the two of them.

"Let's go," Sabae said irritably. "You're going to watch our arrival in Lothal if I have to carry you all the way to the deck and hold your eyelids open."

"You will," Hugh said.

Sabae grunted, then staggered off across the ceiling. The spellbook fluttered off after them.

Hugh could feel his mana reservoirs draining quickly, but all three had started off full, so he should be able to keep this up for a while.

Sabae almost dropped him when reaching up to open his door, and smacked his leg against the door-frame as she stepped out.

To Hugh's surprise, she didn't head straight for deck, instead heading for the cabin she shared with Talia.

"Talia," she called, knocking on the door. "We're almost to Lothal. Come up on deck to watch!"

"No thanks," Talia called back, seeming miserable. "I've

already seen Skyhold and Theras Tel from a ship, they were impressive enough for me."

"Lothal's near as impressive as either," Sabae said, "and maybe even more distinctive. Hurry up already."

Hugh heard a groan from inside the room. A long moment later, a miserable, seasick Talia poked her head out of the room.

"This had better be worth it," Talia said, then stopped as she looked straight into Sabae's upside-down face. "What are you doing on the… Hugh?"

Hugh grunted vaguely at Talia in greeting.

"Hugh here," Sabae said, jostling him a little, "was refusing to come out of his room and decided to be difficult when I tried to drag him out."

"Huh," Talia said.

Hugh felt something bump against his leg, and he glanced back to see his spellbook hiding from Talia.

"Well, come on then," Sabae said.

She turned and started striding towards the hatch to the deck.

"Don't think I don't see you, you dumb book," Talia said. "I still haven't forgiven you for dragging me across Skyhold by my hair."

The book fluttered down the hall ahead of them, towards the exit. Hugh noticed the ship's cat poking its head out of an open cabin, eying his spellbook cautiously with its eight eyes.

Sabae seemed like she would cheerfully call any bluff of Hugh's, so Hugh slowly weakened his levitation cantrip before they got to the stairs. Sabae, well-used to Hugh's overpowered levitation cantrips by now, expertly revolved her body in the air, landing gracefully on her feet.

She kept Hugh slung over her shoulder, though.

The Endless Erg halted a half-dozen leagues shy of Lothal, not reaching the sea this close to the Skyreach Range, which loomed just to the east of them. They didn't have to leave the *Ox,* however— some previous ruler of Lothal had carved a massive canal for the sands of the Erg, leading straight to the edge of the city.

The first sign of the city itself came nearly a league out. A single curious stone column jutted from the ground to the side of the canal. It was pentagonal in shape and around the height of a grown man, fashioned of some dark stone.

Hugh thought about reaching out with his crystal affinity sense, but couldn't summon up the energy or the interest.

Not more than a minute later, another pair of columns came into view along the side of the canal.

"Are they guideposts?" Talia asked, still looking queasy.

Artur chuckled.

Soon, the columns began jutting from the sand with such frequency that they resembled a stubby forest. A large number had fallen and were lying in the sand.

"Seriously, who carved all these?" Talia asked. "And why?"

"Hugh, why don't you use your affinity senses to answer her," Alustin said, from his perch on the railing.

Hugh sighed, but reached out with his affinity sense towards the columns.

Then frowned.

"They're… not carved at all," he said. "They're just… big crystals. They're naturally that shape. And they're not connected to anything, just shoved into the sand."

"Columnar basalt," Artur said. "It's what happens when liquid, flowing magma is allowed ta' cool slowly. As the cooling magma solidifies into lava, it contracts inta' these columns. It's the same formation process as any other crystal, just on a larger scale than most. And as fer these particular columns, they were moved here ta' act as a training ground fer Lothal's stone mages."

"Moved here from where?" Talia asked.

"From Lothal," Alustin said, pointing towards the horizon.

Hugh looked, and saw a dark mass coming into view. At first, he couldn't make it out very well, but the *Ox* quickly drew closer to it as it sailed down the sand canal.

Lothal was nowhere near the size of the mountain Skyhold was built into or the colossal volcanic plateau

Theras Tel rested atop— it reached maybe two hundred feet into the air at its highest point. It was, however, even more astonishing than either in its own way.

All Hugh could see of Lothal was a solid wall of columnar basalt. Countless thousands of the pentagonal stone pillars interlocked together, stretching thousands of feet in either direction. Hugh could see the figures of guards and lookouts patrolling atop the wall.

“Smell that?” Sabae said.

“Ah been smellin’ it fer leagues,” Godrick replied.

“Smell what?” Talia asked.

“Tha sea,” Godrick said.

Hugh sniffed, and thought he could smell salt on the wind.

Ahead of them, the sand canal continued through a vast tunnel in the city’s wall. As the *Ox* entered the tunnel, the temperature dropped immediately in the shade. In the light of the tunnel’s glow crystals, Hugh looked up to see that the ceiling was entirely formed of the basalt columns. He swallowed as he stared up at their pentagonal bases, partially convinced that they’d start falling down on the ship at any moment.

In the distance, Hugh could see a light at the end of the tunnel.

“How’s the ship still sailing through the tunnel?” Sabae said.

Alustin pointed to spellforms near the base of the walls. “The tunnel’s enchanted to keep a constant wind flowing through it. If you look at the sand on the other side of the tunnel, you can see it blowing back outward— the wind blows the other direction on that side of the tunnel.”

The tunnel continued for hundreds of feet before the ship sailed back into daylight. Hugh’s apathy had vanished entirely by that point as he gawked at the stones of the tunnel. When another ship sailed by in the other direction, far enough away he had trouble making out the faces of the crew, he realized that Indris Stormbreaker, the colossal dragon queen of Theras Tel, could likely stretch out her wings to their full extent in the tunnel, though maybe not fly down it.

When the *Ox* approached the end of the tunnel, Hugh cast a cantrip that Kanderon had taught him— one intended to shield his eyes from the light of stellar affinity spells. It should work fine to keep the sun from blinding him.

When they exited the great tunnel, the others all winced and covered their eyes, but Hugh gasped.

Lothal was a gargantuan cooled lava flow, entirely composed of basalt columns.

Lothal's wall wasn't a wall at all. The whole city was built out of the columnar basalt. All of the streets, all the buildings— everything was built with the pentagonal columns.

The harbor itself was a great sand pool near the top of the city. From it, the whole city sloped downward like a great trough, walls of basalt columns rising to either side. At the bottom of the trough was a second harbor, this one of water, not sand, where ocean vessels docked at piers built of columnar basalt. Out past the harbor Hugh could see the ocean stretching to the southern horizon.

The trough was by no means an even, gentle slope of descending columnar basalt. Terraces and switchbacking streets of all different sizes interrupted its descent— some not much larger than a staircase landing, other big enough to fit an entire village onto. Houses and businesses all looked like extensions of the immense lava flow, save for the glass windows and colorful signs. Looming above the lower harbor to one side was a great building that Hugh assumed was Ampioc's palace, also constructed entirely of columnar basalt.

Crowds bustled through the switchbacking streets, congregated in markets on the great terraces, and moved up and down massive staircases. It was one of the densest, busiest congregations of humanity Hugh had ever seen, even rivaling the crowds of Theras Tel.

"Welcome," Alustin said, "to Lothal, the worst city in the world to drop a coin."

Everyone except Godrick and Artur gave him an odd look.

"Because the coin will probably roll into one of the cracks

between the columns and get lost?" Alustin said.

They just kept staring at him.

"It was funnier in my head," Alustin said.

"Yeh probably shoulda' waited 'til we actually set foot on the columns," Artur said. "Would have worked better then."

Alustin just sighed.

CHAPTER THREE

An Entire City of Godricks

The first thing Talia noticed when she stepped off the ship onto the stone pier was the size of the crowd. Not their numbers, the actual physical size of the people in the crowd.

"Oh, lovely," she said to Sabae. "It's an entire city of Godricks."

Talia guessed there wasn't a single adult in the crowd less than six feet in height, and most were well above that. A few even looked taller than Artur.

She just rubbed her still miserable stomach and glared at the crowds.

"I can live with that," Sabae said, a faint grin on her face.

Talia rolled her eyes at the other girl.

Godrick himself strode down the gangplank, carrying both his luggage and Talia's. Not that Talia couldn't carry it herself, but Godrick seemed to suffer mental anguish when he wasn't helping someone with a task. It was a struggle to carry anything of your own when Godrick was around.

"Ah need ta' find a new hammer while we're here," Godrick said. "Keep yer eyes open fer' any smiths or enchanters."

"Ah wonder how long this 'un will last," Artur replied, gently pushing Hugh ahead of him. "Anyone want ta' place bets on when he'll lose or destroy it?"

Talia noticed that Hugh actually seemed to be paying attention to the city around him, rather than just being withdrawn into himself. Maybe he was starting to move past Avah dumping him?

She quickly looked away, not wanting to stare. She was only concerned because she didn't like seeing her friend sad, after all.

"We've got a couple of days until our chartered ship is scheduled to leave," Alustin said. "Let's get all our things to our inn, then you can all take some time to explore Lothal."

Sabae had bent down to feel the top of one of the basalt columns that formed the city. "This rock's almost black. Shouldn't it be hot from the sunlight?"

"Lothal's primary enchantments drain the heat from the stone and store it deep underground," Alustin said. "There's a massive cavern there where they use that heat to boil seawater and separate out the salt. They pump the water up into the city using that same heat, and then use the salt as one of the city's main exports and sources of government revenue."

The group's usual method of maneuvering through a crowd involved simply having Godrick lead the way and following in his wake, but now they found themselves moving at a crawl. While Godrick and his father were still tall, even by the absurd standards of Lothal, they were hardly giants here, like they were most places.

Talia kept getting jostled by ridiculously oversized men and women, all loudly arguing, yelling out greetings across the bustling crowd, and gesturing wildly.

And on top of that, they were all speaking in nigh-incomprehensible accents even thicker than Artur's.

At one point, Talia found herself separated completely from the others. She felt a slight hint of panic at that— she wasn't normally claustrophobic, but she felt like she was about to get trampled at any second. On top of that, she kept tripping on the narrow gaps between the tops of the interlocking stone columns.

She got Alustin's joke now, at least. If she dropped a coin, it’d definitely roll straight down one of those gaps.

She didn’t really have any spells that could help, outside of causing mass destruction and carnage. She wildly pushed around through the crowd for a moment, not seeing the others, until something flitted in front of her eyes.

It was a little paper crane.

Talia sighed in relief and followed Alustin’s origami golem out of the crowd, where she found the others all waiting for her on a slightly quieter terrace away from the crowd at the upper harbor.

And, of course, she tripped on one of the cracks between the tops of the columns and went sprawling forwards.

Before she hit the ground, she felt her fall slow, then reverse, and she came back up to her feet again.

“Thanks, Hugh,” she said, blushing a little.

“That’s what I’m here for,” Hugh said absently, turning away.

“We really do fall down a lot, don’t we?” Sabae said.

“Ah think that’s kinda our specialty,” Godrick replied. “But yeh’ll get used to watchin’ yer steps here before long. In some of the neighborhoods towards the edges a’ the city, there’re no cracks in between the columns, which helps. Construction a’ the city over the years loosened a lot of them.”

Talia ignored their conversation and fumed to herself. She hated this city already.

Sabae gratefully dropped her luggage on her bed in the inn room she was sharing with Talia. The inn was most of the way down the city, almost to the lower harbor. Her legs were burning a bit just from walking down all those countless staircases— she couldn’t imagine how much of a hassle it would be carrying a heavy load all the way from the lower to the upper harbor. There weren’t any wagons, either— cargo hauling was all done by porters or mages.

“I’m going to wander down to the lower harbor,” she told Talia. “Want to come with?”

"Nope," Talia said from where she was sprawled on her own bed.

"That was mostly rhetorical," Sabae said. "You've never seen a proper sea before, right?"

"We're about to be on it for weeks," Talia said. "I'm sure my stomach will hate it just as much."

"Come on," Sabae said, grabbing Talia by the hand and hauling her out of bed. "Quit being all grumpy, your stomach should be feeling better in no time. I'm getting enough sulky from Hugh."

"He's not being sulky, he's just—" Talia said.

"He's being sulky," Sabae said. "Nothing wrong with that; he just had his first breakup. It's normal, but it's still a little exhausting. I bet you were like that after your first breakup, too."

Talia gave her a level look.

"Well, maybe not sulky so much as dramatic," Sabae said. "And angry."

Talia kept staring at her.

"Anyhow, just saying, Hugh's being dramatic, yes, not ridiculous," Sabae said.

"We should drag him out with us, too," Talia said.

"I'd planned on it," Sabae responded. "Keeping him busy will help."

Hugh, at least, came willingly without being dragged— at least in part because he knew Sabae really would drag him. He'd already had a couple weeks to sit around and mope, and it had probably been good for him— better than dwelling on the battle atop Skyhold, at least.

Alustin and Artur were waiting for them in the half-full common room of the inn as they descended the stairs— which, of course, were made of columnar basalt. An absurd amount of magic must have gone into the construction of Lothal— there's no way they'd simply carved buildings straight out of the basalt without many of the columns just falling apart.

She frowned at Alustin, but quickly wiped it off her face. Things had been strained between the two of them since their confrontation in his office. Sabae still hadn't decided whether to tell the others that the events of the last year, including Bakori's breakout and the awakening of Jaskolskus, had been engineered as a coup by Kanderon, with Alustin's help.

Sabae had long accustomed herself to the idea that she and her friends would be pawns in the games of the great powers, like Kanderon or her own grandmother. Or, at least, she thought she had. But something rubbed her the entirely wrong way about the callous manner in which she and her friends had been used as bait for the demon Bakori. There had been safeguards, sure, but those had proven woefully insufficient.

"We've got a lost city to talk about," Alustin said cheerfully, waving them over to the table.

"Should you really be talking about that in the open?" Sabae asked.

Alustin shrugged and turned to a nearby patron at another table. "Hey, do you know where the lost city of Imperial Ithos is located?"

The man just stared at him, confused, then his face went blank and he looked away.

"The Exile Splinter's power hasn't faded entirely yet," Alustin said. "It took a year and a half of me testing you and exposing you to knowledge of it before its hold on you was broken."

Artur grimaced. He'd only found out about Imperial Ithos and the Exile Splinter a week ago. Kanderon, the primary creator of the mysterious Exile Splinter, had the ability to shield others from the effects of the weapon that had cast the capital of the Ithonian Empire out from the world of Anastis. Directly shielding Artur from the effects of it had left him with a debilitating headache for several days, however.

Kanderon wasn't the only great power with knowledge of the Exile Splinter, however, or the impending return of Ithos to the universe. Other great powers and nations had that knowledge as well as the ability to shield people from some of the Exile Splinter's effects— most worryingly, the Havath Dominion, the expansionist power from the east of the

Ithonian continent that considered itself the rightful inheritor of the Ithonian Empire's mantle.

Sabae and the others sat around the table with the two older mages.

"So, we have five major potential sites for Ithos we'll be investigating on this trip," Alustin said. "They're all along the southern coast of Ithos, so we'll be sailing east to check all of them out. There are some other minor sites we'll likely be inspecting if we have time as well."

"How will we know if it's the right place?" Sabae asked.

"First," Alustin said, "it's going to be big enough for a large city to fit. Second, it will be an aether desert that is starting to have rapid and unpredictable increases in its aether density. Third, there should be signs of a lateral mana well— unlike many other great cities throughout history, Imperial Ithos was built on a lateral mana well with a rather stunted labyrinth, not a junction well with a full labyrinth. There shouldn't be a labyrinth there when we find it— the entrance to Ithos' labyrinth was dragged out of our world along with the city itself. There are a few other clues as well, largely based on the distance to historical population centers and the like. Imperial Ithos was somewhat remote and inaccessible for a capital, so far as we can tell— it was only built a couple centuries before the fall of the Empire, and it was built that way deliberately so as to be more defensible."

Alustin paused. "Also, if you see an ancient city pop into existence, you're probably in the right place."

"It's definitely either going to be at the last location we check or at none of them, and then turn out to be a location we never even thought of," Talia said. "Or it's in Emblin."

Sabae sighed. "Is that another of your theories derived from all the trashy adventure novels you read? And why would it be in Emblin?"

Alustin butted in before the two of them could start squabbling again. "It's definitely not Emblin, it's been a mana desert since well before Ithonian times. We'd best hope that it's one of the locations we're searching, or at least one of the locations being searched by other Librarian Errant teams. We're not the only ones looking."

"Yeh mentioned Imperial Havath was lookin' as well?" Godrick asked.

Alustin nodded. "And at least a half-dozen other great powers we know of. There's a good chance we're going to be attacked on this trip."

"How good of a chance?" Talia asked.

Alustin and Artur glanced at one another meaningfully.

"I'd be shocked if we don't get attacked, honestly," Alustin finally said.

Artur grimaced again.

Sabae glanced up, spotting movement above. Hugh's crystal spellbook was lurking among the uneven basalt columns making up the ceiling. Even though it didn't have eyes, a face, or any visible way of expressing itself, she was fairly confident it was giving Talia a nervous look. The fact that she'd threatened to destroy it quite messily had probably contributed to that.

Sabae sighed, and turned her attention back to the conversation.

Godrick frowned at the selection in the weapon broker's shop.

"What da yeh think a' this one?" he asked the others, showing them a particularly hefty morningstar.

"It's not a hammer," Hugh said, glancing at it.

"Godrick's fighting style should still work well enough with it, though," Talia said absently, eying a particularly nasty-looking halberd.

Then she paused and looked apologetically back at Hugh. "But the hammer is kind of iconic for him and his father, though."

Godrick sighed, and set the morningstar back on the rack. He wasn't even sure if Talia realized how ridiculous she'd been acting over Hugh since Avah dumped him, or even if she was aware of her painfully obvious crush on him. Hugh definitely hadn't noticed it, that was for sure.

He glanced over at Sabae, who was flirting with the shop clerk. *Badly* flirting. Now that she'd finally convinced herself it was fine to date, she'd been diving in headfirst at every opportunity. It hadn't gone beyond awkward flirting just yet, but…

It was just a matter of time before someone was crying on Godrick's shoulder over all of this.

Or the other way around. Godrick was under no illusions that he was less of an idiot than his friends at times.

Judging from the frequent looks the clerk was giving Godrick, either he would prefer Godrick to be the one flirting with him, or he'd recognized him as Artur's son. Godrick's da was nothing if not well known in Lothal, even considering how seldom he visited the city.

Godrick had to be honest, he got a little tired of just being recognized as the son of Artur Wallbreaker, and not being recognized simply for being himself. He glanced at the morningstar again. Maybe he should get it, just to differentiate himself from his da? He did know how to use one, albeit not as well as he did a hammer.

"What are all these pamphlets?" Hugh asked, idly browsing the pile of them on a nearby table.

"They're for Ampioc's various cults," Godrick said.

"Cults plural?" Hugh said.

"Weren't yeh paying any attention ta Kanderon when she was telling yeh all this? Or ta me the half-dozen times ah've told yeh this?" Godrick asked.

Hugh gave him a sheepish look.

Godrick rolled his eyes at that.

"Ampioc has relatively little interest in the day ta day runnin a' his cults," Godrick said. "He's controlled Lothal fer about thirty years now, and in that time his cults have fractured again and again. There's actually specific theological reasoning fer it, and the biggest debate is to whether there should be eight or nine different Ampioc cults."

"How many are there now?" Hugh asked.

"Nineteen, maybe twenty?" Godrick said.

His parents had moved to Skyhold from Lothal when Godrick was still a small child, and he didn't remember it very well. They'd only returned to visit his mother's parents a couple of times, and they'd both passed on years ago. Godrick certainly didn't feel any strong connection to the city, and his father had mostly bad memories of it. He still kept up on the news from Lothal, though.

"How about this one?" Talia asked, trying and failing to lift a sledgehammer sitting in a tucked-away corner.

Godrick reached over and pulled out the hammer. The enormous pentagonal steel head of the hammer was shaped like a basalt column, so it had clearly been made here in Lothal. Lothalans were obsessed with making sure things fit the city's pentagonal aesthetic. It was unusually heavy, even for its large size, but still well balanced. Godrick reached out with his affinity senses to find that a long steel rod extended down the inside of the ash-wood handle.

"Ah think a plant or tree mage grew this handle up around the tang a' the hammerhead," Godrick said, turning it over in his hands. "No enchantments, but ah reckon this can take a serious beatin'."

"I bet it can dish one out, too," Talia said.

Godrick spent a few more minutes looking over weapons, but he eventually came back to that same hammer. The head that mimicked one of Lothal's countless columns was a bit silly to Godrick's mind— it's not like Lothal needed any more of them— but it was a sturdy, well-built hammer.

He'd prefer something enchanted, but there's no way he could afford an enchanted weapon right now. His da's services as a battlemage were in high demand, but Artur wouldn't casually purchase Godrick one regardless— decent weapons-grade enchantments were absurdly expensive, and Godrick had lost his last couple of hammers. Well, magically detonated his last one, but still.

A long round of bargaining with the clerk later— which, of course, was as loud, ridiculous, and argumentative as any bargaining session in Lothal— Godrick left the shop with his new hammer slung over his shoulder.

"Why are Lothalan coins blank on one side?" Sabae

asked, looking at a Lothalan blank. The coin's non-blank side had a pattern clearly meant to depict the city's columns.

Godrick shrugged. "Ah heard it's cause Lothal used ta' trade rulers so often that the city mint got sick a' cuttin' new molds. Ah'm not sure that's true, though."

"While we're shopping, I want to try and get some more shards of whale bone— I heard that some of Lothal's water mages harvest it from whalefalls on the seabed, or trade for it from sea dwellers. Anyone want to find a bakery after that?" Talia asked. "Besides Hugh, obviously."

"I actually don't know if I'm hungry right now," Hugh said.

Godrick, Talia, and Sabae all stopped as one to stare at Hugh. They'd literally never seen him pass up a chance to go to a bakery.

That pause saved Godrick's life.

He heard a loud clack, then the world went white.

CHAPTER FOUR

Grovebringer

Hugh had forgotten to stop using the glare-shielding cantrip. He'd just absently kept it fixed in his mind's eye for hours now. It said a lot about how his mana reservoirs had grown that he hadn't even noticed the drain. So, when the dagger-thin lightning bolt impacted the wall just past Godrick, he wasn't blinded by the glare like the others.

As the thunder rolled over them, Hugh reached out with his affinity senses to the basalt columns of the terrace-street as he crafted a second spellform in his mind's eye.

Hugh's crystal mana reservoir level dropped sharply as he

severed the links in the crystal pattern of a row of columns in the street, separating them from the rest of the street. He dropped the second spellform immediately, then crafted a levitation cantrip designed specifically for the columns. His crystal mana reservoir began plummeting again as the entire row of columns shot up, forming a barrier between them and the attackers. Hugh quickly formed a third spellform— the pattern linking spellform that was the basis of most crystal magic. He rapidly began fusing the bases of the raised columns to the tops of the still intact columns around them.

The whole process probably took less than a five-count, and as he dropped all the spellforms save for the glare-shield cantrip, he heard a sharp clacking noise, and the flash of another lightning bolt hit the other side of the ten-foot tall wall he'd just raised in the street. It shuddered a little, but held.

Around them, people screamed and shouted in the street, dodging for shelter inside shops.

"What the storms was that?" Sabae said, rubbing her eyes.

"We're under attack by a lightning mage," Hugh said, running over to Godrick, who was lying on the ground groaning. "Godrick needs healing."

"Ah'm fine," Godrick said, sitting up with a groan. "Sore, but ah hardly got singed."

"You were two feet away from a lightning strike carrying a giant steel hammer, how are you not a crisp right now?" Sabae asked. She started checking over Godrick to make sure he was unharmed, ignoring his protests.

There was another sharp clacking sound, then Hugh's improvised wall shuddered from another lightning bolt.

"Sabae, were you watching that lightning bolt with your affinity senses?" Talia asked. "If you can pinpoint its source, I can return fire."

"My lightning affinity sense is more like hearing," Sabae said, "and wherever it's coming from, it's way out of my range."

"What's that noise before each strike?" Hugh asked.

"Galvanic beacon, probably," Sabae said, peering into Godrick's eyes. "Acts as a target for lightning spells. Lets you fire them more accurately and hit from a farther distance."

"So we wait for the next clack against the wall, then Hugh and I jump out from behind the wall and attack," Talia said.

"Me?" Hugh asked.

Talia gave him a level look. "Are you forgetting about your starbolts?"

Hugh paused. "I… uh, yeah, actually."

Talia strode over to one edge of the wall. "Get ready, Hugh."

Hugh did the same on the other side. "Oh, by the way, I'm using the glare-shield cantrip Kanderon taught me to keep the lightning from blinding me. You should do the same."

Talia nodded.

The seconds seemed to stretch on and on as they waited for the next clack. It was probably only a few heartbeats, but it felt like an eternity. When it finally struck, Hugh hurled himself out from behind the wall and looked in the direction he thought the lightning strikes were coming from.

Immediately after the lightning bolt struck the wall, which was already looking battered and cracked, he threw himself back behind it, without firing a single starbolt. Talia, on the other side, did the same, and they exchanged a startled look.

"What is it?" Sabae asked.

Another clack hit the wall, followed by yet another lightning strike.

"The lightning's coming from halfway across the city," Hugh said.

"They've positioned themselves up on top of the edge of the trough near the upper harbor," Talia said.

Godrick groaned and glared at his new hammer. "This really isn't the timeliest purchase ah ever made, is it?"

Artur was watching the ships in the harbor when the attack began.

Well, more glaring at them from where he was sitting on the roof of the inn.

The tide was approaching its highest point at the moment, so ships were moving freely in and out of the harbor. At low tide, the water level would be a solid forty-some feet lower, and the harbor would become a closed bowl, the ships inside hemmed in by walls of basalt pillars.

Artur sighed, and slowly clambered to his feet.

"Ah don't," he said, not looking around, "know why yeh thought ice would be a decent choice ta use against me."

Around him, the stone began to crack and crumble, flowing upwards in streams towards him.

"Consider it a gamble," a voice from behind him said. "People have tried lightning, poison gas, and every other method they could think of to take you down, and it all fails."

"In fairness," Artur said, as his stone armor started to form around him, "that was while ah was already armored. Ah'm as vulnerable as anyone else when caught unarmored and unaware."

"I didn't take you unaware, though, did I?" the voice asked.

Artur turned around, his armor halfway covering him already.

Facing him was a whip-thin man not much older than his son, wielding a blade of ice engraved in spellforms, and covered in armor fashioned of yet more ice. Beneath the armor, he wore a pristine white uniform with glittering bronze accents.

"Yeh didn't want ta," Artur said. "Yeh wanted ta prove yerself against me, and ah imagine yeh specifically ignored orders ta ambush me. Probably even misled the others in yer Hand ta get a chance at me alone."

"You guessed right," the man said, then launched a spray of razor-sharp ice crystals at Artur, whose armor was still incomplete.

Artur raised an eyebrow and the shards of ice halted in midair, before simply falling to the ground.

The Havathi Sacred Swordsman stepped back. "How did you…"

Artur grinned as the stone of his armor began sealing

around his face. "Ice is jus' another type a' stone, son."

The Swordsman took another step back. "Ice isn't a rock, that's absurd. It's frozen water."

Artur shrugged as a half-dozen basalt columns tore themselves loose and rose to hover around him.

"An' rock is jus' frozen magma. But ah don't really think this is the time ta' be concerning yerself with academic debates. Yeh have better things ta worry about."

The six hovering columns, each weighing most of a ton, shot forwards like spears.

In the distance, lightning began to crackle across the city.

"How, exactly," Talia asked, "are we supposed to take down a lightning mage who can hit us from across the whole city?"

She kicked Hugh's impromptu wall with a satisfying thunk, pretending it was the lightning mage's face.

"I'm assuming that's well out of your range?" Sabae asked.

"I'd be really lucky to hit even a quarter of that distance," Talia said. "Hugh?"

There was another click, then the wall shuddered from a lightning strike.

"You want me to build a lightning ward?" Hugh asked.

Talia rolled her eyes. "No, I want you to fire a starbolt. We just talked about this a few seconds ago."

"Oh, right," Hugh said. "I mean, hypothetically it could travel that far, but I can't really aim it effectively, and I don't have enough mana to keep up the containment shell for the starfire the whole way, so it would just detonate above the city somewhere."

Another click, and another lightning bolt. Slivers of rock cracked off the fused pillars and clattered onto the basalt cobbles.

"Actually, maybe yes on the lightning ward?" Godrick said. "Ah'll start reinforcin' and reshapin' the wall a bit, and yeh put the ward out past the wall."

"It'll take longer because of the gaps between the

columns," Hugh said. "I'll need to grow them together along the path of the ward. If I—"

"No," Sabae said.

The others all turned to look at her.

"If the lightning mage is using a galvanic beacon to hit us, how are they getting it all the way here?" Sabae asked.

Talia blinked, then realized what the taller girl was getting at.

"They've got a spotter!" Talia said.

"What?" Hugh asked.

Another click, and another lightning bolt. More shards of stone broke off the wall, and Godrick cursed and began reshaping the stone columns to reinforce them.

"Galvanic beacons are single use enchantments, so the click each time is a galvanic beacon hitting the wall," Sabae said. "It's extraordinarily unlikely that our lightning mage has the ability to fire a galvanic beacon from this distance—it's almost certainly copper or silver, and there's no way anyone short of archmage level could be controlling or firing metal at this distance, and a copper or silver archmage would have annihilated us by now."

"So there's got to be a second mage launching and activating the galvanic beacons," Talia interjected. "And they've got to be much closer. If we can find them and take them down, the lightning mage is useless."

"How are we supposed ta find 'em, exactly?" Godrick asked, not taking his eyes off the wall.

"That seems like it would be up to you boys," Talia said. "Since you've already got a metal affinity, and metal's sort of crystalline, right?"

Hugh sighed. "I mean, sort of, but not exactly, and only a rare few crystal mages can do anything with it. Kanderon and I aren't among them."

Godrick shrugged, still not looking away from the wall. "Ah can't detect copper or silver with mah affinity senses."

"I'll do it," Sabae said. Gusts of wind were flowing towards her as her armor began spinning up around her limbs. "I'll act as bait. My lightning affinity's not useful for much, but I can still block lightning if I need to."

"This is way different than Rhodes' lightning, or what you faced against the pirates," Hugh said, looking nervous.

Sabae shrugged as the wind started to wrap around her torso. "We don't have a lot of other options, do we? You and Talia just need to be ready to hit the spotter hard when he fires the beacon at me."

Talia glanced at Hugh and realized she felt almost as nervous as he looked— risking her own life didn't bother her too much, but having Sabae risk her life for them felt awful. She'd had more than a few nightmares about what might have happened to her friends if she hadn't made it to the top of Skyhold in time on the summer solstice, and there was only so much her dream affinity could do to affect her own dreams.

Talia looked back at Sabae and nodded. "We'll be ready."

Alustin sighed, set his bookmark into place, then tucked the book into his storage tattoo under the guise of putting it into his satchel.

Then he leapt onto the iron-mesh teashop table as an arrow hammered into the chair he'd been sitting in, his arm still in the satchel. His teacup skittered off the edge of the table, shattering on the basalt floor, but the teapot managed to stay on the table.

Alustin pulled his arm out of the satchel, magically withdrawing a dozen books-worth of loose sheets of paper from his tattoo as he did so. He spun, spotting a tree growing out of the ruins of the metal chair he'd been sitting in.

The other patrons sitting on the teashop's balcony, as if woken from a reverie, began shouting and fleeing for the inside of the teashop.

Alustin sighed, then leapt for the next table as an arrow hammered into his, knocking the whole thing over. The arrow immediately sprouted roots and leaves as it began to grow.

He leapt erratically from table to table as the archer bombarded the balcony. By the time he reached the last table, the first sapling had already reached the height of a man.

The sheets of paper spun wildly around him. A couple of the arrows hit the papers, which, while not strong enough to stop the arrows, were enough to deflect them away from Alustin.

The railing was, of course, just a raised row of basalt columns. Without any hesitation, Alustin leapt from the last table to the railing, then hurled himself off the third-story balcony.

Thunder rolled over the city.

The sheets of paper around him swarmed, wrapping around his torso and forming a set of four dragonfly wings behind him. They began moving in a blur, but Alustin was only head-height off the ground when his fall stopped and he shot forwards, dodging another shot from the archer.

Alustin had faced this bow before— Lothal was going to have a small forest to clean up after this. He'd never encountered Grovebringer on this side of the Skyreach Range before, but then, he'd seldom faced Havathi agents west of the mountains, let alone Sacred Swordsmen.

He hugged the ground as he flew, staying behind what little cover he could find, only going up to dodge the few Lothalans who hadn't hid indoors. Your average Lothalan might be huge, but no more of them were mages than in any other city of its aether density— they knew to get out of the way of a mage battle fast.

Lightning crackled over the city again. Alustin considered heading for the source of the bolts— he'd wager all the gold in his tattoo that either Artur or the apprentices were being targeted— but he needed to shake off the wielder of Grovebringer first.

Which wasn't going to be easy, considering that Grovebringer's warlock wielder had also pacted with some sort of item that granted them invisibility. They'd proven to be one of the longest-lived Sacred Swordsmen the Librarians Errant had faced over the years— both organizations had high fatality rates, in no small part thanks to one another. Given enough preparation time, most Librarians Errant were more than a match for the Swordsmen one-on-one, but the

Swordsmen liked throwing ambushes, and almost always outnumbered Librarians in the field.

Well, always outnumbered them in the field.

Alustin summoned even more paper out of his tattoo, took a deep breath, then released himself from the grip of his wings. The wings kept flying forwards, while Alustin plummeted down towards the street below, without losing his forward momentum. He rapidly assembled a new spellform in his mind's eye, and the loose paper trailing behind him shot forwards, linking together to form a series of blanket-sized sheets of paper.

He tore through them one after another, but by the last, he'd slowed down enough to hit the street, roll, and immediately start running. The rough cobble-shapes of the basalt were going to leave bruises, but it was better to have bruises than having a tree growing out of his ribcage.

A rain of brilliantly glowing droplets tore through his wings, still buzzing over the street ahead of him, and Alustin grimaced and withdrew his magic from the paper wings as they caught fire. They collapsed into hundreds of sheets of loose paper, torn and burning.

Several pedestrians still in the street screamed as they were pelted with the glowing droplets, and the smell of burning flesh rose into the air. At least one person dropped to the ground unmoving.

One of the glowing droplets hit the ground just ahead of him, sizzling. He leaned forward to take a closer look, taking care to keep several sheets of paper with wards drawn onto them floating in front of him.

Molten lead.

Before the lead droplet finished cooling, it started rolling away from him, then leapt into the air. Countless other droplets of lead replicated its motion as the Swordsman responsible called the lead back to themselves.

Alustin sent his vision racing forwards with a farsight affinity spell and spotted the wielder. The arrows from Grovebringer had ceased, so they likely thought the rain of molten lead had taken him down. The Swordsmen would realize he was still alive soon enough, but he had a chance to escape through a building or side-street in the meantime.

He did seriously consider it for a moment, but his feet didn't. Within a few heartbeats, he was sprinting at top speed towards the Swordsman pulling on the molten lead.

Alustin pulled his sword from his storage tattoo as he ran. The spellform lines of its enchantment began to glow, and Alustin smiled grimly.

Moments before Sabae was about to windjump, Hugh caught her attention.

"How are we supposed to know where the galvanic beacon is heading towards you from?" Hugh asked.

Sabae paused. "I, uh…"

Hugh fumbled around in his beltpouch, dropping a couple of Lothalan blanks on the ground, one of which promptly rolled into a crack in the street. He pulled out a lumpy, misshapen hunk of quartz and tossed it to Sabae.

"Launch that at whoever's firing the beacons at us, I can track it with my affinity senses, then Talia can use my starbolt to aim. Both of you use the anti-glare cantrip I showed you," Hugh said.

Sabae bounced the hunk of quartz in her hand a couple of times, then nodded at Hugh.

"Hurry up," Godrick said. The wall shuddered, several large cracks forming in it. Godrick quickly began sealing them, but it was clear the wall wouldn't take many more hits.

"Three," Sabae said.

"Wait, are you jumping at one or at go?" Talia asked.

Sabae sighed. "At go."

She shot Hugh a glance, and he looked briefly abashed.

"Three," Sabae said, and spun her wind-armor up even faster.

"Two."

"One."

Sabae swallowed nervously. "Go."

She detonated the swirling winds around her legs, and blasted straight upward into the air. She immediately started spinning her leg armor back up.

Sabae carefully resisted the urge to look towards where the source of the lightning was or down to check the damage to the wall, keeping her eyes focused on the nearby buildings.

There. From the corner of her eye, she caught a glint from a window, and she turned her head to see a crossbow bolt flying straight at her.

She pitched her arm forwards in a perfect throw, detonating the wind armor around the arm just as the lump of quartz was leaving her hand. It shot forwards like an arrow just as the crossbow bolt struck her wind armor dead center over her chest and was thrown to the side.

She *pushed* outward with her lightning affinity as the lightning struck the crossbow bolt just inches away from her, and she found herself blasting towards the ground, away from the lightning.

As she fell, Hugh's starbolt lanced towards the window, almost bright enough to blind her even with the cantrip protecting her eyes. Just before she fell behind the wall, a ball of purple-green dreamfire followed it. Interestingly, with the anti-glare cantrip protecting her eyes, she could see spots of yellow in it that must be drowned out, normally.

Her armor collapsed when she hit the ground, only a heartbeat behind the thunder.

Sabae groaned. She could feel her limbs tingling, like every other time she'd come so close to lightning. She didn't feel any pain, like she had when she'd burnt the scars into her arms, shoulders, and face, but it still wasn't pleasant. The armor had protected her from the crossbow bolt-shaped beacon and the fall, at least.

Godrick rushed over and said something that she didn't quite catch, and Sabae shook her head.

"What?" she asked.

"Are yeh alright?" Godrick repeated.

"I'm fine," Sabae said, sitting up with a groan. "Did we get the spotter?"

"Without a doubt," Talia said, peering around the wall.

"Wow. Starfire and dreamfire interact really explosively."

Godrick helped Sabae to her feet, and she glanced over at Hugh.

"Thanks for that crystal, Hugh," she said. "Don't you use that to fight with sometimes?"

"I used to," Hugh said, who was still looking past the wall. "Pretty sure it got destroyed just now. It was the first crystal I ever fused."

Sabae rubbed her neck awkwardly. "I'm sorry, Hugh, I…"

Hugh turned to look at her and shook his head. "Don't worry about it. It had sentimental value, but my friends have a lot more."

"Ah think we should get moving," Godrick said. "We're out a' the lightnin' mage's range now, but ah'd rather not let 'im track us down again."

"Right," Sabae said, collecting herself. "We should head back towards the inn and try and find Artur or Alustin."

"I think I see Artur fighting down towards the harbor," Talia said.

Sabae glanced to where Talia was looking and spotted a massive stone figure looming over houses near the harbor, swinging a tree-sized hammer. Blasts of ice and yellow-green gas rolled harmlessly off Artur's immense stone armor.

"And ah think ah see Alustin," Godrick said, pointing.

Sabae glanced over and spotted what appeared to be a forest growing in the middle of Lothal that hadn't been there a few minutes ago. A huge flock of origami golems and darting sheets of paper raced through it. Much of the paper was on fire, as were a number of the trees. Burning ropes of what looked like molten metal tore through the air above the forest.

As Sabae tried to make up her mind about which of the older mages the apprentices should head towards, Hugh spoke up.

"I just killed someone," Hugh said. "An actual human being, not, like, an imp or monster."

He stared at them for a second, then bent over and vomited.

CHAPTER FIVE

The Needle of Leagues

Hugh trailed after the others as they sprinted towards the lower harbor. He was barely paying attention to where they were running, and probably would have gotten lost if Talia wasn't dragging him by one hand.

He'd just *killed* someone.

The past couple years Hugh had been training to be a battlemage, and he'd definitely thought about what it would be like to kill someone, but Hugh couldn't even begin to wrap his head around his emotions at the moment. He'd never even seen the spotter he fired the starbolt at, had never looked them in the eyes. They'd been trying to kill him and his friends, but…

Hugh's stomach churned, and he barely kept himself from stumbling and dry-heaving all over the street.

"Panic later, run now!" Talia shouted back at him.

Hugh nodded and forced himself to run faster.

A couple of years ago, he would have been crumpled on the ground gasping if he tried to run this far, but Alustin had been forcing his students to train physically for nearly two years now, which included daily runs.

In the distance, Hugh could see the looming form of Artur's armor. He knew the stone mage could grow it to a far greater size than Godrick could, but right now it had to be at least twice the height that the demon Bakori had been.

Even from here, Hugh could feel the rumbling of Artur's fight against their attackers. The bursts of ice either shattered harmlessly off his armor or were deflected in midair, presumably by Artur's own magic. The green-yellow mist boiled uselessly around Artur— the stone mage had apparently come up with his own solution for poison gas years ago. He'd also come up with some solution for seeing outside of his armor without any sort of faceplate or hole, but he'd never told the apprentices what it was, and if Godrick knew, he wasn't telling.

Not that Hugh would press— he respected Godrick and Artur's secrets.

"That's what ah'm supposed ta' live up ta'," Godrick muttered. "That'll happen."

Hugh glanced over towards the new forest that had sprung up on the western side of the city, where Alustin was battling more of their ambushers. The forest had continued expanding as the apprentices ran for the harbor, growing at unnatural speed. The roots were visibly growing between and splitting apart the stone columns that formed the buildings and terrain of the city. To make things even more absurd, more of the forest was burning at this point. Swarms of paper danced through the urban forest fire, a good number of them on fire as well.

Hugh was definitely happy staying away from either battle. Thankfully, they were heading for the lower harbor instead.

A few strands of Talia's long red hair got in his face from where they'd come loose from her braid, and Hugh shook his head to get them away from him.

How was Talia so relaxed about killing people? She'd killed more than a few in the time he'd known her, and had apparently killed a raider from a different mountain clan when she was just a girl, but Hugh could never imagine himself being as calm about it as she seemed.

And, for that matter, Godrick had helped Talia drop several tons of rock on the valve room in Indris' palace last summer, killing multiple cultists trying to flood the lower levels of the city. He didn't seem that much more shaken up about it than Talia did.

Hugh… didn't think Sabae had ever killed anyone, but he wasn't sure.

Abruptly, his foot caught the edge of a slightly raised columnar cobble in the street, and he pitched forwards, pulling Talia off balance. He reflexively cast a levitation spell and caught them before they hit the ground.

"Sorry," he told Talia as they climbed back to their feet.

Talia grumbled something, then took off, hauling Hugh behind her.

For someone that short, Talia could run surprisingly fast and far. Maybe because she'd grown up at such a high altitude, where the air was far thinner.

Godrick and Sabae had pulled farther ahead of them and were almost down to the lower harbor. Both were fully armored— Godrick in his own smaller version of his father's armor and Sabae in her wind armor that resembled nothing so much as whirlwinds wrapped around her limbs and body.

Sabae probably could have wind-jumped to the harbor in a fraction of the time it had taken for them to run there, but she had decided they all needed to stay together.

By the time Hugh and Talia had reached the harbor, Sabae and Godrick were already catching their breath at the edge of a harbor-side building. The harbor was otherwise deserted, save for a couple ships untying from the stone docks.

"You can let go of my hand now, Talia," Hugh said.

"Oh, uh… right," Talia said, and let go without looking at him.

Hugh leaned against the wall of the building and looked up past the harbor at Ampioc's palace as he caught his breath.

"So we're heading up to Ampioc's palace to find him?" Hugh asked.

Godrick glanced oddly at Hugh. "Why would we go to the palace to find him?"

Hugh had just opened his mouth to respond when lightning struck the docks.

Alustin dodged around the trunk of a brand-new cedar tree as it grew out of the street, leaping over its writhing roots.

It was somewhat ironic that this forest was only minutes old, and it was already having its first forest fire.

The bow, Grovebringer, was one of the oldest enchanted

weapons Alustin knew of that was still in active use, and it grew more powerful with every year it was pacted with one of the Havathi warlocks that made up the ranks of the Sacred Swordsmen.

Not that there was anything sacred about them, the Havath Dominion merely delighted in seeming like it was on the side of righteousness and order. They didn't even allow cults in their territory, so the name was a bit absurd.

He still hadn't caught any sign of its wielder, but as the urban forest grew denser, the archer had fewer and fewer clean shots at Alustin, making Grovebringer less effective in a protracted battle.

Especially since he suspected the archer was firing from well outside the forest.

Alustin glanced behind him, spotting the other Sacred Swordsman standing in the midst of the forest fire. He'd tried multiple times to get close to the woman wielding the oversized lead sword, but she was surrounded by a whirlwind of droplets and ropes of molten lead. There had to be almost a ton of molten lead swirling in the air around her. Even the papers that he'd painstakingly inscribed fire resistance wards and glyphs onto couldn't make it through without being ignited or shredded by the lead— for that matter, they could barely withstand the heat of the forest fire.

His sword was more than a match for hers if he could get close, but even with his paper armor fully constructed and active, he would burn to a crisp before he got near.

He cursed as he danced over the edge of a column that had been tilted by the roots growing down in between the columns. He could see at least three or four feet down into the crack. He shook his head. Alustin seldom tripped— any citizen of Helicote was trained in footwork from the time they could walk, especially those who would wield one of the Lord of Bells' blades.

Not that there were any other citizens of Helicote left other than himself, of course. At least none worthy of the name. Just a few cowardly survivors hiding their pasts from Havathi assassins. Them and…

Alustin almost tripped on another tilted column. Then he stopped, and stared down at the exposed crevice. He smiled and began sending sheets of paper down into it.

When the Swordsman with the blade of lead approached, not even a minute later, Alustin was simply standing there, covered in his full-plate paper armor, his spellform-covered sabre casually slung over one shoulder.

The woman laughed. "Finally decided to stand and fight? Not much good it will do you. There's not a chance you'll be able to get close to me."

Alustin didn't reply, only shifting slightly.

"Who would believe that I would be the one to take down the Last Loyal Son of Helicote?" she asked. "Valia will be infuriated, but she's had more than her fair share of opportunities to turn you."

Alustin rolled his shoulders, then moved his sabre into a guard position.

"Nothing to say before you die?" the woman asked smugly.

"It looks quite comfortable where you're standing," Alustin finally said. "I'd bet quite a lot that you've got some way to keep the space around you cool."

The Swordsman's eyes widened, then she laughed. "Won't do you much good."

"It already has," Alustin said, and then sheets of paper began rushing up from the cracks between the columnar basalt in a whirling column, completely obscuring the woman. There was a brief scream, then the flying papers turned red.

At that, the whirling cloud of molten lead began to slow. As it came to a halt, the lead rained down, completely coating the dead Swordsman, her weapon, and the paper in still-molten metal.

The lead started dripping down into the narrow spaces between the columns, and Alustin could feel the paper he still had down there igniting. It had been harder to fly the paper through the gaps than he'd expected— they were wide enough for a coin to slip between them near the top, but the gaps quickly grew thinner, until he couldn't even fit paper between them a few feet down. He'd managed to get more than enough into position, though.

He briefly wondered how the city took care of water and garbage that got trapped down in there— they probably had a janitorial mage corps for that, he imagined. Water mages, most likely?

Alustin didn't see what direction the arrow came from, but it punched through his armor like it wasn't even there, embedding itself into the ground nearby. As the newest cedar tree in the forest began to grow, Alustin started to laugh.

And his armor dissolved into loose paper.

With no Alustin inside.

Sheets of paper wrapped themselves around his sabre, and began flying it back to him via a circuitous route.

"Nice try," Alustin said. His voice echoed up from a sheet of paper lying by the new tree, one bearing spellform glyphs that let him speak through it at a distance. "Better luck next time."

Grovebringer's wielder didn't answer, but then, no one had ever heard them speak, nor knew their identity. They also never attacked alone, so he should be safe until they rejoined another member of their Hand.

Alustin took off at a run as his armor and wings began to reform. He needed to get to his students before the remaining Swordsmen did.

Shards of stone hissed through the air, and Hugh felt a sting as one sliced his cheek.

Then the lightning strikes stopped, leaving only a crackling noise.

Hugh looked up to see a mage hovering above the pier. They were covered head to toe in plate armor lacquered white, with elaborate copper spellforms inlaid across its surface.

Lightning crackled around their armor and shivered down to the pier below, where a trio of metal rods were embedded between the basalt columns. It gave the mage the appearance of standing on a tripod of lightning. A vicious-looking harpoon hovered in the air next to them, galvanic arcs rolling between it and the armor.

"I feel a need to apologize," the mage said. Their voice echoed and crackled like the lightning, and hardly sounded human.

Hugh blinked at that. He glanced over at Talia, who was toying with her necklace of bone shards, but hadn't attacked. He readied a starbolt, but decided to wait on the others.

"Apologize for what?" Sabae called out, her own voice distorted by her wind armor.

"I assumed that your friend here," the lightning mage said, "was Artur Wallbreaker. Clearly, however, I was mistaken."

The lightning mage gestured towards where the colossal figure of Artur's armor strode down a city street, swinging an implausibly huge metal hammer. Shard of ice were still dashing themselves against the armor, but the green-yellow mist had largely dispersed— most likely Artur had killed that attacker already.

Hugh started to prepare another starbolt, then paused, and tapped into his crystal mana reservoir instead.

That reminded Hugh of the spotter he'd just helped to kill, and he had to struggle to focus his attention on the current situation.

"Ah hope yeh can forgive me fer not really being happier that yeh were trying ta' kill me da instead," Godrick said.

"Of course," the figure said, nodding its armored head gracefully. The harpoon floating in the air was turning away from them, focusing in Artur's direction.

"What do you want with us?" Sabae demanded.

"I'm afraid my reasons are somewhat impolite," the armored mage said. "Unfortunately, I find myself needing to take you hostage. Nothing personal, I assure you, and I intend nothing untoward."

"Who are you, and who do you work for?" Sabae demanded.

Lightning began to wrap itself around the harpoon.

"My name is Sanniah of the Ceaseless Thunder, and I

have the honor of being one of the Sacred Swordsmen of Havath and the wielder of the Needle of Leagues," the figure said. "I stand to defend humanity from the monsters and petty tyrants that endlessly squabble over territory and power, and I promise to do my utmost to ensure your safety during the unpleasantness that is to follow."

"I have a better idea," Talia said, then launched a dreambolt straight at Sanniah.

It streaked towards the Sacred Swordsman, but as it approached, lightning lanced out towards the dreamfire, detonating it in midair. The lightning withered like a dying vine— which really wasn't something lightning should be doing— but the dreamfire dispersed harmlessly.

"Huh," Talia said.

"I truly mean you no harm," Sanniah said. "It's certainly regrettable that you killed my hireling, but ultimately, the error was theirs for mistaking you for Artur. If I had been close enough to see you personally, I would not have attacked you."

The lightning around the harpoon vanished. Nothing happened for a fraction of a second, and then another massive lightning bolt shot out of its tip, straight as an arrow. If Hugh didn't have his anti-glare spell up, he'd probably be blinking away afterimages for a good while. Hugh swiveled to follow the bolt, and saw Artur stagger in his suit of armor, a crater visible in the stone of its shoulder.

Hugh turned back to see lightning beginning to wrap itself around the harpoon again. He almost lost his focus on the crystal affinity spellform he was channeling mana into in his mind's eye, but he managed to hold on.

"I only need the beacons at longer ranges, of course," Sanniah said.

Hugh swallowed. Artur was still a good quarter of the way across the city.

"Stones with that," Godrick said. "Ah'm not standin' around like a lump while yeh attack me da!"

He lifted his new hammer above his head and threw it. It shot forwards at obscene speeds, clearly propelled by his magic. Almost as if they'd planned it, Sabae launched a gust strike after it, propelling it even faster.

Lightning from the armor intercepted the hammer at the same distance the dreamfire bolt had been disrupted, and the hammer simply stopped in place. Sanniah was blown backwards a little by the gust strike, but the lightning she stood atop pulled her back into a hovering position between the three metal spikes in the pier.

"A word of advice, child," Sanniah said. "A sufficiently powerful lightning mage can quite easily stop metal projectiles in midair. Most projectiles, really."

Several more lightning bolts arced out from the armor to the hammer, which began to glow cherry red. The handle caught fire, and droplets of molten steel began to drip onto the stone of the pier.

"I will give you one more chance to surrender," Sanniah said. "I can't spare any more time than that to humor you, children. I beg of you to make the right decision."

The harpoon launched another lightning bolt at Artur. This time, when Hugh turned to look, he noticed that several trees appeared to have started growing out of the stone mage's suit of armor, and were badly slowing him down.

He didn't take time to puzzle over that, however, as his spell finally completed. He quickly assembled a starbolt spellform in his mind's eye and took a deep breath.

"Ward up!" he shouted, and fired the starbolt.

His stellar mana reservoir had refilled a little since he'd killed the spotter, but he'd still only get one more shot after this.

The instant the starbolt got into range, the armor's lightning dropped the half-melted hammer and slammed into the glowing sphere. Both erupted into a flash of light bright enough to leave afterimages even through Hugh's eye-protecting cantrip. A wash of heat rolled over the students.

"Very well, then," he heard Sanniah say, and even through the afterimages, he could see lightning fire straight from the woman's armor towards them.

It never hit.

The lightning simply scattered and burst in midair before

it reached them. Hugh could feel his crystal mana reservoir draining, but at a rate he could easily handle for the moment.

As his vision cleared, Hugh watched the lightning crawl across the edges of his ward, trying to reach them. More bolts hammered into the ground at its edges, but the ward itself was several feet underground— he'd created it by altering the crystal patterns of the basalt below them. It had been somewhat strange recrystalizing the basalt— they were already essentially perfect crystals, so he'd actually been creating flaws in them in the shape of ward spellforms. The ward had been much more time consuming than the wall he'd built earlier had been, but it allowed them to fire spells out through it without exposing themselves to attack.

The others started casting spells like mad. Talia began launching dreamfire bolt after dreamfire bolt, some of which appeared to be layered. Godrick began tearing up chunks of stone from inside the ward, well away from its spellforms, and hurling them at the Havathi agent. Sabae launched gust strike after gust strike, and Hugh launched his third and final starbolt.

Sanniah handled all of them with ease.

She gracefully swayed about atop her lightning, dodging most of their spells, the lightning from her armor deflecting or destroying all the attacks that she couldn't dodge. Lightning from the Needle of Leagues kept blasting towards Artur in the distance.

And the lightning just kept hammering into Hugh's ward. He started funneling mana from his spatial mana reservoir into the ward as well, but he'd never used that reservoir for anything other than fueling wards and cantrips, and it was by far the smallest and least developed of his three reservoirs.

Hugh briefly wondered where his spellbook was at, but he decided it was better off not near them— he had no desire to see how well it could stand up to lightning.

After firing his last starbolt, Hugh wished he'd brought his sling with him, but he'd left it at the inn, along with the small handful of wardstones he'd crafted since Midsummer.

A small, vicious little part of Hugh began to haul up those old feelings of worthlessness, but Hugh forced himself to watch the lightning hammering into his ward and smiled. He might not be able to attack at the moment, but he certainly wasn't useless in the slightest.

"Godrick!" Sabae shouted. "The spikes in the pier!"

Godrick launched one more rock at Sanniah, then turned to the spikes Sanniah had embedded into the stone pier. Hugh could feel Godrick's stone magic shifting the columns of the pier, and he suspected that he was using his steel affinity on the spikes as well, though Hugh couldn't feel it. He could see the strain on Godrick's face— the bigger apprentice was definitely better trained in melee range magic.

With the high-pitched noise of metal scraping stone, one of the spikes went flying out of the pier, and Sanniah lurched to the side. A shot from the Needle of Leagues went wide and hammered into a city street, leaving a smoking crater among the columns.

The lightning that had been connecting the armor to the spike lurched and began dragging along the pier, burning a crooked path along its surface before it connected to Godrick's half-melted new hammer, which began to melt even farther down into the cracks of the pier.

Hugh was fairly sure that Sanniah hadn't seen Sabae use a gust of wind to hurl something pale and white onto the pier, where it slid into one of the cracks between the columns. Hugh rapidly began adding modifications to his ward— not an easy task while it was active.

Sanniah straightened, crossing her arms. "This is truly regrettable, children. You show such promise."

None of them responded, or launched any attacks at the Sacred Swordsman. Sanniah's lightning continued to carve into the dome that Hugh's ward had formed over them.

"I don't know what your masters have told you about Havath, but we're not evil," Sanniah said. "We're not simply conquerors bent on world domination. We seek to end the interminable feuding of the great powers, to make the weak more than simply cattle for whatever powerful mage comes along."

The Needle of Leagues fired again.

The lightning from Sanniah's armor that had been hitting the ward ceased, and Sanniah continued. "Artur Wallbreaker is powerful indeed, but not powerful enough to withstand an entire Hand of Sacred Swordsmen. Your teacher Alustin is already slain, and Artur will not last much longer. I offer you one last chance to surrender."

Sabae glanced back at Hugh. He gulped, then nodded at her. She, in turn, nodded at Talia.

"Actually," Sabae called out to Sanniah, "I'd like to offer you an opportunity to surrender."

Sanniah simply stared at Sabae. Hugh imagined that if she weren't wearing a helmet, there would be an expression of shock on her face.

Unfortunately for her, she should have been looking down, not at Sabae.

"You're not serious, are you?" Sanniah said.

"Not in the slightest," Sabae said cheerfully.

A loud cracking noise rose up from below Sanniah, and she looked down to see glowing spines of bone rising from the pier.

"Have a nice flight," Talia said.

The pier exploded.

CHAPTER SIX

Ampioc

Shards of burning bone and chunks of broken basalt rained against Hugh's ward, but the modifications he had made held. As the smoke and debris cleared without any sign of lightning, Hugh started to relax.

Only for a moment, though.

The pier was almost entirely gone. A handful of basalt

columns still jutted from the water, at steep angles or with their tops broken off.

And atop one of those pillars stood Sanniah. Her armor was badly damaged, even melted in places. The inlayed copper spellforms were broken and shattered, and the white lacquer of the armor was cracked and flaking all over. The helmet was especially badly damaged, its spellforms actively spitting sparks.

The Needle of Leagues, however, was perfectly intact, hovering beside her.

Sabae exploded forwards, windjumping straight through the ward at Sanniah.

Almost contemptuously, the Sacred Swordsman grabbed the harpoon floating beside her, swinging it like a club. Lightning tore into Sabae, sending her plunging straight into the water of the harbor.

Sanniah plucked off her helmet while Hugh stared at the water, willing Sabae to surface. The Sacred Swordsman tossed the ruined helmet into the water right where Sabae had fallen.

Sabae didn't surface.

Sanniah was a nondescript middle-aged woman with close-cropped grey hair. The only noteworthy aspect of her face were the vicious-looking burns on her cheeks and forehead.

"I'm truly sorry it's come to this," Sanniah said, and lightning began to wrap around the Needle of Leagues.

Sanniah leapt straight towards them, lightning propelling her at terrifying speed. Talia fired a dreambolt at the Havathi, and Godrick followed up with half a shattered column, but bursts of lightning shattered both. Shards of stone cut into Sanniah's face, but she didn't slow at all.

Hugh funneled all his remaining mana into the ward, but he knew it wouldn't be enough to stop a weapon as freakishly powerful as that harpoon.

The Needle of Leagues never impacted the ward, however. Something flickered across Hugh's vision, and there was a massive flash of light. It wasn't as bad as starfire hitting lightning, and Hugh's vision quickly cleared.

Alustin stood in front of them, in half-charred paper armor. The Needle of Leagues strained against a sword in Alustin's hands— an odd looking blade with a slight curve that Hugh had never seen before, covered in a truly absurd number of spellforms.

Sanniah launched herself back a few feet with one of her lightning jumps, and the Needle began charging itself up again. Alustin didn't give her the time she needed, however. In a swirl of paper, he leapt after her, and they began exchanging blows rapidly. Glyph inscribed papers intercepted lightning bolts, and burning bits of paper filled the air around the two.

Then the spellforms on Alustin's sword began to glow, and it began to leave translucent afterimages floating in its wake, almost like visible echoes.

"Ah can't…" Godrick started, then simply trailed off.

Alustin stepped to the side in a move that obviously left one side open, even to someone who knew as little about swordplay as Hugh. He gasped as Sanniah swung the Needle of Leagues straight at the opening.

The harpoon hit one of the afterimages, and simply bounced right off. The afterimage dissolved a moment later, but Alustin was already on the offensive.

He began forcing the Havathi back, dodging gracefully around the afterimages his sword left in the air, while Sanniah found herself being hemmed in closer and closer to the water, each swing of her harpoon blocked by one of the motionless translucent sword echoes.

And then, defying all logic, she simply stepped forwards into the wall of hanging blades. Or, more lurched than stepped. The floating swords cut through Sanniah's armor like it were warm butter, and one of her arms was severed entirely, crashing to the ground.

The afterimages dissolved entirely, and Sanniah's corpse crumpled to the ground.

Out on the water, standing on one of the ruined columns of the pier, stood Sabae, wrapped in spinning water armor, her arm still outstretched from where she'd hit Sanniah with a blast of water from behind.

Hugh's heart unclenched, and he staggered as he dropped his ward entirely. He exhaled, and started to relax as Sabae let her water armor drain back into the harbor.

Only to immediately tense up again.

Something immense was rising out of the water.

"What is *that*?" Hugh demanded.

"That," Godrick said, "is Ampioc."

Ampioc was an octopus. Hugh had seen octopuses before, hauled in by fishermen in Emblin in his childhood, when his parents took him and his little sister to visit the coastal towns on business. They'd just been little creatures, no more than a foot or two in length— most much smaller than that. There had also been little freshwater octopuses in the streams near his village, no longer than a child's finger.

Ampioc, however, was the single biggest creature Hugh had ever seen. The immense red octopus must have been half again the length of Indris Stormbreaker. He took up a considerable portion of the harbor by himself, and what Hugh could see of the octopus's arms looked big enough to tear a ship in half.

Hugh gulped.

One of Ampioc's eyes, which was big enough to fit Godrick inside it twice over, slowly turned to focus on them. His pupil was a long, slightly curved rectangle.

Around him, Hugh spotted the others bowing, and he quickly followed suit.

After a moment, they all straightened, but nobody spoke as Ampioc surveyed the damage to his city.

Hugh took the time to look around as well and winced. They'd done quite a number on the city in just a few short minutes. A new forest was growing in the middle of the city. The apprentices had blown up a pier, and heavily damaged the docks. Several full streets were torn up and broken by Artur's battle— which appeared to have ended. Artur himself was striding down towards the docks, his armor much reduced in size, his enormous hammer nowhere to be seen.

Ampioc slowly shifted his attention back to the group, and his color turned an even deeper red.

Except for one patch. Specks of blue appeared on his rubbery skin facing the group, and they quickly grew and merged together, forming letters.

<Explain,> the letters on Ampioc's skin said.

Alustin raised a hand. Hugh noticed that his sword had vanished.

"I am Alustin Haber, servant of Kanderon Crux. I wish we had met again under better circumstances. I was traveling with my apprentices and Artur Wallbreaker on business for Kanderon, when we were ambushed by Havathi agents. Sacred Swordsmen, to be precise. We were in no way the aggressors, and were merely waiting for our ship to arrive."

He nudged the Needle of Leagues lying on the ground with his foot.

"We successfully dispatched several of the attackers. I feel that their weapons are best used to recompense Lothal's city treasuries for the damages," Alustin said.

Hugh felt momentarily miffed at that— they'd worked hard at fighting Sanniah, and the Needle of Leagues would be a perfect complement to Sabae's shield and powers.

The letters spelled out on Ampioc's skin shifted into new words. <A fair and just proposal.>

One of Ampioc's massive arms rose from the water, a deluge of seawater running off it. Almost gently, the tip reached out and clenched the Needle of Leagues with one of the suckers on its underside and slowly withdrew it under the water.

"There's another sword up in your new forest, buried under a mound of mostly-molten lead," Alustin said.

The letters on Ampioc's skin faded, but none replaced them immediately. Hugh wasn't sure, but he thought that the octopus's skin had grown a little less red.

"Ampioc!" Artur's voice called out.

Hugh turned to see the stone mage arrive at the docks. He was clutching two swords in one stony fist— one bearing a sickly yellow-green pommel stone filled with writhing mist, the other apparently made of solid ice. His helmet had retracted, exposing his face.

<Artur,> Ampioc replied. <It has been too long.>

The octopus's skin tone cooled even further, taking on a distinct purple tinge.

Artur exchanged glances with Alustin, who nodded. Almost gently, Artur took the sword with the green-yellow pommel stone and slid it towards the edge of the pier. Another of the octopus's arms reached out and gently slid the sword into the water.

"If it is acceptable ta yeh," Artur said, "Ah have a use fer the other weapon."

More letters formed on Ampioc's skin, this time in yellow.

<If I had been in the harbor, rather than out hunting, I could have ended this incident immediately,> Ampioc said.

Given the octopus's sheer size, Hugh suspected Ampioc could spell out impressively long speeches if it so chose. He wasn't entirely sure what Ampioc meant by his comment, but Artur just nodded and held onto the sword.

<Have you considered my offer further, Artur?> Ampioc spelled out.

Artur shook his head. "Ah'm sorry, Ampioc. Ah simply have too many bad memories a' Lothal."

Ampioc turned a deep blue that looked almost regretful to Hugh, then shifted to a pale olive green.

<Very well. How many members of the Havathi Hand can you account for?> Ampioc asked in black letters.

"Two," Artur said. "Grovebringer's wielder escaped me."

"Grovebringer's wielder escaped me as well," Alustin said. "So we took down four of the five."

<How much longer do you intend to stay in Lothal?> Ampioc asked.

"Our ship should arrive in the next couple of days," Alustin said. "We'll be leaving as soon as it finishes loading supplies."

Ampioc didn't respond to that, but one of his arms rose out of the water and, with surprising delicacy, picked Sabae up off the broken column and set her down gently next to the others.

Sabae squeaked a little, but looked more surprised than anything.

Ampioc turned away from them, turning eggshell white. Broken basalt pillars began lifting themselves out of the water, their cracks fusing together.

"I think that's us dismissed," Alustin said.

As Alustin escorted them away from the lower harbor, Hugh looked back to see the destroyed pier reassembling itself. One of Ampioc's great eyes flicked upwards and met Hugh's gaze. He couldn't even begin to guess what lay behind that inscrutable alien gaze.

Hugh turned away and followed the others back to the inn.

CHAPTER SEVEN

Helicote

By the time they reached their inn the destroyed pier was almost entirely restored, and hundreds of broken and scattered columns across the city had begun to heal and float back to their proper place. The sheer scale of Ampioc's spellcasting was stunning— it dwarfed even Headmaster Tarik's legendarily huge stone spells or Artur's colossal stone armor.

The only spellcasting Sabae had ever seen that compared to it had been from other great powers— Indris, Chelys Mot, or her grandmother. Well, and Hugh, when he'd shielded Theras Tel from the sandstorm, but that had been a trick, a ward fueled by the storm itself, using the windlode spellform Sabae had provided him.

The last sight Sabae saw as the inn door closed was a trio of massive, tree-tall columns floating down the street.

"So Ampioc is a stone mage?" Hugh asked as they all sat down at one of the inn's common room tables.

Sabae noted that Hugh still hadn't drifted back into his unhappy mood yet— when there was an emergency, Hugh snapped immediately out of whatever unpleasant mental space he was in. It was inactivity that gave Hugh time to dwell and be miserable. He'd drift back out of things soon enough, but he'd be useful and alert until then.

Sabae was pretty sure that Hugh was going to be in an especially bad place when he did drift away, though. Hugh wasn't the type to easily deal with killing someone else.

For that matter, Sabae was feeling pretty shaken up about Sanniah. She hadn't told the others how bruised and battered she was, not to mention the large numbers of new burns she'd picked up. She could heal herself, but it would take a few days. She'd come terrifyingly close to dying out there.

Her hands started shaking a bit, and she sat on them to hide the trembling.

She wasn't entirely sure Sanniah was the first person she'd killed— or helped to kill, anyhow, Alustin had done most of the work. There'd been a gravity mage in Theras Tel she'd hit pretty hard who hadn't gotten up afterward, but she had no idea if they'd survived or not. She was pretty sure she was handling it better than Hugh, though.

"He's a basalt mage," she said. "Which Kanderon told us already."

"Strictly speaking," Alustin said, "He's nine basalt mages. Each of his arms has their own mana reservoirs, and can semi-independently spellcast. Ampioc more coordinates and guides his arms than controls them."

"That makes me somewhat less happy about being picked up by him," Sabae said.

"They're usually well behaved," Artur said, waving the innkeeper over.

"Usually?" Sabae asked, feeling increasingly skeptical.

"It's… complicated. But it went jus' fine fer yeh," Artur said. "And Ampioc's arms are the reason there are so many cults in Lothal. Yeh can't swing a stick without encounterin' another one worshippin' this arm or that."

They all took a moment to order food— which, at the moment, was just a pot of fish stew that was kept warm in the kitchen between meals. They were the only ones in the common room, and there was only a single nervous cook and the inn keep here at the moment— everyone else was in hiding until they were sure things had calmed down. It wasn't cowardice, just common sense when there was a battle between mages.

"You have a lot of explaining to do," Sabae said, pointing at Alustin. "Starting with why Havathi Sacred Swordsmen attacked us."

Artur glanced up from the ice sword he'd claimed. "Ah'd say it's a wee bit unusual yeh haven't been attacked by 'em before, around Alustin. Yer teacher's killed more a' them than anyone livin'."

"Not enough of them," Alustin said quietly. In a more normal tone of voice, he continued. "Apart from the longstanding rivalry between the Librarians Errant and the Havathi Sacred Swordsmen, there's also the ongoing hunt for Imperial Ithos and the Exile Splinter. They're almost as close to finding it as we are."

Sabae had known for a while that Alustin had some sort of grudge against the Havath Dominion, but she was starting to think it was a bit more intense than she'd imagined.

"Why didn't you try and keep the Needle of Leagues for Sabae?" Hugh interjected. "A lightning enchanted weapon seems perfect for her, especially one that powerful."

Sabae gave Hugh a surprised look at that. She hadn't actually considered that.

"It wouldn't have worked for her," Alustin said. "First, because Sabae's difficulties working magic at range would still apply to the Needle. Second, because it's been pacted to Havathi forces for too long."

"Pacted?" Talia asked.

"The Sacred Swordsmen are all warlocks," Alustin said. "Ones who exclusively pact with magical weapons. I believe I've mentioned that before. There are some limitations to what magical weapons they can pact with— they need to have artificial mana reservoirs— but when they do, they gain the affinities used in creating the weapons, an unusual amount of control of the weapon, and often a few odd abilities related to the enchantment of the weapon. The weapon, in turn, grows gradually more powerful, slowly grows its mana reservoirs, and even tends to become intelligent. The oldest weapons used by the Swordsmen have grown alarmingly powerful, and many are actively loyal to the Havathi Dominion. The Needle of Leagues is one of the oldest weapons of the Swordsmen— it never would have accepted serving anyone else. Grovebringer, the bow that created the forest out there, is another of their oldest and most powerful weapons."

"So why did Ampioc want it?" Talia said.

"I'd like to think he wants to keep the weapons out of Havathi hands, but most likely he intends to gift the younger weapons to his own warlocks, if he has any, and likely intends to ransom back the Needle of Leagues to Havath," Alustin said. "If I thought I could have gotten away with it, I would have kept it."

"Shouldn't we be worryin' about Grovebringer?" Godrick asked.

Alustin shook his head. "Grovebringer's current wielder never attacks on their own, only in the company of other Swordsmen. We're not sure why, but they're probably long gone by now."

"Do the Sacred Swordsmen only carry a single enchanted item, or—?" Talia asked.

"They usually carry three or so, though it's rare they pact with all of them. Most warlocks have mana reservoirs too small to pact multiple times. Sanniah's armor was a powerful enchanted item on its own, and I suspected she was pacted with it as well. Being pacted to multiple items with lightning enchantments is probably why she was so powerful."

Sabae decided to steer things back in the right direction.

"What happens if Havath gets to Imperial Ithos first and claims the Exile Splinter?" Sabae said.

Alustin shrugged. "It would probably take them years, perhaps decades to figure out its use. They have a handful of crystal mages, but none as brilliant as Kanderon. Still, for someone as long-lived as Kanderon, that's a short enough time period to be unacceptable. More concerning to me would be the likelihood they'd recover enchanted items from the ruins of Imperial Ithos— there were quite a number of extraordinarily powerful ones lost with the city. Or, perhaps, the odds that some Ithonian mage managed to transition into lichdom and is hanging around still, but that seems unlikely— liches were rare prior to the fall of the Ithonian Empire, and they destroyed many of the existing ones over the centuries of their expansion. There are some very notable exceptions, but liches and empires don't get along well."

Sabae could see that. Given their largely stationary nature, and their strong incentives to maintain close control of their demesnes, liches would be a major thorn in the side of anyone who wanted to expand their power widely. None of the liches of the Endless Erg or the southwest coast of the Ithonian continent were particularly powerful, but the Kaen Das family had cultivated alliances with as many as possible— they were useful tools for preventing expansionist ambitions in the region. Not to mention, reliable allies that stuck around for centuries were rare enough. Few families or great powers were stable over the long term.

Of course, Indris and Kanderon did the same. Kanderon had probably sponsored and helped half the liches in the region, if not the whole continent, achieve lichdom.

Alustin was being too nonchalant about those specific threats, however. *Something* had him deeply worried about the return of Imperial Ithos, but Sabae couldn't think of what else it could be.

Artur stood up, his stew somehow finished already.

"Hugh," Artur said, "when yer finished eatin', ah've got a project fer yeh ta' help me with."

Hugh nodded at Artur, then dug into his own stew.

Sabae kept staring at Alustin, who gave her a bland look, then picked up his own bowl of stew.

"I need to report this to Kanderon," Alustin said.
"The stew?" Talia asked, an annoying smirk on her face.
Alustin started to reply, then smiled. "That would actually be quite entertaining," he said. "But no, she needs to know that the Sacred Swordsmen were active so close to her territory."
Sabae noticed that Godrick was antsy about something, but he didn't speak up until the two older mages were both up the stairs.
"Yeh all saw Alustin's sword, right?" Godrick said in a low voice the instant they were alone in the common room.
"Did we see the crazy sword that left murder-echoes hanging in midair?" Talia said. "I dunno. Did we also maybe see a giant octopus?"
Sabae poked Talia in the side. Talia gave her a dirty look, but settled down. Sabae grinned a little bit— she kind of got why Talia enjoyed poking and jabbing people.
"Alustin's sword was a Helicotan sabre!" Godrick hissed.
Sabae's eyes widened.
"Drakeshit," Talia said. "There's no way."
"What's a Helicotan sabre?" Hugh asked.

Everyone stared at Hugh.
"Have you… have you literally never heard of Helicote before?" Sabae finally asked. She was used to Hugh being in the dark about things, considering how much of a backwater Emblin was, but this was ridiculous.
"Should I have?" Hugh asked, then ate another spoonful of stew.
"There's no way it's an actual Helicotan sabre," Talia said, glaring at Godrick. "Only Helicotans can wield them. And there aren't any more Helicotans."
"It's definitely a Helicotan sabre," Godrick said. "Ah've read enough about them. Nothin' else has an enchantment like that."
"What's Helicote?" Hugh asked.
Sabae spoke up quickly, before Godrick and Talia could

start arguing again. “Helicote was a city-state in Eastern Ithos, a few days south of Tsarnassus’ southern border. It wasn’t a particularly large or powerful city-state, but it was old and highly respected— it had been ruled by the same lich since shortly after the fall of the Ithonian Empire.”

“And it’s known for its swords, apparently?” Hugh asked.

“Was known, yes. Helicote doesn’t exist anymore,” Sabae said. “Their ruler, the Lord of Bells, was one of the greatest enchanters ever.”

Godrick interrupted. “He forged every single one a’ their sabres personally. The enchantments aren’t inlaid, they’re actually folds in the metal that he beat into ‘em during the forging process somehow. They’re nigh-indestructible, sharp enough ta’ cut through any lesser weapons, and can leave those deadly after-images.”

“Murder-echoes,” Talia said.

Sabae glared at both of them.

“It apparently took years to learn to master one of them,” Sabae said.

“Yeh had ta’ start trainin’ as soon as yeh could walk,” Godrick interrupted again. “Wearin’ a blindfold all the time ta’ master yer situational awareness, ‘cause those after-images—”

“Murder-echoes,” Talia interjected.

“Are just as dangerous ta’ the wielder as their opponent,” Godrick continued. “Explains why Alustin can walk backward without trippin’ and such. Years and years a’ trainin’. Plus, they had some sort a’ enchantment that kept anyone not Helicotan from usin’ them.”

“And there aren’t any Helicotans left,” Talia said, “So it must have been some weird counterfeit or something.”

Sabae sighed.

“So it’s… a powerful enchanted weapon?” Hugh asked. “I mean, it doesn’t exactly seem surprising that Alustin would have a powerful weapon.”

“If Godrick’s right,” Sabae said, glaring at the other two to make sure they didn’t keep interrupting, “then Alustin would have to be Helicotan. Which would be huge.”

“Why, exactly?” Hugh asked, looking genuinely

bewildered at this point. “And why doesn’t Helicote exist anymore?”

“Because it picked a fight with the Havath Dominion single-handed!” Talia said excitedly, waving her spoon. “Thousand to one odds! Almost won, too!”

Sabae sighed. “It’s a lot more complicated than that. This all started over twenty years ago. Havath’s last major war of expansion had been halted by a huge alliance of nations, city-states, and various great powers a little over a decade before that. That was the war that Sulassa Tidecaller and Artur both made their names in as mercenaries. Headmaster Tarik fought in it as well, but she was already famous. Helicote had served in that alliance, but by the time Havath was forced to a halt, Helicote went from being weeks away from Havathi territory to being right up against the border of the Dominion. The war bankrupted and crippled both Havath and the alliance that fought them, so both sides were still licking their wounds and recovering. Helicote, however, knew it was only a matter of time until Havath tried again, and this time, there wasn’t much chance of the alliance reforming in time to keep Helicote independent.”

“So the Lord of Bells attacked them!” Talia said, excitedly.

“Not… well, sort of,” Sabae continued. “The Lord of Bells wasn’t the one who decided to attack. It was the Helicotan Forum who decided to. The Lord of Bells allowed the dwellers in his demesne considerably more independence and power than many liches do, and the Lord-Citizens of the Forum decided they would try to disrupt Havath rebuilding. They managed to convince the Lord of Bells to back their effort, and, well… a city of less than a hundred thousand souls invaded an empire of millions.”

Hugh gave her a suspicious look like he thought she was messing with him.

“It wasn’t a normal invasion, though,” Sabae said. “They didn’t have a great power to lead it— the Lord of Bells could no more leave his demesne than any other lich, and they were outnumbered to a ridiculous degree. Havath had over a dozen great powers of its own, and countless archmages on top of that. Helicote had a few advantages, of course— Helicotan mages were notoriously dangerous, well-trained, and numerous for a city its size— their aether was rich enough to support huge numbers of mages. Their Lord Citizens were especially dangerous and were all armed with the sabres crafted by the Lord of Bells. Rather than attack head-on, well…"

"They started a campaign of mass assassination!" Talia blurted out.

Sabae sighed. "Essentially, yes. Not simply of high-ranking governors, dominion officials, and archmages, however— they also targeted massive numbers of scribes, logistics officers, and clerks. They also destroyed infrastructure on a massive scale. They sabotaged dams, poisoned wells, grew forests right across major roads, and demolished granaries. It took nearly two weeks for Havath to fully mobilize against the threat, and by then, their economy had been crippled for years to come, and they'd suffered a massive loss of institutional and bureaucratic expertise. But mobilize they did, and they crushed Helicote. It took almost a year, but they hunted down every saboteur and assassin, and eventually managed to slay the Lord of Bells and destroy Helicote itself. It cost them the lives of three of their own great powers to do so. Helicote sent out countless letters and messengers for aid, but the old alliance failed to send more than token efforts against Havath. Since then, Havath has systematically hunted down every Helicotan they could find, and placed bounties on their heads. I'm sure there are plenty hiding here and there, but if that's a real Helicotan sabre, that means Alustin is from the family of a Lord Citizen."

"That's insane," Hugh said. "Why… I don't understand why they'd do something like that. They couldn't know the future for sure, or know they'd be doomed. Why would they do that?"

Sabae shrugged. "Honestly, I don't know. They were proud, but if pride was their inspiration, it was to the point of insanity. It worked, though. They did as much damage to

Havath as the last war had done, and there hasn't been another major war of expansion since. A few minor border squabbles and annexations, but Havath has only been back to full strength for six or seven years now."

Godrick pointed up at the ceiling with his spoon. "Ah'm tellin' yeh, it makes perfect sense. He's about the right age, an' there's the whole walkin' backwards bit, not ta' mention his obvious grudge against Havath."

"And his paper affinity would explain why he was sent to Skyhold," Sabae said. "The Lord Citizens of Helicote valued their abilities as warriors equally as highly as their artistic or scholarly talents. A paper mage would have been considered useless as a battle mage, so he gets sent away when his affinities develop, which I'm guessing was probably a year or two before Helicote invaded Havath. And it explains how he survived Havath's purge."

"Why wouldn't your dad have told you about it?" Talia asked Godrick.

Godrick gave her a serious look. "Me da doesn't share others' secrets with anyone, for any reason."

Hugh ate a last spoonful of his stew and got up. "I should go see what Artur wants."

Sabae eyed him critically as he trudged up the stairs. The battle-stress was clearly wearing off, and she could already see him starting to slouch again.

Then she turned towards Talia, who was very determinedly not looking towards Hugh's retreating form, and was staring at her stew.

She glanced over at Godrick, who rolled his eyes and nodded.

The instant she was sure Hugh was out of hearing range, she poked Talia in the side again. "We need to have a little talk about Hugh."

Talia immediately tensed up. "What about Hugh?"

"Yer holdin' a torch fer him," Godrick said. "More of a bonfire, really."

Talia's face turned almost as red as her hair. "I, uh…"

Sabae reached out and gave Talia a quick hug.

"Relax, Talia, it's fine," she said. "These things happen."

"Fallin' in love's like fartin'," Godrick said. "Yeh can try ta keep it hidden, but it'll make itself known eventually."

Talia actually giggled a little in surprise at that, while Sabae gave him a dirty look.

"Gross analogies aside," Sabae said, "I'm pretty sure Hugh hasn't noticed yet."

"Ah don't think ah've seen Hugh pay attention to just about anythin' since Avah dumped him," Godrick said.

Sabae spotted movement out of the corner of her eye, and spotted Hugh's spellbook floating up in the corner of the room watching them again.

"Little weirdo," Sabae muttered.

The other two gave her weird looks, and she rolled her eyes. "Hugh's spellbook, not Hugh. I think it's still afraid of you, Talia."

Talia gave the book a glare, and it darted upstairs in a flash of green. "It should be," she said. "Still going to get it back for dragging me around by my hair."

"Ah don't think Hugh would like that much," Godrick noted.

Talia groaned, and dropped her head down onto the table. "I hate feelings. I tried to pretend I didn't have any for Hugh for ages, but then I talked to Avah after she dumped Hugh, and she pointed out how obvious it was how I felt, and I've just felt like an idiot ever since, and…"

"You talked to Avah after the breakup?" Sabae said. "Is she alright? You didn't injure her, did you?"

Talia shot Sabae a glare. "What? No, we had a good talk. I've got no problem with Avah."

Sabae blinked. She hadn't been expecting that.

Godrick chuckled, and the girls both glanced at him.

"Ah just realized that we're on an epic quest with huge stakes, and we're more worried about our datin' lives than the city destroyin' weapon we're lookin' for," Godrick said.

Talia glared at Godrick, and Sabae arched her eyebrow, but Godrick just grinned right back at them.

Sabae started laughing first, and soon all three were laughing hysterically in the empty common room.

That night, Sabae dreamt of fire and molten stone. Of being trapped on a floating disc over a sea of magma, waves of molten rock cresting above her. Of an armored figure crackling in lightning floating above the magma, pointing a harpoon at her.

She woke from the nightmare with a start, her heart racing.

Talia was fast asleep in the other bed. Sabae staggered out of bed and over to the window, pulling back the curtain.

The moon was full tonight, wider than her outstretched hand. She could see Lothal clearly in its light. A surprising amount of the damage had already been repaired, though the new forest was mostly still there.

There was a wall of basalt columns separating the harbor from the sea, and keeping a certain amount of water in and ships afloat. During the high tide, when the water was a solid forty feet higher, even the largest ships could pass over the wall without much difficulty. At low tides, it became an isolated bowl.

It was low tide now, and even with the larger full-moon tide, the harbor hadn't emptied entirely, unlike the Ras Andis harbor. Of course, the Ras Andis harbor had sand at the bottom that ships in docking cradles could comfortably rest in, while she imagined the bottom of the Lothalan harbor was just more basalt.

Sabae idly wondered whether Ampioc was lurking at the bottom of the bowl, was out to sea, or whether he had some sort of cave or lair to hide in. She suspected the third, knowing what she did about octopuses.

Out past the harbor wall, there was another pool of water, kept in by yet another thick wall of basalt that would be submerged at higher tides, followed by another, and then another. Past those, there were countless thousands of basalt columns jutting upwards as much as twenty feet into the air from the half-mile of exposed seafloor. They extended well past where the columnar basalt ended, in fact.

If Sabae had to guess, the extra walls and the scattered columns were a combination of storm surge protection and marine fortification constructed by Ampioc. Ampioc never ventured into the deeps any longer, and lurked in the shallows to hide from enemies he'd made in the past.

The Kaen Das family had more contact with the marine great powers than most, but undersea politics were strange and arcane. Civilization as such didn't quite exist in the same way as it did on land, though it wasn't entirely absent either. As such, they'd never been able to tell whether Ampioc's exile was a formal one or not.

For the first time in a long time, Sabae thought about her mother, serving as a storm-mage escort to trade fleets. She didn't feel as much bitterness towards her as she used to, but it wasn't gone entirely.

Sabae wondered how often her mother thought of her these days.

It was a long time until Sabae turned away from the window to try and get back to sleep.

CHAPTER EIGHT

The Rising Cormorant

The amount of repair work that had been done in Lothal overnight was astonishing. The evidence of the battle was still obvious, of course— debris was everywhere, and there was still a forest growing in the middle of the city— but if Talia didn't know better, she'd say the battle had happened at least a week ago. Many of the trees were already being chopped down and milled by mages into lumber on the spot, and broken columns of basalt still danced down the street.

In one corner of the harbor, Talia spotted one of Ampioc's

massive eyes jutting out of the water, two of his eight arms just barely breaching the surface.

The massive octopus only held her attention for a short time, though, before she resumed glaring at the ship they'd be taking eastward, the *Rising Cormorant.*

It was one of the biggest ships in the Lothal docks by a considerable margin. The *Cormorant* was far longer than Kanderon was, and it absolutely dwarfed any ship Talia had ever ridden on before. Despite its huge size, however, the ship was a graceful, elegant, and well-kept vessel. The figurehead was, obviously, a massive cormorant, its beak pointed skyward.

Talia had never sailed on a proper ocean before— one with, well, water instead of sand— but she was fully anticipating being miserably sick on their long trip eastwards. The sea moved much more than sand did, after all.

That wasn't the reason she was glaring at the *Rising Cormorant*, however.

No, she was glaring at it because it was a Radhan ship, and somehow, she just knew there'd be a Radhan girl around her age who was prettier than her and who would start flirting with Hugh.

Who, of course, was staring at the *Cormorant* like an idiot, probably thinking of Avah.

Talia walked behind Hugh and shoved him off the edge of the pier.

He caught himself with a levitation cantrip before he could fall in the water, and magically lifted himself up onto the dock.

"What was that for?" Hugh asked, giving Talia a hurt look. His spellbook, slung over his shoulder, slipped behind him to hide from her.

"You can space off when we're on the ship and safely out to sea," Talia said. "Stay alert for now, in case more Havathi decide to make trouble."

Hugh gave her an irritated look, then turned away.

Sabae and Godrick both gave her incredulous looks. Talia

just glared at them and turned away.

That had been stupid, she had no idea why she'd done that. So, so stupid.

It was only a few more minutes before the ship was done loading cargo, and Talia spent the whole time fuming at herself for being an idiot before they boarded.

Once they did, she lurked at the back of the group, mostly hidden behind Artur and Godrick.

To her immense displeasure, there wasn't just one beautiful Radhan girl onboard, there were *several.* And cute boys as well, for that matter. She was fairly sure Hugh was only attracted to girls, but given how much of an idiot she was, they likely still had more chance with Hugh than she did.

Just about all the Radhan close to their age were pausing in their work to look them over. One of them winked at her, and she just glowered back at him, fantasizing about burning down the ship.

Hugh managed to pay polite attention during introductions. Alustin hadn't ever sailed on the *Rising Cormorant* before, so introductions were much more formal than they'd been on the *Moonless Owl*. The *Cormorant*'s captain was a stern looking older woman, Grepha, with a steel-grey braid down to her knees. They were also introduced to the first mate, the head mage, and several Radhan teens that would show them to their rooms, but Hugh didn't catch their names.

He knew the others would be irritated with him— for that matter, he was irritated with himself— but he just couldn't seem to stay outside his own head for very long unless he was actively doing something. His head was a jumble of confusing thoughts about Avah, his conflicting feelings about killing the Havathi spotter, and his irritation at Talia's weird stunt on the pier.

Preparation to cast off had started the instant they boarded, but it would be a little while before they actually left the harbor and set sail. Godrick wandered off to the deck to watch the preparations the instant he got his bags stowed, but Hugh decided to wait down below until they actually set sail. Sabae would drag him out if he didn't come out then, but right now he really didn't feel like being around others.

He spent a couple minutes laying in his bunk, staring at the ceiling— or whatever Sabae would have called it. His spellbook nestled under his arm, dozing contentedly.

At least, until his pack began shrieking at him.

Hugh sat up too quickly and smacked his head against the ceiling, then clambered down to open up his pack. His spellbook began shifting awake irritably.

After some rummaging, he found the source of the sound— it was the little book Kanderon had given him.

The instant he opened the book, the horrid shrieking stopped.

Hugh. I did not give you a means of rapid communication for you to simply forget about it.

He looked at Kanderon's distinct handwriting for a moment, so similar to the writing of the Index in the Great Library that was somehow an extension of her. It was livelier, more flawed, however, than the Index's own neat, precise script. Then he sighed, got out a pen, and clambered back into his bunk, and began to write back to the sphinx.

Apologies, master, Hugh wrote.

You should have reported in much more quickly after a major incident like that, came the response. **I expect prompt and detailed reports from my agents, which includes you. The instant you're safe and secure after a combat situation, you report in. Try not to pick up Alustin's bad habits about timely reporting.**

Hugh's spellbook slowly leaned upright against his side and began glaring at the communication book.

"Are you… are you being jealous?" Hugh asked his spellbook. "I'm allowed to read other books, you know."
Hugh returned to writing.

Honestly, master, I entirely forgot I had this book in my possession. I was exhausted, tired, and confused.

The spellbook's glaring had redoubled, and Hugh could swear its crystal had shifted to a slightly darker shade of green.
"Oh, is it me writing in other books you have a problem with?" he asked. "Because you're going to have to get used to that."
The spellbook shot him a wounded look, then drifted up off the bed and down into the room, probably to hide under the bottom bunk.

Understandable, but you need to train yourself to immediately report in the future, Kanderon wrote.

Kanderon spent the next few minutes interrogating Hugh on various details about the ambush. Hugh meant to stick to just the facts, but somehow, when it came to the death of the spotter, Hugh found himself confessing all his conflicting feelings to Kanderon. How he knew he'd done the right thing, and helped protect his friends, but somehow still felt ashamed, awful, and conflicted. And how he even felt ashamed for still missing Avah, which just seemed so petty alongside his new concerns and their mission.
Kanderon was silent for a time after that, but eventually resumed writing.

In all my centuries of life, Hugh, if there's one thing I've learned, it's that emotions cannot truly be controlled. They can't be harnessed, and they will never obey your expectations. We can control our reactions to our emotions, and we can slowly wrestle them into the directions we desire, but we will always have to understand them and fight them on their own grounds.

Which is to say, we have to understand ourselves. As much as some fools crave it, all attempts to become beings of unalloyed logic and reason fail. There is no shame to being emotional any more than there is to breathing air, Hugh. This is true of humans, it is true of sphinxes, and it is true of dragons. To live is to feel. Not even liches escape that fact.

And you can't expect to simply solve your turmoil, as wonderful as that would be. You'll have to work it out over time. We all hold vast reservoirs of emotion, but you can only channel those reservoirs so fast, Hugh. They'll drain over time, but they'll also refill continuously as you experience new things and encounter new pains. Little droplets of your emotions now will stay in there for a long time, and they'll emerge years later when you least expect them to. They'll grow diluted by new emotions, but they'll never go away entirely. I have old griefs and regrets of my own, Hugh, ones older than nations. They still surprise me when I expect them least, and I still have to deal with them. And I wouldn't have it any other way, Hugh. My pain is what keeps me connected to those weaker to me, what keeps me from simply considering myself a god to humans.

It hurts, but the only way past the hurt is through it. Pain is never shameful. And while I may not understand every emotion you feel, for the emotions of sphinxes are in many ways far different than those of humans, I am always willing to listen.

Kanderon stopped writing, and Hugh just stared at the page. He… he didn't know what he'd been expecting, but it hadn't been that. He'd expected some callous remarks about human frailty, some curmudgeonly orders to distract himself with ridiculous amounts of study, or just an utter dismissal of the importance of the spotter's death.

Not…

Hugh wiped the corners of his eyes. It must have been a second since this cabin had been cleaned. It was too dusty in here.

Kanderon resumed writing.

Anyhow, when you're keeping humans as pets, you need to tend to their emotional health as well as their physical. It's just good sense. And what you need right now is a distraction. Do you have *On the Nature and Growth of Crystalline Solids* with you?

An image of the sphinx getting embarrassed at being sentimental and changing the subject abruptly popped into Hugh's mind, and despite himself, a faint smile crept across his face. Kanderon was many things, but comfortable with sharing her emotions was definitely not one of them.

"Hey, spellbook," Hugh said. "*On the Nature and Growth of Crystalline Solids.*"

His spellbook took its time, but floated back up to him. It flipped its crystal pages open, and detailed writing and diagrams began forming on the pages.

Hugh wasn't entirely sure how, but his spellbook had the ability to replicate the contents of any books or papers it consumed into its internal pocket dimension. He definitely didn't mind, though— he'd long since fed it most of the books he owned, just for the convenience.

As Kanderon began to lecture him on water-soluble crystalline substances, his eyes couldn't help drifting back to her advice every couple of minutes.

Hugh came out onto deck just as they began leaving the harbor.

Off to one side, he could see Ampioc lurking just below the water as he repaired the damage to the city. Hugh stared at the immense octopus thoughtfully, wondering what sorts of emotions it felt, considering how much farther from being human it was than a sphinx or a dragon.

"Hugh!" Sabae called.

Hugh turned to see his friends standing in the prow of the ship waving at him. He waved back, then wandered over to them, feeling somehow lighter than he had in a while. He still missed Avah, and he still felt torn and sick about the spotter, but it wasn't quite as overwhelming as it had seemed before.

"I thought I was going to have to come drag you out of your cabin," Sabae said.

He gave her a wry grin. It didn't last long, but it felt good.

The four of them stood quietly in the prow as the crew bustled about behind them.

As they sailed out of the harbor, Hugh gazed at the massive columnar basalt seawall. Hundreds of seadrakes and seabirds basked in the sun or squabbled over fish atop it. He reached out with his affinity sense, and could feel the columnar basalt wall's submerged section as they sailed over it, and all the ways in which Ampioc must have magically reinforced its structure over time. He stretched his senses even farther out, feeling the further retaining pools the city used to assist as stormbreaks.

"Ampioc seals the entrance to the harbor entirely during a storm or attack," Alustin's voice said, from just behind them. "Builds a huge wall to close it off entirely."

The four of them jumped and turned around, to find, instead of Alustin, a hovering origami golem in the shape of an octopus. Unlike most origami golems, it didn't seem to be flapping wings or anything to keep itself in the air.

"Look up," the octopus said in Alustin's voice.

Hugh looked up to see Alustin waving at them from the drakes's nest atop the mainmast, standing beside a tall sailor with a spyglass.

"What are yeh doin' up there?" Godrick asked.

"I like having a good view," Alustin said.

The tall sailor lowered the eyeglass and said something, but his words didn't come through the origami octopus.

"I'm wounded you'd think my motives would be so base," Alustin said, though he didn't actually sound offended. "I'll have you know—"

Sabae interrupted. "We can still hear you, Alustin."

"Ah, right," Alustin said. If Hugh didn't know better, he'd say Alustin sounded embarrassed. "Well, uh, I meant to give you a bit of a history lesson, but for now, why don't you just go ahead and enjoy the view? Of the ocean, that is."

The octopus dissolved back into loose sheets of paper, which fluttered back up towards Alustin.

"I liked it better when he hid his flirtations from us," Sabae said, then turned back towards the ocean.

Hugh nodded in agreement as they all turned away.

It had been years since he'd last been out on the ocean. Before his family had died in the fire, his parents had once taken him to one of Emblin's fishing villages, high up on the green-grey cliffs of ancient welded ash. They'd hired a fishing boat to take them out for the day. Hugh remembered clinging to his parents as they walked down the steep cliff-paths to the floating docks, which went up and down twenty feet or more with each tide. They'd spent hours sailing along the coast and back.

He hadn't thought about that day in years.

Hugh turned his thoughts away from Emblin, before they could move forwards to darker times. He sent his affinity senses back down into the water, where he could feel the columnar basalt below. This far out, much of it was covered in sand and seaweed.

He paused, and then formed a spellform and began channeling mana into it. A few moments later, a trickle of sand began rising from the waves, congealing into a ball in front of him. Or, rather, trickles of a specific type of sand grain.

"Hugh, what are you doing?" Sabae asked him, looking at the wet sand ball.

Hugh just shrugged, then envisioned and activated a second spellform. The ball of sand began to writhe visibly as it shrunk.

Within a couple of minutes, a fist-sized transparent crystal hovered in the air. It was a hexagonal column, with the characteristic pyramid shaped spike at the top and bottom. It was just quartz, but compared to his cloudy, lumpy, misshapen old lump of quartz, it might as well be a different type of crystal entirely. The shape of this crystal was perfectly matched to the underlying pattern of the quartz, meaning his control over it with his magic would be far more precise.

He hesitated briefly before the next step, making sure he remembered the spellform correctly— it had been almost a year since he'd used it. His memory was pretty good, though, and it wasn't nearly the hardest spellform he'd ever used.

He took a deep breath, then assembled the proprioceptive link spellform in his mind's eye, casting it on his new quartz crystal. When it gently floated over to him and began slowly orbiting his head, he exhaled softly. He let go of all his active spellforms, but the quartz simply kept orbiting his head without him needing to pay attention to it. In addition, it used so little mana that his reservoirs could easily refill from the aether around him faster than it could drain away.

"Hey, Hugh?" Talia said.

Hugh turned to her, startled. He'd almost forgotten she was there— she was usually the loudest of his friends by far.

"I, uh, wanted to apologize for pushing you into the water earlier," she said. "Or trying to, I guess, since you didn't get wet. Not that it makes that better. I was nervous about getting on the ship and… some other stuff, and I just… I dunno, tend to get a little aggressive when I'm nervous? "

"I've noticed," Hugh said. "I tend to accumulate bruises a lot more quickly when you're stressed about things."

"Likewise," Godrick said.

Sabae just glanced back with a wry look, but Talia had always been a lot more cautious about jabbing, elbowing, or hitting the taller girl. Hugh highly doubted Sabae would be nearly as tolerant about it as Godrick or himself.

Talia turned red— or, redder— and looked down at her feet. "I'm sorry."

Hugh sighed. "It's annoying, but if it was really that big of a deal, we would have told you to stop."

The others all shot Hugh skeptical glances at that, even Talia.

Hugh sighed. "Fine, I would have just suffered in silence, but Godrick or Sabae would have done something about it."

"It might not be a big deal to you guys, but it is to me," Talia said. "I want to stop being so ridiculous about hiding my emotions behind being a belligerent jerk, and actually talk with you guys about them. And I don't want to hit my friends anymore like some spoiled child."

Hugh almost said something snarky, then stopped. Talia might be tougher than him, but he knew how hard it was to confess difficult things even to friends.

Instead, he stepped over to her and gave her a hug. He felt Talia tense up for a moment before she relaxed and hugged him back. He let go after a little longer and stepped back.

"I really appreciate that," Hugh said. "But don't beat yourself up if it takes time to get better at being more open. Stuff like that takes time."

It wasn't nearly as eloquently phrased as Kanderon's advice to him, but Talia smiled at him.

"Thanks, Hugh. I—" Talia started to say, before she was interrupted.

Not by a person, but by Hugh's new crystal running into the side of her head. It slowly rolled across her cheek and then tumbled off her nose at glacial speeds.

Everyone just stared at the slowly orbiting crystal.

"Maybe I should just have it float over my shoulder," Hugh said.

"Ah think that might be fer the best," Godrick said, visibly struggling to contain his laughter.

Sabae just nodded, shaking with suppressed laughter of her own.

Hugh blushed a bit at that, embarrassed at ruining the moment.

"Sorry about that, Talia," he said.

"It's fine," Talia said, fixing a strand of hair.

Godrick leaned over and wrapped Talia in a hug of his own. "Ah really appreciate yeh bein' open with us. Trust me, ah know it's not easy."

Sabae joined in the hug as well. "It means a lot. I also really, uh… appreciate the facial expression you made when that crystal hit you in the face."

Both she and Godrick burst out into laughter again, and

even Hugh's lips turned up at the corners, despite his embarrassment over the crystal.

"Hugh," Talia said, "is it alright if I wait a few seconds to start keeping my promise to hit you guys less?"

Hugh nodded as somberly as he could, trying not to start laughing. "That seems perfectly fine to me," he said.

Talia smiled at him, then punched Sabae in the shoulder and Godrick in the thigh.

"Ow! Hugh, you traitor!" Sabae said between laughs.

Hugh did burst out laughing then.

CHAPTER NINE

Old Philosophies

Alustin finally came down to join them about an hour later.

"Lesson time!" he said cheerfully.

"Don't you have more flirting to do?" Talia said.

"Don't you have more seasickness to deal with?" Alustin said.

Talia blinked in surprise. "I… I don't feel seasick!"

She grabbed Hugh and shook him. "I don't feel seasick!"

Hugh gently extricated himself, eying his floating crystal over his shoulder. He'd only just managed to get it to hover in place where he wanted it to, and he wasn't entirely sure it was stable. He'd have to double-check the spellforms when he went back to his cabin.

"Wave-going and dune-going ships have very different motions," Alustin said. "Getting seasick on one and not the other isn't uncommon."

"How did you not get yelled at by Captain Grepha?"

Sabae asked. "Most ship's captains hate their lookouts getting distracted."

Alustin tapped his glasses. "Farseer, remember? I've volunteered my services for the trip, so the captain will be happy to give me more leeway. Anyhow, as I said, it's lesson time. We're doing double duty on this one— I have a training exercise for each of you to perform while I lecture you."

Sabae's exercise involved maintaining wind armor on one arm and water armor on the other— something she complained was like trying to pat your head and rub your belly at the same time. Talia had to channel her magic into a tiny fragment of bone, and keep it from igniting for as long as possible while holding it. Godrick had to use his scent affinity to keep the smell of sea-salt from the group. When he complained that he didn't have a spell that could do that, Alustin smiled and presented him with a spellform for that very task.

Hugh didn't understand why there was a scent spellform for something so specific, but then, he didn't really understand scent affinities at all. They were, to say the least, really weird.

Alustin had apparently been communicating with Kanderon as well, because he assigned Hugh a practical exercise in growing salt crystals in seawater. It was surprisingly more challenging than Hugh expected. While he was just using the same pattern linking spellform he used to grow quartz crystals out of sand or feldspar crystals inside a boulder, there were several unique challenges here. The big one, obviously, was the fact that the salt was actively dissolved in the water. It wanted to stay dissolved, too, so Hugh had to use much more mana to cause the salt seed crystal to start growing, rather than dissolving. On top of that, there was the fact that there were quite a few different salts dissolved in the water, not just normal table salt, so he had to focus to make sure the salt crystal he was growing wasn't filled with impurities.

The pattern linking spellform was the most versatile spellform he'd ever used, but that very versatility made it aggravatingly difficult to use at times. He definitely understood why Kanderon didn't want him tinkering with the spellform— he'd be more likely to make it fail or injure himself than to improve things.

"Alright, then," Alustin said. "Everyone ready?"

They all glared at him. He laughed, then stepped between them to perch on the railing directly behind the figurehead—which also served as the bowsprit for the *Rising Cormorant.*

"So," Alustin said. "I've been talking to Artur about your educations, and he believes you've all become too focused in your studies. I've come to agree with his arguments."

"Being focused is a good thing, though, right?" Talia asked.

"It certainly can be, and narrow courses of study can be useful in a lot of respects, but many of the greatest mages achieve their mastery not just via depth of study, but breadth as well," Alustin said. "Quite a few mages have developed entirely new techniques and spells by studying affinities other than their own. Artur's a great example of that, in fact."

They all glanced at Godrick, who looked blank for a moment, until a look of realization crossed his face. "Right! Me da developed his armor after studyin' illusion magic fer years, ta figure out how ta make it work. Lots a' stone mages have developed armor before, but it always either took active shapin' and intense focus, or was prohibitively mana hungry, but da figured out how ta pull it off by modifyin' the techniques illusionists use when they create illusions based off physical objects— illusion anchors."

"Which, I can assure you, isn't as nearly as easy as it sounds," Alustin said. "Plenty of people have tried to mimic Artur's approach, but there's clearly more to it than just that. I've met few other mages as brilliant as Artur."

Godrick smiled proudly at that.

"So for the rest of this summer, along with many of my other planned lessons, I'm going to be introducing you to the abilities and techniques of various other affinities," Alustin said. "Not only in hopes of inspiring you to think of new techniques or new ways to use your own affinities in creative ways, but also so that you have more familiarity with different affinities if you need to fight them in the future."

The tiny bone shard between Talia's hands started expanding, and she hastily threw it overboard. The resulting explosion was small enough that it likely wouldn't have done more than burn her fingers, but Hugh thought it was pretty obvious why Talia wouldn't want that.

"Start again, Talia," Alustin said. He waited for her to pull out a new bone shard before continuing. "I decided I'd start with one of the strangest affinities— shadow affinities. Does anyone know what, precisely, shadow affinities affect?"

"Shadows?" Sabae guessed, somewhat sarcastically. A bit of water sprayed out of her spinning armor and splashed Hugh, and he almost lost control of the salt crystal he was growing in the waves beside the ship.

"And what's a shadow?" Alustin asked.

"It's… a lack of light?" Hugh ventured.

"Exactly," Alustin said. "It's a lack of light. That's the weird bit, though— how many affinities do you know of that affect a lack of something, rather than a thing?"

They were all silent for a moment as Alustin stared at them.

"Ah guess… ah haven't seen another like that?" Godrick said.

"So why is shadow unique like that?" Alustin asked. "How is it the only affinity that affects an absence, rather than a presence?"

The bone shard in Talia's hands grew a little bit, and its cracks shone slightly brighter for a moment, but then it seemed to stabilize.

"It's affecting something other than the shadows?" Talia said. "Like… the light, maybe?"

Alustin grinned at her. "Right on the mark, at least half the time. That was actually something of a trick question, because shadow affinities are what is known as a compound affinity. That is to say, there are two entirely different forms of shadow affinity. Compound affinities are actually fairly common— there are, for instance, at least six different versions of ice affinities. There's one that functions via draining and moving heat, almost like a fire affinity, and there's another that works like a crystal affinity specialized for just ice crystals. There's yet another that is a water affinity variant, and so on and so forth."

"What about stone affinities?" Godrick asked.

Alustin shook his head. "Stone affinities are, rather, a form of cluster affinity. It's a subtle difference, but with compound affinities, you essentially have multiple versions of an affinity for a single substance, whereas with cluster affinities, you have a single affinity for multiple substances, like the different types of stone or, alternatively, different types of trees for tree affinities. Cluster affinities are where you most clearly see specificity translating into more power, though that rule still remains true of all affinities."

"And is that why ah'm stronger with some types a' stone and weaker with others? And likewise with me da, but different stones fer him?" Godrick asked.

Alustin nodded. "Most likely, though the specific mechanisms of how those variances occur aren't known."

"Are there other categories of affinity?" Hugh asked.

Alustin nodded. "Quite a few. There are structural affinities, like crystal or fiber affinities, which target structures or arrangements of material rather than varieties of material. Then there are monolithic affinities, like solar, wind, or flame affinities, which only affect a single material in a single manner."

"I hadn't heard the term compound affinity before, but fire is definitely a compound affinity," Talia said.

Alustin raised an eyebrow at her. "That… is certainly a bold claim."

Talia shrugged. "I can't tell you more— because it's a clan secret— but are you really going to argue with a member of Clan Castis about fire?"

Alustin grinned at that. "That would be even bolder of me, so no."

Sabae raised her hand. "I hadn't heard those terms either,

but my family suspects there are different types of wind affinities too— we haven't been able to prove it, but we suspect air has different components to it, and that a lot of what we see as variations in wind affinity power is actually variations in what part of the wind the mage is affecting? So I guess it would be a cluster affinity."

"Different components of wind?" Alustin asked, visibly intrigued.

"I haven't spent a lot of time looking into it," Sabae said, "but some of my family members believe it's why a candle goes out when you place a glass jar over it— because it's burned through some component of the air as fuel."

"So, what yeh're saying is that the world will run out of air someday because a' fire?" Godrick asked.

Both Talia and Sabae shook their heads at that.

"Plants produce whatever part of the air it is that fire needs," Talia said. "Clan Castis has known that for a while now."

Sabae nodded in agreement.

"I'm definitely going to want to speak to both of you more about this later," Alustin said. "All of this, I should note, is on the theoretical end of things, not so much the practical, but neglecting the study of magical theory is a good way to stifle your ability to innovate. Purely practical education makes effective battle mages, but it won't make you an archmage or a great power. Of course, neither will purely theoretical education— a balance is needed between the two. And for all that taxonomies like this one are often among the more arbitrary theoretical constructs, they're still highly useful."

Talia cursed and threw her bone shard overboard, where it detonated. Alustin waited patiently while she started the process all over again.

"Anyhow, back to shadow affinities," Alustin said, once she was charging a new bone shard. "There are only two types of shadow affinity. One is, like Talia guessed, a close relative of light affinities. It effectively acts as a light barrier, creating shadows. It can be used to turn invisible and has limited illusion-generating ability. Yves Heliotrope, one of the Skyhold Council members that died in the battle against Bakori, had both a light affinity and a shadow affinity of this sort— which allowed her to generate shadows for her light-based illusions, something purely light-affinity based illusionists can't do. That's the easiest way to identify a light-based illusion, by the way— look for missing shadows, at least for entirely constructed illusions. Illusions that are just masking another object might still have something of a shadow, though it will be distorted. Other illusions based in different affinities have different weaknesses you can learn to identify."

Hugh shuddered, thinking about Yves' body impaled on Bakori's tail, and his salt crystal began to dissolve. He quickly stabilized it, and dismissed the image from his mind.

"The other type of shadow affinity is a lot more interesting for our purposes," Alustin continued. "Not to mention, it's significantly more powerful, and one you've encountered before."

"Eudaxus, the high priest of Indris' cult," Sabae said.

Alustin smiled at her, and then clambered all the way up onto the railing, until he was standing atop it.

"Eudaxus," he agreed. "He can make shadows tangible, transmit his voice through them, even teleport through them across short distances— which, by and large, is one of the rarest abilities any affinity can have. Of course, Eudaxus is one of the most powerful shadow mages alive, and stands fairly high in the ranks of archmages, but it's still astonishing. His variety of shadow affinity is sometimes called a darkness or night affinity, but I prefer simply calling it a greater shadow affinity. Less ambiguous and confusing, to my mind, since I've heard regular shadow affinities called night or darkness affinities quite often as well."

"Will Hugh ever be able to teleport with his spatial affinity?" Talia asked.

Alustin shook his head. "Probably not. It's possible, of course— it's one of the other rare affinities that can do it. It's so prohibitively difficult that you basically have to spend years mastering it at the expense of almost all other applications of the affinity— both due to the opportunity cost, and due to the fact that teleportation can disrupt extraplanar spaces. And, as those are Kanderon's specialty as a planar mage, she doesn't personally use it."

The smell of sea salt rolled over them, more apparent for its previous absence, and it was Godrick's turn to curse. Alustin waited patiently for the smell to recede again before continuing.

"I could have you play an elaborate guessing game to figure out how Eudaxus does that," Alustin said, a grin on his face, "but I think I'm being hard enough on you already today. A greater shadow affinity is a type of affinity known as a meta-affinity, a vanishingly small category. In fact, the only other I know of off-hand are dream affinities and language affinities, the latter of which only the Ithonian Empire ever developed. Meta-affinities mimic the abilities of multiple otherwise non-contiguous affinities. In the case of greater shadow affinities, it's a blend of spatial, shadow, light, and force affinities. This isn't an exact metaphor, of course— someone with all four of those regular affinities would be hard-pressed to replicate greater shadow affinities, since it's not truly a blend of those abilities, but rather just mimics their effects. Rather, greater shadow affinities work by, well, ignorance."

The ship hit a particularly large wave, and all four students cursed. Talia's bone shard went skidding across the deck before Sabae sent it flying into the water with a well-timed gust strike. The water spinning around her other arm, however, drenched the other three. Hugh lost his magical grip on the salt crystal, and he had to frantically reach out with his affinity sense to find and retrieve it as it sank.

Godrick's loss of control wasn't as dramatic as the others, but still resulted in the smell of salt flooding back.

Alustin, meanwhile, simply stepped with the lurching of the ship over their heads, to the railing on the other side. He was hardly even splashed by Sabae's loss of control.

Someone— Hugh was guessing Alustin— cast a drying cantrip on the group. Their teacher waited patiently standing atop the railing for them to all resume their practice before he resumed.

Several Radhan children, the youngest barely old enough to walk, watched them from near the foremast, laughing at them.

"Essentially, Eudaxus and other greater shadow users seem to be able to, for lack of a better description, trick places into thinking that they are other places, with other properties, or even to link them together somehow. Almost as though the lack of light inside of a shadow makes its contents less certain, less *real*."

"That's bizarre," Talia said. "And it seems entirely different than what a dream affinity does."

Hugh shrugged. "Seems pretty similar to me, at least in how weird it is."

"Maybe," Talia said, "but I don't know what lessons we're supposed to draw from this, either about how to fight a greater shadow affinity or how we're supposed to apply this to our own affinities."

Alustin fixed her with an ominous smile. "As to the first, fighting greater shadow affinities is straightforward enough. Prevent a shadow from staying in one place or becoming too clear, and it becomes difficult for a greater shadow mage to affect. Weakening the shadows with more light also does the trick. The latter question, that of applying it to your own affinities, however, is a lot more interesting. It would take several weeks of lecturing to explain in detail, but it reflects on a concept much bandied about by pre-Ithonian philosophers— the idea of representation space. Representation space was a hypothetical transcendent location where affinities came from— where the ideal form of all things was located. Both real objects and affinities were supposedly just representing what was found in that space, with each affinity there representing a node in a sort of strange, multi-dimensional conceptual grid."

"Ah thought yeh told us the Ithonians proved that wrong, though," Godrick said. "That nothin' a' the sort existed."

Alustin pointed at him. "Precisely correct. They did not, however, do away entirely with the idea of representation space. It transfigured, as some ideas do, into something the Ithonians called description space. Rather than a transcendent plane where the true forms of all things existed, it was a purely notional space where the *descriptions* of all things existed, and that affinities were nodes in the multi-dimensional conceptual grid of description space, along intersections of axes of physical properties like hardness, density, melting point, size, and so on and so forth."

"Purely notional meaning fake?" Hugh asked.

Alustin swayed on the railing as he tilted his head to one side, then the other. "Well… it's certainly not real except as an idea, but not being real is hardly the same as being fake."

"I'm still not seeing the relevance of this," Talia said, though there was a note of apprehension in her voice.

Alustin's smile grew even wider. "In essence, meta-affinities, rather than being nodes in description space, are claimed by some philosophers to be axes in description space. Not axes for any normal physical property, however, but for stranger ones, that intersect non-contiguous nodes in description space. As for the relevance of all this, well… you, Talia, are going to be spending the next few weeks reading pre-Ithonian philosophy, Ithonian studies that disprove that philosophy, and a long, long list of post-Ithonian essays and texts on description space, and then at the end, *you'll* be telling *me* what the relevance is."

A glowing blue tattoo appeared on Alustin's forearm, and an impressive stack of books appeared in midair above his hand. He levitated the stack down in front of Talia.

She glared at it for a moment, then glared at Alustin.

"So you're having me investigate an imaginary space that even its creators don't believe exist, that was made up to respond to another imaginary space that was disproven," Talia said.

"Essentially, yes," Alustin said.

"I hate this more than any other assignment I've ever received," Talia said.

Alustin just smiled at her.

Talia scowled and threw her newest bone shard overboard.

By sheer bad luck, it detonated right alongside Hugh's submerged salt crystal, cracking it apart and sending it towards the depths.

Hugh sighed, and prepared to start the process of growing a salt crystal all over again.

CHAPTER TEN

Unfortunate Dietary Choices

By the time their lesson was over, Godrick was exhausted and wrung out. His scent reservoir had given out fairly early on, so Alustin had set him to solving complex blacksmith puzzles using only his magic. Alustin had borrowed an enchanted blacksmith puzzle from Sabae for that— one that Godrick had actually given her for her birthday. Solving it with only his magic was far, far more challenging than solving it with his fingers— complex motions like that were harder to perform with magic than one's hands. Listening to Alustin lecture them about different types of affinities had only made it harder. After shadow, he'd taught them about hair affinities, which were bizarre, and then an introductory lecture on the different types of illusion magic. Those ranged from light to dream to mirage, all the way to the absolutely terrifying perception affinities. Thankfully, those last were vanishingly rare, and their users tended to die horribly or drive themselves insane. There were also, apparently, illusionists that used cloth, pigment, and other such affinities to perform more physical illusions. Much of it was recap for Godrick, having heard many lectures on illusionists from his father, but Alustin put a fascinatingly different spin on things.

There were, apparently, many more such lessons to go on illusions— not just on how they worked, but how to spot them, how to see through them, and how to disrupt them.

At one point, Artur had wandered by to check on them, curious about the periodic explosions Talia was producing. Godrick was a little surprised to see his da on deck— on those rare occasions when Artur had to travel by ship, he seldom left his cabin. He seldom talked about his seafaring days, and most of what Godrick knew his mother had told him when he was young, before she died. It was pretty grim stuff, even with her clearly leaving a lot out of the stories. He'd never pressed his da to hear more, but he definitely understood why Artur didn't like ships.

His da hadn't stayed on deck very long— just enough to check up on them and remind Hugh to come help with whatever mysterious project they were working on when the lesson was over.

By the end of the lesson, Lothal had long since drifted out of sight behind them, and the *Rising Cormorant* had drawn alongside the beginning of the Skyreach Range. He could see a flight of dragons winging together amongst their peaks, recognizable only by their shapes as anything but a flock of sparrows in the distance. The mountains seemed to rise straight from the sea and land like great stone spikes driven upwards, ignoring foothills like they were frivolities for lesser mountain ranges.

That wasn't actually true, of course— the foothills on this side of the range were buried by the seas bordering it. To the west, they were covered by hundreds of feet of sand, while to the south where the *Cormorant* sailed, they were inundated by saltwater. Farther north, or on the east side of the range, you could see more in the way of foothills— not just because they weren't covered up there, but because the foothills to the east were far larger and far more numerous.

Godrick took a couple more minutes to enjoy the view, then left Talia and Sabae at the prow to follow Hugh down below.

Godrick smacked his head against the ceiling twice on his way to the cabin he shared with Hugh. He didn't curse, however, just sighed heavily— he was long since used to hitting his head almost wherever he went, except for Lothal.

That was one thing he loved about Skyhold— all the ceilings and doors were more than tall enough, there.

As Godrick fixed his hair, he wondered at how Kanderon got in and out of the mountain. She was far too big to travel through most of the hallways or entrances.

There was a certain irony to that, to be sure. She effectively ruled over a small city whose streets she could not walk. But then, that was true of many of the nonhuman great powers— Indris could fly over her streets, but not walk most of them, and while Ampioc could technically roam the streets of Lothal with surprising grace, he seldom did so— not least because it left things rather slimy.

There were several ship's cats clustered outside his door, for some reason. Actual cats, for the most part, not overgrown spiders. There was one seadrake among them, as well— seadrakes were far better-tempered than sand drakes, and were sometimes kept as pets by sailors. They got along well with cats as well, though likely just to take advantage of their body heat as much as anything.

Godrick sighed, and gently began moving the cats and the seadrake out of the way, though one of them decided to climb up his legs and up to his shoulders as he did so. He gave it a dirty look, but the young cat just butted its head against his cheek.

He carefully slipped inside, so as to not let any of the other animals into their cabin.

Only to find, when he got inside, an utter disaster.

There were papers strewn *everywhere*. Across the floor and on both bunks. Some were loose sheaves of papers, some were crumpled balls, and a few were even chewed up books. Countless torn up scraps covered everything. There was, inexplicably, a chewed-up hat lying on the floor as well.

There was an unpleasant noise like a book ripping, and

another cloud of papers fired itself off the top bunk. The cat on Godrick's shoulder reared up to bat at the loose pages, and Godrick sighed.

He stepped over to look, though he already suspected what he'd see.

Hugh's spellbook lay atop the bunk, its crystal a much paler shade of green than usual. The strap Hugh used to sling it over his shoulder was all tangled up, and it was trembling slightly.

Godrick awkwardly reached out to touch the book, and it cuddled up to his hand, looking miserable. He gently scratched its spine, and the book seemed to relax slightly.

The cat hopped onto the bunk and sniffed the book curiously.

"There, there," Godrick said. "Yeh wait here, and ah'll get Hugh, alright?"

The book responded by vomiting paper scraps all over him.

Godrick knocked on his da's door, the cat back on his shoulder.

"Hey, Da, is Hugh there?" he called.

"Just a moment," Artur called.

There was some clattering, then Hugh opened the door, his new crystal still floating over one shoulder. Behind him, Godrick could see something covered in a sheet on the narrow table in his da's room— Artur's cabin was huge for a ship but small by any other measure. His da, sitting next to the table, waved at him.

"Why do you have a cat on your shoulder?" Hugh asked.

"Ah'm just bein' fashionable," Godrick said. "Why don't either of yeh have one?"

The cat chirped happily at that.

"Thanks fer remindin' me," Godrick told the cat. "Hugh, ah think yer spellbook is sick. It's vomitin' paper scraps all over our cabin."

Hugh just stared at him for a moment, then sighed. "I swear, it's always something with that book."

"Yeh still haven't named it?" Artur asked. "It definitely needs a name."

"Is it alright if I go check on it?" Hugh asked Artur.

"Ah'll come with yeh," Artur said. "Ah'm definitely curious what a sick book looks like."

The three of them strode down the hallway— or, Godrick supposed, the passageway, as Sabae would call it. She was constantly getting on the other three for getting the names of ship's features wrong. There were just so many alternate names for things on board a ship, though— it seemed really unnecessary to Godrick.

The cats and the seadrake all flooded into their cabin when they entered— there was no way to keep them all out while all three of them entered.

There was barely enough room to stand for all three of them. Poor Hugh was in danger of being squashed between Godrick and his da.

"It looks like the poor thing ate somethin' that didn't much agree with it," Artur said, as Hugh comforted the miserable-looking book.

Hugh paused for a moment, then lifted up his pillow to check and scowled.

"That's exactly what happened," he said. "It ate the magic journal Kanderon gave me to keep in touch with her. I'd bet the enchantment on it is giving it indigestion."

Artur stepped back as much as he could in the cramped cabin, looking nervous. "That's, ah… really not good. Long distance communication enchantments are fairly high-energy."

"How high energy?" Godrick asked. His da knew quite a bit about enchantments— he'd pursued enchantment as a potential career when he was younger, though he'd decided against it, ultimately.

"Blow a hole in the side a' the ship an' sink it high energy," Artur said.

"We should probably go get Alustin," Hugh said. "He's got a journal too, he can contact Kanderon for us."

Hugh gingerly lifted the spellbook off his bunk and began

carefully walking it down the passageway, Artur close behind. Godrick took a few seconds to clear the cats and the seadrake out of the room, then shut the door behind him and followed.

He felt a bit like Hugh, thinking it, but Godrick would absolutely love it if this was the last interesting thing that happened on the voyage. Boring sounded wonderful right now.

That was, of course, when the whole ship shuddered, and the yelling and screaming started abovedeck.

CHAPTER ELEVEN

Here Be Serpents

Sabae was having more trouble with this whole flirtation thing than she had anticipated. It had always seemed easy enough from outside, and she had never had any trouble advising friends about their dating lives— or even manipulating Hugh's dating life, because he definitely never would have gotten together with Avah without her meddling.

She still needed to decide whether to intervene in the whole Hugh and Talia situation. She certainly could, but she felt rather less relaxed about meddling in her friends' lives now, largely thanks to her persistent anger at the way Kanderon, Alustin, and her grandmother had manipulated them over the last year.

Somehow, though, dating became a problem of a whole different order when she was involved, and not observing.

And a cute boy asking what she liked to do for fun should *not* be this difficult to answer.

It had all started innocuously enough— after Hugh and Godrick had left, several Radhan teens around their age had approached them. Two boys, and a girl who turned out to be the twin of the shorter boy. Tollin, Dell, and Yarra.

Talia, for whatever ridiculous reason, was just glaring at Yarra the whole time.

Introductions had gone easily enough— Tollin and Yarra were both water mages, and were curious about Sabae's unusual magic. Sabae had been happy to answer a few questions, though she wasn't going to give away the whole fishing fleet when it came to talking about her magic. Other mages might advertise their affinities and capabilities, but battle mages needed to be a bit more circumspect.

Then Yarra's twin brother, Dell, the lone non-mage in the group, apparently bored with all the technical discussion of magic, had decided to change the subject. He apparently got more than enough of it from most of the other teens onboard— the Radhan trained many more of their youth in magic than most populations. Dell was blind in his mind's eye, however, so he couldn't learn magic. Nothing wrong with that, of course— the aether wasn't thick enough for everyone to be mages.

So he asked Sabae what she liked to do for fun.

It's not that Sabae's mind went blank. No, lots of potential answers came to mind. The problem was that she rather doubted that Dell would be that interested if she said she enjoyed studying magic, even though that was true. She'd probably sound insane if she said she enjoyed getting involved in the deadly politics played between the great powers. Hanging out with her friends just sounded too boring.

Her pause had dragged out just to the point where it was getting awkward when the pack of sea serpents attacked the ship.

It probably said something about her that her immediate response was feeling relieved that she didn't have to answer Dell's question.

Sabae had seen sea serpents before, of course. Ras Andis' fleets brought in dead ones every now and then— they attacked fishing boats regularly along the southern coast of

Ithos, hence the need for mages to guard the fishing fleets. There were far, far more dangerous creatures in Anastis' oceans, but most, like krakens, leviathans, and the countless aberrations of the depth, generally kept to themselves and avoided the shallows. Sea serpents were surface hunters with voracious appetites, and had no compunctions about targeting ships. They were as cunning as wolves, and far more powerful.

Sea serpents traveled in packs of a half-dozen to a dozen individuals, ranging in length from ten to twenty feet. They were slow and sluggish most of the time, save while hunting. While pursuing prey, they were faster than nearly any ship over short distances, save for a few coursers that were the seagoing equivalent of her grandmother's sandship, *That Old Pile of Junk*— built to travel at terrifying speeds propelled by storm archmages or the like.

Despite the name, they weren't snakes at all, nor reptiles nor dragon-kin, but fish. They possessed strange, lobe-shaped fins that they could move in any direction, which along with their sinuous, snake-like bodies, gave them unparalleled agility in the water. And though they weren't snakes, they were just as good at climbing as snakes were, and had a nasty habit of climbing silently up the sides of ships and snatching sailors off the decks.

Not for the first time, Sabae would have died if it weren't for Talia. One moment, Sabae was making a fool of herself, and the next, a bolt of purple-green dreamfire was traveling right past her face.

She whirled to see a serpent looming over her, looking confused, with a smoldering patch just beneath its jaw from the impact. The great fleshy whiskers and the corners of its fang-filled mouth quivered, and then the smoldering patch ruptured, spilling out thousands and thousands of what looked like coins. The serpent began to deflate like a balloon as the coins kept flowing onto the deck, before it finally just collapsed into the water.

The coins, of all things, appeared to be made of wood.

Sabae only hesitated for a moment before she began to spin up her wind armor, but that moment of hesitation was enough to give the next sea serpent a chance to strike. It closed its jaws around Dell's leg, then threw itself back into the water, dragging the Radhan youth over the railing.

She didn't hesitate this time. Sabae leapt atop the railing, then dove headfirst towards the water, detonating the wind armor around her legs to propel herself forwards into the water like a spear.

Talia had absolutely no interest in admitting it, but the only reason she was able to kill the awful fish-snake thing before it grabbed Sabae was the fact that she'd been fantasizing about blasting the Radhan teens with dreamfire.

It's not that she hated the Radhan in general, just their youth. They were unnecessarily friendly, even more unnecessarily pretty, and almost certainly all planning to seduce her friends, especially Hugh.

Self-reflection wasn't always Talia's strong suit, but she definitely knew that none of her friends would look fondly on her for fantasizing violence against others for petty personal reasons like that.

But then, it saved Sabae's life, because her mind's eye was already primed for the dreamfire spellforms.

The second awful snake-fish thing took her by surprise, however, and she cursed as it dragged Dell over the side of the prow. Before Talia could do more than curse, Sabae had launched herself straight after Dell.

Talia briefly considered chasing after, but she had only gone swimming a handful of times in her life, in placid ponds and narrow streams in the valleys of the Skyreach Range. Before she could make a decision, however, screaming came from farther down the deck.

More of the hideous creatures had clambered up the sides of the ship, and at least three sailors had already been grabbed by them.

Talia formed the spellform for guided dreambolts in her mind's eye— she didn't want to accidentally hit any panicking sailors or rigging with a normal, unguided dreambolt. Before she'd even finished, however, the attack was already over. One of the creatures was blasted over the side by several Radhan water mages, another was impaled by a dozen massive wooden spines that erupted from the deck, and at least four of them had been slaughtered by Alustin. He'd sliced them into thin, finger-width discs with a storm of paper.

Not for the first time, Talia was glad Alustin was on their side. She could easily imagine him doing the exact same thing to a human being.

She turned to Tollin and Yarra, who were gaping in confusion and horror.

"Can either of you feel Sabae or Dell with your affinity senses?" she demanded.

They both just looked blankly at her.

"You're water mages, aren't you?" she demanded.

"Right, sorry," Tollin muttered, and closed his eyes.

Yarra started to close her eyes as well, but Talia jabbed her with a finger. "And keep a watch out for out for more of those awful creatures."

"Sea serpents," Yarra said, but nodded and closed her eyes.

Talia raised an eyebrow at that. That was *not* what she was expecting a sea serpent to look like.

The seconds crept by like hours as Talia scanned the railings for more serpents, waiting for the young water mages to find Sabae.

Finally, Tollin opened his eyes. "I can't find them," he said.

She turned to Yarra, who was on the verge of tears. "I can't sense my brother or your friend at all."

Talia struggled not to scream and curse.

"Neither of us are very powerful yet, though," Tollin said. "They could have easily dropped behind the ship or something and left our range."

Talia took a deep breath.

"Keep looking," she ordered them.

Sabae's wind armor on her upper body meant that when she entered the water, only her legs actually got wet at first. She quickly spun up water armor around herself, trapping the remnants of her wind armor inside so she could breathe. She couldn't use both armor types at once yet, so the vast majority of her air escaped before she sealed it inside her water armor.

While Sabae could propel herself by detonating her water armor around her limbs in the same manner she wind-jumped, she'd been practicing a rather different method of swimming locomotion. It had taken direct intercession by Alustin to get her the chance to practice it in the great water holding tanks below Skyhold, but given that the water wasn't purified until it was to be pumped upwards to the top of the mountain, where it would then travel downward through pipes, getting it dirty hadn't really been a concern.

Sabae focused on pulling water in towards her head, spun it down her body, then released it off her hands and feet. She shot downward into the water.

She couldn't see the sea serpent at first, but she could feel it with her affinity sense as it dove downward, Dell still struggling in its mouth. Sabae redoubled her efforts, panicking a school of scrap-feeders that often followed sea-serpents as she jetted past them.

As Sabae dove, she felt something— no, a whole group of somethings— deep in the water below her.

Her eyes, dry in the bubble of air held in by the water armor, widened.

Juvenile serpents.

They were floating with their head downward and tails pointing upwards— for whatever reason, serpents spent most of their time not hunting in that pose, from what Sabae had been told. Each juvenile was about the size of Talia, but she had no doubt their needle-teeth were just as sharp as their parents'.

Sabae flooded even more mana into her armor and blasted

forwards dangerously fast.

The water was already growing murky with depth, so when she slammed into the adult serpent, she only had a moment's notice from her eyes. She'd been watching the serpent carefully with her water affinity sense, however. At the last second, she flipped around and slammed into it with both feet, detonating the water armor around her legs as she did so.

The serpent was sent tumbling off course, and Dell slipped out of its mouth, floating limply in the water. She could see clouds of blood billowing from his leg.

The juveniles, apparently, could detect Dell's blood too, because they'd turned upwards and were racing towards him.

Sabae accelerated down towards him, but the momentum she'd lost hitting the big serpent cost her most of her advantage in getting to him. The juvenile serpents were just feet away from him when she arrived.

She shifted her water armor from its chase spin pattern to a more combat focused spin pattern, then sent the first pair of juveniles tumbling away with a powerful water-burst from each arm.

That, unfortunately, sent her tumbling backward— she hadn't had nearly enough experience using her magic underwater for her comfort, and this was her first ever underwater combat situation.

She frantically rolled to orient herself just as the next juvenile lunged for Dell.

Talia was pacing back and forth irritably when Hugh, Godrick, and Artur raced onto the deck. It probably hadn't been more than a minute, and the rest of the water mages on board had already started looking for Sabae and Dell with their affinity senses, but it felt like it had been an eternity. Even Alustin, standing up in the rigging, was looking with his farseeing affinity, but it likely wouldn't help much— he apparently had as much trouble seeing through water with it as he would with his eyes normally.

"What's going on?" Hugh asked as he rushed over to her. "Where's Sabae?"

For some reason, he was cradling that damn crystal spellbook in his arms. Irritably, she drew two of her daggers— the one Hugh had found for her in the dungeon with the kinetic anchor enchantment on it, along with the one carved out of dragonbone. For a moment it almost seemed like it was trembling in anticipation, but that was surely just her own nerves. There was nothing— *nothing*— Talia hated more than feeling helpless.

Talia scowled and pointed into the water. "Sea serpents took one of the Radhan boys," she said. "Sabae went after him."

"My brother's name is Dell," Yarra said, sounding offended.

"Hugh doesn't know that, and it's no time for introductions!" Talia snapped. "Keep looking."

She felt her arm with the dagger tremble again, and an idea came to her.

"Hugh, your spellbook doesn't need to breathe, right?" Talia said. "Send it down to look for them."

Artur shook his head. "Bad idea. The pesky little book went an' made itself sick, eatin' somethin' it shouldn't a."

Talia raised her eyebrows incredulously at that. "It did *what*?" she demanded.

Hugh shrugged and gave her an apologetic look. "It ate the journal Kanderon gave me to communicate with her," he said.

Talia snarled in frustration and channeled mana into her dragonbone dagger, which burst into flame. She was about to release a few choice curse-words when she felt a curious buzzing in her hair.

Then the back of her head decided to catch on fire explosively, sending her flying face-first into the deck.

Rather than try and blast the juvenile serpent out of the way, Sabae sent a water-strike towards Dell. Not a strong one, but enough to send him tumbling out of the serpent's path. She rapidly switched her armor back to her chase spin pattern, and shot after him.

She barely reached Dell before another juvenile did, grabbing him around the waist with an impact that sent them both tumbling wildly through the water. She cursed as the water blasting off her arms exacerbated the tumbling even more, and quickly switched to a combat spin pattern again.

Another juvenile rushed her, jaws agape. Sabae frantically twisted her legs into position, pulling as much water as she could into the armor spinning around them.

Just as the juvenile began to close its jaws around her feet, she detonated the water armor around her feet as hard as she could. The juvenile simply exploded from the inside out, and Sabae and Dell were sent jetting away from the cloud of gore.

As Sabae got their motion under control, she took a moment to take stock of their situation. Her heart was racing and her muscles were already screaming, and it was starting to get harder to breathe the air she'd brought down with her. Dell wasn't moving at all, but she didn't have time to check for a pulse.

The scattered juveniles were regrouping to come after her again, and the adult was recovering from her attack, and was turning back towards her.

Sabae made a frustrated sound in the back of her throat and rapidly began pulling more water into her spinning armor. Her mana reservoir, already heavily depleted, began draining even faster.

She carefully adjusted her grip on Dell, then envisioned a spellform in her mind's eye.

Other than cantrips and healing spells, Sabae seldom used spellforms these days— most of her magic involved completely spellformless casting. This wind spell, however, was absolutely essential if she wanted to survive the next few seconds— or, for that matter, if she wanted Dell to survive.

If he even was alive.

It wasn't a spell that she'd learned at Skyhold, either— this one was a spell taught to all Kaen Das mages who went to sea.

The juveniles were only a few feet away when she reached the limit of how much water her armor could hold. The enraged adult serpent wasn't far behind them. She'd pulled Dell partially into her armor, at least as much as she could without disrupting its spin.

Sabae took one final deep breath, flooded the spellform in her mind's eye with mana, and detonated her water armor downward. Not just the water around her legs, but *all* of it. The remainder of her air even went with it in a cascade of bubbles.

They blasted upwards faster than Sabae had ever moved in the water before. She almost lost her grip on Dell, and she was fairly sure that she'd sprained something in her shoulder. Behind her, she could feel the juveniles go tumbling through the water with her water affinity sense, and farther back she could feel the adult racing upwards.

She switched her armor into chase mode almost immediately, and the spin began accelerating her upwards before she could lose much of her momentum.

The spellform in her mind's eye was draining mana from her wind reservoir at a truly terrifying rate. It was her largest reservoir by far, however, given how much more she'd used it than the other three, so she shouldn't be overly worried about it running out. Still, she couldn't help but be nervous— she'd heard countless horror stories about what could happen to mages that ascended through water too quickly without its protection. It curdled your blood, somehow, turning the air you'd breathed into your lungs and veins toxic. If the spell failed, she and Dell would die a gruesome death, even ignoring the sea serpents.

The adult sea serpent's pace while swimming with Dell in its mouth turned out to have been a leisurely swim for it— it was swimming faster than anything else she'd ever sensed in the water, and despite her absurd speed, it was steadily gaining on her.

Sabae's heart was pounding and her body was struggling with her lack of air as the water around her lightened. She could feel her whole body trembling, and her lungs ached as they demanded she take a breath.

When she erupted from the waves into the air at speed, her armor collapsed entirely, as did the spellform. She tried to spin up wind armor, but she couldn't focus between gasping for breath as she and Dell hurtled skyward.

Below her, the surface erupted in spray as the sea serpent launched itself into the air, its jaws agape. Sabae frantically tried to summon her wind armor, only to have her grip on both her magic and Dell fail entirely.

She reached the pinnacle of her ascent and began to fall straight downward towards the serpent.

Sabae took a deep breath and closed her eyes, hoping her death would be a quick one.

Even through her closed lids, the light that followed was blinding.

Her fall began to slow, then she came to a stop entirely, floating in midair.

She blinked the afterimages away, then swiveled, where she spotted Dell hanging beside her. She kept turning and spotted, nearly a full ship's length away, the *Rising Cormorant.*

Hugh was standing at the stern railing, waving at her.

CHAPTER TWELVE

Destructive Resonance

Several Radhan sailors carefully guided Dell onto the deck as Hugh levitated them in. The ship's healer was already examining his injuries before he even touched the deck.

Hugh carefully looked Sabae over as he guided her in. She seemed exhausted, but he didn't see any visible injuries.

Sabae staggered as she landed, and Hugh caught her—

with his arms, this time, not a spell.

"Are you alright?" he asked.

"I'm fine," Sabae said raggedly. "Just exhausted."

They embraced for a long, quiet moment. Hugh was just barely tall enough to see over her shoulder, where a water mage was drawing seawater out of Dell's lungs while the healer worked on his leg.

"Hey Hugh?" Sabae said quietly.

"Yes?" he asked.

"If I ever catch you talking badly about yourself again, I'll beat you till you're more bruise than not. I literally can't even count how many times you've saved my life now," she said.

"You've saved my life before too," Hugh said. "I don't…"

Sabae squeezed him a little harder. "Till you're more bruise than not," she repeated.

Hugh felt a smile work its way onto his face.

"Thanks, Sabae," he said quietly.

They stepped apart, and Hugh's smile turned into a smirk. "Even if you're turning into Talia."

Sabae rolled her eyes at him, and sent a lazy punch his way that he easily dodged.

Then his smile vanished. "Oh, crap, Talia!"

He grabbed Sabae's hand and dragged her back towards the prow.

"What's going on?" Sabae asked. "What happened to Talia?"

"I have no idea," Hugh said. "Her hair just kind of randomly exploded when we brought my spellbook near her."

"What?" Sabae demanded, as she stumbled and almost fell on a coil of rope.

"I don't know!" Hugh said. "The healer stopped the worst of the bleeding, and the others are looking her over right now."

They got to the prow, where a small crowd was gathered.

"Uhhh… pardon me," Hugh said, awkwardly shuffling at

the edge.

Sabae rolled her eyes at him.

"Hey!" she shouted. "We saved Dell. He's back towards the stern!"

Most of the Radhan immediately headed towards the back of the ship.

"How did you know I was coming up behind the stern?" Sabae asked.

Hugh shrugged, feeling a little awkward still. "Most of the water mages on board were watching for you with their affinity senses. They tried to stop the ship as fast as possible, but we figured we'd still passed you by, so I waited at the stern for you. They also let me know you were being chased by the serpent, so I got the starbolt ready."

Sabae started to say something, but was interrupted by two of the Radhan nearly tackling her with hugs. Hugh recognized them as the boy and girl Talia had been waiting with.

"You saved my brother," the girl said.

"You're amazing," the boy said simultaneously.

Both showered her with further praise for a little while longer, then each kissed her on a cheek and were gone.

Sabae just stood there blankly, slightly in shock.

"I think you have some admirers," Hugh said.

"Um," Sabae said.

"Don't get greedy, though," Hugh said.

"Uh," Sabae said.

Hugh rolled his eyes, then led her over to where the others were clustered around Talia, who was sitting slumped on the deck, staring at her own lap. He carefully stepped over the piles of wooden coins lying everywhere as Godrick and Artur made room for them.

"Ow," Talia said. "Ow, ow, ow!"

Talia was in rough shape. The healer had reset and healed her broken nose before Sabae had retrieved Dell, but blood still caked her mouth. Her hair was a charred mess, with big clumps of it simply gone. Her blue spellform tattoos extended all the way across her scalp underneath her hair. There were bleeding wounds in her scalp cutting through the tattoos. Alustin was picking bits of metal out of the gashes, an irritated look on his face.

"Can I help somehow?" Sabae asked. "I do have a healing affinity, after all…"

Alustin shot her a flat look as his storage tattoo lit up on his arm.

"What have your healing instructors told you about head wounds?" he asked, pulling a sheet of paper from midair.

Sabae sighed. "Don't do anything until you're a fully trained healer. You're more likely to hurt the patient than help."

Alustin nodded. "Go back over to the healer. See if she needs any help with the Radhan boy. We need her back here as quickly as possible, with as much mana left in her reservoirs as possible. Oh, and congratulations on saving him, and I'm glad you're safe, Sabae."

Sabae gave Alustin a look that seemed almost suspicious to Hugh, then nodded and left.

"Have you figured out what happened yet?" Hugh asked.

Alustin yanked another bit of metal out of Talia's scalp, then turned towards Godrick.

"Could you do something about the smell of burnt hair?" he asked.

Godrick, who was still cradling Hugh's spellbook, just nodded, but the smell immediately started to diminish, replaced by the smell of… fresh bread?

Alustin turned back to Talia's scalp. "Yes, Hugh, I believe I have figured it out. Talia, were your hairpins enchanted?"

"They could turn into lockpicks," Talia said. "Godrick gave them to me."

"And you had how many of them in your hair?" Alustin asked.

"…five?" Talia said.

Alustin sighed. "And how many other enchanted items did you have on you?"

Talia winced as Alustin yanked another fragment of hairpin out of her scalp.

"Two enchanted daggers and a couple magic needles in

the backs of my shoes," Talia said.

Alustin exchanged an exasperated look with Artur.

"Resonance cascade?" the huge stone mage asked.

Alustin nodded. "Resonance cascade."

"Resonance cascade?" Godrick asked.

"A chain reaction in the aether between enchanted items that can cause them to fail catastrophically, often triggered by having too many in close proximity," Alustin said. "How many enchanted items do you think I carry with me?"

Talia shrugged.

"Just two," Alustin said. "I have plenty of papers inscribed with glyphs, and my extra-spatial storage tattoo, but my only actual enchanted items are my sword and the book I use to communicate with Kanderon and the other Librarians Errant. Artur?"

"Mah hammer, a ring that filters poisons, an', well, one other," Artur said. "Ah've got ta keep some secrets."

Hugh realized that he'd never actually seen Artur carrying his hammer outside battle. Did he have a storage tattoo like Alustin? The big stone mage wore three rings— one of bronze, one of stone, and one of iron. He assumed one had to be the poison-filtering ring— was one of the other two enchanted?

Alustin turned back to Talia. "I specifically warned you, I believe, about carrying too many enchanted items."

"You told me that they could interfere with each others's function, not that they would just randomly explode," Talia said. She sounded angry and miserable, but also a bit off, somehow.

"Enchanted items exploding is a rather… extreme outcome," Alustin admitted. "In this case, it was most likely triggered by your large number of enchanted items in proximity to Hugh's spellbook suffering gastric distress. Especially if you were using any of them. It probably set off a cascading resonance between your enchanted items."

"That spellbook is the worst, and I hate it," Talia said.

Hugh frowned. Talia was definitely slurring her words. He crouched down to take a closer look at her.

"It wouldn't have been a problem if you'd been careful

enough to listen to my advice," Alustin said. "Just be thankful it was your weakest enchanted items that detonated. It usually is during a resonance cascade, but on rare occasions it can detonate a more powerful item. One of your daggers would have killed you for sure, and if it had been a more powerful magic item, like my sword, it could have torn the entire ship into splinters. A enchantment on the scale of Grovebringer or some of the other truly powerful items out there could level a large village."

"Is your sword really Helicotan?" Talia asked, looking up at Alustin. "Are you really Helicotan?"

"Hold still," Alustin snapped at her. Then he sighed, and continued in a calmer tone. "And I don't like to talk about it, but yes, I am. And I'm sorry, but I'm going to have to cut your hair off entirely. It's too thick for me to get all of the shards out, and it's definitely not safe to remove the shards with magic or heal you with them still in."

"What? No!" Talia said, struggling away from Alustin. She lost her balance immediately, and Hugh barely caught her in time with his magic.

Hugh briefly considered how odd it was that his first reaction was now to catch someone with his magic and not his arms, but most of his attention was fixed on Talia's eyes.

"Alustin," Hugh said, alarmed, "Talia's eyes aren't focusing right."

"That," Alustin said, reaching out to pull Talia upright, "is because she's very badly concussed. We need to get these shards out of her quickly so the ship's healer can fix the damage, because we have a short window to work here. Treating concussions is tricky, time-sensitive business. Not to mention, enchanted items are generally created using some very nasty alchemical compounds, so it's best not to leave pieces of them in wounds for long. I'm very sorry, Talia, but I don't have a choice."

Hugh glanced at the sheet of paper, noticing a particularly complex spellform in its center, with smaller spellforms running along its edges. He thought they were wards for a brief moment, but they were structured entirely wrong for that.

"Hold very still," Alustin told Talia.

"Alright," she said, but kept shifting around.

"Artur," Alustin said. "A hand, please."

Artur crouched down and gently cradled Talia's neck and chin.

Alustin waited for a moment to make sure Artur was keeping her still, and then the spellform glyphs on the paper lit up— the center glyph first, followed by the ones along the edges. With a slow, smooth, cautious motion, he guided the paper over Talia's head, the paper slicing through Talia's hair less than a finger width from her scalp. As it moved, the paper's shape perfectly shifted to curve around and keep an even distance from Talia's scalp. The paper's edge sliced through Talia's hair like it were just an illusion, which was pretty alarming, given how thick it was— Hugh doubted a sword could chop through her hair so easily. He knew for a fact scissors had trouble with it, from Talia's many complaints on the matter.

The burnt remains of Talia's hair slumped to the ground, mixing in with the scattered wooden coins.

Alustin sighed, then, with a flick of his hand that was probably entirely unnecessary, he sent the sheet of paper flying off the side of the ship.

Hugh's eyes widened when he saw it slice through the top inch of the railing as easily as it had chopped through Talia's hair, but he didn't say anything, not wanting to alarm her.

Artur let go of Talia's head, and Alustin returned to her scalp, carefully picking out the shards of metal from her cuts.

Without her hair, Talia looked tiny and oddly vulnerable. Hugh was so used to thinking of Talia as a terrifying, unstoppable juggernaut that it felt deeply uncomfortable to see her like this. He had to force himself not to look away in discomfort.

Then he noticed, with some alarm, that several of the cuts had broken the lines of Talia's tattoos.

"Sir, Talia's tattoos…" Hugh began, but stopped, not knowing what to say without further upsetting her.

"Her tattoos will be fine," Alustin said. "Any decently constructed magical tattoo has self-repair functions, and they're as much aether construct as physical construct. I've heard of tattoos that have even remained functional when the limb they were on was lost before, though that's something of an extreme case. And I believe I've told you not to call me sir before."

Hugh would need to eventually ask what, exactly, an aether construct was, but for now he just filed it away.

He glanced back down at Talia, and realized, to his shock, that she was weeping silently.

Hugh glanced over to Godrick, who looked back helplessly. Hugh's spellbook was looking a little less ill in his friend's arms, and was staring at Talia with what looked like shame in its… binding? Spine?

One of these days, Hugh was going to figure out exactly how his spellbook conveyed emotions without facial features, or features of any sort.

He made himself look back to Talia, feeling just as helpless as Godrick looked. He did know a hair mage back at Skyhold who could help her grow her hair back out, but that did nothing for her at the moment. He couldn't make her healing go any faster, or…

Then he thought back, and remembered a time when Talia had simply sat with him and offered him kindness when he'd needed it, when he'd still been broken inside, before he'd really believed he deserved friendship or happiness.

Hugh swept a section of decking clear of wooden coins and sat down next to Talia. He quietly reached out and took her hand in his, not saying anything.

She squeezed his hand hard.

They sat like that as Alustin finished cleaning out the wounds in her scalp. As Sabae returned with the healer. As the healer had worked her magic and Talia's eyes started focusing properly again. As the healer lectured Talia, telling her not to sleep until at least after sundown, and not to use any magic for at least two days.

He only let go of her hand when the healer ordered Talia

belowdecks to rest.

CHAPTER THIRTEEN

Hiding

Hugh watched quietly as Sabae escorted Talia belowdecks, the healer pacing along and reiterating her orders that Talia wasn't to sleep.

When he looked back to the others, Godrick was giving him an odd look.

"What's that look?" he asked Godrick.

Godrick just shook his head. "Yeh're a good friend, is all. Talia's lucky ta have yeh in her life. We all are."

Hugh rubbed the back of his head awkwardly and picked up a handful of the wooden coins to look at. The first one had what looked like a bee on one side, and… Hugh didn't even know what the thing on the other side was.

Captain Grepha came striding up towards them, an inscrutable expression on her face.

"I need to both apologize to and thank you all," she said.

"Apologize for what?" Alustin said from his seat on the railing.

"If we'd had a proper serpent-watch set," Grepha said, "none of this would have been a problem. We—"

Artur raised his hand to interrupt. "It woulda' been silly fer yeh ta set yer mages ta that this time a' year an' this close ta' Ampioc's territory. There shouldn't be any serpents this close ta shore in summertime."

Hugh shot Artur a surprised look, then Godrick a curious one. He thought Artur hated ships, so how did he know so much about sea serpents, of all things?

Godrick just shook his head.

"Nonetheless," Captain Grepha continued, "it's still my

responsibility as captain of this vessel to—"

Alustin made a farting noise with his mouth. Everyone shot him surprised looks.

"You're being absurd," Alustin said. "You're apologizing for something that was out of your control and utterly unreasonable to predict. It is a waste of your time and ours, and so far as I'm concerned, you and your crew reacted commendably fast to anomalous circumstances. I'm far more interested in hearing the news of the victims, and if there's anything we can do to assist further."

Captain Grepha stared at Alustin for a long count, and Hugh wondered whether she'd take offense.

Finally, her shoulders slumped.

"Thank you," she said. "Not just for the kind words, but for the aid you and your students rendered. We would have lost quite a few sailors if not for you all."

"How bad was it?" Alustin asked quietly.

The captain sighed unhappily and massaged the back of her neck. "Two dead. One missing, almost certainly dead. Three badly wounded. A few lesser wounds. I need to especially thank your tall apprentice with the scars— we've never gotten anyone dragged under by serpents back before. I apologize, but I didn't catch her name."

"Sabae Kaen Das," Alustin said.

Captain Grepha's jaw dropped.

"You're messing with me," she said.

Alustin shook his head.

"She's some by-blow or distant cousin, surely?" the captain asked.

Alustin shook his head again as he took Hugh's spellbook from Godrick's arms.

"She's Ilinia's granddaughter," he said. "Hugh, I'll look over your book, but it seems the worst has passed. I'll get in touch with Kanderon as well to see what she has to say about the situation."

Grepha's eyes got even wider at Kanderon's name.

Hugh reflected that perhaps he took his relationship with Kanderon a bit too much for granted.

"Is there anything else I can assist you with, Captain?" Alustin asked.

"Uh, I—" Grepha started, then paused to collect herself.

"Yes, actually," she continued. "If there's one sea serpent pack this close to shore in summer, there's almost certainly more. We're considering taking the Silent Straits instead of the southern route. If you could scry it for us to check whether it's safe, I'd appreciate it."

Both Alustin and Artur looked at Grepha in surprise, but Alustin finally nodded.

"I can do that," he said. "I haven't heard any rumors of the Listener stirring of late, so it might be feasible. I'll check with Kanderon on that as well."

"Much appreciated," Grepha said, swiveling to return to her duties. She gave them one more searching look before she left. "Kaen Das girls and Kanderon Crux. Next you'll tell me green-eyes here is a Prince of Highvale."

"No," Godrick said, a mischievous look in his eyes, "but he is arch-rival to one."

Hugh just scowled at his friend as Grepha strode off, muttering to herself.

Artur leaned down and picked up a wooden coin. "Some kind a' wingless dragon on one side an' a chamber pot on the other," he said.

Godrick picked up another. "Ah've got a smilin' guy on one side and the same guy frownin' on the other."

Hugh sorted through the wooden coins he was holding. "I've found at least three bees, a fire-breathing goat, a sand drake, and a pile of books."

Alustin arched his eyebrows at them, and leaned down to pick one up. He didn't say anything for a moment.

"What's on yours?" Hugh asked.

"A sea serpent," Alustin said.

No one said anything for a moment.

"An' the other side?" Artur asked.

Alustin flipped the coin over. "Looks like… a pigeon."

The paper mage shot Hugh a curious look. "How does Emblin deal with sea serpents and other threats, by the way? The mana desert extends well out to sea, doesn't it?"

Hugh shrugged. “I suppose it does. I’d guess that most of the biggest monsters just avoid the low aether density, and Emblin has a deal worked out with a few intelligent sea monsters. Dunno what, exactly, but we trade them beef and mutton and such to keep our shores safe.”

Alustin grunted at that. He tossed the coin off the ship, then stood atop the railing.

“I’ll be getting started on my scrying, then,” he said. He strode off down the railing with the relaxed gait of someone walking down a road, not someone walking on the railing of a sailing ship at sea.

“E’s in a particularly bad mood,” Artur said.

“How can yeh tell?” Godrick asked.

Artur shrugged. “Known ‘im since before ‘e got so good at actin’,” he said. “Hugh, yeh up fer some work on our project?”

Hugh nodded, and tossed the wooden coins back on the pile.

“Ah guess ah’ll go check on Talia,” Godrick said. “Try not ta’ blow up the ship with yer secret project, huh?”

“No promises,” Hugh said.

“Go away!” Talia yelled, when Godrick knocked on the door to her and Sabae’s cabin.

“It’s me,” Godrick said.

“Come in, Godrick,” Sabae called. “Ignore Talia.”

Godrick opened the door and ducked under the frame, then carefully shut it behind him.

Talia was curled up in a ball on the corner of the lower bunk, Sabae sitting next to her. Talia had pulled the blanket around her like a cloak, hiding all but the lower part of her face.

Rather than try to cram onto the too-small bunk, Godrick snagged the blanket and pillow from Sabae’s bed and made himself a cushion to sit on the deck with, and settled down next to the girls.

"I want to be alone," Talia said quietly.

"And we're under healer's orders to not leave you alone until nightfall at least," Sabae said.

Talia sniffed, but didn't argue further.

None of them spoke for a few minutes. Finally, Sabae broke the silence.

"You saved my life again," Sabae said. "That first serpent would have gotten me if it weren't for you. Thank you, Talia."

"It's not—" Talia started, but Godrick interrupted her.

"Yeh best not be sayin' it's not a big deal, Talia," he said. "Cause far as ah'm concerned, it's most certainly a big deal."

Talia made a few grumbling noises, but then she poked a little more of her face out from under her blanket.

"It was pretty amazing how you went into the water after Dell," she said.

Sabae grimaced. "I'm still amazed I didn't die," she said. "I definitely would have at the end if Hugh hadn't killed that last serpent."

Talia seemed to retreat a little bit at Hugh's name, and Godrick grimaced.

"Ah was the only one who was useless today," he said. "Yeh three all saved lives, an' ah was just standin' there like an idiot holdin' a book."

Both Sabae and Talia glared at him, Talia's face mostly emerging from the blanket to do so. Her eyes were much more focused than they'd been before the healer had seen to her.

"You've saved our lives more than enough in the past," Sabae said. "None of that nonsense."

"If I don't get to talk down on myself, neither do you," Talia said.

Godrick sighed. "Fine. Ah just feel so useless out here on the water," he said. "None a' my affinities are much use here. If we were in the north and there were ice around, ah'd feel more useful, but…"

"Ice?" Sabae asked.

"Ice is a type a' rock," Godrick said, readying himself for the inevitable argument.

"No it's not," Sabae said. "It's frozen water."

Godrick rolled his eyes. "And rock's just frozen magma."

"It's different," Sabae insisted.

"Only in that it freezes at a cooler temperature than magma," Godrick said.

"There's no way ice is a rock," Sabae insisted.

Godrick shrugged. "Well, technically it's a mineral. But ah can affect minerals with mah stone affinity too. Not as powerfully as rocks made of mixed minerals, but ah can. And ice is one a' the hardest minerals fer me ta' affect, but ah can still do it."

"Can you make armor out of ice?" Talia asked.

Godrick nodded. "Ah prefer not to— it's ice still, and ah can't say ah enjoy gettin' frozen— but me da's had me try it a couple times."

"There is something deeply wrong with all of this," Sabae said. "Are you sure you don't just have an ice affinity as well?"

Godrick rolled his eyes. "Ah think ah'd notice if ah had a fourth affinity, Sabae."

"Can you affect water like you can lava?" Talia asked. She'd perked up a little more and was leaning forwards out of curiosity.

Godrick noticed Sabae wince a little as Talia mentioned lava.

"Not unless it has little bit a' ice in it," Godrick said.

"Can you—" Talia started, only to stop when the blanket slipped off her head. She immediately yanked the blanket back over her nearly-bald scalp and curled up tighter again.

Godrick sighed, and gently reached out to pat Talia's shoulder. "Yeh don't need ta' hide from us," he said.

"I'm hideous," Talia said.

"No you're not," Sabae said, sounding exasperated. "Quit being ridiculous."

"Yes I am," Talia said.

"You're not hideous in the slightest," Sabae said. "Nor

have you ever been."

"I am too," Talia insisted.

Godrick snorted. "Yeh're bein' petulant, Talia, quit that."

He reached out and pulled the blanket off Talia's head. She glared at him miserably.

"Yeh're not the first mage ta' burn off their hair," Godrick said. "These things happen, and yeh can't beat yerself up about it. It'll grow back. And honestly, with yer tattoos, it doesn't look bad at all. Yeh look kinda scary, honestly."

"You're just saying I look scary to make me feel better," Talia said, but she seemed a little pleased by that.

"And because you actually are terrifying," Sabae said.

Talia sniffled a bit, but gave them a small smile.

"I really loved my hair," she said. "I know I complained about it a lot, but it was my favorite feature."

"It was pretty amazing," Sabae said.

"Ah always felt Hugh was the odd man out there," Godrick said. "We all have amazin' hair, but he's just got pretty normal hair."

"I like his hair," Talia muttered.

"You like everything about him," Sabae said, rolling her eyes.

Talia pulled her hand out of the blanket as though to hit Sabae, then scowled at her fist. She tucked it back into the blanket.

"I'm being a total idiot about him, aren't I?" she asked. "I doubt he's ever even thought of me as anything but a friend."

Godrick shrugged. "Ah've got no idea. If he has, ah doubt he ever thought it was a serious possibility. He's better than he used ta be, but he still doesn't think much of himself."

"Godrick's right," Sabae said. "I don't think he believes that anyone could actually have feelings for him, even after Avah. Plus, you know, Hugh's completely thick when it comes to this sort of thing."

"Not like it matters much," Talia said. "One of the girls on this ship is going to snag him while I'm hiding away down here, I know it."

"He's workin' with me da on their secret project right

now," Godrick said. "The one that ah need ta' keep pretendin' ah haven't already guessed is doin' somethin' with that ice sword me da seized from the Havathi ta replace mah lost hammer. Besides, that would be absurdly fast fer someone to move on Hugh."

Talia didn't say anything, and Godrick frowned.

"Unless yeh meant that yeh were plannin' ta stay hidden down here the entire time until yer hair grew back?"

Talia curled up a little more.

"There is absolutely no chance I'm letting that happen," Sabae said. "You've seen me drag Hugh out of his rooms, do you think I won't do the same for you too?"

"Hugh's not going to be attracted to this," Talia said, pointing at her scalp. "I doubt he'll even want to look at me."

Godrick rolled his eyes at her. "Who exactly was it that sat holdin' yer hand ta' comfort yeh for a half-hour just now?"

"That's different," Talia said, in a tiny voice.

Sabae rolled her eyes now. "What would one of the characters from your ridiculous novels do in this situation?"

Talia considered that for a moment. "Repeatedly try and fail to work up the nerve to confess their feelings to their love interest over and over again, with lots of amusing accidents and misunderstandings between them that make things seem impossible, only to finally find their courage during the final battle?"

Sabae and Godrick exchanged glances.

"First off," Sabae said, "you are absolutely not going to confess your feelings to Hugh during a battle. That's a good way to get both of you distracted and killed."

"But—" Talia started.

"Ah've got ta agree with Sabae on this one," Godrick said. "That's a terrible idea."

Talia sniffed, but nodded.

"Second," Sabae said, "that sounds like it would be absolutely exhausting and annoying for everyone involved. Especially me and Godrick."

Godrick just nodded at that.

"So what then?" Talia said.

Sabae shrugged. "Do you think you could actually just, you know, work up your nerve and tell Hugh how you feel?"

Talia just shrugged.

"Ah mean, we're on this whole expedition with the future of the continent at stake," Godrick said. "Ah think it might help if yeh just get it over with one way or another, so yeh can keep focused on the mission."

Talia eyed him oddly. "Isn't the usual advice here to avoid complicating things altogether when you're in the middle of a crisis like this?"

Godrick shrugged. "Do yeh seriously see us ever *not* bein' in the middle of some crisis or another?"

Sabae chuckled at that, and even Talia snorted in amusement.

CHAPTER FOURTEEN

The Listener in the Silent Straits

The Radhan held a funeral for the deceased two evenings after the sea serpent attack.

The crew of the *Rising Cormorant* had been lavish with praise over the past couple days, and Hugh couldn't even count the number of times they'd been thanked by crewmembers. Most of the attention was reserved for Sabae and Alustin, thankfully. Hugh and Talia were occasionally congratulated for killing one sea serpent each, but for the most part, he, Artur, and Godrick were left out of the praise. That being said, the crew had begun treating all of them as though they belonged to one of the families on the ship.

For all that warmth, however, they weren't allowed to attend the funeral. The group from Skyhold was asked to stay belowdecks, and the mess hall was made available to them during the funeral. The Radhan religion was, apparently, as secretive as their language. All Alustin would say about it, as he poked at Hugh's spellbook, was that he was fairly sure it was an invisible cult— the only stable one he knew of— and that he had absolutely no interest in using his magic to spy upon the mourners.

The atmosphere the next morning was somber, but not just because of the funeral the night before.

"There are four rules for traveling through the Silent Straits," Alustin said. "First, your ship must not be built of cedar, and you must be carrying as little as possible on board. Second, you must use as little magic as possible. Third, you do not stare towards the demesne of the Listener for sustained periods. Quick glances and panoramic sweeps of the mountains are fine, but no staring. And fourth, and most importantly, you *must not speak.* No casual greetings, no muffled curse words, nothing. It is called the Listener for a reason. The Silent Straits are called such not because they are silent, but because you need to be silent to pass through it safely. The Listener's demesne isn't currently blooming, so we shouldn't attract its interest if everyone obeys the rules, most especially the fourth. No matter what you do, stay silent."

Hugh raised his hand. "Sir, I could construct a noise ward around the ship to make it quieter?"

Alustin shook his head. "What's rule two, Hugh?"

"Don't, uh, use magic, sir?" Hugh said. He was somewhat taken aback by Alustin's intensity. He hadn't even told Hugh not to call him sir like he usually did.

"Use as little magic as possible," Alustin said. "Using small amounts is safe enough, but we'll be restricting that to the ship's mages. And our concern isn't noise, it's spoken words. The Listener doesn't pay attention to non-speech sounds like footsteps, the creaking of the ship, or coughing. Unusually loud noises sometimes cause it to stir, but a full-ship noise ward would draw its attention far more swiftly. If you don't think you can follow these rules, the ship's healer has prepared sleeping draughts so you can sleep through the transit. All of the young children on board will be taking it, as well as several of the more… gossipy crewmembers."

"And me," Artur said. "Ah've got no intention ta' ever be awake for another transit through the Silent Straits again."

Hugh shot Artur a curious look. He'd always assumed Artur got seasick or something, but it was becoming clear that Artur had a history with sailing ships. He didn't want to pry, though.

"What is the Listener?" Talia asked in a quiet, subdued voice from where she was sitting tucked between Godrick and the mess hall bulkhead. She'd barely spoken since the sea serpent attack, and wrapped a patterned cloth around her head on the rare occasions she left her cabin. When Hugh had asked, she'd just told him she was reading the books Alustin had assigned her.

Alustin shrugged. "I have no idea," he said. "I suspect Kanderon might know, but she's never told me what the Listener is, save that she believes its borders to be stable, and unlikely to expand anytime soon. Galvachren likely knows what it is as well, though he's never admitted as much in any of his writings."

"My grandmother might know as well," Sabae volunteered. "I'm not sure, though. She dislikes admitting ignorance about things like that."

Alustin nodded at that. "What I do know is that the Listener is a strong contender for the single mightiest great power on the continent. It's laid waste to countless fleets, dragon flights, and great powers. The only real rival it has is the Sleeper in the Sand."

"The what?" Godrick asked.

"A giant sunmaw the size of a town," Alustin said. "It's buried under the sand of the western Endless Erg somewhere. So far as we can tell, it's essentially unkillable, and could probably devour Indris in a few bites. Remember how difficult it was to hit the normal sunmaw we faced with spells, thanks to the way it distorted the aether around it and made spells fail?"

Talia, Sabae, and Godrick nodded.

"The sleeper's mana disruption field extends hundreds of feet away from its body. It's older than human civilization on Anastis, and it's been imprisoned and kept asleep beneath the sands for over a millennium now."

"It tries to awaken every century or two," Sabae said. "My family is among those who help force it back to sleep every time."

Alustin nodded. "As are Kanderon, Indris, Chelys Mot, the rulers of most of the city-states of the Endless Erg, and countless wandering dragons and the like. Nobody wants that thing to awaken again."

Their teacher took a bite of his breakfast— one of the curries that the Radhan seemed to enjoy for most of their meals— before continuing.

"There's one other thing you need to know along with the four rules," Alustin said. "Which are, by the way?"

"Your ship mustn't be built of cedar," Sabae said. "Though that one's really weird."

"They're all weird," Alustin said. "Next."

"As little magic as possible," Talia said quietly.

"Don't stare at the Listener's demesne," Hugh said. "Just glances."

"And no speaking at all," Sabae finished.

"Right," Alustin said. "So the other thing you need to know is about the Listener's demesne's blooms."

"Is the Listener a lich?" Sabae asked.

Alustin shook his head. "I don't think so," he said. "We just call its territory a demesne because it never leaves and because of, well, the massive changes it has made to it. I was telling you about the blooms, though. Normally, the demesne is an ugly, dusty grey-brown. When it blooms, huge patches of yellow, red, and orange appear. When the blooms are dense and wide enough, it is absolutely unsafe to venture anywhere near. It's guaranteed death to do so, even more surely than if you break the four rules."

"A gruesome one," Artur said, an uncharacteristically gloomy look on his face.

Alustin nodded. "The Listener's demesne is in bloom now, but not nearly enough to be a danger."

"Why does anyone sail through the Silent Straits?" Hugh asked. "This seems insane."

"It's the fastest route past the Skyreach Range by sea, for one," Alustin said. "For another, it's far safer in many regards— you won't find any kraken, sea serpents, or anything else dangerous enough to threaten a ship. Even in the depths of winter, when the serpents come closest to shore, they avoid the straits. That's a big part of why we're taking this route— the southern routes through the islands are more dangerous when serpent infested."

"Ah'm still worried about why the serpents came so close in summer," Artur said. "Ah've not heard of that happening before."

"Maybe the storm-paths have shifted?" Sabae suggested. "I know my grandmother sometimes shifts storms to alter serpent migrations."

"Best not repeat that too loud," Alustin said, glancing around. They were eating breakfast late, so the mess hall was half empty. "I don't think that's a possibility that would endear you to the crew, even with how grateful they are to you for saving Dell."

Sabae nodded seriously at that.

"We've got another few hours before we reach the straits," Alustin said. "Once we're there, the actual trip through the dangerous section, where the strait is narrowest, should only take four to six hours, depending on how much the winds want to cooperate. Decide soon whether you want to sleep or not."

Hugh already knew he'd be staying awake. Terrifying unknowable monsters aside, it wasn't often you had daylight hours where you were guaranteed that nobody would try and start a conversation with you.

The narrowest section of the Silent Straits, where the demesne of the Listener bordered on the sea, was only a little bit over a league in width. It stretched perfectly east and west along the southern shore of the continent, and was bordered by the first of the mountainous Shattered Isles to the south.

Before taking the sleeping draught, Artur had told them how the Shattered Isles had once been a part of the Skyreach Range, in eons past when the world was colder and the seas were lower, long before humanity had come to the world of Anastis. The Silent Straits had been a great pass then, where a river ran straight through the mountains. Powerful earth or stone mages could still feel the ancient riverbed below the seafloor with their affinity senses.

The summer heat's grip on the sea air struggled against the fierce winds that blew between the mountains to either side of them. The wind raised whitecaps on the waves, and the *Rising Cormorant* lurched and shuddered without the magic of its wind and water mages to steady its course through the center of the channel.

To the south, the Shattered Isles loomed, far bigger than the mountains Hugh had known in Emblin. Even at the height of summer, with the sun nearly directly overhead, he could see snow and ice at their peaks. The sky held only scattered clouds that seemed to mirror the whitecaps on the waves.

Sparse, scrubby forests speckled their slopes, and drakes and seabirds, including the ship's namesake black cormorants, hunted fish in the waters below them, noisily squabbling over their catches. They hardly even had to put forth any effort to capture fish, however— schools of boarfish thick enough to walk on hunted swarms of arm-length basking squid. Flying fish escaped predators in the water below, only to be seized on the wing by flying predators above. Seals rested on cliff ledges twenty feet above the water, waiting sleepily for high tide to lift the ocean up to them once more so they could hunt and play in the water. Wild gryphons and mountain goats watched their ship pass by from great boulders and clifftops.

If that had been all the scene, it would have been one of the most beautiful sights Hugh had ever seen. He could have lived happily in such a place.

It wasn't the whole scene, however, and no matter how wondrous he found the Straits, his eyes kept being drawn inevitably northward, as though pulled by hooks.

He made sure not to look for more than a few breaths at a time. He'd worried, at first, that he wouldn't know how long it was safe to look at the Listener's demesne, but he found no difficulty with that. More than a few moments, and his vision began to waver, his stomach twisted, and even his heart began to stutter, as though some arrhythmic patternless cacophony tried to impose itself over his heartbeat.

Those brief glances, however, unsettled him deeply.

He hadn't known *what*, exactly, he'd been expecting. Mysterious structures, bizarre growths, or maybe shadowy movement. Twisted, demonic wildflowers for the blooms Alustin had spoken of, perhaps.

The Listener's demesne, however, contained none of that.

Instead, the great mountains of the southern edge of the Skyreach Range seemed to be covered in a dull grey-brown blanket. Not a tightly woven, well-made blanket, but a loose, fuzzy, dusty mass, slumping over boulders and cliffs, covering everything, even the peaks that would normally be bare far above the tree line. Great streaks of vivid yellow, angry chains of red specks, and misshapen rosettes of orange were all scattered about the blanket, but other than their garish colors, seemed no different than the rest of the surface. A gently shifting haze of dust seemed to drift above the cloying blanket that was the Listener's demesne.

These few leagues of the Silent Straits were the only place the demesne touched the sea, but Hugh could easily see the enormity of it, as it covered mountains that stretched past the horizon, widening as it extended northward. The Silent Straits were only the narrowest tip of its reach.

The Radhan worked in absolute silence, communicating only by gesture and carried note. The captain, stationed by the helmsman's ornate wheel, carried with her a pad that she jotted quick orders on to be carried by runners. Some of the Radhan had improvised thick veils over half their face that blocked the view to their left, to limit their glimpses of the

Listener's demesne.

For all the noise of wind and birds, of leaping fish and irritable seals, and even of the creaking ship itself, the human silence was shockingly oppressive. Hugh could feel it weighing on him like silence had never done before. The fear and nervousness of the crew combined with the horrible, unmistakable feeling of being *watched.* As though the Listener knew perfectly well they were on its doorstep, yet simply had no reason to care yet.

Hugh kept waiting for some sort of crisis to occur— a broken mast, a sailor overboard, something. Anything to break the awful monotony and pressure. But the ship just kept plowing through the choppy seas, and the silence beat against them all constantly.

The crew, his friends, and Alustin took frequent rests belowdecks, where the awful sense of being watched was lessened a little. Hugh felt strangely compelled to stay on deck, spending most of his time at the prow or at the starboard railing, watching the pristine, life-filled wilderness of the Shattered Isles drift by. The only communication he had came in the forms of the comforting touches everyone on deck began to give each other as the hours drifted by— a hand rested on a back or a quick squeeze of the shoulder.

The only other person who stayed on deck the whole time was Captain Grepha, who looked more tired and worn out with each passing mile. Near the end of the third hour, she locked glances with Hugh and gave him a single approving nod, and Hugh felt as though he had passed some sort of test.

It was a quarter of the way through the fourth hour when the sense of being watched lessened. Another quarter of an hour after that, it broke entirely.

No one spoke just yet, however. They all kept casting glances backwards, as though the Listener's demesne demanded their attention still.

Hugh cast one, final glance backwards as they rounded a curve in the strait. There, halfway up a mountain, rested a great cancerous splotch of bloom, the reds and oranges and yellows following a winding curve that looked like nothing so much as a great, malformed eye.

He shuddered, and the eye passed silently, blindly behind a cliff.

CHAPTER FIFTEEN

First Site

The *Rising Cormorant* anchored in a sheltered cove an hour after exiting the Silent Straits. A token watch was set, and the rest of the crew collapsed in their bunks and hammocks, as though they hadn't slept in days. It was only midafternoon, but Hugh slept in well into the next morning, far after he normally would have risen.

As the ship prepared to leave the cove, he found himself, of all things, wondering if Avah had ever passed through the Silent Straits. He knew she'd voyaged on water a few times, though she'd spent most of her life sailing the sand. She'd told him stories of hidden oases in the far west of the desert, and of an abandoned city carved into canyon walls. She'd told him a few scattered stories of her time on the water, but it simply never seemed to hold her attention in the way the sand did.

If she had sailed the Straits, would she have told them? Hugh couldn't ever imagine bragging about sailing the straits. Just a day later, it seemed akin to a fever dream, not some daring feat. He didn't know if he'd ever find the words to really explain what it had felt like. Both Alustin and Artur had sailed the Straits before, and their descriptions beforehand had utterly failed to do it justice. Would Avah have even tried?

He almost found it a little odd that he was brooding about Avah again. So much had happened in the short time since they'd left Skyhold that Hugh felt overwhelmed with new memories, as though the events of recent days were trying to force others out of his mind.

Then he thought about the Havathi spotter he'd killed, and he realized that Avah had been right. His life wasn't ever going to be the quiet, peaceful life he wanted, not so long as he was pacted to Kanderon and studying under Alustin. Avah wanted adventure, but ones of discovery, of visiting natural wonders and ancient ruins. Avah chased the thrill of bargaining with merchants and seeking new trades, not the stress of battle, and Hugh couldn't blame her at all. That's all Hugh had to offer her, and no matter how she felt about him personally, he realized that he understood her not wanting everything that came with him.

Most of the time, *he* didn't want everything that came along with his life, so he most certainly couldn't blame her.

But… he didn't hate his life. He could do with less violence, with less danger, but he was coming to love seeing the world and learning new magics. He'd accomplished things that he was genuinely proud of, no matter how hard it was to admit.

And most of all, he had Sabae, Talia, and Godrick.

As the ship left the sheltered cove behind, Hugh felt like he'd left some part of himself he no longer needed in it, and as he turned away from the railing to join a lesson from Alustin on, of all things, the different varieties of dirt affinity, he found himself focusing a little more easily. He didn't feel better, necessarily, just not as overwhelmed.

They reached the first potential site for Ithos a week after the Silent Straits.

Passing ships had reported changes in the aether surrounding an island towards the edges of the Shattered Isles, and it only required a couple days detour in their journey.

They spent the entire morning hiking up into a mountain pass into the heart of the island, starting out at daybreak. The aether was too thin here for Alustin to fly up and check, and scrying was insufficient— Kanderon demanded that they check each location in person.

All the physical training Alustin and Artur had put the four of them through over the last two years was coming in handy now— Hugh doubted he could have successfully ascended the pass when he'd first arrived at Skyhold. He'd hardly been out of shape then— he'd spent years wandering the alpine woods of Emblin during the days to avoid his family as much as possible— but the pass was steep as a staircase, and the ground largely unstable, crumbling shale. Hugh and the others found themselves scrambling up on all fours as often as not.

Godrick and Artur had a particularly difficult time of it— given their greater weight, the shale crumbled far more easily beneath them. They used their magic to help stabilize it, but Godrick ran out partway up, and Artur was reluctant to let his mana reservoirs get too low.

All of them save for Alustin and, a little surprisingly, Talia, were exhausted by the time they reached the top.

"Ah'm used ta' Alustin bein' annoyingly chipper," Artur said from his seat against a boulder, "but how are yeh just prancin' around, Talia?"

Talia smirked at him. "I grew up in the Skyreach Range; I'm comfortable at far higher elevations than this. Plus I'm not carrying around a couple hundred pounds of unnecessary muscle."

Both Godrick and Artur made rude gestures at her, and Hugh and Sabae exchanged amused glances.

Talia wasn't fully back to her usual brash self just yet, but she was far more confident and energetic than she'd been following the sea serpent attack. She still wore the bandanna over her scalp, but Tollin and Yarra had scrounged up a truly ridiculous broad-brimmed hat from the ship's stores for her. It had numerous gaudy decorations, and a trio of massive, battered, colorful feathers from some unknown tropical bird jutting up from it.

It was far too large for Talia, and was continually sagging in front of her eyes. It looked absolutely ridiculous, but Talia was delighted by it. One of her many brothers apparently had a similar hat.

After only a few minutes of rest, Alustin had them back up and moving. The trip down into the valley in question was shorter and easier than the trip up. The valley was barren, rocky, and completely empty, save for a single rain-fed pool with some shrubs next to it. It was bordered by cliffs and steep mountain slopes, with two other exits leading in and out. It was a bit on the small side to fit a city in, to Hugh's mind, but then, maybe Ithos had been built more vertically than horizontally?

Alustin spent quite some time taking measurements with various arcane instruments, the largest of which resembled the offspring of a telescope and a tuning fork, taller than Hugh and Talia. Meanwhile, the rest of them aimlessly poked around the valley. Hugh had wandered over to the pool, intent on trying to skip a rock all the way across the small body of water, when he saw something reflected in its waters.

Hugh quickly glanced up, and there, perched atop a cliff, was a sphinx.

He was less than half Kanderon's size, and his fur was a rich grey, rather than the tawny amber of Kanderon's coat. His wing-feathers started off grey as well, but as Hugh's eyes traced along the sphinx's immense wings, they became a pattern of alternating black and white feathers towards the tips.

The sphinx was definitely male— his face was sharp-browed and severe, though he was visibly younger than Kanderon, with skin darker of hue as well. The sphinx's eyes were a brilliant gold as he stared unblinkingly down into the valley at them.

Hugh wasn't sure how long he stared up at the sphinx before he heard the crunching of feet on the rock beside him.

"Not often yeh see a sphinx this close," Artur said. "Magnificent, isn't he?"

The sphinx blinked for the first time, as if acknowledging that as his due.

Artur chuckled softly. "Of course yeh can hear me from

up there. Well, yeh don't need ta' worry about our intentions in yer territory. This is just a temporary stopover on our voyage."

Artur clapped a hand gently on Hugh's shoulder. "Alustin's done with his measurements, Hugh. Let's get headin' back ta' the ship, eh?"

Hugh and the others were silent on the way up out of the valley. At the top of the little pass, the whole group stopped and looked back. The sphinx was still perched atop his cliff, watching them.

Hugh, feeling a little self-conscious, waved goodbye to the sphinx. To his surprise, the sphinx gave a deep, deliberate nod, before spreading his wings and launching himself off the cliff. He flew in a huge circle around the valley, giving them a magnificent view, then gained altitude and soared off, deep into the mountains filling the island.

The group set off down the pass. It was, annoyingly, just as difficult descending the shale as it had been climbing it. They marched alongside the steeper edge of the pass, so they could steady themselves on the rock wall to their side— not that it was that useful, as it was made of the same crumbling shale.

Halfway down, Sabae spoke up.

"Why was it so much smaller than Kanderon?" she asked.

Alustin, in the lead, turned back to look at them all.

"He was a younger sphinx, I believe," Alustin said. "Probably no more than a century or two old. Not that he'll ever reach Kanderon's size— she's by far the largest sphinx I've ever even heard of, and by all accounts the oldest, too. None of the others even come close. Of course, none of them have crystal wings, either. I'm amazed this sphinx let us see him. Many of them were hunted by the Ithonian Empire, and most on the continent that survived still lurk deep in the wilderness, far away from civilization. There's only one other I know of that's regularly involved in human affairs, and it's a member of the Alikean Parliament. It's different on other continents, but—"

"How old is Kanderon?" Talia asked.

Alustin shrugged. "She's never said, but she was already

fully grown when the first Skyhold Council used the Exile Splinter on Ithos. So very likely seven or eight hundred years, at least."

The rest of the trip down the pass was, despite its difficulty, filled with stories and rumors about sphinxes. Talia and Artur had the most stories to share, having spent the most time in the Skyreach Range. Talia had never seen any sphinxes other than Kanderon this close before, but she'd seen some at a distance, and she had more stories to share about encounters members of Clan Castis had with sphinxes over the years. A surprising number of the stories involved sphinxes battling dragons for territory. Despite their smaller size, sphinxes won more often than not. Their senses were far superior to dragons, so they usually managed to pull off ambushes, and their parents seldom let them leave the nest before they were capable of practicing magic at a level comparable to a human archmage, which was a huge advantage for ambushes.

Artur had quite a number of surprisingly close encounters with sphinxes as well, and had actually helped a nesting pair rescue a nestling from a collapsed cave once. Sphinxes apparently mated for life, and had a child only once every few decades. No one knew for sure whether they gave live birth or laid eggs— sphinxes were notoriously secretive about many parts of their life.

Though, reflecting on a conversation Hugh once had with Kanderon, he suspected that part of it might be embarrassment on the part of the sphinxes, rather than them just being secretive.

When they got back to the ship, Hugh wanted nothing more than to take an immediate nap, but, to his surprise, his spellbook was flapping around the rigging making a nuisance of itself.

It had spent most of the time since it ate the communications diary hibernating, only rousing itself to demand attention or pets from Hugh once or twice a day.

When Hugh managed to finally coax it down from the rigging, it snuggled up in his arms happily. He couldn't help but notice that it had only come down once Talia had gone belowdecks— he'd have to do something about the squabble between those two. So far as he could tell, he was fairly sure the spellbook felt bad about all the inconvenience and trouble it had caused Talia, but Talia was still happily holding onto her grudge.

"Should we give it a try?" Alustin asked him.

Hugh hesitated, then nodded. They'd consulted extensively with Kanderon via Alustin's book about the spellbook situation, and they'd worked out a plan of action for when the spellbook was finished… digesting… the communications diary.

Hugh opened up his spellbook to a random page. It didn't really matter which page he used— the spellbook could display any of the pages Hugh had written in it, either from before or after it had transformed, as well as the pages of any book it had devoured.

"Alright, spellbook, are you ready for this?" Hugh asked.

The spellbook didn't move, but it projected a sense of readiness towards Hugh.

"You really need to name that thing," Alustin muttered.

Hugh ignored him. He'd name the book when he thought of a good name for it.

"Alright," Hugh said, "contact Kanderon."

The spellbook's crystal pages seemed to strain, and a wash of blue-green rippled through the normal steady green.

Hugh took a deep breath, channeled mana, and began writing in the spellbook with his finger.

Kanderon?

Nothing happened for a few moments, but then a familiar bold script began to scrawl across the page.

Ah, Hugh! It worked, I see. Excellent. That book of yours isn't a completely useless annoyance, it seems.

A ripple of irritation reached Hugh from the book, but it didn't do anything to interfere with Kanderon's words. His spellbook seemed to take its duties as a book very seriously.

We just finished checking out the first site, Master. It wasn't what we were looking for— Alustin said it was just a natural shift in the aether. The localized mana desert around this island is starting to collapse, apparently.

Unsurprising. We suspected this site was an unlikely one to start with, though not firmly enough to rule it out.

We did see something you might be interested in, though.

Hugh spent the next few minutes describing the sphinx they'd seen. Kanderon seemed quite pleased to hear the news— she seemed to believe it was a sign that the younger sphinxes on the continent were growing bolder, and more willing to interact with the rest of civilization. She didn't have much hope for the older sphinxes that had survived the Ithonian purges to rejoin society, however.

Hugh spent the next hour or so discussing the events of the voyage so far with Kanderon before he finally begged off, exhausted and badly needing a nap.

Before he shut the book and went belowdecks, Kanderon shared one more piece of news with Hugh that she thought he'd find interesting. Rhodes Charax, Hugh's old bully, had gotten in an argument with his master, Aedan Dragonslayer, that escalated to a battle that had leveled a good part of the Skyhold docks. Shockingly, Rhodes had actually fought his master to a standstill before escaping into the Skyreach Range. Nobody had seen him since, though most suspected he was returning to Highvale. Kanderon, however, wasn't so sure, and she warned him to be cautious, as there was no telling what Rhodes' intentions towards Hugh might be.

Hugh, however, found that rather than being scared or apprehensive, he was just thoughtful. He was fairly sure he knew exactly why Rhodes and Aedan had argued and then fought, and he was oddly sure that, wherever Rhodes was going, it wasn't after him. Hugh would never forgive the cruelty Rhodes had shown him— not least because Rhodes had never actually apologized for it, or anything but abandoning him in Skyhold's labyrinth— but after his confrontation with Rhodes near the end of the school year, Hugh realized he no longer seriously worried about Rhodes as an enemy.

Plus, Rhodes kind of owed him for telling him the truth about Bakori and the events in the labyrinth.

He didn't tell Kanderon any of that just yet, however— he wanted to think about it a while longer first. So, he simply thanked her for letting him know and bid her farewell.

As he closed the book and descended belowdecks for his nap, Hugh realized to his mild surprise that this had been the longest conversation he'd ever had with Kanderon that wasn't a lecture or lesson.

CHAPTER SIXTEEN

Stormward's Gift

At the far eastern edge of the Shattered Isles, there was a small island with a natural harbor that the Radhan knew about.

The rock layers of the cliffs surrounding the harbor were tilted up at a shallow angle from being horizontal. One of those layers was a soft mudstone resting atop a particularly strong, erosion resistant sandstone. Over the eons, the mudstone had worn away more swiftly than the sandstone, leaving a wide exposed ledge that formed a natural road all the way from the water to the very tops of the cliffs, accessible from the lowest to the highest tides.

The previous few days had featured considerable

argument by Captain Grepha and the other Radhan elders aboard the ship about dates and calendars, though they shut up whenever they realized one of the party from Skyhold was near. Hugh even overheard them speaking in the secretive Radhan tongue a few times. Despite knowing nothing of the language, it was pretty obvious there was a lot of cursing involved. The Radhan tongue seemed especially well suited for cursing, if Hugh was any judge.

The arguments were finally resolved with the announcement that a major Radhan holiday was occurring the next evening, and they'd be laying harbor at an uninhabited island they knew of. When asked how they could have only just figured out a holiday was the next day, they merely began muttering about conflicting calendars, and avoided any further questions.

The island was a battered, broken-looking thing, whose outcrops were too jumbled to be called hills. Given the tilted rock layers of the island, it looked more as though some immense giant had broken a great stack of leaning boards.

Hugh never would have noticed the half-concealed harbor if they hadn't sailed straight into it on the morning of the mysterious Radhan holiday. The Radhan spent half a day preparing the feast-site atop the cliffs. They refused any help, so Hugh and his friends spent much of the day exploring the jumbled rocks of the island. The cliffs near the harbor were fairly flat and open, but farther towards the back of the small island they turned into an impassible mass.

In the afternoon, Hugh noticed the Radhan drawing a ward in chalk around the feast site. He took his leave of his friends, who were waiting on Godrick to shape a ladder into the stone of a particularly tall rock spire so they could get a view from the top.

Artur was using his magic to help flatten the stone they were constructing the tables atop of, while Alustin was nowhere to be seen.

Hugh spent a few moments following the curve of the ward the Radhan were constructing, frowning and muttering to himself. Finally, he strode up to the Radhan ship mages drawing the ward. They were drawing it out of a book, arguing about it as they went.

"This," Hugh said, "is one of the worst wards I have ever seen in my life."

"Excuse me," one of the mages said, clearly offended, "we've been using this ward for decades. It's a time tested design, and—"

"It's terrible," Hugh said. "It's supposed to be a concealment ward, I take it?"

"It *is* a concealment ward," another mage said. "It's hardly safe to just have a celebration out in the open on an exposed island like this. A dragon or something could easily spot it from a distance and decide to drop in if we didn't put up a ward."

"They could probably spot it from a distance even with this ward," Hugh said. "*I* will take care of the warding, because this offends my professional sensibility as a warder."

"No offense," one of the mages said, "but you are just a student, and…"

Hugh began assembling the pattern unlinking and pattern linking spellforms in his mind's eye.

"By any chance, did you hear about the attempted coup in Theras Tel a year ago?" Hugh asked.

"Yes, but I don't see…" one of the mages began.

"Did you hear about a ward someone built to shield the city from a storm while Indris Stormbreaker lay poisoned?" Hugh asked.

"Well, yes, but…" the same mage said, looking confused.

"That," Hugh said, "was me. I made that ward. I'm Hugh Stormward."

He flooded mana into the pattern unlinking spellform, then snapped his fingers for show. The chalk ward puffed into a dust cloud off the rough stone. Hugh then dropped the unlinking spellform and channeled mana into the pattern linking spellform. The chalk dust flooded past his legs and back into the sticks of chalk the mages were holding, rapidly growing them back up to size.

The instant that spell was complete, Hugh turned his

attention, and the pattern linking spellform, onto the rough stone. A band of stone, as wide as a long stride, simply flattened itself out as Hugh reshaped the crystals of the stone into something stronger and harder— a particularly strong variety of sandstone cemented with quartz. Within the band, Hugh began to grow the ward's spellform structure out of pure quartz. Within moments, the rough, uneven stone began taking the appearance of dressed stone inlaid with shining quartz crystals.

Hugh walked at a steady pace behind the ward as it grew. It cut across the different-angled rock layers its roots running several feet deep. The lines of the spellform were precise and flowing, and Hugh took no shortcuts with his work. His will-imbuing abilities let him take those sorts of shortcuts quickly and easily, with little risk of failure, but the wards he made that way weren't as durable over the long term, and right now, Hugh was aiming to impress.

He honestly couldn't believe he'd claimed the title of Stormward out loud. It had seemed a cruel joke to him for some time, and he'd been happy just being Hugh of Emblin.

Well, maybe not happy about it. He'd long since gotten tired of the weird looks that people gave him for being a mage from Emblin. And he didn't really have any attachment to Emblin any longer, nor any desire whatsoever to visit it again.

So, alright, he kind of hated being Hugh of Emblin. But Hugh Stormward sounded so… pompous and overblown, and it almost seemed like bragging to use the title.

But, then, as awkward as it felt to admit to himself, he'd earned it. Not by himself— he never could have done it without the help of Sabae and the crew of the *Moonless Owl*— but he had done it, and if there was one thing in his life he was unabashedly proud about, it was his skill with wards. Even without his will-imbuing warlock powers, he was already better with wards than many professional warders. There were definitely lots of better warders out there, but none he'd ever met. The only better warder he personally knew of was his teacher, Loarna of the Vault.

Who, admittedly, he'd never actually met in person, as she gave her classes as a series of elaborate tests, challenges, and riddles, never showing herself to her students.

It took him a little over an hour for him to curve the ward all the way around the party site. He likely could have done it in ten minutes or less, if he had been alright with a rush job, but Hugh intended to build something that would really last. He ignored the questions bombarding him from the Radhan mages as he went. His ward was considerably larger than the one they had planned, and far more intricate, with three interlocking layers of ward stretching all the way around.

"Your old ward blocked outgoing light," Hugh said. "It did so indiscriminately and completely, meaning that on a bright night, the inside would have been just a mysterious dark splotch. It blocked all sound just as indiscriminately, so anything that navigated by sound would surely have noticed the mysterious dead zone. Your ward also used a gratuitous amount of mana that would have required a mage constantly on duty."

He tapped the new ward with his foot. "My ward, on the other hand, only blocks out light in excess of the ambient light while active, meaning that light passing in from one side will still pass out the other normally. It only blocks out sound generated inside the ward, but lets outside sound pass through easily."

One of the Radhan mages raised their hand. "Couldn't something with sufficiently good night vision still see the revelers inside it with ambient light levels?"

Hugh nodded. "They could, but I've also taken care of that. I had a couple of choices there. First, I could have effectively turned the ward into an illusion field that projected an illusion of blank stone there, but that would have been prohibitively difficult on short notice, especially since I'm not trained as an illusionist at all. The other option, which I ended up going with, is constructing an attention ward. Anything that goes by that doesn't already know what's behind the ward will simply have its attention turned away from it. It's easier to construct, uses less mana, and is less prone to failure. On top of that, it uses half as much mana as your ward would have and should last for decades."

"I feel like a big fancy ward like this is a little noticeable," one mage said.

Hugh smiled and channeled a bit of mana into part of the ward. Unlike almost all the other functions, once started, this one would be able to sustain itself off ambient mana from the aether from here on out, unless this island became a mana desert.

"Step outside the ward," Hugh said, and did so himself.

The instant he did so, the ward simply vanished from sight, and looked like rough stone again. The people inside were still clearly visible as they went about preparations for the celebration, as was his spellbook, who had stolen a tablecloth and was attempting to abscond with it, but when Hugh's eyes tried to focus on the ward, they just slipped right off it. The instant he stepped back inside, the ward became visible again. The ambient mana was more than enough to keep attention off the ward itself.

The other mages moved in and out of the ward for a while, clearly excited, while Hugh lectured them on activating the ward for the party, and on its other functions— most notably the other one that ran on ambient mana, the one that dealt with damage to the ward. If the damage was below a certain threshold, it would slowly heal the crystal structure of the ward over time. If, however, the damage exceeded that threshold, it would collapse and destroy the ward. Damaged, malfunctioning wards were a danger to anyone around them, and many warders made entire careers around removing aging and damaged wards, often after they'd killed or wounded some innocent. Building a collapse function into a ward intended for more than temporary use was absolutely essential for any ethical warder.

There were a couple other functions as well— if you pumped more mana into it, it could also turn aside strong winds and inclement weather.

Hugh left the mages to play with the new ward, then

headed for the cliff edges overlooking the harbor. He constructed another ward there by reshaping the crystals in the stone, this ward buried deep inside the stone out of sight. It plunged vertically downward from the top of the cliff all the way to the bottom of the natural harbor, and well out under the seabed.

Around that time, his friends wandered down to see what he was up to, having noticed his construction of the first ward from their outlook. Hugh explained his plans, and they eagerly signed onboard. Godrick and Talia went down the ramp to start, while Sabae went to fetch Artur to help.

Hugh, meanwhile, used a levitation spell on himself to lower his weight down to almost nothing, then took a running leap, soaring across the mouth of the harbor. He barely made it across to the other side— he'd underestimated the force of the levitation spell he'd needed, but that was easily fixable mid-leap. He made sure to use his stellar mana reservoir to power the levitation spell— his crystal mana reservoir was by far the largest, but he'd need it to finish the ward.

His landing was less than graceful, however. It was more of a crash than a landing, really.

After he dusted himself off, he constructed another, identical vertical ward inside the cliff running down to and under the seabed, eventually connecting it to the ward coming down from the other cliff underneath the seabed.

He had to take a break for a half hour after that— growing wards in the crystal structure of stones at those distances was immensely draining, both mentally and on his aether reservoirs. Last summer, his affinity senses could never have reached all the way down the hundred-some foot cliff, nor could his mana reservoirs have handled its construction in such a short time.

Once his mana reservoir had refilled enough, Hugh drew another segment of the ward branching off the second vertical ward. It curved along in the stone deep beneath the clifftop around the harbor, eventually reaching all the way around to connect to the top of the other vertical ward. The final shape of the ward was something like a pair of horseshoes connected at the tips, sitting at right angles to one another.

Hugh climbed down the ramp for the final step. He consulted with Sabae again, because he'd only ever constructed the spellform once before, when building the Stormward around Theras Tel. He reshaped the crystals in the stone beneath the seabed especially carefully for the windlode spellform— it needed to be absolutely perfect to work. He then built a series of false spellform lines to further confuse anyone trying to analyze it. He was, so far as he knew, the only person outside the Kaen Das family who knew the windlode spellform, which allowed the caster to tap into the thickened aether that drove before storms. The resulting mana was somewhat limited in terms of what it could be safely used for, but wards were one of those things.

The massive new ward that covered the top and entrance to the harbor had many of the same functions as the party ward did, though it didn't need to conceal itself from direct sight, being buried beneath the stone. It performed all those functions on a much greater scale, however. On top of that, it had the capability to shield the entire harbor from storms using the windlode. It drew more heavily from the ambient aether than the first ward, but a mage would have to be paying exceptionally close attention to the decently thick aether here to notice the draw-down.

Godrick and Artur, meanwhile, had greatly improved the quality of the tilted sandstone ledge, making it into a proper road leading up, and roughening the stone so it didn't get as slick while wet. They'd also shaped several benches along the cliff wall to rest on the way up. Talia, meanwhile, had carved a series of caves into the mudstone layer using dreamfire. That process had sent lambent smoke, melting ice butterflies, and unpleasant sounds into the harbor. The caves could be used for emergency shelter, storage, or whatever purpose the Radhan saw fit.

Their work had drawn the attention of quite a few Radhan, but they refused to explain until they were done— at which point they were happy to explain and bask in the attention.

The five of them had turned the nameless little island with the natural harbor into a far more secure, permanent refuge. Only someone who already knew about the harbor's existence could find it now, and so far as the Radhan knew, they were the only ones who ever came there. Even the ladder Godrick had shaped into the stone spire earlier out of boredom could be used as a lookout, and the handholds would be almost invisible from a distance. That hadn't actually been part of the plan, but Hugh couldn't help but notice that Godrick didn't mention that part.

If the Radhan had been fans of theirs before, they were absolutely thrilled now. Quite a few of the Radhan were already speaking of permanently shifting some of the trade routes to use this harbor as a rendezvous point and stopover.

To Hugh's irritation, Sabae proposed that the until-now nameless island be renamed Stormward's Gift. Hugh glowered at her for that one, especially when the Radhan adopted it happily. They even had Godrick and Artur carve the name into the harbor wall. He might have come to grips with it as a title, but naming the island after him was just too much.

It did occur to him that it benefited her family as well, given how the title Stormward was associated with the Kaen Das family. Weirdly, that actually made him feel better about it, since it took some of the pressure off him.

It honestly didn't bother him that Sabae tended to have multiple motives for everything she did. Hugh genuinely trusted that she meant the best for him and the others, and it wasn't like he, Talia, or Godrick were any good at scheming or politics.

It was about at this time that Alustin showed back up, looking a bit disheveled. Hugh couldn't help but notice the tall sailor Alustin had been flirting with when the *Cormorant* left Lothal looked equally disheveled, and had also only recently shown up.

Hugh just rolled his eyes at that.

To his embarrassment and discomfort, he kept getting hugged and thanked over and over by the Radhan. It was actually a bit of a relief when the sun hit the horizon, and the party from Skyhold were all banished to the ship.

CHAPTER SEVENTEEN

Sphinx Eyes

They weren't banished to the ship for the whole evening, of course. Just for the actual religious ceremony.

Their banishment also included a fairly sizable feast for them, with about twice as much food as six people could reasonably be expected to eat.

They certainly gave it their best shot, though.

After they ate, Hugh dragged himself back to his cabin and managed to struggle into the upper bunk, feeling as though he'd tried to eat his own body weight. The others were still in the mess hall enjoying themselves, but Hugh was feeling a little mentally exhausted from the day and wanted a chance to be alone for a little while.

He vaguely considered trying to take a quick nap, but figured he'd be better off just staying awake, so he called his spellbook to him to try and get a little bit of reading done in the light coming in from the passageway.

He spent a few minutes persuading his spellbook to show him a list of books it had stored within it. Most were dry texts on wards and spellform construction, but as much as Hugh enjoyed that sort of thing normally, he was definitely looking for something a bit lighter to read at the moment.

Finally, Hugh settled on a novel Alustin had given him when he first refurnished Hugh's secret room in the library. Hugh had fed his spellbook nearly every book he owned at this point. Hugh always intended to read more novels, but it always seemed to slip his mind when he was choosing a new book to read.

Something odd happened when his spellbook tried to form the text of the novel on its crystal pages, however. It wasn't the print of the book that appeared at all, but Kanderon's distinctive handwriting.

Lasnabourne is dead.

The handwriting that responded to her was graceful and precise, each letter flowing into the next.

Was it the current Kaen Das ruler?

No, it wasn't Ilinia. And it is astonishing that you cannot bother yourself to learn the name of a mage that could so easily defeat you in battle, and that even I would be hard-pressed against.

I'm sure she could, but she's still just one of the ephemerals. She'll pass away of old age soon enough. Besides, I'm most of the way across the continent from her, and we have no reason to clash. Not least because she is a part of your... what did the Havathi call it? Your Coven?

Your complacency will be your undoing someday, Keayda.

So you've claimed for centuries now, Kanderon, and it's not come true yet. Tell me, though— if not the current Kaen Das, then who?

Who do you think? Lasnabourne was warned about his diet. Again and again those of us old enough to remember warned him to change it. Even leviathans and kraken are not so foolhardy as he. Lasnabourne might have been old, but only in comparison to humans and dragons. He was a hatchling the last time they were on Anastis. You remember how powerful they are.

I have heard nothing of their return from the Council. Are you sure?

The Council is divided, and we cannot trust them to tell us everything. Half of them oppose our purpose. Besides, I personally visited Lasnabourne's island just two days past.

I saw them offshore, Keayda. They may bear us no ill will, nor even much interest, but we must watch them nonetheless. If they begin to depart again, so soon after arrival, we will know our fears are coming true. We must watch and see whether they are the harbingers of their greater kin's arrival, or are merely here to evacuate their lesser kin from the coming of the…

The text collapsed into the opening pages of the novel. Hugh tried to call it back, but the spellbook seemed utterly bewildered at his command, as though it didn't know what he was speaking of.

That… that had been a conversation between Kanderon and the lich Keayda. One speaking of the death of another great power, Lasnabourne. Somehow, his spellbook digesting the communications diary must have meddled with its enchantments somehow. That was an absolutely terrifying thought, and not one he had any desire to share— Kanderon would *not* react well to finding out that his spellbook had accidentally violated the sanctity of her correspondence.

If Hugh remembered correctly, the phoenix nested in the islands southwest of the Ithonian continent. He wished he had his copy of *Galvachren's Bestiary*, but it was one of the only books he hadn't fed to his spellbook so far.

Over the last couple of years he'd come to realize that the *Bestiary* was, at least in part, a guide to the great powers of the Ithonian continent. It was where he had first learned of Keayda, Lasnabourne, and many other great powers, but he had doubted his spellbook could digest the book— both thanks to its enchantments that let every copy change when Galvachren altered his master copy, and thanks to its sheer, mind-boggling size. Hugh had trouble lifting the tome even with both hands.

Hugh was wracking his brain trying to remember more details about Keayda and Lasnabourne, while also trying to desperately commit every detail of the message to memory. He didn't dare recopy it into his spellbook— accidentally eavesdropping on one of Kanderon's private conversations was bad enough, but recording it?

No, no thank you.

And what was the Council? The Coven? *Who* had just returned to Anastis, and from where? And what had Kanderon been about to say when Hugh's access was cut off?

His mind was still racing in circles when the floorboards creaked and Talia stepped in.

"Hugh?" she said, in a near whisper.

"Did the Radhan send for us to rejoin them?" Hugh asked.

"Not yet," Talia said, still quietly. "You weren't trying to nap, were you?"

Hugh shook his head. "No, I was just getting some reading done."

Talia was silent for a moment, then said, in a much more normal voice, "What?"

"I was reading," Hugh said.

"How?" Talia demanded, giving him a confused look.

"With… with my eyes," Hugh said.

"It's pitch black in here, Hugh," Talia said.

Hugh furrowed his brow in confusion. "No it's not. There's plenty of light coming from the passageway."

Talia looked in his general direction, then back out the door.

"There's really not, Hugh. Are you using some kind of night vision cantrip? Do those even exist?"

Hugh shook his head. "Are you alright, Talia? There's plenty of light for me, did you hurt your eyes somehow?"

Talia stared at him silently, then stormed out of the room.

A few moments later, she was back, dragging the others with her.

"Huh," Sabae said. "It is, in fact, pitch black in here."

"Are yeh reading from yer spellbook?" Artur asked. "Maybe yeh're using yer crystal affinity sense to read the letters?"

"What are you all going on about?" Hugh asked, genuinely perplexed.

"I don't think that's it," Alustin said, entering the room.

He tapped a finger against the glow crystal by the door, and light filled the room. The others all blinked and shielded their eyes, but Hugh only needed to blink once or twice.

Then Alustin climbed right up onto the bunk with Hugh and was staring directly at his eyes from only inches away.

"Fascinating," he said. "Hugh, can you think of any incidents where you had an easier time seeing in the dark recently than others around you?"

"I mean… maybe?" Hugh said. "I honestly don't know?"

"Someone deactivate the glow crystal, please," Alustin said.

The light in the room dimmed a second later.

Alustin put his finger right next to Hugh's eyes, then flared an abrupt light cantrip from his fingertip. Hugh blinked and pushed away Alustin's finger.

"Did anyone else see that?" Alustin demanded.

"Ah did," Artur said.

"Likewise," Sabae said.

"I didn't," Talia muttered.

"Ah'm still stuck out in the hallway," Godrick muttered.

"What?" Hugh demanded.

"Eyeshine," Alustin said, climbing down from the bed. "Have you ever seen a cat or a dog's eyes reflecting a light cantrip or a campfire? They reflect it brightly. It's how they see in the dark better than we do. It's called eyeshine, and you have it. Not especially strong, but it's there."

"What?" Hugh demanded, even more confused. "Why would I have eyeshine?"

Sabae put her finger in his face and set off her own light cantrip.

"I saw it that time," Talia said. "It's really faint, but you're right, it's there."

"Still stuck in the hallway," Godrick said.

"Why are my eyes turning into dog eyes?" Hugh said.

Alustin shook his head. "They're not. They're turning into sphinx eyes."

Everyone was silent for a moment at that.

"Ohhhh," Hugh said, finally understanding what Alustin

was getting at.

"I don't understand," Talia said.

"It's the warlock pact," Alustin said, turning the glow crystal back on again. "Warlock pacts often result in not just altered magical abilities, but altered physical characteristics as well. It's fairly unpredictable what effects, if any, a warlock will develop from this process, but Hugh's been pacted long enough already for it to start happening."

"Still can't see," Godrick said.

"Hugh's pacted with a monster the size of a large building, and all he got was night vision?" Talia asked, sounding less than entirely impressed.

"Probably more than that," Alustin said. "Sphinx eyes also have incredible distance vision, impressive ability to make out small objects close up, and significantly improved color vision as well. Sphinxes have some of the best overall vision I know of. Hugh's eyes won't ever get quite as good as Kanderon's— for one thing, a lot of their increased distance vision comes from their sheer size, but more importantly, traits acquired by warlocks are seldom as powerful as the original."

"I suppose that's not bad, then," Talia said, sounding a bit less skeptical.

"Sounds like someone's boardin' the ship," Godrick said. "Ah'm guessin' we can head back up now. Also, ah still haven't gotten ta' see yet."

"Right then," Alustin said. "Let's all get ready for a party."

CHAPTER EIGHTEEN

Constellations

Alustin had insisted they all pack formal wear for the trip. Not their best, but nice enough. To Hugh's amusement, it had been Artur who complained most about that, insisting that bringing formal wear on a combat mission was "ridiculous Librarian nonsense."

Hugh rather liked wearing his. He couldn't explain why, but dressing nice felt a little like wearing social armor or something. He did leave his floating quartz crystal in his cabin, though— probably best not to have it at the party in case he accidentally hit someone with it.

As they climbed the ramp up to the top, Artur gave them all dirty looks, as though daring them to comment on his formal-wear.

Talia and Sabae had even worn dresses to the party— which was definitely a rare occasion. Talia wasn't wearing her ridiculous new hat, but she'd found a headcloth that went with her blue dress, which while not overly fancy, matched the color of her tattoos perfectly. Sabae's dress was mostly just… green. Really, really green. Possibly too green.

Hugh couldn't help but notice that the party ward was working perfectly. Unless he focused as hard as he could, his eyes simply skimmed over the party space as though it were empty stone.

The instant he stepped over the ward, however, the atmosphere completely changed.

The Radhan had set up a huge bonfire, burning what smelled like dried seaweed and driftwood, both of which were plentiful among the rocks around the base of the island. A small group of Radhan were playing musical instruments, many of which looked to be homemade. The music wasn't as… technically proficient as the music Hugh had heard at Skyhold's Midwinter celebration, but it was far more enthusiastic, and Hugh couldn't help but be reminded of the sandstorm festivals in Theras Tel, albeit with a little bit over a hundred people rather than a city of hundreds of thousands.

There was a sizable crowd dancing off to one side of the

bonfire near the musicians, while some of the children ran and played near the center of the warded space. Glow crystals rested atop the tables, in the middle of a massive demolished feast. Or, partially demolished, at least. The cooks had made enough food for at least twice as many people as were on the ship.

Someone pressed a wineskin into Hugh's hand, and he turned to see one of the mages who'd been working on the ward earlier.

"I don't suppose you'd be interested in talking shop during a party," the middle aged man said.

"Honestly," Hugh said, "I can't think of many things I'd prefer more than talking about wards at any point."

Sabae straightened a couple wrinkles in her dress nervously as she stared at the dance floor, looking for Tollin or Yarra. She saw plenty of married couples, and a few unattached Radhan flirting with members of other Radhan families— one family onboard had split onto two ships recently, and another new one had moved in to take the cleared space. It wasn't an acrimonious split, by any means— the Radhan had a highly complicated method of determining who would live on what ship, and moved between various ships quite frequently.

As she scanned the crowd, she saw Alustin somehow already on the dance floor with his tall friend, despite the fact the Skyhold party had only arrived a couple minutes ago.

She heard muffled cursing behind her, and saw Talia glaring off at a crowd of mages, all clustered around Hugh, who was talking animatedly.

"They wanted him to talk about wards," Talia said helplessly. "Now how am I going to get my chance to talk to him?"

"Yeh'll find it. That's what parties are fer," Artur said, patting Talia on the shoulder. "Ah'm in a bit of a music makin' mood mahself."

With that, Artur strode off towards the musicians.

"Your dad plays music?" Sabae asked Godrick.

He shrugged and smiled. "He's a man a' many talents."

Talia made another high pitched noise. "How does he know about me and Hugh?"

Sabae sighed. "I think everyone but Hugh knows, Talia. Godrick, let's find something to drink and distract Talia until Hugh's not busy anymore, so she can go talk to him and totally fail to work up the nerve to tell him how she feels."

"Hey!" Talia said, glaring. She made to kick Sabae, but then stopped, and settled for sticking out her tongue.

"Ah'll distract Talia," Godrick said, chuckling. "Yeh're going ta go over ta' that table over there and chat with some very pretty Radhan youths that are keepin' their sick friend company. They keep looking over at you. Yeh're going ta' have a nice conversation with them, and then yeh're goin' ta' ask one of them ta' dance."

Sabae looked over and spotted Tollin and Yarra keeping company with Dell at one of the tables. She took a deep breath.

"And remember," Godrick said, "yeh need ta' pick jus' one a' them."

"Why do people keep saying that?" Sabae muttered.

Godrick just sighed. "Come on, Talia, let's get a drink then do a little dancin'. Yeh'll need to work up your nerve at some point, though."

He dragged a grumbling Talia off behind him. Sabae watched them for a moment, then shook her head. There was no way Talia was going to go through with telling Hugh her feelings tonight, and she'd be willing to bet they'd be dealing with weeks more of her pining, at least.

Sabae took a deep breath, smoothed her dress one more time, then strode over towards Tollin and the twins.

"Sabae!" called Dell happily as she arrived. "My hero!"

He burst into a fit of coughing, but it only lasted a few seconds. He'd breathed in a lot of seawater when the serpent had dragged him underwater, and his lungs had suffered a lot of damage. He was already doing considerably better under the attention of the *Cormorant's* healers, however. He hadn't been able to speak above a whisper the first day after he woke up.

"Hi Sabae!" Yarra said, tucking a strand of her long brown hair behind one ear.

"Glad you made it!" Tollin said, shaking his own shaggy black hair out of his eyes.

Dell took a sip from a wineskin, then handed it to Sabae. She took a sip to hide her nervousness.

This was absolutely ridiculous. She shouldn't be getting this nervous just because of a couple pretty faces. So she'd never dated before or kissed anyone, but she'd manipulated Hugh and Avah into dating. She'd observed other people dating enough to know it wasn't that complicated. People just liked to make idiots of themselves. It wasn't that scary, not in comparison to the other things she'd done. Sabae had fought pirates, sea serpents, and demons, and she had survived the labyrinth of Skyhold twice, not to mention…

She quickly turned her mind from thoughts of magma.

Dell cleared his throat. "Sorry about that. I should clarify that you're my hero because you're about to take one of these idiots off my hand so I can actually have a conversation about something other than how amazing and pretty they think you are."

Both of them turned bright red, and Yarra swatted her twin brother gently on one shoulder.

"Careful, I'm still wounded," Dell said, laughing.

Sabae spent a few minutes chatting with the three of them and passing around the wineskin. For someone still recovering from a near-death experience, Dell was surprisingly relaxed and sociable.

They finished the wineskin, and Dell asked the other two to fetch another. There was a little argument that it was hardly a task that needed two people, but Dell just waved them off.

When Yarra and Tollin were out of earshot, Dell's face turned more somber.

"Sabae…" he started, and she found herself tracing the

scars on her hands with her fingers, a nervous habit she'd thought she'd broken years ago. She'd never quite understood Hugh's discomfort with praise until this last week, when the Radhan had started relentlessly sending it her way.

Dell smiled wryly. "I'm sure you're sick of being thanked and congratulated, so I'll make this the last time, I promise. But you really did save my life. I really thought I was going to die down there."

He rubbed the back of his head awkwardly, in a move almost identical to Hugh when he was feeling awkward.

"I can't even stand near the railing without panicking now," he said. "I have nightmares every single night about deep water. I know it hasn't been that long since the attack, but I've been seriously thinking about asking to be moved to a ship on the Endless Erg. I don't know how you can be as strong as you are about things like this. It's more than just your magic— I've known plenty of mages who weren't half as brave or confident as you. I know you probably think I'm weak or a coward for being so afraid, but I just want you to know how much it means to me."

Sabae sat down next to him, and spent a moment thinking about her words. Finally, she took a deep breath.

"I've been having nightmares too," she said. "During midsummer, a rogue mage and a demon attacked Skyhold, and, well… I got trapped. Stuck inside a little warded space, with waves of magma crashing against it. I really thought I was going to die too. More nights than not, I get woken up by nightmares of molten stone. And the serpent that snagged you, the one that chased us up to the surface? It's been showing up in my dreams too, swimming in the magma. So has this one lightning mage who…"

She stopped, noticing Dell's wide eyes.

"My life's a bit over the top, right?" she said, nervously.

"Just a little bit," Dell replied. "Only a tiny bit, though."

They both burst out laughing at that.

Sabae wiped tears of laughter out of her eyes. At least, she was fairly sure they were tears of laughter.

"I'm glad you made it too, Dell," she said. "And you don't need to be ashamed of your nightmares and fear."

"You either," he said. "And it looks like your admirers have finally found the wine. Have you picked whose heart you're going to break yet?"

"Why do people keep asking me that?" Sabae groaned. "Why do I have to be the one to make that decision? And why is it so difficult?"

Dell gave her a thoughtful look. "You… haven't dated much before, have you?"

"Is it that obvious?" Sabae said, scuffing her sandal on the ground.

"I mean, a little," Dell said. "Either that or you're just, uh… really, really ambitious, and, uh… I'm leaning more towards the inexperienced end of things."

Sabae groaned.

"Here they come," Dell said. "But… since you saved my life and all, I think I can help you out a little. Try not to cause any drama for me to deal with, alright?"

Sabae gave him a confused look, but she didn't have time to ask what he meant before Yarra and Tollin arrived.

Yarra handed her brother the wineskin, and Dell drank deeply, then sighed. "As much fun as I'm having, I'm about done in for the night. Tollin, I hate to be a bother, but would you be willing to help me back to the ship? I'm not sure I can make it back on my own, my leg's killing me tonight."

"Of course," Tollin said.

"Should I help too?" Yarra said.

Dell waved her off. "I'm not a complete invalid, and besides, we don't want to abandon Sabae completely, do we?"

Yarra beamed at her brother, and Tollin suddenly cast a suspicious look at his friend, but Dell just smiled and waved back at Sabae. She smiled and waved back at him as he limped off, his arm around Tollin's shoulders.

Sabae shot a glance at Yarra, and there was a moment of silent awkwardness as Sabae tried to figure out what to say.

This really shouldn't be this difficult. She'd seen other people flirt successfully so many times before, it really wasn't that complicated. She didn't know why…

Yarra spoke up, interrupting Sabae's thoughts. "So, uh… would you like to dance?"

Sabae blushed, then nodded, not trusting her tongue not to say something stupid. Yarra blushed too, but she grabbed Sabae's hand and led her towards the dancers by the fire.

Sabae realized she was grinning like an idiot, but made no effort to stop.

Along the way, Sabae noticed Hugh's spellbook sitting suspiciously close to the edge of the fire. It noticed her and abruptly started giving her an innocent look, as though it were just enjoying the heat.

Sabae scowled at the ridiculous thing, sure it was up to something, then shook her head. Someone else could worry about that absurd book. She had much better things to focus on tonight.

To Talia's surprise, dancing with Godrick was really easy. Despite the massive height difference, Godrick was a skilled dancer, and he didn't seem to be bothered by her repeatedly stepping on his feet while she kept sneaking glances over towards Hugh.

Or, not too bothered, at least.

Over in the band area, Artur had borrowed some clearly homemade stringed instrument, and was playing it with gusto. He kept the beat with one foot, and each time he tapped it, the ground produced a surprisingly resonant, deep sound.

"He hollowed out the rock under his foot," Godrick said. "Turned it inta a sort a' drum."

Talia blinked at him in surprise, and Godrick shrugged. "Me da's the first thing yeh looked at other than Hugh all night. Wasn't hard ta' guess what yeh were thinkin'."

Talia sighed. "I'm sorry, Godrick. I'm being pretty terrible company tonight, aren't I?"

Godrick shrugged. "Ah don't think a friend's company is

ever bad company," he said. "An ah'm happy ta' tease yeh about this sort a' thing, but ah also have yer back. Take yer time."

Talia turned their dance into a hug for a moment, almost tripping them both.

"Thank you," she said. "But you're definitely getting interested looks from some of the Radhan, and I'd be a bad friend if I stole all your time tonight."

"Well," Godrick said, "ah think yeh might be about ta' have yer chance. Hugh's leavin' that group a' mages."

As they turned on the dance floor, Talia spotted Hugh storming towards the fire.

"No!" Hugh shouted. "Stop that! What are you even doing?"

He reached down and yanked his spellbook away from the fire, then shook it upside down. A number of hot coals fell out onto the stone.

"Why were you even eating those?" Hugh demanded. He was silent for a moment, then made a frustrated sound. "No! That's absurd! Spitting hot coals at annoying children would *not* make you a dragon."

There was another moment of silence, then Hugh sighed. "Absolutely not. Go find some fish or sleeping seabirds to harass or something."

He threw the spellbook up in the air, and it flapped away in the direction of the ship. Hugh visibly sighed, then strode away from the fire and crowds.

"Looks like he's had enough a' crowds fer the moment," Godrick said. "Go after him!"

"Maybe he's just looking for somewhere to relieve himself," Talia said.

Godrick stepped back and crossed his arms. "Then yeh turn around and wait fer him ta' finish, and yeh get a funny story out of it. Go!"

Talia took a deep breath, nodded, and started off after Hugh.

"Hey, Talia?" Godrick said.

She turned around to look at him.

He clapped her on the shoulder. "Ah believe in yeh, bud.

Yeh'll do fine."

Artur was taking a break from playing music to get something to drink when Alustin suddenly appeared next to him.

"There is absolutely no way," Alustin said, "that I was as ridiculous as my students when I was their age."

"Yeh were considerably worse," Artur replied.

"Why can't my apprentices be as sensible as your son?" Alustin complained.

Artur rolled his eyes. "They're a good lot. Ah've told yeh already, they're just enjoyin' themselves. They haven't had much time ta' jus' be young lately."

He offered the wineskin to Alustin, who shrugged and took a sip.

"These wards Hugh built today… ah've got ta' admit, they're a bit scary fer someone his age," Artur said.

"He's still not on Loarna's level, but he's far beyond even most fully trained warders at this point," Alustin said. "If I were going to try and break one of his wards, well… I'd have to either brute force it or be tricky about it. I don't honestly think I could break his wards in the traditional manner."

"Yeh seldom do anythin' in the traditional manner," Artur noted.

Alustin smirked at that. "True enough. When are you and Hugh going to be done with your little project? I'd like to get them training with it sooner rather than later."

Artur shrugged. "Ah'd hoped tomorrow, but…" He gestured at the party. "Should be soon, though."

The paper mage took another drink, then handed the wineskin back to Artur. "Both Hugh and Godrick are going to be at a bit of a disadvantage once we head north from Zophor, if the Themeseren site or the third site aren't the right one. Neither of them have affinities particularly well-suited towards the jungle."

Artur raised an eyebrow at that. "An' either a' us do?"

Alustin gave him a wry look. "We have the advantage of years of using our affinities in more adverse conditions. And your equipment means you're never at a loss for material to work with, and much the same for my tattoo."

Artur nodded at that, and took a drink.

"So," Alustin said. "What do you think will happen with Hugh and Talia? I'm personally betting she chickens out and doesn't go through with telling Hugh tonight."

"It's almost painful ta' watch," Artur said. "But ah'll take that bet. Ah'm guessin' she kisses Hugh, panics, runs away, an' that leads ta' weeks a' nonsense."

They shook hands on the bet.

"At least Sabae and Godrick won't be so dramatic," Alustin muttered.

Artur raised an eyebrow, then nodded over at Sabae, who was dancing with one of the Radhan girls. There was a Radhan boy standing irritably on the sidelines staring at them both.

Alustin sighed. "At least Godrick won't be so dramatic."

"Hey now," Artur said, giving Alustin a mock offended look. "Don't count mah boy out a' this, he's no underachiever."

Alustin just rolled his eyes at that.

Hugh was sitting on the edge of the cliff watching the waves crash against the rocks beneath his feet when Talia found him.

She sat down next to him, without saying anything. They stayed there quietly for a long time. Of all his friends, Talia was the one most comfortable with silence, which Hugh greatly appreciated. Most people were terrible at just being silent and enjoying someone else's company.

He took a sip of the wineskin he'd brought with him, and then offered it to Talia. She took it from him with both hands, and started drinking as though she planned to drain it dry.

"Don't forget to breathe," Hugh said.

Talia handed it back to him and caught her breath. "Haven't actually had anything to drink yet," she said. "Got pretty thirsty dancing with Godrick."

Hugh lay down on the clifftop, his calves dangling over the edge, and stared up at the stars. The moon wasn't out at the moment— it was usually bright enough to wash out many of the stars, even as far as it was from being full. The stars weren't as bright as they were out in the Endless Erg, or up in the mountains of Emblin, but they were still brilliant.

Talia followed suit. They started pointing out constellations, but they'd both grown up far to the north, so many of the ones they were familiar with were in vastly different positions than they were used to in the sky. Interestingly, Talia was having an easier time seeing them than Hugh did— he could, apparently, see a lot more stars than she did, so it was harder for him to pick out the specific stars that belonged in the constellations.

"So how'd you miss realizing you were developing night vision?" Talia asked. "It seems like the kind of thing you would notice."

Hugh grimaced, a little embarrassed. "I dunno," he said. "I think it must have developed slowly over time, and with me spending most of my time inside Skyhold over the last year, it must have just crept up on me. I'm sure there were signs of it, and I just didn't realize. In case you hadn't noticed, I'm not the most observant person ever."

"I've definitely noticed," Talia said dryly.

Hugh snorted at that.

Neither of them spoke again for a long while. He felt an itch in the back of his mind that usually indicated his spellbook was nearby and up to something, but at the moment, he was too content to be bothered.

He'd almost figured that Talia had fallen asleep when she spoke up in a quiet voice.

"Hugh?" she asked.

"Yes?"

"I, uhhh…" Talia paused for a long time. "I was wondering how you were feeling about Lothal."

"Lothal?" Hugh said.

"It's just… you were really upset about the Havathi spotter we killed in Lothal," Talia said. "You've been pretty quiet about it, but I've been worrying about you. For all that I'm more comfortable with violence, a lot of it's because I'm familiar with it from being taken on Clan raids and such. And I'm not actually as comfortable with it as I act sometimes, honestly. A lot of it is just bravado on my part. And, well, you've fought monsters and such before, but there's a big difference between that and killing an intelligent being."

The itching in the back of Hugh's mind grew a little more, but he ignored it, and tried to think of what he wanted to say.

"I don't know anything about them," Hugh finally said. "I don't know their name, what they looked like, or if they were close to their family. The only thing I know is that they were trying to kill us, and I feel like that should be enough to feel justified about the whole thing. I was protecting my friends. But… I just keep trying to imagine what they looked like, over and over again, putting different faces on them. I just can't stop imagining what they look like, and it feels ridiculous to me. And when I feel sad about Avah dumping me, I feel guilty, like I'm a bad person for thinking about something as trivial as a breakup when I should be thinking about the person I killed, who I just can't stop wondering what they…"

Hugh forced himself to stop talking and breathed in raggedly. He felt Talia reach out and grab his hand, and he squeezed hers in response.

"Of all people, Kanderon has been giving me advice on it, and letting me talk to her about it," Hugh said. "I feel guilty sometimes, that I'm wasting the time of someone that important with my ridiculous anxieties. She even listens to me talk about Avah, which seems absurd to me, but she hasn't complained once. Or, about anything other than my studies, at least."

"You can always talk to me, Hugh," Talia said.

Hugh squeezed her hand. "I know, I just… you've seemed so stressed out about your hair lately, and I was worried I'd start talking about Avah and annoy you, because I know you didn't like her very much, and I just didn't want to be a burden. You and Sabae and Godrick do so much for me, and I know I'm not really completely useless, but it's felt so hard to ask even more from any of you lately, like I need to try and balance things out and do more for you all before asking even more from you."

"Hugh," Talia said. "I'm really regretting promising not to hit you right now. You're being stupid. There is no ledger between us. I'm not keeping track of what good deeds my friends owe me, and when I do nice things for you or Sabae or Godrick, I'm doing them because I simply want to do them, because doing nice things for my friends makes me feel good. And I can guarantee that the others feel the same way. Do you bother keeping a mental ledger for the nice things we do for you, or are you just keeping track of how far behind you think you are?"

"I guess just the latter?" Hugh said.

"Friends don't need to keep track," Talia said. "Also, your annoying spellbook is hovering over us, and I'm pretty sure it wants something from me."

Hugh glanced over and saw that the spellbook was indeed hovering there. It shot him a pleading look.

"I think it brought you an apology gift?" Hugh said.

"A what now?" Talia said.

The spellbook opened its pages and flapped them convulsively, almost like it were coughing, and something dropped on the ground between them.

They both sat up and stared at it, letting go of each other's hands.

"It's a fish," Talia said. "Or half of one, anyhow."

"A mackerel, I think," Hugh said.

"What could I possibly want with half a mackerel?" Talia demanded. "What possible use could I have for it?"

Hugh's spellbook sent him another pleading look, and images raced through his mind.

"It, uh… stole it from a shark, and the shark reminded my spellbook of you, so…" Hugh shrugged.

Talia glared at the book, then pulled up one foot and kicked the half-mackerel off the cliff.

"Go away, book," she said.

It flew off slowly, looking dejected.

Talia laid back down and adjusted her head covering. Hugh stared after his spellbook for a moment longer, then followed suit.

"Sorry about that," Hugh said. "What were you saying?"

"Just… if you need to talk to me about anything, you can, Hugh. Always."

"Thanks," Hugh said. "Same goes to you. Whenever you need to talk about something, I'm always here."

Talia was quiet for a moment, then started cursing.

"Uh… Talia? Is something wrong?" Hugh asked.

Talia sighed. "I didn't hate Avah."

"She dumped me, and we're not getting back together," Hugh said. "You don't have to lie to spare my feelings."

"I'm not… I really didn't dislike her, Hugh." Talia said. "I was jealous of her. I was jealous about how open she was with her emotions, about how comfortable she seemed with the expectations others had for her, about how much prettier she was than me, and… I was jealous of your relationship with her."

Hugh was silent for a moment as he tried to process that.

"You had a crush on Avah?" he said.

Talia was silent for a moment, then started laughing.

"What?" Hugh asked, confused.

It took a few moments for Talia to regain control of herself. She sat up, then reached over Hugh and grabbed the wineskin. She took a deep drink, then just held the wineskin in her lap for a moment.

"Talia?" Hugh asked, sitting up as well.

"I didn't have a crush on her, you idiot, I had a crush on you," Talia said. "I still do."

Hugh just gaped at her like a fish, trying to think of what

to say.

Talia started growing visibly nervous.

"Hugh?" she asked.

"Talia, I…" Hugh started, but he didn't know what to say.

Talia started to stand. "I'm sorry. That was unfair of me. I should get going. I'll—"

Hugh reached out and grabbed her wrist. Talia froze, then slowly sat back down.

"My words aren't really working right now," Hugh said. "Could you give me a second here?"

"Alright," Talia said, in a tiny voice.

It felt like an eternity as Hugh stared at the ocean in front of him, his thoughts racing around and refusing to collect themselves in any sensible order. Finally, he said the first thing that came to mind.

"What about Phusan?" he asked.

Talia shrugged. "I think I was just trying to make you jealous. He was cute, but boring."

"How long…?" Hugh asked.

"I don't know," Talia said. "I think I was trying to deny it to myself for a long time, but I think the first seeds were planted, when, well… when I discovered your secret room."

Hugh gave her a confused look. "When we had that argument because I was hiding things from you guys?"

Talia shook her head. "It wasn't a fight, Hugh. I violated your privacy, triggered your defensive wards, then blamed you for my own mistakes. I was miserable for days, because I absolutely knew I was in the wrong even when I did it, but, well… I was a real spoiled brat growing up, Hugh. I got away with everything, and I never had to apologize for anything. Then my affinities appeared, and they didn't work, and I got a chip on my shoulder the size of a mountain from that, and I'm rambling, but I'm trying to say that I wanted to apologize, but I didn't really know how, and I was terrified you'd throw it back in my face and hate me. And then I made myself do it, and you just… forgave me. Just like that. And I think that was the moment I realized that you weren't just… waiting for me to show weakness so you could tear me down, prove you were better than me, or something like that. I think… I think that was like a seed, and my feelings grew from that? That sounds stupid, doesn't it?"

"No," Hugh said. "It doesn't sound stupid at all."

He stared out at sea again, his thoughts still racing, but feeling like they were taking more of a shape now.

"You're thinking of a way to let me down gently, aren't you?" Talia asked, finally.

"Honestly," Hugh said. "I don't think I've ever thought of you romantically."

"Oh," Talia said. "I… Thank you for being honest with me. I should—"

Hugh shook his head. "No, I don't think you understand. It's not that there was something wrong with you that I never considered it, it's that I literally wouldn't let myself consider you romantically."

"I think it's my turn to be confused," Talia said.

"Even though you literally just told me I could tell you anything, this is still really hard to say," Hugh said. "But… I kinda live in constant fear that I'll do something to drive you and Godrick and Sabae away. Most of the time I feel like you three, and I guess to a lesser extent Alustin and Kanderon and Godrick's dad, are literally the only reasons I'm a functioning person at all. If I didn't have you all around me, I wouldn't be able to stand up on my own at all. Or, maybe more that I wouldn't really feel like a person at all, like all I am is just the pieces of yourselves that you all share with me, and if you weren't in my life any more, I'd just be… hollow, I guess. I really try not to think what would have happened if I hadn't met you all, because I… I just don't want to think about that, is all. And so… yeah, I just literally never allowed myself to even consider romance with you, because it might have threatened our friendship, and I just couldn't risk it. I couldn't… I can't lose any of you. I can't lose you, Talia."

Hugh realized his hands were shaking, and then suddenly Talia was squeezing him so hard he could barely breathe.

"I'll always be your friend, Hugh," Talia said. "That's never going to change. Ever."

Hugh hugged her back, and neither of them said anything for what felt like the longest silence yet.

Finally, Talia let go of him, and scooted back to her spot.

"So…" Hugh said. "I guess what I'm saying is that I honestly don't know. I think I just need time to think about things. And I know that won't be fun for you, because waiting is the worst, but…"

Talia reached out and squeezed his hand once, then let go and stood up.

"I'm going to go turn in for the night, I think," Talia said. "I'll see you tomorrow?"

"Of course," Hugh said.

After Talia left, Hugh just sat there, staring out to sea. A few party-goers wandered past, but they somehow sensed that he didn't want to speak to anyone at the moment, and they left him alone.

He watched the stars move across the sky, the waves crash on the rocks below him, and the moon rise.

When Hugh got up to return to the ship, the celebration had long since ended, and the eastern horizon was already turning light.

CHAPTER NINETEEN

Oddly Timed Lightning

Talia wasn't avoiding Hugh, she was just… giving him space. She didn't want him to feel pressured or uncomfortable.

And, admittedly, perhaps walking barefoot to avoid having audible footsteps, checking around corners on the ship with mirrors to make sure she didn't accidentally run into him, and avoiding long sight-lines on deck were slightly… aggressive methods of avoiding him.

She spent most of the morning finding places to hide. It wasn't hard— she was small enough to fit in all sorts of places no one else but children could fit into. She tried to get a little reading done from her assigned homework from Alustin, but constant nervous checking for Hugh kept her from focusing.

Hugh didn't trudge onto deck until well into the early afternoon, and Talia had grown complacent by that point.

The *Cormorant* had gotten off to a late start that morning, with a big chunk of the crew still hungover from the night before. The Radhan were still moving capably enough, but there was a lot more complaining going on, and everyone seemed to be moving just a little bit slower.

Hugh was yawning as he stepped onto the deck, and by the time he finished and looked around, Talia was well on her way up into the rigging of the mainmast.

She made it all the way to the drake's nest, where an amused Radhan weather mage she vaguely recognized helped her up. The gentle rocking of the ship in the waves was greatly magnified up in the drake's nest, and her stomach sent up a mild protest at it.

To her surprise, she found Sabae curled up in the bottom of the drake's nest, wrapped in an old, weather-stained blanket that had obviously been up here for some time. The drake's nest was quite cramped with all three of them in it.

"What are you doing up here?" Talia asked.

"Hiding," Sabae said. She looked miserable.

"From what?" Talia asked.

Sabae gave her a dirty look. "Unanticipated consequences."

The weather mage snorted at that, and Talia gave her a curious look.

"Your friend danced with and kissed both Tollin and Yarra last night," the woman said. "She very much surprised the night watch by doing her magic jump thing from the cliff-top right into the water, then sneaking on board."

"It was a cunning escape stratagem," Sabae muttered, and pulled part of the blanket over her head.

The weather mage chuckled. "I heard you were aiming for the ship, and were drunk enough you missed by two ship lengths. You're lucky you didn't drown. Anyhow, you shouldn't feel too bad, kid. Tollin and Yarra are trouble."

Sabae made a miserable noise. "Dating should not be more complicated than politics. Or involve as much yelling."

Talia gave the two of them confused looks.

"Tollin and Yarra date and break up every few months," the Radhan woman explained, leaning against the mast where it jutted up through the floor of the drake's nest. "I think they were legitimately impressed with your friend, and really do like her, but they were definitely also trying to make each other jealous. Not to mention, Tollin's father is the first mate, and Yarra and Dell's family captained the last ship they were on, and Captain Grepha doesn't have an heir, and they've both been jockeying around that."

"So they're… enemies?" Talia asked. "Rivals for the captaincy after Grepha?"

"There are no enemies on a Radhan ship, kid," the woman said. "Friendly rivals, maybe, but not for the captaincy. Neither family actually wants that, because that would bind them to the *Cormorant,* and there are rumors that there are several new ships being added to the fleets soon, and nice ones, at that. Both want a chance at those."

"I'm supposed to be the one scheming and manipulating," Sabae muttered. "And yet I keep being the one manipulated lately."

"What?" Talia said.

Sabae pulled the blanket off her face a little and sighed. "Nothing. So how'd last night go for you? Did you talk to

Hugh?"

Talia glanced down automatically, seeing Hugh sitting in the prow. Godrick and Artur had just joined him, and the three appeared to be juggling chunks of rock between them with magic, presumably for training.

"I, uh…" Talia said, cautiously. She looked at the Radhan woman nervously.

"I can keep a secret, no need to worry," the woman said. "My name's Renna, by the way."

"I'm…" Talia started, but the woman waved her off.

"Everyone on board knows who you lot are, Talia. Kinda hard after the craziness of this voyage," Renna said.

"Well?" Sabae asked.

"Yeah, I talked to him," Talia said, sitting down. There wasn't much room, so she sat down on top of Sabae.

"Really?" Sabae asked.

"Yes."

"Seriously?"

"Yes, Sabae."

"About your feelings for him, or something totally unrelated?" Sabae asked.

"About my feelings," Talia said, and sighed.

"Wait, really?" Sabae said, and pulled the blanket completely off her face.

"Yes, really," Talia said, irritably. "Did you not believe I would?"

Sabae gave her an awkward look. "I was actually expecting a long, complicated comedy of errors. I take it Hugh shut you down, since you're hiding up here with me?"

"Not… not exactly," Talia said. She spent a while telling Sabae and Renna the story, though she left out a few details Renna didn't need to know, like about Hugh's eyes.

"Huh," Renna said. "I feel like I'm missing a lot here, kid, but I'm cheering for you. And, uh, no offense, but… your friend Hugh seems a bit broken."

Talia glowered off into space. "I pretty regularly fantasize about paying Hugh's family in Emblin a visit, and not a friendly one. They're monsters worse than the ones we faced down in the labyrinth, if you ask me."

"You're not the only one," Sabae muttered. "Godrick and I have discussed the logistics of the expedition in detail. The main problem is keeping Hugh from noticing our absence for a couple months."

Talia made a long, frustrated noise in the back of her throat.

Sabae patted Talia comfortingly, then pulled the blanket over her head. "I'm too hungover to give coherent advice right now. I'm going back to sleep."

Talia just sighed.

The first storm hit them the day they finally passed the eastern edge of the Skyreach Range— which also happened to be Talia's seventeenth birthday.

It had been three days since the party, and Talia had successfully avoided Hugh a lot of the time, save at lessons. Every time they did talk, it just felt awkward and terrifying, and part of Talia was worried that maybe she had damaged their friendship somehow.

The three days had been stressful for more than just that reason, though. On no less than five occasions, the water mages on guard duty had detected packs of sea serpents. The ship mages steered around them, diverted them with water currents, and even killed a couple sea serpents, but it had everyone on edge. The sea serpent killings were far less dramatic than the first attack had been— the ship's water mages just levitated a bubble of water containing a sea serpent out of the air, withdrew the water from their gills, and held them in the air near the ship until they suffocated, which took quite a while.

Everyone agreed that there were far, far too many serpents for this time of year. Even in winter, this many serpents would be unlikely to be seen in this region.

The mages also spotted various other sea monsters, including, ironically, a massive sea snake nearly as long as the ship. It paid them no attention, but it did surface nearby for a time, digesting some meal it had swallowed whole— a large shark, perhaps, or maybe a sea serpent. Its body was a brilliant scarlet mottled with burnt orange spots, and its tail flattened out towards the end, looking almost like a great paddle stood on its edge, which allowed the reptile to swim at great speeds. If Talia hadn't seen how voracious sea serpents were, she'd have given the name to sea snakes instead. Sea serpents were, after all, just big elongated fish with weird fins. The serpents were, however, for all their smaller size, the far greater threat to ships and sailors than sea snakes. Sea snakes, and most other sea monsters, for that matter, simply didn't like the taste of humans.

The eastern edge of the Skyreach Range trailed off much less impressively than the western edge. In the west, Skyhold and the other mountains rose almost straight out of the ground, with comparatively little in the way of foothills. Many of them approached the size of the largest mountains towards the center of the range. In the east, however, the mountains slowly decreased in size, trailing off into foothills.

It was still a majestic sight, though. The great rainforests of Southeast Ithos started right in those foothills.

The increasing humidity, however, Talia could have lived without. She had enough trouble with the heat.

The storm didn't come from the sea. It rolled right off the Skyreach Range, almost without warning. The crew had less than an hour to prepare for its arrival, and Talia's birthday dinner had to be put off.

Not that Talia particularly minded the delay. She had bigger problems at the moment— the storm had proven that, in fact, she was still vulnerable to seasickness on the water as well as on sand. The creaking and shuddering of the *Rising Cormorant* were, if anything, even worse than they had been on the *Moonless Owl* during the sandstorm.

Godrick and Alustin were both banished to the lower decks with her during the storm. Godrick was quite content with that fate— his affinities weren't particularly useful in a storm, and it didn't seem to wound his pride very much not to be able to help on deck. He seemed quite happy just to be able to be there to help Talia— as happy, anyhow, as someone could be when holding a chamber pot for someone to vomit into, or using his scent magic to help deal with the results.

Interestingly, a couple of the ship's cats didn't seem to mind the smell either, and had curled up with her and Godrick.

Alustin, meanwhile, was anything but content. Unlike Godrick, he clearly was used to being able to help in any situation, but Captain Grepha had been quite clear that they didn't need a paper mage in a wind storm. Every now and then, the captain would send a runner to have him scry some detail of the storm, but it was clear they didn't consider it vital— for all the unusual timing and direction of this storm, the Radhan were more than capable of weathering it on their own. He paced around the passageways relentlessly, muttering to himself and taking frequent breaks to scry on the events above deck. At one point, he wanted to give them a lecture on how various nations and city-states deal with the introduction of invasive new species into their territory from labyrinths, but Talia just locked eyes with him and glared while she dry-heaved until Alustin got the message and left.

The others, however, were still useful on deck, and each took an opportunity to come visit when they were on break.

Artur's affinities were no more useful than Godrick's, but as had long since become clear, for all he hated ships, he had experience as a sailor, and the more sailors that were on duty during a storm, the better. The Radhan were, thanks to their ships being crewed by families, fanatically opposed to losing crew-members during a storm, and made sure to rotate sailors frequently so as few people were working while exhausted as possible. Artur always made sure to stop in on Godrick and Talia to check on them. His huge beard and hair never actually seemed to dry out during the storm— even drying cantrips couldn't seem to get all the water out.

Sabae, meanwhile, was kept on rescue duty. Her magic made her uniquely suited towards rescuing anyone swept off the decks by a wave or blown from the rigging. Other water mages could pluck them from the water if need be, but having Sabae on duty left them to use their strength to help weather the storm instead. She was the only one who was dry when she came to visit, thanks to her wind armor. She didn't even need to use it at full force to keep dry, so she could keep it up almost indefinitely. Her visits were few and far between, since she was by far the least exhausted, given that she hadn't been called on to do anything yet.

Hugh wasn't being used as a warder, surprisingly. The Radhan of the *Cormorant* didn't want a storm ward on the ship. They didn't know how the ship would handle with a storm ward, and they didn't want to test it in a storm this fierce— according to Captain Grepha, the sea was far more treacherous than the sand.

Instead, Hugh was being used for his stellar magic. Kanderon had recently provided him with a new spellform—one similar to his flare spell, but which released light slowly, instead of in a blinding burst. The added light was a blessing in the murk of the storm.

Talia was actually surprised when Hugh came to visit her and Godrick. Maybe she was just too miserable to feel awkward and nervous, but his visit made her feel a little better.

Of course, Hugh loaning Talia his stink-absorbing glass marble helped even more. It was more powerful and reliable than Godrick's scent affinity, even though Godrick had helped manufacture it.

The inside of the hollow sphere had once been clear, but there was now visible grime filling the spellforms etched into the inside surface, and unpleasant looking vapors filled it. According to Godrick, though, it would work fine until the whole inside of the sphere was filled with the gunk. Then, of course, it would need to be very carefully disposed of.

Talia was too sick and exhausted to remember exactly what they talked about, but the last thing she remembered before falling asleep in Godrick's lap was Hugh wishing her a happy birthday.

By the end of the storm, Artur was exhausted. Physically, yes, but even more so emotionally.

Part of him had forgotten how much he'd once loved the sea, and the camaraderie of working together alongside other sailors to fight through a storm.

Part of him was in constant terror. Artur had to keep fighting to remind himself that he wasn't on the *Hydra's Kiss* again. That he didn't need to be on constant guard, that he was safe from everything but the storm around them.

No matter how hard he pushed against them, though, his fears wouldn't go away.

But the *Rising Cormorant* was just a ship, not the mad ruin of a wood lich that had been ambitious enough to try and make a ship its demesne, whose mind had fragmented at being forced into a demesne too small for it. The *Rising Cormorant* had no vicious illusionist for a captain, as mad as her ship, who delighted in trapping her sailors in nauseating, terrifying visions at the least sign of insubordination.

The *Rising Cormorant* had no decks stained with blood. It was a merchant vessel, not a pirate ship.

He wasn't onboard the *Hydra's Kiss* anymore.

Artur shuddered and forced the memories aside as he adjusted the lashings holding tight a sail locker that had flown open in the storm's chill winds.

A great circle of calmer waters stretched around the ship, two ship-lengths in diameter. Calmer was a relative term, of course— the waves were still twice his own height and more, and the larger ones still regularly washed onto the deck.

The waves outside the circle were monsters, one and all. Without the ship's complement of water and wind mages, they'd surely have swamped the ship by now.

In all the years Artur had spent at sea, he'd only twice seen a storm like this. It wasn't that this storm was the worst he'd ever seen— in fact, not even close. The great typhoons that struck the southern shores of Ithonia dwarfed even this one. Most sailors, at least in the southwest, were able to shelter in the lee of the Kaen Das magics, which could turn aside even those immense spiral storms.

No, this storm wasn't alarming due to its power. It was alarming, rather, due to the fact that it was so clearly and obviously unnatural. Part of it was just the fact that the storm's existence was just so untimely. A storm this fierce shouldn't be rolling off the Skyreach Range at this time of year. Or at all, really. And it definitely shouldn't be heading to sea, carrying frigid mountain air. What's more, the waves and wind all traveled in an astonishingly straight line towards the southeast.

And the lightning was entirely wrong. Great stretches of time would pass without a single bolt, the only lights the pale glow of the mage lights and the actinic, burning light of the starfire sphere Hugh held aloft above the stern. That light reached out across the sea around them, illuminating their circle of safety and casting shadows among the immense waves past it.

Then, as if out of nowhere, the sky would erupt with lightning, as though it had been storing it all for a single moment. Dozens if not hundreds of lightning bolts would hammer into the sea at once in every direction. It was so loud that not just the lightning was visible, but the thunder as well, as it blasted the driving rain sideways. Then, just as fast, the lightning would be gone again, for another long period of darkness, wind, and torrential rain.

The *Cormorant*, as befit a ship of its size, bore enchantments to repel lightning, but the ship's mages in charge of monitoring them were clearly growing nervous. They were built to prevent periodical strikes over long periods of time, not entire forests of lightning.

When the storm ended, it wasn't gradual. The edge simply rolled up behind them, then past them, and they were out as the storm overtook them entirely. The back end of the storm ended unnaturally smoothly, and Artur shuddered at the unnatural sight.

Someone had *made* this storm. Either Ilinia Kaen Das or Indris Stormbreaker could easily have done it, but their reach ended at the Skyreach Range. Ephyrus, the dominant weather mage in this portion of the continent, simply wasn't known for randomly sending storms out to sea, though, in fairness, no-one really understood how Ephyrus thought, or had ever successfully communicated with the creature. There were many other weather mages on the continent that might have been able to raise a storm working in concert, but acting on weather beyond a local scale was a surefire way to attract the irritation of one of the greater weather mages. Even Ephyrus, as alien and inscrutable as it was, would react against a transgression like that. Weather spells cast by the great powers often acted on the scale of weeks, months, or even years, and interference with that would readily draw their ire.

In the distance behind them, Artur could see another storm.

CHAPTER TWENTY

Storm Armada

"We have a problem," Alustin said, dumping out a huge load of assorted paper scraps from his satchel onto the patch of decking that he'd just dried off with a cantrip.

Hugh knew that his teacher had dumped all those paper scraps into his satchel from his arm tattoo, but there were clear and obvious advantages to people not knowing where you were actually storing things.

The paper scraps abruptly formed themselves into a moving paper sea, with tiny swells and a miniature model of the Rising Cormorant in the center.

"The second storm is, like we expected, going to miss us

by leagues. Unfortunately, I scryed at least a half dozen more already on their way, and even more forming in the edges of the Skyreach Range. I think we can all agree they're unnatural, but there's nothing we can do to stop them. This is clearly the work of one or more of the great powers," Alustin said.

Stylized storm clouds rose up from the little paper sea behind the model of the *Cormorant.*

Most of the group stole glances at Sabae, though Hugh found his sliding over to her side, where Talia was standing. Their eyes locked, and to Hugh's surprise, Talia looked away first, blushing.

"We're well ahead of schedule, thanks to the boost the first storm gave us," Alustin said. "But getting to the second or third potential locations for Imperial Ithos' return is going to be a problem."

The Radhan all got confused looks for a second, then Captain Grepha shook her head.

"This would all be so much easier if you could tell us what you're looking for," she said.

"Unfortunately, I can't," Alustin said. "The Themesere harbor is impassible during storm surges. Its gravity enchantments can keep the water in bowl shape under normal conditions, but they're overwhelmed during storms," Alustin said. "Even if we made it in, we've got at least a week's march overland to get to the site, and it's a middling quality one on a ridge that stretches out from the Skyreach foothills into the jungle. Then we'd have no way to get out, and the *Cormorant* would be trapped in the holding pools atop the cliffs until the storms ended, and we don't know when that would be."

Artur leaned over to Hugh at his confused look. "The gravity enchantments in Themesere pulls the water and ships sailin' in it against the cliffs, sa' that the ships can jus' sail straight up the side, then over ta' the holdin' pools. It's a sight ta' see. Not a' particularly large city, but ah reckon a lot a' ships jus' add it ta' their routes fer the view."

Alustin nodded at that, and a tiny seaside city atop a line of cliffs formed, the paper sea crawling up its cliffs unnaturally.

"The third site," Alustin continued, "is in an open patch of ocean to the southeast of Themesere."

A mark formed on the paper model of the sea.

"Wait. Why would Imperial Ithos be out in the ocean?" Hugh asked.

Several of the nearby Radhan shook their heads, confused.

"It probably wasn't," Alustin said. "Odds are it's none of the sites we'll be checking. This one is an especially low probability. Successful floating cities are exceptionally rare, and they seldom survive more than a couple generations. The tides and storms are simply too much for them, no matter how well-built or designed. It's also dead center in the path of at least four or five storms."

"So are yeh thinkin' site four or site five, then?" Godrick asked.

Talia started to perk up at that, and Hugh could see Sabae visibly rolling her eyes. Hugh recalled Talia's guess that it would be the last site they checked.

"Site four," Alustin said. "Zophor is closer than Nidassus, and it's one of the highest priority sites being investigated."

Talia deflated.

"Hold on," Sabae said. "Isn't Zophor both in a swamp and in a fairly high aether density region?"

Alustin shrugged. "It's a tidal delta, which is a fairly specific type of swamp, but yes, it has fairly high-density aether. It also has a junction mana well with a complex labyrinth. The actual site in question is Lake Nelu, about a week's travel upriver from Zophor. It's a huge, shallow lake that the Ylosa River passes through on its way to the delta and Zophor."

The paper scraps swarmed and twisted, and the sea was replaced by a map of the shore, showing a great river delta, with a sort of crude grid of channels formed by the tide overwhelming the river's current twice a day. The islands were completely covered in a shockingly detailed rainforest. As Hugh traced the paper river upwards, it slowly grew more and more dominated by the river current, until it was a vast, interlocking braid of rivers, filled with great islands. Hugh seldom saw anything like a distinct bank to the river on a paper map. Instead, the waters seemed to intrude into the forest, and the trees of the forest into the river. In fact, many if not most of the islands in the channel, on second glance, were more groves of trees protruding from the paper waters than anything.

Hugh didn't know how accurate Alustin's paper map was, but…

"Hold on a second," he asked, not looking up. "Where's Zophor? I don't see a city on here."

A bit of a laugh went around the deck.

"It's definitely there, Stormward," Captain Grepha said. "You'll understand when we get there."

Hugh glanced up, confused. Even Godrick and Sabae seemed a little amused at the question. Only Talia also seemed confused. Then she froze, and looked up towards Alustin with a smile.

"Wait, is it like Hold Yehal?" Talia asked.

Alustin nodded. "Even more impressive in some ways," he said.

"Hold Yehal?" Hugh asked.

"The closest thing ta' a capital city the Clans have," Artur said. "Beautiful place."

"We don't have a capital," Talia said, glaring at Artur. "It's just the biggest clan hold is all."

"Ah'm not sure Hold quite does Yehal justice," Artur said. "It's a full city on its own."

Alustin raised his hand to quiet them, and the paper delta collapsed into scraps on the deck.

"One important difference between Hold Yehal and Zophor is that Zophor is the demesne of the lich Zophor. He created it wholesale a little over a century ago," Alustin said.

"Humble sort, sounds like, to name a whole city after himself," Talia muttered.

"Zophor is one of the most powerful liches on the continent," Alustin said. "He's no ally to either Kanderon nor the Havath Dominion. We need to be careful not to offend him while we're there."

Waves began to form slowly in the piles of paper scraps, then the *Rising Cormorant* seemed to rise out of the waves.

Off to one side of the map formed a clear representation of the Ithonian coastline, with paper Skyreach Range foothills to the west and the Ylosa river delta to the East.

"Here's the problem," Alustin said. "Or, problems, I suppose. First, the storms."

Stylized storms rose all throughout the paper map. Hugh glanced behind him, where he could see the second storm near the horizon, while off to one side, he thought he could see yet another storm forming.

"Even assuming they were our only problem, we'd likely have to pass through at least five more of those storms before we got to Zophor," Alustin said. "We could try and avoid them, but that would add days, if not a full week, onto our trip. And given how quickly the Exile Splinter's hold on Imperial Ithos is fading, we don't know how long it will be until the city merges back into our world."

The Radhan all looked confused to the point of pain, and several of them were clutching their heads now. Alustin's face turned grave, and the Skyhold party exchanged worried looks. The Radhan's confusion grew worse and lasted longer every time the city was mentioned. It had taken a year and a half of Alustin mentioning it regularly for the Exile Splinter's hold on Hugh and his friends to collapse, but it appeared to be progressing far more swiftly for the Radhan.

Hugh couldn't help but notice Sabae was practically glaring at Alustin. Hugh was used to others keeping secrets from him— in all honesty, he rather liked being ignorant of the dangerous political currents that often moved around him— but Sabae and Alustin definitely knew something that they hadn't told the others, and it had been splitting the two of them steadily apart since the aftermath of midsummer.

Hugh might not be the most observant person ever, but this was hard to ignore.

Finally, after what had to be almost a full minute, the Radhan all seemed to refocus. The other Radhan sailors on deck cleaning up the damage from the storm didn't seem to have even noticed their confusion.

"The storms aren't our only problem, though," Alustin said. "Then we have the sea serpents. We could normally handle that one well enough, save for the fact that the ship's water mages are already exhausted from just a single storm, and keeping watch for sea serpents while dodging or crossing storms would be a nightmare."

"What do yeh want to bet the storms are behind the serpents stirrin'?" Artur said.

No one took him up on that bet.

"So, then we've got our third problem," Alustin said.

More ships began to assemble on the paper sea— forming out of clouds of scraps, not rising whole from the waves.

"Havathi privateers," Alustin said. "They might not have a navy worth a pair of old socks, but they've got the money to hire as many independent ships as they could ever want. I've found at least a dozen so far, all with complements of Sacred Swordsmen and assorted battle mages on board, and there might be more caught in the storms as well. They even have a war ammonite in the area. It looks like they're actively hunting for us. They don't appear to be heading to Zophor, so I suspect they don't know about that site yet, though they do seem aware of Nidassus, Themesere, and the third site."

There was a moment of silence, then quite a few moments of cursing from nearly everyone.

"How, exactly, are yeh proposin' we get through storms, sea serpents, and ships huntin' us?" Artur said.

"Fairly easily," Alustin said, smirking. "There's a reason I picked this ship, after all. Same reason it's called the *Rising Cormorant.* It should also let us safely check sites three and four."

All the Radhan went still and silent, and finally Captain Grepha sighed. "Of course you know about that. It won't work, though. It's a short-term solution, it won't work across these sorts of ranges. There's no way we can supply that much mana to the enchantments for that long."

Alustin's smirk grew even wider. "No, but Sabae and Hugh can handle that."

Hugh shifted uncomfortably as all eyes turned to the two

of them.

Despite the cryptic pronouncements, Alustin didn't tell them what he'd been talking about. Instead, he, Captain Grepha, and some of the ship's officers spent several hours arguing and debating. Whatever Alustin's plan was, it wouldn't be starting until the next morning.

And he gave them all training to work on in the meantime, at that.

Talia was assigned a series of exercises meant to help her cast increasingly small dreambolts, using minuscule amounts of mana. Alustin had been somewhat irritated when he'd found out how she'd killed Abyla Ceutas atop Skyhold. He was happy she'd saved the others, but Talia had received a long, pointed lecture about the difference between siege magic and battle magic.

Siege magic— especially artillery magic— focused on expending the entirety of a mage's mana reservoir on a single spell, meant to punch through powerful defenses. Depending on the aether density around them, they could often only cast a single spell per hour. Even mediocre artillery mages could fire archmage level spells, and powerful siege mages were a serious danger even to great powers.

The problem was that once a mana reservoir was trained to do siege magic, it became almost unusable for other magic. The change was irreparable as well. Siege mages were simply only useful as part of an army, not as independent operatives. And while the vast majority of battlemages Skyhold trained were destined to serve in armies across the continent— save, apparently, for in the Havath dominion and a few unfriendly city states— Alustin was most certainly not putting in the time for something so mundane. Even most army mages weren't trained in siege magic— it was a very limited duty.

And if Talia kept using monstrous attack spells like the one she'd used against Abyla, ones that simply used all mana she had available in her mana reservoir, it could start happening to her. It wouldn't happen immediately, or even quickly, but Alustin knew quite a few mages who had slowly degraded their abilities to use more delicate magic over time. Apparently, Headmaster Tarik's obsession with mana efficiency wasn't just for the purposes of making her already absurd mana reservoirs stretch even farther, but was also to help her retain her ability to do fine work with her magic. There wasn't a set size where magic started counting as siege magic, however. Instead, it had to do with the size of the spell related to the size of the caster's mana reservoir, and to how precise the mana requirements for the spell were.

So Talia had to sit there for hours on end, manifesting and holding swarms of tiny, fingernail-sized dreambolts in front of her, gradually progressing to smaller sizes and larger swarms. To everyone's surprise, Talia hadn't complained in the slightest, but had taken Alustin very seriously.

"It might make me more powerful," Talia had said, "but it also leaves me less capable of defending myself or others. What use is more power if it leaves you less battle-ready?"

Sabae, meanwhile, was progressing in using wind and water armor at the same time. Rather than just holding one on each arm, Alustin had her passing segments of each around her body. The ship's sailors had been instructed to call out commands to her whenever they passed— move the spinning water to her left arm, or the wind to her right leg. They quickly jumped into the spirit of the training, giving her contradictory commands, elaborate patterns to follow, or making her move the two spinning sections of armor in time to the beat of sea shanties.

They didn't come close to her, though. The armor had a nasty habit of exploding off her when the wind and water passed over or even too close to each other when she wasn't focusing, and it could easily knock a person down. It definitely knocked Sabae down quite a bit. Hugh spotted her surreptitiously healing her own bruises every now and then.

Hugh and Godrick had been assigned training together, under Artur.

Specifically, working with what had once been a sword made of ice, and was now a ring of ice.

Godrick stared at both of them in slight horror as they showed him what they'd turned the weapon into.

"Neither of yeh are enchanters," Godrick said. "Couldn't yeh have sunk the ship, alterin' an enchanted weapon like that?"

"We didn't make a single change ta' the enchantment, Son," Artur said. "It was never a sword at all."

"It was always a ring," Hugh said. "The Swordsmen had just… persuaded it to form a sword-shaped shell around itself."

"It's alive?" Godrick asked. "Ah'm supposed ta' wear a livin' ring that might still be loyal ta' Havath?"

Hugh shook his head. "It's… not like my book. I'm pretty sure your average snail is considerably smarter than it is. Most of our work was just persuading it to change its shape."

"Hugh's spellbook is somethin' special," Artur said. "Ah've never heard about an item pacted by a warlock gettin' that smart that fast. Reckon it might have ta' do with the way the labyrinth stone is part of Hugh's pact with Kanderon, not ta' mention merged inta Hugh's attuned aether crystal. Plus, ah don't know anyone who really understands labyrinth stones. They don't work by Anastan spellform rules, growin' in labyrinths as they do. Anyhap, an enchanted weapon would have ta' be bonded ta' a person for years an' years before it gets that smart. Some a' the older ones, like Grovebringer, are nearly as smart as people."

A thought occurred to Hugh, and he looked around with a little alarm. He hadn't seen his spellbook since just after the storm ended. It had stayed slung around his shoulder for the whole storm— for all its mischievousness, it seemed to understand exactly when there was danger and it needed to behave.

He would bet money that it was up to something right now.

"Regardless, ah couldna have done this without Hugh," Artur said. "Ah doubt anyone but a warlock could talk ta' this little lass with any ease. Ah'll be right back."

Artur got up and walked off. Godrick stared uncertainly at the ring in his palm.

"Is this ring really female?" he asked.

Hugh shook his head. "It barely even has self-awareness or a personality. I think your dad just likes assigning personalities to things."

Godrick snorted at that. "Yeh're not wrong there. Ah can't even tell yeh how many times ah've caught him bein' disappointed at a cooking pot like it burnt the food ta' spite him."

Artur returned carrying a pair of water barrels, one under each arm. So far as Hugh could tell, he wasn't even using any spells to lighten them. Even ignoring how powerful a mage Artur was, he was kind of terrifying. They were smaller barrels, but each of them had to weigh considerably more than Hugh did.

Artur set both down with a loud thud, then the nails simply flew out of the lid of one barrel. He snagged them out of the air and shoved them into one of his pockets before removing the lid.

"Toss her in," Artur said.

Godrick looked askance at him, then shrugged and tossed the ring in the water. It sunk briefly, then bobbed immediately back to the surface.

There was a loud crackling noise, and the ring began to grow, but not out across the surface of the water, as ice normally would. The center of the ring filled in, then expanded vertically. The water level in the barrel began to visibly drop as a shaft of ice began to rise from the water.

Within five heartbeats, it had finished growing, the water level far below where it had started. The spellform-engraved shaft of ice rose up out of the water, bobbing faintly. The only reason it didn't fall out of the barrel was that the tilt of the shaft was holding the bottom against the inside of the barrel.

"Yeh goin' ta pull it out or just look at it?" Artur asked Godrick with a smile.

Another detonation came from Sabae's direction, but they only spared her a glance as she picked herself up from the deck, dripping wet.

Godrick reached out and touched the shaft.

"It's not as cold as ah was expectin'," he said. "Still cold, but not painful ta' hold."

"One a' the enchantments on it," Artur said. "Go on, then."

Godrick closed his fingers around it, then pulled it out of the barrel, revealing a massive hammerhead. As the water coursed off the ice, Godrick spun it, showing off the icicle-shaped spike coming from the back.

"This is way bigger than any hammer ah've wielded before," Godrick said. "Lighter, though."

"Ice doesn't weigh as much as iron," Hugh said.

Godrick and Artur gave him almost identical looks with raised eyebrows.

"Right," Hugh said. "Sorry. Bit obvious."

"Ah named her Hailstrike," Artur said. "And yeh and Hugh are goin' ta be spendin' a lot a' time trainin' with ice over the next few days. There isn't any naturally occurin' stone in the Ylosa River delta, which is a' big disadvantage for both a' yeh. An' ice isn't near as easy ta' use as normal stone is."

"What about you, sir?" Hugh asked.

Artur sighed. "Yeh call me sir again, and ah'll throw yeh in the ocean. Yeh're a great friend ta' me son, yeh've saved his life on multiple occasions, and yeh're pleasant company. As far as ah'm concerned, yeh're the next thing ta family, so call me by mah name."

"Yes, si… I mean, Artur," Hugh said, a little uncomfortable. He couldn't help but smile, though. "But won't you be at the same disadvantage in the delta without stone?"

Artur chuckled. "Don't yeh worry about me, Hugh. Ah'm never at a disadvantage."

As he eyed the stone mage's broad smile, Hugh was really, really glad Artur was on his side.

They all turned at the sound of Talia yelling and cursing. She appeared to be covered in live, panicking eels, and

Hugh's spellbook was hovering excitedly nearby.

Hugh sighed. "I really don't think my spellbook understands how apologies or apology gifts work."

CHAPTER TWENTY-ONE

A Ship Lives Up to Its Name

Midmorning the next day, the *Rising Cormorant* was preparing to sail straight into another storm.

Alustin had eventually won his argument with Captain Grepha, and he and Artur had spent the rest of the day training Hugh and his friends mercilessly. Hugh hadn't minded being worked so hard in the slightest. When he was busy, his brain wasn't the useless morass of confusion it had been lately. By evening, Hugh had been so tired he fell asleep the instant he crawled into his bunk.

Of course, Godrick was already asleep in the lower bunk when Hugh had gotten to their cabin. Hugh had forced himself to take the time for an important conversation with Artur. He'd needed to talk to someone, and he didn't feel comfortable talking to his friends about it, and even considering how open his conversations with Kanderon had been lately, he didn't think she'd fully understand.

He considered talking to Alustin about it, but somehow he couldn't imagine Alustin giving him non-ridiculous advice.

It was still on his mind the next morning, though he tried to turn his thoughts to more immediate matters.

"So, uh… you still haven't told us what this is supposed to do," Hugh said from where he stood in the bow.

"That would ruin the fun," Alustin said, from his perch atop the railing.

"Just… funnel mana into the figurehead?" Hugh said,

gesturing at the carved wooden cormorant, bigger than Godrick or Artur.

"That feather right there," Captain Grepha said irritably, pointing at an innocuous section of carving.

"And make sure to use that secret technique Sabae taught you," Alustin said.

Hugh glanced back to the base of the foremast, where Godrick, Artur, Talia, and much of the crew stood watching. He took a deep breath, then envisioned the windlode spellform in his mind's eye. Immediately, he felt the aether around him respond, almost like it was twitching, and he hadn't even started funneling mana into the spellform yet. Given the sheer number of storms in the region— now close to two dozen, both over land and sea— the aether had thickened far, far more than it had during the sandstorms Hugh had survived in the Endless Erg.

"Any time now," Captain Grepha said, as they drew closer and closer to the unnaturally sharp rear edge of the storm. This one wasn't moving anywhere near as fast as the first, and the wind mages were easily able to push the ship fast enough to catch up to it.

"If you're not comfortable, I can take the first shift, Hugh," Sabae said. "But you'll do fine."

Hugh gave her a nervous smile. He'd never cast the windlode spellform directly before, only built it into wards. Its mana had also never run directly through him before. Sabae had said it should be fine, as long as he didn't try to cast any spells, but…

"Any time now," Captain Grepha repeated.

Hugh took one more deep breath, placed his finger against the carved wooden feather, and reached out to it mentally. He felt a link form between his mana reservoirs and the figurehead, and then Hugh pushed some of his mana into the windlode. It ran through the lines of the spellform floating in his mind's eye, then came out the other end, but when it did, it came out leading a flood of mana straight from the aether. With an effort of will, Hugh connected the windlode mana to the figurehead, and the wooden cormorant began to draw on the storm aether.

It didn't feel pleasant in the slightest. The sheer amount of mana rushing through him was more than he'd ever experienced, save for when he had attuned his aether crystal and formed his spellbook during the construction of the stormward around Theras Tel.

Hugh could feel the mana being sucked through the figurehead and into a set of truly massive artificial mana reservoirs somewhere belowdecks. He could feel multiple enchantments connecting into them— at least four of them— but only two started drawing on the mana. There was something of a delay as the artificial reservoirs began to convert the unattuned aether from the storm into what Hugh suspected was water mana, as well as two other types of mana he couldn't identify.

"We're sinking," Sabae said. "Are… are we supposed to be sinking right now?"

"Why, yes," Alustin said. "Yes we are."

Hugh looked away from the back of the wooden cormorant and realized that Sabae was right. The swells were considerably closer to the deck than they'd been before.

The *Rising Cormorant* was sliding down into the waves smoothly and without protest.

"Do you know why the Radhan named this ship the *Rising Cormorant*?" Alustin asked, stepping off the railing.

The water kept rising around the ship, and Hugh swallowed, but he kept his hand pressed to the feather. He actually could have let go if he wanted— he only needed to be in a certain physical proximity to channel mana into the figurehead— but he didn't move his hand at all.

"Alustin?" Captain Grepha said.

"Yes, Captain?" Alustin replied.

"Shut up. I'll tell it. You're just guessing," the captain said.

Alustin sighed dramatically.

"Have you ever watched a cormorant hunt?" the captain asked Hugh and Sabae.

Sabae nodded, and Hugh shook his head.

"Cormorants dive deep," Grepha said. "They swim farther down than any other seabird while fishing— sometimes multiple ship lengths beneath the water. They're not the most graceful fliers. Their wings are short and they have to work harder than any other seabird to take to the air and stay there. Beneath the water, though…"

Grepha trailed off as the sea rose to the deck. Hugh winced, sure it was about to wash through the gaps in the railing.

But it didn't. The water just kept rising along the sides of the railing, then atop it, as though there was an invisible wall keeping the water out.

"Beneath the water," Grepha continued, "they're among the most graceful of hunters. They'll pursue schools of fish, explore nooks and crannies in submerged rocks, and easily evade sharks and other marine hunters."

The walls of water kept rising and rising— past Hugh's head, then to the level of the sails. The walls subtly ballooned outward as they rose, so only the tips of the yardarms touched the water. They dug into the walls and trailed wakes behind them. Hugh realized they were still moving forwards as they sank.

"And when cormorants rise from the depths," Captain Grepha said, "they're like arrows launched towards the sky."

The walls of water closed atop them, and the *Rising Cormorant* sank completely below the surface of the sea.

When Talia had left Hold Castis to travel to Skyhold, escorted by three of her brothers, she'd doubted that she'd see anything so awe-inspiring as the sights of her home. She'd grown up in a high valley in the greatest mountain range in the world— amazing, awe-inspiring sights had been a regular occurrence for her. One of her earliest memories was of watching two dragons battle for dominance above a deep ravine whose bottom was barely visible, with snow-capped peaks on each side.

She'd been so, so very wrong.

Anastis seemed intent upon overwhelming her with its wonders at every turn. Skyhold, its library, Theras Tel, the great sandstorms of the Endless Erg, Lothal— it seemed as though she'd never run out of things to see.

Talia had never seen anything even remotely like this, though. It wasn't the grandest, or the most overwhelming sight she'd ever seen, but it was utterly unique.

The light of the sun filtered gently down through the waves. Ripples of light and shadow cast by the waves flickered gently across the deck, and Talia laughed as they raced across her outstretched arms.

To either side of the *Rising Cormorant*, fish swam alongside, seemingly curious about the strange thing that had sunk into the water to join them. Several of the Radhan children were making a game of reaching through the invisible barrier that held back the water and trying to snatch smaller fish with their hands.

In the distance to one side of the ship, Talia could see a school of dog-sized fish being pursued by some sort of brilliant red squid three times the length of a man.

The light dimmed a bit as the ship sank farther, but the ship's dive stabilized a few ship-lengths in depth.

Talia wandered over to the other side and reached out her fingers, stopping inches away from the water. She hesitated for a moment, then dipped her fingertips into the wall of water.

It just felt like… water. A little colder than at the surface, and with a notable current from the ship's forward motion. Little wakes in the barrier formed behind her fingers, and she laughed in delight.

"Haven't heard you sound this happy in a while," Sabae said from behind her.

Talia plunged her arm fully into the water, then whipped it out, splashing Sabae.

Or, tried to, at least. The water she sent towards Sabae got caught in an invisible current rotating around the taller girl's torso, before being sent spiraling down one arm, which Sabae leveled at Talia.

"I surrender! Have mercy," Talia said, raising her arms in

defeat.

Her splash had hit Godrick, at least, who sighed heavily at her.

Sabae rolled her eyes at Talia, then sent the water blasting into the wall of water. It splashed, but the water droplets sent cascading away from the wall fell back against it, as though the wall were down and not to the side.

Godrick's clothes dried out, presumably from a cantrip.

"This is amazing," Talia said. "How could I not be happy?"

"Ah'd have ta' agree," Godrick said. "Yeh might be used ta' this sort a' sight, Sabae, but fer the rest a' us…"

"Some of my aunts and uncles would regularly take the children down to the bottom of Ras Andis harbor at high tide," Sabae said, walking over to the wall. "They'd form a big bubble, and we'd walk around the bottom of the harbor in it, catching crabs and scaring fish. In my first few months living at Stormseat after my father died, it was one of the only things that ever really made me happy. I didn't realize how much I missed it until now."

Talia reached up and squeezed Sabae's shoulder.

Godrick walked over to the wall beside them and stood staring out. In the distance, Talia could see what she thought might be a sea turtle with a shell as broad as a man was tall.

"Pretty romantic down here, ah think," Godrick said.

Talia gave him a confused look.

Her friend sighed. "Yeh should go talk ta' Hugh again."

Talia glanced at the bow of the ship, where Hugh was standing with Alustin and Captain Grepha.

"He's busy," Talia said. "And I told him I'd give him space to think."

"There's a difference between giving him space and avoiding him like he's poisonous," Sabae said. "Go talk to him. Doesn't need to be any sort of serious conversation or anything. Whatever else he is, he's still your friend."

Talia opened her mouth to give some sort of excuse, then closed it. She looked back out to sea, where the shape had resolved itself as definitely a sea turtle. Several more turtle silhouettes were visible as well past it.

"Do you really think I should?" Talia asked quietly.

Her friends both nodded at her— Sabae exasperated, Godrick encouraging.

Talia took a deep breath and carefully adjusted her headwrapping. Then she turned and started walking towards Hugh.

She made it three steps before she turned and darted back towards the other two.

"Alright, really though," she said. "Have either of you talked to Hugh about all this? Is there anything you can tell me?"

Sabae just glared and crossed her arms, while Godrick just smiled and shook his head.

"Ah offered," Godrick said. "He declined, though. Whatever he decided, he wanted yeh to know before me or Sabae."

"Go," Sabae said. She gave Talia a gentle shove.

"He really wouldn't tell you?" Sabae asked, as they watched Talia slowly walk towards the bow of the ship, trailing her fingers in the water.

Godrick shook his head. "He really wouldn't. Said it wasn't fair to Talia if he did."

"Hugh really does have a little bit of a romantic streak, doesn't he?" Sabae asked Godrick. "There was that thing with the fountain in Theras Tel, too."

Godrick nodded at that. "Do yeh ever wonder what Hugh might have been like if his parents never died, and he didn't get so… broken?"

"All the time," Sabae admitted. "But I also feel like we may have never gotten a chance to meet him then. Who knows what his parents might have done when he showed the first signs of magic."

Sabae glanced towards the stern. Several of the ship's water mages had pulled great spheres of seawater inside the ship, some filled with schools of small fish. The Radhan children and a few older youths leapt in and out of the bubbles, swimming around in them and leaping between them. And, for that matter, so was Artur— he'd taken up residence in the largest floating sphere, only his head and shoulders jutting out of the water. He was laughing uproariously as children swarmed him, trying to dunk his head inside the bubble.

She noticed Yarra and Tollin, each standing with a different group, and both clearly ignoring one another, and Sabae, for that matter. Dell sat on a crate reading a book— he was thoroughly irritated with all three of them for being dramatic idiots at the party.

"I think Hugh's going to say no," Sabae confessed as she turned back to Godrick. "I think Talia's about to get her heart broken. They've known each other long enough that if Hugh were going to develop feelings for her, he would have shown something ages ago. And confessions of love don't just make people fall in love themselves."

Godrick raised an eyebrow at her, then slid his new ice ring off his finger, closed it in his fist, and shoved his fist into the water. His hammer began growing out in the water.

"It's a bit slower in salt water than fresh water," Godrick said.

Sabae crossed her arms and raised her eyebrows back at him.

"Remember what Talia told us Hugh said?" Godrick asked. "About how when Talia confessed that she was jealous, he thought she was jealous a' him, and had a crush on Avah?"

Sabae shrugged. "I mean, it's Hugh, he's notoriously thick about these things."

Godrick shook his head, then drew Hailstrike out of the water.

"Ah've come ta realize he's really not that thick," Godrick said, idly toying with the hammer. "He's actually pretty keen-eyed fer noticin' when one a' us is in a bad mood, fer instance. He didn't notice Talia's blindingly obvious crush for a totally different reason. Ah mean, she was followin' him around starin' at him like a hungry dragon stares at a herd a' aurochs."

Sabae looked at the bow to see Talia approaching Hugh, Alustin, and the captain.

"What's the different reason?" Sabae asked.

Godrick shrugged. "Ah've basically told yeh before. Hugh doesn't think he deserves ta' be loved."

He squeezed the shaft of the hammer at a specific spot, and Sabae could see the spellform lines start to glow. Then the whole hammer collapsed into tiny fragments of ice, so thin that they drifted to the ground rather than fell. Godrick opened his hand to reveal the ring of ice again.

"Of course Hugh deserves to be loved," Sabae said. "That's ridiculous."

"Ah fully agree with yeh," Godrick said, slipping the ring onto his finger. "But Hugh doesn't. He honestly thinks he's not. It's why he gets so embarrassed when yeh say nice things about him. Part a' him doesn't trust the compliments. He thinks, deep down, yeh're mockin' him somehow, or plannin' some cruel trick. Deep down, his awful family, and Rhodes fer that matter, has him convinced he really is worthless. He was only comfortable pursuing Avah, ah think, because yeh and Talia kept treating it as a shallow, meaningless thing early on. He could fool himself inta' thinkin', at some level, that Avah was only interested in him because he was such a good mage."

He frowned and looked up. "Shouldn't we have passed under the storm already?"

Sabae shook her head. "We're traveling slower underwater than we were on the surface. Not much slower, but enough that it'll take a lot longer to catch up to the storm. Are you sure about Hugh, though?"

Godrick nodded, and stuck his hand in the water. The ice ring glowed slightly on his finger, but didn't start growing into the hammer.

Sabae ran her fingernails down the scars on her cheeks. "That is… incredibly sad, and I want to go hug Hugh immediately."

"Yeh should probably wait a bit," Godrick said. He turned and focused on the ring, and a lump of ice grew above his palm in the water. He made a grab for it, but it floated towards the surface.

Godrick frowned, and the ice stopped ascending, then shot down towards his hand.

"That's really a lot harder ta' control than other rocks," Godrick said.

"Ice isn't a rock," Sabae said automatically, but her heart wasn't in it. "But what does that have to do with Talia?"

"Ah mean, ah've only got her retellin' of the story," Godrick said. "But Hugh said he wouldn't let himself think of her that way. He didn't say he wouldn't let himself think a' any a' his friends that way. Just Talia. And yeh don't need ta' force yerself not ta' think a somethin' if it's not on yer mind."

"…Huh," Sabae said.

"Ah could be wrong," Godrick said. "Ah'm genuinely not sure either way. But… ah suspect, that maybe Hugh had considered it before, but then he just buried the idea away, because he didn't think he deserved Talia, or that she'd ever have even the remotest interest in him. And no offense ta' Hugh, but ah suspect he develops romantic feelin's pretty easily, even if he hides 'em."

"And if you're wrong?" Sabae asked.

"Then ah'll be there fer Talia ta cry on, and ah suspect ah'll need ta' be there fer Hugh, 'cause ah can't imagine anything that would make him more miserable than hurtin' a friend. But ah hope ah'm right," Godrick said.

Godrick let go of the piece of ice, which promptly floated back upwards. He withdrew his hand from the water, then clapped Sabae on the shoulder.

"Ah'm not gonna watch ta' see, though," Godrick said. "Going ta' give them what little privacy they can get on the deck of a ship. Reckon ah'll go swimmin' with me da instead— looks like those kids could use some help dunkin' him."

He started to walk off, then looked back at Sabae. "Ah reckon yeh've probably got someone yeh need ta' talk too as well."

Sabae watched Godrick stride towards the bubbles, feeling deeply lucky to have him as a friend.

Then she started walking that general direction herself. She found herself rubbing the scars on her hands anxiously, but didn't make herself stop.

Tollin started to say something as she approached him, but she just walked right past him.

Yarra had a slightly triumphant look on her face as Sabae approached her, but Sabae just walked past her as well.

She came to a stop in front of Dell on his barrel. He was looking a little better today, though still not great.

"I don't suppose you've come to apologize?" Dell asked, glancing up at her. He scowled, then looked back at his book. "I still owe you for saving my life, but that doesn't mean I'm not mad. I tried to help you out at the dance, and you really made a lot of drama for me. Not that my sister and Tollin don't make enough of that on their own, but…"

"I didn't come to apologize," Sabae said. "Though I really should be, you're right. I'm sorry I made trouble for you, and for Yarra and Tollin as well. I… I've never done any dating before, so I think I let things go to my head. I, uh… got a little greedy."

Dell sighed. "I'm still a little grumpy, but I forgive you. And you're not about to confess your love for me, are you? Because I'm not interested in dating or romance with anyone in the slightest."

Sabae shook her head. "I actually kinda figured that already. No, I was actually coming over because I wanted to see if you wanted to go for a swim."

Dell froze.

Sabae waited patiently.

Finally, Dell spoke up in a quiet voice. "I'm alright, but thank you. I'm trying to get some reading done."

"You haven't turned the page once since we submerged," Sabae said.

Dell looked up at her, his expression studiously blank.

Sabae sat down on the barrel next to him. "This is awful for you, isn't it? It has to be terrifying being underwater again, even like this. And yet, you're staying on deck, not going below."

Dell looked away and surreptitiously wiped at his eyes with his sleeve. Sabae waited patiently.

"I don't want to go live on a sandship," Dell said. "I used to love the water, and now I can hardly look at it."

"You should go swimming with me," Sabae said.

"In the bubbles?" Dell asked, hesitantly.

"No," Sabae said. "Not in the bubbles."

"I… I should go below," Dell said. "I'm sorry."

"You'll be safe, Dell," Sabae said. "The ship's mages are monitoring the waters around us carefully, and more importantly, you'll be with me. I saved your life once, I can do it again if need be."

She held out her hand, and Dell just stared at it.

"Why do you care so much?" he finally asked.

"Because maybe if I can help you with your fears," Sabae said, "I can start dealing with my own."

Dell looked her in the eyes, then hesitantly took her hand.

Hugh was watching a school of tiny, brilliant blue fish dart and play around the wings of the figurehead when Talia interrupted the quiet conversation between Alustin and Captain Grepha.

"What happens if we run out of mana?" Talia asked.

"We won't," Alustin said.

"If we did, though…" Talia said.

Hugh didn't look back, just kept watching the fish.

"When the enchantment mana reservoirs are low enough, the ship will surface automatically," the captain said.

"That seems difficult to build into an enchantment," Talia said.

"I'm not an enchanter, but from what I understand," Captain Grepha said, "it's just a matter of linking the spellforms of the enchantment that keep us submerged to the mana reservoirs at a higher level than the enchantments that propel us or maintain the bubble. Not that up and down really exists as we understand it in the aether, but there's some equivalent in regards to mana reservoirs. It actively takes mana to keep us submerged, so once that enchantment deactivates due to low mana levels, we'll rise right to the top. Though, according to our enchanters, we're supposed to avoid surfacing that way, if possible. Not good for the enchantments, the ship, or the crew, apparently."

"While I encourage your curiosity, Talia," Alustin said, "the captain and I are having an important discussion."

"Sorry," Talia said. "I, uh… was actually wanting to talk to Hugh."

"Ah, I see," Alustin said. "Well, Captain, shall we give my students some space so as not to bore them?"

Captain Grepha sighed loudly.

"Try to not get distracted and abandon your post, Stormward," the captain said.

Talia didn't say anything as they walked away, and Hugh just kept watching the little blue fish.

"You don't mind, do you?" Talia asked. "I know I said I'd give you space, so if you'd prefer me to…"

"It's fine," Hugh said.

He shoved his hands in his pockets and moved to one side. After a long pause, Talia stepped up beside him.

Neither said anything for a moment.

"Those fish are nearly the same color as your tattoos," he finally said, nodding at the fish.

"I suppose so," Talia said.

Hugh wasn't sure how long they stood there for. Twenty minutes, an hour, more? They watched the sea turtles that had been shadowing the ship cruise along in their stately way, and a great school of boarfish cross their path in the distance, with their distinctive jutting teeth. A school of curious squid, each no longer than his arm, spent several minutes slapping at the invisible wall around the *Cormorant* with their tentacles. They were known as curious squid for good reason, and it certainly wasn't for their foul taste.

And the little blue fished danced in endless circles around the figurehead.

Not too far ahead of them, he could see the edge of the

storm above the water. They were slowly catching up to it again. It looked like a wall of shadow from where the storm clouds loomed overhead.

Then, to Hugh's surprise, something bounced off the figurehead, then slid along the wall of the bubble in slow motion.

It was a jellyfish. It was a gentle pastel orange, its body about as wide as a human head. Its tentacles hung several feet below it in a lacy fringe.

The dancing fish had vanished when he looked back, but several more jellyfish were visible floating towards the ship. In the distance, he saw several of the sea turtles moving towards the jellyfish.

"It's like there's something new to see every few minutes down here," Talia said.

"Apparently some of the water mages detected a pod of leviathans yesterday," Hugh said. "They weren't coming anywhere near us, though."

"What is a leviathan, exactly?" Talia asked. "They and krakens are both octopus things, right? Or… squids?"

Hugh shook his head, though he still didn't look at Talia.

"Nope. According to Galvachren, krakens are close relatives to both octopuses, squid, and ammonites, but they're larger than any of them get. Which is already pretty huge, so I have trouble imagining how big kraken are. Leviathans are even bigger, and they're basically giant cuttlefish, another squid relative. They're the biggest things in the ocean, save for a few freakish oddities and large icebergs, and they're relatively slow, placid, and unaggressive. They host entire ecosystems on, in, and around them."

"What do they eat?" Talia asked.

"Fish, sharks, sea serpents… whatever they want, really," Hugh said. "Less than you'd suspect for something their size, though. But they never eat or harm anything intelligent, and Galvachren suspects that they're highly intelligent themselves, and use their color-shifting skin to communicate with some language of color and pattern, but no one's ever been able to translate their complex color shifts. They're even better at altering their colors than any other tentacled creature. There's a story in Galvachren's Bestiary about one that used its natural camouflage to make itself effectively invisible while floating on the surface, then actually created a painting of a ship so lifelike that a nearby ship didn't realize the other ship was false until they sailed within a ship's length of the leviathan."

Hugh realized he was rambling nervously, and shut up.

"I'd love to see one of those someday," Talia said.

"Me too," Hugh replied.

More and more jellyfish were rising in a great column from the depths ahead of them, and many were bouncing off the sides of the ship's bubble. In the middle distance, the sea turtles were snacking on the jellyfish in surprising numbers, but it didn't even make a dent in the rising column.

Hugh glanced over his shoulder— the one facing away from Talia— and saw the ship's officers calling everyone away from the walls, though they didn't seem too alarmed. One Radhan teen, apparently trying to impress his friends, appeared to have touched one of the jellyfish and gotten stung. He had a huge welt across one arm, but wasn't otherwise hurt.

Most of the jellyfish were the pale orange ones, but there were a few that were smaller and more of a peach shade, and every now and then there was a huge one, bigger across than a person, in a much deeper orange, with brilliant yellow fringes around the edges of its body.

Hugh heard a splash, and looked back again to see Sabae and Dell crash-landing onto the deck near the stern, laughing.

"This is incredible," Talia said.

Hugh looked back, and the rising column of jellyfish had grown so thick that Hugh couldn't see more than a few feet ahead of them. The light around them was starting to take on an orange tinge as it passed through the great undulating cloud of jellyfish swimming above the ship's envelope.

Then, like an onrushing wave, the shadow of the storm swept over them.

For a moment, Hugh couldn't see a thing. Then his eyes adjusted, and the jellyfish came back into view.

"Hugh?" Talia said, sounding nervous. "I can't see anything."

Hugh was briefly confused until he recalled his night vision. He had just opened his mouth to say something when the lightning struck.

It didn't blind him, filtered as it was through so much water and countless jellyfish. Instead, the whole ship was lit up in a brilliant cascade of orange shades as the lightning began hammering down in the unnatural way it had in the last storm.

Talia gasped.

After a few seconds, the lightning ceased, and the ship returned to darkness. Slowly, though, it began to lift, as sailors cast light cantrips and began activating the glow crystals on the railing and in the rigging.

Around them, it looked as though they were traveling in a world made of nothing other than undulating jellyfish. They looked almost like hallucinations in the gentle light of the glow crystals.

Hugh finally turned to look at Talia. She looked at him nervously.

"You really have feelings for me?" Hugh asked. "This isn't some weird joke?"

"I wouldn't do that to you," Talia said.

Hugh sighed, and tried to assemble his thoughts.

"It's a no, isn't it?" Talia said. "You're trying to think of a way to break it to me kindly, I can tell. People don't need time to think about these sort of things if they're really interested. You can't talk yourself into liking someone. Just… just don't. Tell me outright, Hugh. I'm not so fragile that I'll break. I…"

Hugh reached out and yanked the knotted handkerchief off Talia's scalp. She stopped talking, her mouth agape.

Her hair had already grown out a surprising amount— in just two weeks, it had gone from less than a finger-width in length to more than twice that. It was already thick enough that Hugh could only see her scalp tattoos at specific angles through it.

Talia's mouth was gaping like a fish.

"You know," Hugh said. "You look pretty tough like this. I kind of like it."

"What?" Talia said. "I don't…"

Hugh leaned in and kissed her.

After a moment, he leaned back. Talia just looked… shocked and baffled.

"Why…?" she finally got out.

"Why what?" Hugh asked, looking around. He'd vaguely expected a bunch of Radhan to burst out into applause or catcalls. Though, in fairness, his relationship with Avah had probably been a little unusual in that regard.

"Why did you just kiss me?" Talia asked, perplexed.

Hugh gave her a confused look. "Oh, that? I put poison on my lips to kill you."

Talia punched him. Hard.

"Sorry," Hugh said. His shoulder was definitely going to have a bruise from that. "I was trying to break the tension a bit, and it sounded funnier in my head? Why do you think I kissed you?"

Talia just stared at him, and Hugh rubbed the back of his head, feeling awkward and nervous all of a sudden.

"This all went much more smoothly in my head," Hugh said.

"I'm just…" Talia said. "I honestly came up here expecting you to tell me you weren't interested. I've been preparing myself since the party for you to reject me. I'm still not sure I didn't just hallucinate that kiss."

Hugh kissed her again. And this time he took his time about it.

"I told you I was going to think about it," Hugh eventually said. "If there hadn't been a chance I'd say yes, I would have just told you that."

Talia leaned her head against his shoulder.

"I'm not complaining, I just… Why?" Talia said.

Hugh took a moment to collect his thoughts.

"Part of me was all for it the instant you said something,"

he said. "And part of the reason I wanted time to think was that I thought I was just being a fickle idiot. At first, I thought that I was only seriously considering it because I was still broken up about Avah, and I didn't want to just use you as a bandage for my hurt feelings. I dunno. I was just kind of a mess of confusion ever since you told me."

Hugh realized he'd stopped letting mana funnel into the figurehead, and rapidly reassembled the spellforms in his mind's eye. Thankfully, the ship's mana reservoirs hadn't drained enough to cause a problem.

"Hugh?" Talia asked.

"I just… wasn't getting anywhere trying to think it through, and I didn't think it was fair to talk to Sabae or Godrick, so… I went to Artur last night," Hugh said. "And I told him about the whole situation, and how I felt, and how I didn't want to hurt you."

"What did he say?" Talia asked.

"He said there was no way around hurting you, either way, because that happens in every relationship," Hugh said. "All you can do is try and make things better afterward, and try not to repeat the same mistakes."

He paused, then grinned. "He also told me I was being an indecisive idiot and to just tell you how I feel already."

"So just to be clear, this means we're dating now, right?" Talia asked.

Hugh kissed her again.

CHAPTER TWENTY-TWO

Conspirators

When they arrived at the third site, the Havathi were already there. No less than four privateers were sailing above them. None approached the size of the *Rising Cormorant*, but given their heavy armament and contingents of battle mages and Sacred Swordsmen, half that many would have been more than sufficient to take down the Radhan merchant ship.

Thankfully, the war ammonite wasn't one of the ships. The spiral-shelled squid-kin were sometimes captured young and trained to stay on the surface as war ships. Their tentacles hung deep underwater, though, meaning it was the greatest danger of any of the Havathi-funded ships.

They never even realized the *Cormorant* was there.

It took Sabae and Hugh both channeling the windlode into the ship's enchantments to let it go deep enough to evade the Havathi water mage affinity senses. The deeper the ship went, the more mana it consumed, at surprisingly disproportionate rates. Not to mention, the third site was a localized low mana zone, so it was much harder to get enough mana into the enchantments than normal.

Alustin was able to finish his readings in just a few minutes, and they were able to move on rapidly.

"Something bizarre is going on here," Alustin muttered out loud, glaring at his notes, then at the water around him. "It's like a mana desert, but not exactly."

Sabae arched an eyebrow at him.

"The aether in mana deserts is simply less permeable to mana," Alustin said. "This is permeable to surprisingly large amounts of mana, but it just moves incredibly slowly through it. I'm not sure what to make of it. It's definitely not what we're looking for, and probably just a curiosity, but it's probably worth an expert in these sorts of things investigating it in the future. Otherwise, though, the only notable thing about it is the sheer number of curious squid."

Sabae just grunted and turned back towards the water.

It was much darker at these depths, and the ship's glow-crystals were dimmed to the absolute minimum needed for the crew to work, so the Havathi above couldn't spot their lights. Light from the sun still penetrated down this far, but the water below them was a deep, inky blue that her eyes couldn't penetrate. They were even deeper than she had gone while rescuing Dell from the sea serpents. Sabae thought she could see something shifting down there, but she wasn't sure.

"Hugh?" she asked. "Can you see down into the water below?"

Hugh looked up from his quiet conversation with Talia, confused.

"What?" he asked.

Sabae rolled her eyes. While she was happy that Talia and Hugh were a thing now, they were in classic new couple mode. Less making out in public than Hugh and Avah, but they were clearly both having trouble paying attention to anything but each other.

"Does your night vision let you see into the darker water below?" Sabae asked.

Hugh blinked, then turned to look.

He stood there for a moment, then turned away, a disturbed look on his face.

"Yes," he said. "Yes it does, and I regret looking."

"Is there something big down there watching us?" Talia asked, looking oddly excited by the prospect. Ever since she and Hugh had started dating, she'd stopped wearing her head wrapping, as well as that ridiculous hat.

"Big, yes," Hugh said. "Watching us, I have no idea. I couldn't see any eyes. It had a huge mouth and what looked like lots of rotting flesh hanging off it, though. Oversize fins and lots of randomly placed tentacles, as well."

"Rotgrubber," Artur muttered, from where he was sitting nearby, drawing spellform diagrams in a notebook. "They're scavengers. Slow movin', not particularly dangerous, but one a' the ugliest things in the oceans. They'll eat anythin', then store any toxins in their flesh, so not many creatures want ta' eat them. The rotting flesh is just that— rasps an' other cleaner fish that eat dead skin and parasites off bigger fish won't come near a rotgrubber. And the tentacles are actually worms that burrow inta' their flesh. Not sure whether they're parasites or do somethin' fer the fish, but yeh never see a rotgrubber without them."

Sabae shuddered, and resolved not to ask Hugh to look anymore.

Eventually, they drew far enough away from the third site and the Havathi ships that they could rise to a higher cruising depth, and Hugh left Sabae to channel the windlode on her own. There were so many storms crossing the sea at the moment that the aether levels in the region were perpetually high.

Alustin was the last to leave the prow after he'd finished stowing his instruments, leaving only Sabae and Artur.

"Yeh don't trust him anymore," Artur said quietly. "Yeh've been starin' at him like yeh're tryin' ta figure out how big a threat he is ever since midsummer."

Sabae gave Artur a surprised look. She hadn't realized that she'd been that obvious about it.

"I still trust him in some things," Sabae said. "I trust him as a teacher, and I trust him not to let harm come to us via negligence. I don't trust him or Kanderon not to actively risk us in their schemes anymore, though."

Artur raised an eyebrow and opened up a small pouch on his belt. What looked like iron filings started flying out, and scattered themselves across the deck around them. Within a few moments, they'd resolved themselves into the shape of a ward around the two of them.

"Ah'm not the only one who noticed, then," Artur said. "We should be safe ta' talk now."

Sabae only had to consider for a moment before deciding to trust Artur. There was no way she could work through this on her own, and of all the adults around her, Artur was the only one who she was sure had her and her friends' best interests at heart.

"Midsummer was a coup," Sabae said. "Kanderon baited out Bakori, and left her political foes to take the brunt of the damage, then persuaded my grandmother to take care of Bakori for her. And I think that these storms have something to do with whatever price Kanderon paid my grandmother."

"Not just yer grandmother," Artur said. "Indris, too. Ah've got ah lot a' friends across the Endless Erg, and ah've been hearin' rumors a' high-level negotiations goin' on fer much a' the last year. Not ta' mention, ah heard from Alustin that great windstorms have been rollin' down from the Skyreach Range north a' these storms."

"Neither of them have ever been able to affect the weather past the mountains before," Sabae said. "They're too tall."

Artur shook his head. "Kanderon and the Skyhold founders built great weather wards inta' the Skyreach Range. They wanted ta' restrict future weather mages from gettin' as powerful as they did durin' the Ithonian Empire. There's a reason yeh get weather-related great powers more commonly than just about any other type, after all. Ah'm guessin' Kanderon bribed yer grandmother and Indris by shuttin' the wards down."

Sabae's mind raced at that news. A large part of any weather mage's power came down to how much of the great wind currents they could control, and they grew rapidly more powerful as their territory increased. It wasn't the only secret to Kaen Das power, of course— there was the windlode, a long list of other secret spells, the power of the Storm Seat itself, and quite a few great enchantments and the like— but the sheer amount of sky her grandmother controlled or influenced was prodigious.

For Kanderon to offer even more power to her two mightiest rivals in the region was astonishing, and spoke to the sheer urgency of this whole crisis around the return of Imperial Ithos. Kanderon *never* gave up long term advantage in normal situations.

"Those in the know have started callin' those three the Coven," Artur continued. "Ah've never seen great powers at this level cooperate so closely before, outside a' alliances against Havath. Ah think it might be all about this Exile Splinter."

Sabae shook her head. "That's part of it, but there's something more going on. When I confronted Alustin about my suspicions, I saw something in his eyes. Something about Ithos' return terrified him."

Artur gave her a surprised look. "Are yeh sure? Ah've known Alustin since he was younger than yeh are, and ah've never seen him terrified before. Even when we got the news a' Helicote's fall, an' that the Havathis had a bounty out on any survivin' Helicotans, he responded with anger, not fear."

Sabae just nodded.

Artur sighed. "That's alarmin', but we don't know enough ta' confront him about any a' this yet. Have yeh told the others yer suspicions?"

Sabae shook her head. "I doubt any of them would even want to know yet, and all telling them would do is hurt their relationship with Alustin, and now's a bad time for that."

Artur frowned. "Ah genuinely think that Alustin will do everythin' he can ta' keep yeh from harm, but yeh need ta' remember— his first priority is and will always be revenge on Havath. Even if he has ta' choose between his loyalty ta' Kanderon and revenge, he'll choose his revenge every time. An' keep in mind, he's *very* loyal ta' Kanderon. Ah know a' multiple times he's acted independently or even against her orders ta' strike at the Havathi."

"Why does she put up with that?" Sabae asked.

"Until the gorgon incident a few years back," Artur said, "Alustin kept a very low profile fer an' archmage. An' make no mistake, he's a canny, powerful one. Ah'm not sure many other archmages could take him in a fight, especially not if he has any time ta' prepare. Kanderon's not goin' ta' dispose an asset that powerful readily. Not ta' mention, she's got a clear soft spot fer him. Fer all that Kanderon can be a ruthless, schemin' terror, she's got a habit of gettin' emotionally attached ta' her minions, an' Alustin's been her special favorite fer a long time now. Though, ah wouldn't be surprised if Hugh's challengin' him fer that spot."

"You could beat Alustin if it came down to it, right?" Sabae asked. "You're already powerful enough to challenge many of the lesser great powers in the region."

Artur shrugged. "Ah don't think ah'll need ta. Ah could easily take Alustin when it comes ta' raw power, but ah've got no idea the extent of his tricks. He comes at everythin' sideways. He doesn't plan like the rest a' us do— he doesn't have any attachments ta' his specific plans, just ta' his goal. He spends all his time creating more options ta' improvise with and recombine, not buildin' up some master plan. Not ta mention, fer all his schemin' and plottin', Alustin is still mah friend, and ah've got no desire ta' fight him. Ah've got no love fer Havath, either."

"But you also don't trust him enough to let him take us on this trip alone," Sabae said. "You're worried enough that you're taking a ship again, and you obviously have some sort of bad history with ships."

"Ah've got plenty else ta' worry about yeh kids over," Artur said. "Like sea monsters and the Havathi."

Sabae couldn't help but notice that he hadn't denied her claim.

Artur opened the pouch on his belt, and the iron filings flew back into it, breaking the ward.

"Yeh've got few hours left before we surface, right?" Artur asked.

"Then Hugh's got a shift after me," Sabae said. "Then we'll have a gap between storms that we'll be surfacing for, try and make some better time to Zophor."

"So let's get some trainin' in, then," Artur said. "Get spinnin' up that armor of yers. Wind on one arm, water on the other."

Sabae gestured at the figurehead. "But what about…?"

"It's good trainin', learnin' ta channel multiple spells at once. And ah reckon yeh usin' formless magic alongside spellforms will give yeh an especially good challenge," Artur said.

Sabae sighed, and pulled seawater to one arm, wind to the other.

"And ah'm goin' ta be lecturin yeh on various schools a' thought about mage armor," Artur said. "If yeh'll forgive me fer a little immodesty, no one knows the topic better. Yeh need ta' start thinkin' about more than just how yeh're makin' yer armor— yeh need ta' start considerin' the end goal, and even more importantly, what yer philosophy and theoretical principles are regardin' yer armor."

Sabae sighed. She might trust Artur more than Alustin, but Alustin was, shockingly, the more easy-going teacher.

It could be worse though. It could have been Kanderon.

Sabae dreamt of magma again.

She was trapped on the Skyhold council chamber seal, Abyla Ceutas' lake of magma writhing around it. Only instead of being a small lake of it on the peak of Skyhold, it was a sea that stretched from horizon to horizon, and it was slowly rising.

Shapes were swimming about beneath the magma, and Sabae, in that way peculiar to dreams, knew they were sea serpents, and she knew they were coming for her.

She knew she was dreaming, knew that she wouldn't be harmed, but she still cowered and covered her head when the first serpent launched itself out of the magma at her.

It never struck, though.

She slowly looked up, and to her shock, the sea serpent was dissolving into little bird-winged mice.

Another sea serpent reared up from the water in the distance, with purple-green flames tearing through it, dissolving it into luminescent golden smoke that sang quietly.

Patches of dreamfire began racing across the magma, leaving behind a madcap, bizarre dreamscape in their stead. Crystal trees, rabbits the size of houses, and cloud fortresses drifted through her mind as the dreamfire burnt away the last of the magma.

Her awareness that she was in a dream began to fade, and the last thing she recalled was Talia's voice, echoing as if from a great distance away.

"You're safe, Sabae. I'm here."

Sabae awoke both well rested and confused the next morning. It took her a second to remember why, and then she recalled the abortive nightmare.

What had that been about? Talia had saved her life plenty in the past, including from Abyla's magma in real life, but she'd never had her show up in a dream like that. She…

A sudden suspicion popped into her head, and she stared up at the planks above her head.

Oh no.

Had she been secretly forming a crush on Talia?

That was *not* what she needed right now. She did not need that kind of drama, she needed to forget that had ever happened, and…

"You awake?" Talia said from the lower bunk.

"Y-yes?" Sabae said, trying to sound normal and not panicked.

"I hope it's alright that I intruded on your nightmare last night," Talia said.

Sabae blinked at that. "What?"

Talia's head poked up over the side of Sabae's bunk. One of the ship's cats was sitting on her shoulders, wrapped around the back of her neck.

"You had already fallen asleep when I came in last night," Talia said. "And you were thrashing around having nightmares, so I used my dreamfire to get rid of that one for you."

"What?" Sabae said, still confused.

"That's the main use of dreamfire, remember?" Talia said. "All dream magic has a use in dreams, and it's possible but difficult to manifest those abilities in waking life as well. Dreamfire is intended to clear away unwanted dreams. It's incredibly easy to do."

"I… oh," Sabae said. "I totally forgot about that. Uh… thank you."

"What was your nightmare about, anyhow?" Talia asked.

"Abyla and her magma," Sabae said. "I've been having nightmares about being trapped back on that seal with the magma battering against its barriers ever since midsummer."

Talia's curious look turned into a glare. "I really wish I hadn't promised to stop hitting you all right now. You've been having nightmares for this long and you haven't said anything? I could have been helping you this whole time!"

The cat chirped, as if in agreement.

Sabae groaned and pulled a pillow over her head, and stopped trying to repress a blush of embarrassment. She couldn't believe that she'd thought that she might be developing a crush on Talia over something so dumb as forgetting the other girl could use dreamfire on dreams.

"You're a heavy sleeper, and I didn't want to bother you," Sabae said.

Talia did jab her in the side with a finger at that.

"I can cast a lot of these spells on you before we even go to sleep," Talia said. "They're not going to stop the nightmares entirely, but they'll make them less frequent and less powerful. Dreamfire should also help you work through the actual fears causing the nightmare a little faster. Seriously, stop trying to carry everything on your shoulders."

Sabae pulled the pillow off her face and gave Talia a look that she hoped was exasperated, but which was probably still embarrassed.

"Why did you have to pick now to get your confidence back?" Sabae said. "I was just getting used to sad, lovesick Talia."

Talia just smirked at her.

A thought occurred to Sabae as she was climbing out of bed.

"Actually, you know who else has been having nightmares lately?" Sabae asked. "Dell, from when the sea serpents took him. Do you think you could help him too?"

"Of course," Talia said. "There's only so much I can do in the time we have left on the ship, but it should help a bit."

Sabae reached out to scratch the cat's head, then, on a whim, mussed up Talia's hair as well— which did essentially nothing, considering how short it was still.

Talia rolled her eyes at her. "Oh no, you've ruined literal hours of work brushing my hair."

Sabae stuck her tongue out at her.

CHAPTER TWENTY-THREE

Delta

Hugh's spellbook intercepted another one of Kanderon's messages a few hours out from the Ylosa River delta.

More eyes are coming to rest on Anastis, Kanderon. The Council is displeased, and none have forgotten that all of this is ultimately your doing.

I was not a member of the Council when I ended the Empire, and I have never and will never apologize for my actions in those years.

The greater Radhan fleet is assembling in case they must rescue their brethren from the coming of the Cold Minds. Galvachren is no longer updating his bestiary, and we have lost track of his actions, and he is the biggest wildcard of all. Even the Wanderer is rumored to have returned. Not, of course, that we expect either you or Keayda to tell us if that were true. We're only lucky the Liar hasn't turned their attention back to Anastis, and that our enemies still fear our defenses.

I am, as always, reciprocal with the degree of trust I offer the Council. And I note who you leave out of your list.

Half of us still consider you a threat, Kanderon. You would do well to remember that. If your Exile Splinter has brought the Cold Minds to us…

The messages abruptly vanished, morphing into the lessons Kanderon had sent him a couple days ago on the theory behind starfire spellcraft, and Hugh frowned, thoroughly disturbed by what he'd read. He knew of

Galvachren, of course. The Wanderer was just a children's tale, though, a semi-mythical archmage with a bag of ten thousand tricks from the years following the fall of the Ithonian Empire. They told tales of her even in Emblin—how she'd traded away a throne she'd won for a swift horse and a treasure map, how she'd overthrown a hundred warlords, and how she even once tied a kraken's tentacles in a great knot. If the messages were to be believed, she was not only real, but still alive.

And Hugh had absolutely never heard of anyone called the Liar. He had no idea who Kanderon was claiming had been left out of the list, except for maybe whoever had killed Lasnabourne. And what was the greater Radhan fleet?

Somehow, Hugh felt asking one of the Radhan about that would be a bad idea.

And what were the Cold Minds?

"What's wrong, Hugh?" Talia asked, walking up to him where he sat in the bow, channeling the windlode into the figurehead.

Hugh hurriedly shut his spellbook and set it down. Talia scowled at it as he did so, and it quickly scuttled away across the deck to get out of her sight. Technically slid, Hugh supposed, since the book didn't have appendages, but it looked more like a crab scuttling than anything despite that.

"Stuff I probably shouldn't talk about?" Hugh said uncertainly. "Something I'm pretty sure I'm not supposed to know."

Talia frowned. "That doesn't sound good."

Hugh shook his head. "Definitely not. I think I need to talk to Sabae about it soon, I have no idea what to do now."

Talia nodded. "That's probably a good plan. Though I feel like I should be getting jealous that you're not telling me first instead of her? Not that I am, but girlfriends in novels are always doing that."

Hugh blushed a little at that. He was still getting used to this whole dating Talia thing, and he was pretty sure he'd used up his store of confidence for the next year or so when he'd kissed her.

"I'm glad you're not," he said, rubbing the back of his

head. "I'm trying to think of a non-weird way to say that, but I don't think I'd be very good at handling that?"

Talia sat down in his lap, and turned to kiss him.

"I think I understand what you're trying to say," she said. "I'm not going to start acting completely different because we're dating. I mean, it'll definitely be different, but…"

"I think I understand what you're trying to say," Hugh said.

Talia smiled at him, then leaned back against his chest.

He wrapped his arms around her and stared up at the water surrounding the ship.

They'd crossed into the outflow from the delta a few hours before, and the closer they got, the murkier and more sediments filled the water. At this point, Hugh couldn't see more than a foot or so into the cloudy brown waters. It blocked almost the entirety of the sunlight, so the only light came from the ship's glow-crystals. Every now and then, a fish brushed up against the invisible barrier, but most of the time it felt like the *Cormorant* was burrowing through the earth.

He still felt a little awkward about dating Talia. It had all happened alarmingly fast for him, and he was still a little worried whether he'd made a mistake or not, but… he also felt more comfortable than he had with Avah, in some weird way.

It was something of a relief for Godrick when the ship surfaced for good. He'd never had a problem with enclosed spaces before, but being submerged more often than not for days on end had really started to weigh on him, especially the last few hours while sailing through the sediment-filled water leaving the delta.

"We timed it well," Captain Grepha said. "We'll be arriving right with high tide, so we'll be able to coast straight up to Zophor. There should be a channel guide waiting for us near the entrance to the channels."

"There had better be," Alustin said. "Because the Havathi seem to have finally realized where we're going, and they have several ships heading this direction at high speed. We should get to Zophor before they reach the delta, but odds are they'll be close on our heels following us to the next site."

"And if Lake Nelu isn't the right site, what then?" Sabae asked. "How are we supposed to get out of the delta?"

Alustin didn't have an answer for her.

The mangroves appeared as a smudge on the horizon at first, but rapidly resolved themselves.

The shortest of the mangrove trees jutted thirty feet above the water, but they would apparently have their trunks submerged all the way up to their lowest branches soon. Godrick could see a few roots jutting straight up into the air, oddly enough.

There were hundreds, if not thousands, of interlocking channels entering the partially-submerged rainforest. At least a half-dozen were in sight of the ship, but the *Cormorant* took none of them. A ship entering without a guide was liable to get lost, then beached or stuck on a sandbar at low tide. Even having water mages wasn't much use, for the currents were complicated and ever-shifting in the delta.

"Ah don't see our guide," Artur said.

Godrick sidled over to his da. "We just got here, what's the problem?"

"There's usually a guide already waitin' as soon as a ship arrives," Artur said. "Ah've rarely heard a' them bein' late. Zophor has mages with all sorts a' different affinities scryin' fer arrivin' ships, includin' a couple farseers like Alustin."

It was only a handful of minutes later that the channel guide arrived, but even that short wait was a little alarming for the Radhan, it seemed. The guide, a naga woman, was delivered to the deck of the ship by a pair of fliers— a wind mage and a gravity mage working in concert, Godrick suspected, though it was hard to tell. Apparently the *Cormorant's* underwater approach had surprised the seers, simply appearing well within their range out of nowhere.

As they wound through the channels, Godrick took the time to chat with a few of the Radhan he'd befriended on the trip, including a couple of cute ones he'd danced with, though nothing more had developed there. Godrick just felt awkward about trying to date on a ship with his father on board. Artur would likely be relaxed and supportive about the whole thing, which, for whatever reason, made Godrick feel even more awkward about the idea.

"Hey, Godrick!" Hugh called.

Godrick strode over to where Hugh and Talia were standing at the railing. Godrick suppressed a smirk when he noticed Hugh and Talia holding hands.

He would be gloating about being the only one to correctly predict the outcome of all that silliness for quite some time.

"Reach out with your affinity senses towards the mangrove leaves," Hugh said.

Godrick's smirk turned into a puzzled look, but he did so.

"There's bits a'… is that salt?" he asked. "Why are there salt crystals on the leaves? Do the waves submerge the mangroves that high up?"

"No, actually," Alustin said from behind them. "The mangroves actually secrete the salt crystals from their leaves as one of the ways that they prevent themselves from being poisoned by the sea salt. It's why they're nearly the only trees that grow in seawater."

Godrick jumped a little at Alustin's sudden interjection.

Alustin walked past him and hopped up onto the ship's railing.

"We might as well get a bit of training in," he said.

Alustin pulled a sheet of paper out of his satchel, and tossed it up into the air, where it folded itself into an origami golem in the shape of a seagull, then fluttered off.

"Ah thought yeh needed ta draw spellforms an' glyphs an' such onto an origami golem?" Godrick asked.

"I did. I spend several hours every day simply drawing glyphs and other spellforms onto paper for later use. I keep the next best thing to a warehouse-full of specially prepared paper in here," Alustin said, patting the satchel at his side, likely for the benefit of the Radhan around them. "The better prepared I am for different situations, the more effective I am as a battle mage. You all have actually made me even more effective of a battle mage— it takes a lot of work and research to figure out how to teach non-standard magic, and it's inspired me to add quite a bit to my arsenal. Not least a significant number of wards, split across dozens of sheets of paper. I can easily mix and match the ward papers to vary the effect. I'm still not as good as Hugh with them, but Hugh's a specialist."

"What about me?" Talia asked.

Alustin chuckled. "Actually, yes. I've been experimenting with glyphs that try and force effects through spellforms that are completely unsuited for them, similar to your early magical problems, and I've been getting some fascinating results. Mostly explosions."

"Not many problems explosions can't solve," Talia said.

"Ah'm pretty sure there are," Godrick said. "Ah'm pretty sure, in fact, that most problems can't be solved with explosions."

"Well, I'm not saying that they make the best solution, or even a good one," Talia said, "but they're definitely a solution."

Godrick just sighed at that. He knew better than to argue with that logic.

The paper seagull returned, leading Sabae over to them, and Alustin unfolded the bird. He showed Godrick the glyphs and spellforms on it, then stored it back in his satchel.

"So," Alustin said. "Training!"

Hugh's training consisted of simply firing starbolts up into the sky until his mana reservoir was empty, then growing salt crystals in the channel water. After weeks of training, Hugh could now launch four starbolts before running out of mana. Hugh had grown much faster at growing salt crystals in the water, but the channel water was brackish and far more difficult to get salt out of than ocean water.

Sabae, meanwhile, had finally progressed up to spinning different types of armor around multiple limbs at once— she could now maintain wind armor on two limbs and water on two limbs at the same time. Alustin had the crew playing the same armor transfer game with her, but her explosions were coming far less frequently.

Talia was having to now hold mana in bone shards for even longer than before, while also maintaining a swarm of the tiny dreamfire bolts at the same time. Everyone was making sure to stay especially far away from her, and more than a couple mangroves took damage from her training.

Godrick was proud of the name he came up with for the swarms of tiny dreamfire bolts, however. Sabae had proposed dreamfire-flies, which Hugh had shortened to dreamflies. Godrick's name, however, was the one that stuck— dreamwasps.

Godrick, meanwhile, was being taught an entirely new spell type. It was one he'd heard of before, and one his father was excellent at, but then, the famed Artur Wallbreaker was good at *everything* he tried.

He felt a brief flash of resentment, which he promptly quashed. His father had literally never been anything but supportive, and didn't treat Godrick with any sort of disappointment for not being as powerful as he was.

The new spellform type was referred to as lithification spells, and they were fiendishly difficult to use. In essence, it was the process of turning non-stone materials into stone— usually mud or sand, though other materials like shells could be used.

The reason it was so difficult was that there were a half dozen spellforms that had to be used over the course of the process, often two or three at the same time. And there wasn't just a simple checklist of what order to use them in, either— it was a process with a complexity coming close to alchemy, though not nearly so dangerous. It was more art than anything. If you applied the concretion spell to the mud too soon, the matrix of the rock would be insufficiently well-consolidated, and it would collapse. If you applied the heating or the pressure spells while there was too much water, the mud would explode. If you drained too much water with the dehydration spells, the mud would just turn to dust instead of water. If you drained the water too quickly, it would leave air bubbles that would cause cracks, even if you took precisely the right amount of water out.

There were literally dozens of ways to ruin the process, if not more. And on top of that, the half-dozen spellforms had to be swapped out with others from situation to situation depending on the contents of the mud, sand, or soil in question. The amount of mana needed for each spellform changed based on both the contents of the ingredients and the conditions around them— not just parameters like the temperature, but on the humidity, the elevation, and more.

Artur had claimed before that the best training for lithification spells was learning how to cook. Godrick, unfortunately, hadn't spent nearly enough time learning to cook from his father yet.

Not to mention, the process was slow and intensely mana hungry. Hugh's ability to simply grow crystals was far swifter and more effective. Lithification was simply too slow for use in combat.

When Godrick brought that up, however, Alustin's response was simply to ask whether Godrick thought magic for battle preparation was important. Godrick felt a little embarrassed at that, considering how Alustin had literally just told him about the hours he spent drawing spellforms and glyphs each day.

Getting more proficient with them would also slowly improve his control over stone over time, which he wouldn't sneer at.

Alustin spent the whole practice-time lecturing them on the magical principles for filtering toxins, and the techniques various toxin mages used for getting venoms and poisons past magical defenses, and in turn the means for defeating those techniques, and so on and so forth.

Finally, Alustin let them rest, just before they arrived at Zophor.

The mangroves grew taller and more densely packed the deeper they sailed into the channels of the delta. Thousands of birds flitted back and forth among the branches, ranging from cormorants and other seabirds to brilliantly colored parrots and hummingbirds. Seadrakes competed for nesting space with their larger forest drake cousins— usually winning, thanks to the fact that sea drakes flocked in large numbers, while forest drakes nested as separate mating pairs.

Hugh also couldn't help but notice his spellbook trying to blend in with a group of bright green parrots, which seemed surprisingly tolerant of the intruder in their midst.

Monkeys raced through the trees, following the *Rising Cormorant* curiously. Hugh spotted a tree reach out and snatch a monkey off a branch at one point, before he realized that it was a man-sized octopus that had camouflaged itself as a section of trunk. The octopus eyed the ship as its skin shifted from the color of the bark to a bright purple, then dropped down into the water, its struggling prey still wrapped in its arms.

The closer to the delta they got, the taller the trees grew, until they passed a bend in the tidal channel and saw Zophor itself.

The living mangroves that made up the tree-city of Zophor towered hundreds of feet into the air, looming high over their natural brethren, which were themselves enormous. At their bases, the city trees were wider across than any other tree he'd ever heard of.

Immense branches intertwined in midair, creating roads between the various trees of the city. More roads spiraled up and down the trunks of each mangrove, with shop-fronts and homes carved into the trunks. Then Hugh blinked and realized that the buildings of Zophor weren't carved, but were actually grown into the trees.

Thousands of people walked the streets of Zophor, and there were even small wagons pulled by what looked like boar-sized iguanas.

There was no land below Zophor— the whole city grew

straight out of the water of the Ylosa Delta.

None of that was the most impressive part of Zophor, however.

There were faces in the trees. Or rather one face, grown again and again. A stern faced middle-aged man, with high cheekbones and a bold jaw. The faces were all bald and beardless. They varied in size, but even the smallest dwarfed Kanderon's face, and the largest dwarfed even the head of Indris.

He looked like a distant relative of Sabae's, Hugh thought.

Then one of the faces moved, the great wooden eyes turning to fix on the *Rising Cormorant,* and Hugh froze.

Several more faces shifted to look at the *Cormorant* with looks of idle interest. Most turned their eyes away soon enough, though a couple stayed focused on them.

As the *Cormorant* sailed between the first trees of the city, Hugh realized they were even taller than he thought, and that the lowest level of the city was well over fifty feet above them, and they were at high tide now.

He was about to ask Alustin how they'd get up there when one of the great mangrove branches began to move.

The branch was immense, far larger by itself than any tree Hugh had ever seen. At its end was a cluster of branches that looked almost like fingers, and as it drew closer, Hugh realized that the branches did, in fact, form a skeletal-looking hand, only with far more fingers than any human hand.

He couldn't help but step back nervously as the branch approached, but no-one on the ship seemed panicked. The Radhan were bustling about and reefing the ship's sails, while the captain was paying the channel guide.

His fellow students, at least, looked a little apprehensive.

As the great branch-hand slipped underneath the ship, Alustin spoke.

"Welcome to Zophor, demesne of the lich Zophor, home to a third of a million people, and one of the greatest tree-cities ever grown. Do try and behave."

The ship shuddered gently as it was lifted up into the air.

CHAPTER TWENTY-FOUR

Lich-City

"How are they powering these enchantments?" Hugh asked, as the branch slowly lifted the *Cormorant* higher into the air. "The aether here is about on par with Theras Tel, but this absolutely dwarfs their lifts."

He stumbled a little as the deck shifted, and Godrick steadied him.

"They're not enchantments, exactly," Alustin said. "Or, they are enchantments, in a sense, but it's mostly just Zophor's control over his demesne."

"What?" Hugh asked.

The deck shifted again, and Talia stumbled into Hugh. Judging by the smirk she gave him, Hugh somewhat doubted it had been an accident.

"Haven't I explained liches to you yet?" Alustin asked.

"They're undead skeleton mages?" Hugh asked.

Alustin took off his glasses and rubbed the bridge of his nose.

"Clearly not," he muttered. "Do the rest of you at least know what a lich actually is?"

Sabae nodded and Godrick shrugged, but Talia shook her head.

"Alright," Alustin said, putting his glasses back on. "A lich is, simply speaking, a mage who has imbued their entire consciousness into a location. Or, more precisely, a massive enchanted construct known as a demesne. And by massive, I do mean massive— a fortress is about the smallest sized demesne that can successfully contain the consciousness of a sapient being. Brains are far, far more complex than any structures we can build, so liches have to build to huge scales to contain a mind. Even a fortress-size demesne is a bit on the small side, and liches inhabiting them are more limited mentally and magically than in larger demesnes. Most liches who can achieve it prefer to build on the scale of a city or a mountain."

"Ah've seen what happens when a mage tries ta' inhabit a demesne too small fer it," Artur said. "It's not pretty."

Hugh started a bit— he hadn't realized Artur had joined them. Of course, he'd been more than a little distracted by the giant tree-city.

"So why would anyone build a small demesne?" Talia asked.

Alustin shrugged. "Most mages who attempt the transition to lichdom do so in old age, out of fear of death. Even if they have the capability to fill an entire mountain with enchantments, they seldom have time to do so. Likewise constructing a whole city. And the number of mages capable of actually doing either is incredibly rare."

The ship shuddered again as it reached the height of the lowest roads. Hugh could see people in a market haggling over fish, and most of them only casually glanced at the ship as it was slowly carried into the air. People could get used to any sight, no matter how astonishing, Hugh supposed.

"Some liches also like ta' try fer mobility," Artur muttered.

"That's a persistent dream of liches," Alustin agreed. "A lich cannot leave its demesne, because, for all intents and purposes, it *is* its demesne. Most of them have avatars, but they're little more than animated puppets. Keayda has a stone naga statue he puppets, Zophor has his faces and his own wooden statues, but their avatars cannot leave their demesnes. Lichdom is a path to incredible lifespans and incredible power, but it also effectively imprisons the mage for eternity. You can't blame a mage for wanting to avoid that fate."

"Ah sure can," Artur said.

"Long lifespans, not immortality?" Hugh asked.

"Even the best made demesne fails eventually. Nothing is

eternal," Alustin said. "There are a few other limitations on liches as well. Their demesne needs to correspond to their affinity, first off, and not all affinities work. It has to be an affinity that can be made into a long-term structure. A fire mage couldn't become a lich, both because it has no solid structure and because there is no way to keep a large enough fire in fuel for long enough. A stone or ice mage could become a lich, however. In fact, stone liches, like Keayda, are probably the single most common type of lich. As an interesting side note, Keayda is so old that no one but him knows whether he was actually a naga in life. The avatars of liches don't have to have any sort of resemblance to them in life."

The branch finally stopped ascending around seventy-five feet above the water. It held still for a moment, then started shifting to the side. Quite a few people on deck, including Hugh, stumbled. He frowned and assembled a modified levitation spellform in his mind's eye to counteract the shifts, and applied it to the group.

"The process of becoming a lich is a gradual one that can take years," Alustin said. "Bits of the mage's consciousness are slowly transferred over to their demesne as they construct it, and it's a process with an extremely high failure rate. The farther along the process goes, the closer you need to stay to your demesne, and near the end of the process you can no longer leave your demesne for any appreciable amount of time. One of the most common failure states of transition to lichdom is running out of your affinity's material you need for the construction partway through the process, whether due to miscalculation or outside interference. Running out of the alchemical compounds necessary for enchantments is also common, as are failures in the enchantments themselves. There are few more complex enchantments out there, if any."

A mangrove leaf bigger than Hugh fluttered down past the ship, and Hugh realized that the size of the leaves must be proportional to the size of the tree.

"Can there be multi-affinity liches?" Hugh asked. "Like, a

stone and steel one?"

"Yeh tryin' ta' turn me inta' an undead monster already?" Godrick asked with a smirk.

Hugh rolled his eyes. "They were just the first affinities to come to mind," he said.

"You can, in fact, have multi-affinity liches," Alustin said. "They're rare, though, because the difficulty of constructing a demesne grows more challenging with each material used. But if you don't use one of your affinities in the construction of your demesne, you lose it for good."

Hugh's eyes widened as he saw another great hand-like branch coming for them.

"Can you keep enlarging a demesne after it's built?" Talia asked.

"Absolutely, though it's far more difficult than building it larger in the first place," Alustin said. "In fact, Zophor is a great example of that. His story is fascinating in general, really. He was actually born in Ras Andis, Sabae, I don't know if you knew that."

Sabae shook her head. "I didn't, actually. I knew he's something of an ally of my family, but I didn't know why."

"He's said to have something of a soft spot for Ras Andis still," Alustin said.

The first branch passed the *Cormorant* gently over to the second, but gently for something this large still shook the ship alarmingly. Hugh's spell, however, kept them all steady. Several of the others shot him curious looks, and he nodded.

Hugh kind of enjoyed having the job of keeping people from falling down. If he was being honest, it helped keep the part of his mind that told him he was useless quiet.

"Zophor was born over a century ago into a body he despised," Alustin said. "He was a particularly powerful and precocious mage with a mangrove affinity. Given that more specific affinities are more powerful than more general ones, mages with affinities for specific species of plants are powerful indeed when surrounded by their plant. Zophor was absolutely brilliant, and began the process of growing his demesne here in the Ylosa delta, the largest mangrove forest on all of Anastis, right on top of a small submerged labyrinth. He wasn't much older than you all when he reached archmage status and began constructing his demesne— just over twenty, in fact. Since he started early for the purposes of gaining a new body, rather than trying to escape death later in life, he had far longer to construct his demesne than other liches. He chose the challenging path of growing a living demesne out of the mangroves, which has the advantage of being able to repair and extend itself over time more easily. He has even greater control over his demesne than the average lich, and it would be absolutely foolish for anyone to attack him head-on without assembling multiple great powers at the very least."

The second branch carried them around the curve of a trunk, and Hugh spotted the docks ahead of them.

It was a series of massive, water-filled wooden bowls, suspended in a spiderweb of branches connecting multiple giant mangrove trunks, fifty feet above the water. The bowls ranged in size from ones just large enough to contain little fishing schooners to ones large enough to contain ships half again the size of the *Cormorant*. Around two-thirds of them were occupied at the moment. There were also a number of dry storage areas for smaller ships, including canoes and dinghies. Hugh could spot at least seven of the great branches moving ships around the docks, as well as innumerable smaller branches moving cargo and smaller ships around.

"It should also be noted," Alustin said, "that Zophor constructed his demesne entirely without a patron. Most liches have the backing of a great power, a city-state, or a nation, and nine out of ten still fail. Kanderon is, in fact, the leading patron of liches across much of the continent, and even with her assistance, the number of mages that fail is still around seven in ten. Zophor, however, figured out the process entirely on his own, and achieved the task single-handedly. People started moving into his demesne before he even finished, and it's said that when his transition into lichdom was complete, he tossed his old body in the river like it was trash. Under no circumstances should you underestimate or disrespect Zophor— he's a living city of unbelievable power, and he's hardly humble or understanding."

As the branch-hand lowered the *Cormorant* into one of the great water-filled bowls of the docks, Hugh looked up at the great wooden faces of Zophor looking down at them, then shuddered.

The docks were apparently so crowded due to the storms. Half the ships that were there were taking shelter from them and waiting for them to subside. The storms had started within a couple days of Midsummer, and hadn't abated since.

Hugh saw goods of an astonishing variety being loaded onto ships around him. Planks and logs of rare jungle hardwoods from upstream were loaded alongside exotic animal pelts. Rare herbs for alchemy went onboard the ships side by side with tropical fruits, all to be stored behind preservation wards. Heavily warded lead casks of alchemical mixtures were loaded alongside beautifully carved furnishings.

Most of all, though, Hugh saw salt. Huge crates and barrels filled with salt littered the docks. Everywhere he looked, he could see little piles of fine salt that had been spilled on the docks.

According to Alustin, Zophor was one of the chief producers of salt on the continent. The great mangroves of the city excreted the salt on their leaves just like any other mangrove, and the city's salt mages regularly harvested it before the rain washed it away, especially during the dry season. Zophor was Lothal's main competitor for salt exports in the south, but the market was still far from glutted— civilization's demand for salt was just about endless.

Hugh thought of Avah while Alustin was explaining the Zophoran salt industry— she would have been absolutely fascinated by it. Unless she'd already visited Zophor? She was far better traveled than he was.

Then Hugh glanced at Talia, by his side, and felt an abrupt pang of guilt. He didn't think she would be upset with him for thinking about Avah— if nothing else, she was too busy being upset about the heat and the humidity— but he still felt a little uncomfortable about it.

"Hey Talia?" he said.

She looked over at him and smiled.

"Is it weird that the docks are reminding me of Avah? Should I be trying not to think of her, or… It's probably weird that I'm asking you, isn't it? I don't think I'm very good at this boyfriend thing yet." Hugh asked. He realized he was about to start rambling, then rubbed the back of his head awkwardly.

Talia's smile faded into a thoughtful look, then to his surprise, she smiled at him. "It's fine, Hugh. It's not healthy to demand that someone you're dating pretend like you're the entirety of their dating history. Besides, I don't have a problem with Avah. After all, I won in the end, right?"

Hugh smiled back at her, relieved.

"Did you get that from one of your novels?" Sabae asked. "Also, Hugh's not a prize to be won, he's a person."

Talia stuck out her tongue at the taller girl.

Hugh glanced over at Sabae. She traveled lighter than any of them, only carrying her enchanted shield and the warded travel pack Hugh had given her— it could clean clothes going into it. He couldn't help but notice that she had her shield stuck to her arm in battle-ready position— she seemed determined not to get caught unawares and unprepared like they had been in Lothal.

Hugh saw fewer weapons on the docks of Zophor than he had on docks in other cities— the lich-city was apparently one of the safest places to live or visit. There were still a few to be seen, though, so Sabae wasn't getting any odd looks.

They had a long walk to their inn— it was a solid hundred and fifty feet higher than the docks, and two trees over. It would have been miserable to carry their luggage without levitation cantrips, but Hugh's feet and legs were still aching before they were halfway there.

The crowds on Zophor's streets were the most diverse he'd ever seen. Naga slithered along the roadways in great numbers. Gorgons, their distant cousins, strode about the streets as well. The shortest of them was as tall as Godrick and Artur, and several they saw were pushing ten feet in height. They were entirely scaled, but the scales were so fine as to look like brightly-colored skin from a distance. Hugh was surprised to see that they really did have snakes for hair, but of wildly varying types. He saw one with a matched head of dozens of small black snakes, another with at least a half-dozen different species of snakes, and a third especially tall gorgon with a single massive python coming from his or her scalp— it was difficult to tell— which wrapped multiple times around the gorgon's torso, and watched the group as they passed, though the gorgon's actual face didn't look their way.

"They're not born with the snakes," Alustin said when Hugh asked. "It's a sort of symbiotic absorption process. Their choice of what snakes to bond with is a hugely important one, and determines a lot about how they'll fit into gorgon society. The sheer weirdness of it is one of the strongest pieces of evidence in favor of the old legend that dragons originally created the gorgons and naga from humans to act as servitors."

Hugh also couldn't help but notice that a few of the gorgons seemed to recognize Alustin.

Gorgons and naga were only the tip of the iceberg, however. Hugh spotted at least three dragons resting on roosts or platforms clearly built for draconic visitors, with merchants coming to the dragons to hawk their wares. An octopus of Ampioc's species, though only a third of the size, had clambered partway up the trunk, and was bargaining with at least four different merchants over what appeared to be a sunken ship the creature had salvaged. Bids and counteroffers raced across the octopus's skin in brilliant colors.

There were endless humans as well, of every color and appearance Hugh had ever seen or heard of, and then some. The majority, though, were the coppery-red so common among the inhabitants of southeastern Ithos— Phusan likely would have blended right in, as immigrants from Sica were one of the most common groups in Zophor, according to Alustin.

Sica was also a tree city as well, apparently, though not a lich-city. It was comparably impressive to Zophor, but wildly different, being grown out of baobabs by generations of tree mages, rather than mangroves like Zophor.

Hugh's spellbook, meanwhile, was having a grand time flapping around over the crowds' heads, drawing far more attention than the Skyhold group did. Several people Hugh could see were eying his spellbook acquisitively, but he wasn't particularly worried. Hugh's spellbook was absurdly strong for its size— it could more than lift the weight of a person into the air, at least for a short time.

Looming over everything were the immense faces of Zophor himself. Most of the time they stayed still, but it was rare not to see several in any direction monitoring the city.

When they finally reached their inn, Hugh's feet wanted nothing so much as to lay down for an hour or three, but…

"We should do something to celebrate Talia's birthday tonight, since we didn't get to at sea," he said.

"You don't have to," Talia said.

"No, we don't have to," Sabae said. "We want to, though, so we will."

CHAPTER TWENTY-FIVE

Tea in the Park

They split up for the afternoon. Alustin and Artur went to arrange things for their expedition upriver, while Hugh and Godrick went to go figure out their plans for the evening.

Talia and Sabae, meanwhile, almost got in a fight against Havathi Sacred Swordsmen.

It had started out innocuously enough— they'd intended to just do a little shopping and explore the city a bit.

After visiting a number of weapon shops and bookstores, Sabae decided to breach the conversational topic Talia had been avoiding the whole time.

"So are we just not going to talk about you and Hugh?" Sabae asked.

Talia blushed. "Sorry. I didn't want to be one of those people who talk about nothing but their new relationship and annoy their friends."

Sabae rolled her eyes at that. "Two of my best friends just started dating. It's definitely something I want to talk about."

"Honestly," Talia said, "I'm still a little in shock about the whole thing? I spent more time preparing myself to get turned down than actually expecting Hugh to decide he was interested. I'm still halfway convinced that he's going to change his mind at any moment."

"Not going to lie," Sabae said, "I thought the same. Godrick was the only one who actually expected you to get together, I think. I doubt Hugh's going to just up and dump you, though. That would be really out of character for him."

Talia sighed and put a volume back on the bookstore shelf in the wrong spot. "I really hope you're right about that."

"So… how are things actually going, then?" Sabae asked, moving the book to its proper spot.

"Good, mostly?" Talia said. "In a lot of ways we were just more immediately comfortable together than anyone else I've dated, but there's also a lot of confusing awkward moments too? I'm trying to take it slow because I don't want to make Hugh uncomfortable, and I've dated more than he has."

"So, uh… there is one thing I've been wondering for a while," Sabae said. "Since you, uh… well, since your tattoos tend to interfere with your cantrips and make them set things on fire, how do you handle casting, uh…"

Talia gave her a confused look for a moment, then turned alarmingly red.

"Anyone I'm dating has to cast them for both of us if we don't want to have healers get involved again," Talia said finally. "So I can't date anyone who is mind-blind or bad enough at magic that they can't cast those kinds of cantrips."

"Wait, again?" Sabae asked. "Did you set fire to some poor Clan Castis boy?"

Talia turned even redder, though Sabae didn't see how that was possible.

"Myself, actually," she finally said. "Anyhow, I'm taking it slow with Hugh, so can we change the subject to literally anything else now, please?"

Sabae nodded, struggling not to laugh.

She failed badly.

Talia was still red in the face and shooting glares at Sabae when they stepped out of the bookstore, which was probably the only reason she didn't attack the Havathi Sacred Swordsmen the instant they crossed paths.

Sabae was the first to spot the Swordsmen. There were five of them— an entire Hand, with several attendants as well. Only two of them were actually carrying swords— two others carried spears over their shoulders, while the last carried a whip made out of a living vine on their belt. The Swordsmen were all dressed in their white and bronze uniforms, and marched abreast, forcing other pedestrians to go around them.

She almost went for her shield on her back, but remembered where she was just in time. She grabbed at Talia's wrist instead.

The Swordsmen and Talia noticed each other the instant Sabae moved, and two of the Swordsmen immediately went for their weapons, including the whip wielder. The others were as quick to stop them as Sabae was with Talia.

Which, to Sabae's surprise, proved totally unnecessary in

Talia's case. She didn't even twitch to move for her own weapons, and her expression was a flat glare towards the Havathi. Sabae slowly let go of her wrist.

The silence dragged out for a long moment until the Havathi woman in the center carrying a spear spoke.

"Sabae Kaen Das and Talia of Clan Castis," she said. "You know, until recently, our intelligence reports spoke of Talia as the most dangerous of Alustin's apprentices, and you as the least dangerous, Sabae, but you were the one to deliver the killing blow against Sanniah, weren't you?"

"A bit rude of me, I suppose," Sabae said, "but in fairness, she ambushed us from a distance. Worse, she turned her back on a Kaen Das. Never a smart idea."

Several of the Swordsmen glared, but none made a move.

"Has your master even told you what you're looking for, Sabae?" the Havathi leader asked. "Do you even know?"

Sabae raised an eyebrow and put her smuggest smile on her face. "Find Imperial Ithos, retrieve the Exile Splinter, activate the Heartburner."

A brief look of surprise crossed the leader's face, but was rapidly suppressed. To Sabae's pleasure, however, the Swordsman with the whip took her bait.

"Activate the what?" he demanded.

Sabae smiled even wider. "Seems our masters aren't the ones hiding details about the contents of Imperial Ithos," she lied.

The crowd seemed to sense that something was up, and people were rapidly ducking into shops and dodging away nearby.

"You know, Sabae," Talia said. "I'm disappointed. For an elite combat unit, they're walking depressingly close together. Some malicious mage could take them all out with a decently destructive spell."

"It is disappointing," Sabae said. "Tragically low standards on the part of the Havathi."

The whip wielder opened his mouth, but the Havathi leader raised her hand to interrupt him. Sabae got a better look at the woman's spear as she did so— it appeared to be carved entirely from volcanic stone filled with deep cracks in the shape of spellforms. Deep inside the cracks, Sabae could see what looked like a hollow space in the center of the spear, with something moving slowly through it.

The Havathi woman stared thoughtfully at her for a moment before she spoke. "I can't imagine your first encounter with us gave you much reason to like us, did it? That is unfortunate, and entirely our fault. I'd like to offer our apologies for Sanniah's attack upon you all."

From the corner of her eye, Sabae could see Talia giving her a confused look, but Sabae kept her expression flat and her gaze on the Havathi.

"Despite what many would have you think of us," the woman continued, "Havath does not seek to extend the borders of the Dominion merely for the sake of conquest or power. The Dominion's goal remains what it has always been— to bring peace to the masses, and keep them from being constantly swept up in coups and power struggles between the great powers. Surely you've seen the results that can have on the commons, on innocents who merely want to live their lives and take care of their families. The means we must pursue to ensure their safety is at times regrettable, but gentle means are seldom enough to bring drastic change."

Sabae smiled, recognizing the territory she was in now.

From what she knew of the Havathi, they were absolutely convinced of the rightness of their cause. For all the destructiveness of their conquests, they weren't overly cruel to their conquered populations, and were quite dedicated to preventing famine and disease in their territories. Though many more resources flowed in from Havath's provinces to Havath City, the tribute was hardly crippling. And they certainly weren't wrong about the destructive results the constant feuding between great powers brought to the people of the Ithonian continent.

Frankly, Sabae doubted she'd be able to defeat an intelligent Havathi in an argument about the moral imperative of their empire. Not that she thought they were correct— the failures of the Ithonian Empire and its brutal cruelties in its later years were both damning indictments of imperial ambitions, to her mind. Empires required an outward frontier, or they'd inevitably turn their violent attentions inward on their own populations. Likewise, no matter what they claimed, the primary purpose of an empire was always funneling resources inward.

No, the problem was that cleverly winning a debate against an opponent of strong convictions didn't change minds. That only happened over time via the planting of seeds of doubt and their patient cultivation.

Pursuing winning a debate against an opponent in circumstances such as this was, more often than not, just a way to impress one's own allies and assuage one's own pride.

Her grandmother had spent years warning her of the idiocy and uselessness of that path in most situations.

But, when you don't think you can win one game… play another game entirely, and don't let your opponent know you've switched.

"Why does that matter?" Sabae asked.

The Havathi blinked in surprise, and Sabae struggled to keep a smile off her face.

"Why does what matter?" the woman asked.

"I am, as you pointed out already, a Kaen Das. Why would you possibly think I care about the fates of the weak or of petty moral concerns? Any justification for power beyond power itself is foolish, and merely shows your own weakness and dishonesty with yourself," Sabae said.

The Havathi leader gave her a shocked look, then collected herself.

"Very well, then," she said. "If it's crude power you respect, then consider this— Havath's victory is inevitable. We are better organized, wealthier, and have more great powers than any other nation. Allying with us is the smartest course of action."

Sabae laughed. "It's not crude power I respect. How power is wielded is even more important than how much power one has, and Havath is nothing if not crude with its power. And the Havath Dominion won't last long against the Exile Splinter and Heartburner."

Sabae really hoped Talia didn't take her seriously, and knew that she wasn't actually so callous. She'd spent her early childhood among the poor of Ras Andis, moving to Stormseat only after her father's death, and she didn't think so little of them at all.

The whip wielder opened his mouth to say something— probably angry bravado— when a cough interrupted him.

Not the Havathi leader's cough.

Everyone turned to see a wooden statue watching them. It wasn't a particularly large statue— only around Sabae's own height. It seemed to be more grown than carved, and was spectacularly lifelike. High cheekbones, stern expression, and a bald scalp that took shiny to a whole new level— it was literally polished.

Zophor.

It also seemed worth noticing, to Sabae, that the statue stood atop a branch large enough to swat Indris out of the sky with ease, which had moved alongside them without making a sound.

Zophor's statue stepped gracefully forwards, and smaller branches wove themselves into a ramp that he descended to the street. The ramp unwove as he stepped off it, and the whole branch shifted back a bit, but remained in sight.

"Now then," Zophor said, in a smooth baritone, "this does seem a tense situation, doesn't it? Everyone heavily armed and on edge? Why, something unfortunate could happen if someone got too worked up. And that would be tragic, wouldn't it?"

Sabae saw her chance and seized the initiative.

"Tragic indeed, sir, and it would be entirely my fault," Sabae said. "My grandmother's often warned me about my bad habit of getting worked up over petty annoyances, and that I need to learn that they simply aren't worth my time."

Zophor's avatar smiled widely, and most of the Havathi glowered at her, though their leader simply watched her expressionlessly.

"Your grandmother sounds like a delightful woman," Zophor said. "Is it anyone I might have heard of, by any chance? You seem familiar to me, somehow."

Zophor definitely already knew who she was— Sabae suspected he'd listened to every word of their confrontation— but she played along anyhow.

"Ilinia Kaen Das, sir," Sabae said.

"How delightful," Zophor said. "The granddaughter of my young friend Ilinia! Come, walk with me— I would love to hear how she's doing."

As they followed Zophor, Sabae made sure to smile sweetly at the Havathi.

Quite a few citizens of Zophor shot interested looks at the lich's avatar as Sabae and Talia strolled through the streets alongside him, but they didn't appear surprised or shocked. Sabae suspected Zophor interacted with his subjects more often than most great powers did.

Zophor had quite a few questions about Ilinia— many of them about the incident at Midsummer, of which the lich seemed surprisingly well informed.

Eventually they came to a park, built onto a great suspended platform between three of Zophor's trunks. The park was filled with gentle, grassy hills, and a stream ran from one support branch, across the park, then flowed into another support branch.

Sabae hadn't considered it before, but the city's water and sewage systems must run through the insides of the various branches and trunks.

Children laughed and played among the grassy hills, and clambered over a cage in the shape of a dome rising out of the ground, woven entirely of living mangrove branches. There was a great mangrove fence surrounding the park keeping any of them from falling, even higher than the chest-high railing surrounding the streets and bridges.

Zophor led them to a small table with several chairs around it. The furniture was all grown out of living mangrove branches, and had leaves protruding from out-of-the-way spots. It rose straight out of the ground, and Sabae was certain it was just a part of the greater tree.

"You know," Zophor said. "When I was a child in Ras

Andis, there was a folktale about an enchanted mirror called the Heartburner, which turned the hearts of anyone who lied about loving someone to ash when they looked into it. I wonder if it's still popular?"

Sabae smiled at him as they all sat around the table. "You know, I actually seem to recall hearing that same story when I was young. I wonder how well-versed your average Havathi is on children's tales from Ras Andis?"

Talia burst out laughing as she understood, and to Sabae's surprise, Zophor chuckled with her.

"I don't believe we've been formally introduced," the lich said. "I am Zophor, at your service."

"Talia of Clan Castis," Talia said. "I love your city, by the way. I doubted it when I heard, but it's even more impressive than Hold Yehal."

"High praise indeed," Zophor said. "I visited Hold Yehal when I was young, along with a few other tree cities, and it was far and away one of my favorites. Most tree cities only utilize one or maybe two types of trees in their construction, but Clan Yehal has included every type that thrives at such a high altitude. It's delightfully heterogeneous. Could I offer the two of you tea?"

Sabae nodded, and within moments, one of Zophor's huge branch hands descended and set a steaming iron teapot on the table, along with three cups. The lich had clearly already prepared the tea before asking.

Zophor noticed that she was eying his teacup and smiled. "Some liches dismiss the importance of eating, drinking, and other pleasures of ephemerals like yourself. I'm far from one of them, and I can't help but note that most of the oldest liches around still concern themselves with such things. Attempting to distance yourself from ephemeral life seems a recipe for eventual madness, I fear. But, of course, retaining the ability to taste is one of the trickiest parts of transitioning to lichdom, and most seekers of lichdom are fleeing old age, and have little time to spare for such things."

Zophor poured tea for each of them.

"Besides, I would simply miss tea far too much for this.

Have you ever had Tsarnassan fermented tea before?" Zophor asked.

Sabae and Talia shook their heads.

"It is something of an acquired taste, and many never learn to enjoy it, but you two seem to be the types to be comfortable enough with risking something new," Zophor said. "The Tsarnassans select the tea leaves carefully, from only the plants with the richest flavor, and then, after drying the tea, they ferment it in buried clay pots high in the mountains for at least two years."

Sabae eyed the tea cautiously. She'd never seen tea this dark before, and it gave off a powerful— almost pungent—smell. It wasn't a bad smell, just a strange one.

"I am afraid that I need to apologize to you both," Zophor said. "For I eavesdropped on your conversation with the Havathi. I confess that I am curious as to how truthful you were, Sabae. Is that what you actually think about power in and of itself?"

That was not what Sabae had been expecting to hear. She quickly took a sip of the tea, burning her mouth a little.

Zophor was right about it being an acquired taste. It wasn't bad, just… strange, and a bit overpowering.

"Do you know much about Clan Castis?" Talia asked.

Both Sabae and Zophor turned to Talia in surprise. Zophor's expression was more polite than Sabae's, who was desperately hoping Talia wasn't about to offend him.

"I've never had the pleasure of meeting anyone from your clan," Zophor said, "but I've heard much about you. It behooves a wood lich well to keep track of powerful fire mages, for obvious reasons."

"Do you know what Clan Castis' greatest weapon is?" Talia asked, then took a sip of her tea.

"I can't help but feel," Zophor said, "that this is something of a trick question. The obvious answers would be your peerless fire magic or your fabled tattoos. I suspect you're about to say that it is neither of those."

"This is really good tea," Talia said, taking another sip. "I might have to pick some up. But yes, you're right, it was a trick question. Clan Castis' greatest weapon is its reputation— as fire mages and belligerent barbarians. It colors and constrains others' opinions of us, and limits their predictions of our behavior. Because that's the thing— people want to believe the reputation. People prefer to believe that reputations are reliable, and they'll focus on anything that helps them to believe that. We've learned to use that to easily manipulate others into overestimating our combat prowess and aggression or into underestimating our intelligence. Not a unique lesson, by any means, and one that I'm sure Sabae's grandmother taught her."

Sabae smiled at Talia, relieved that she knew Sabae wasn't as callous as she had acted.

Zophor stared at Talia thoughtfully, then smiled.

"I'm delighted that you enjoy the tea," he said. "It's always good to find another who shares my good taste."

Both Talia and Zophor drank deeply, while Sabae took a sip to be polite.

"So," Zophor said. "You're hunting Imperial Ithos."

Sabae nodded, there being no point in denying it.

"I must admit," Zophor said, "that this whole situation is of significant interest to me. I only became aware of it a few years ago, and I never imagined the ancient capital of Ithos might be so close to my demesne. I suspect there is much I still don't know, however. It is, I think, quite curious the way that the great powers hunting it go about their pursuit. The younger and brasher powers pursue Ithos avariciously, but the wiser great powers— like your grandmother and her little Coven— seem strangely terrified by the city's return."

Sabae took another small sip to give herself time to think. Talia, meanwhile, just looked puzzled.

"I've noticed something similar," Sabae finally said.

"Do they perhaps think the Ithonians survived their exile, and seek revenge?" Zophor asked. "Or does Imperial Ithos carry back with it ancient weapons of great power?"

"I don't know," Sabae admitted. "But I suspect if she believed any of the Ithonians had survived, Kanderon at least would be hunting the city out of something other than fear."

"I suspect you are correct," Zophor said. "And likewise, there are quite a few mighty magical weapons in existence already— many in the vault at Skyhold, in fact, so it seems strange that might work up so many elder great powers into such a frenzy."

Zophor gently tapped a wooden finger on the table, contemplating.

"Regardless of what the reason is," he said, "I tend to take the opinions of the elder great powers more seriously in this case. They might tend towards the conservative and cautious, but they have one and all survived far more than us younger powers, which is worthy of respect. And while your grandmother may be an ephemeral like the two of you, it is your family that is the true great power, not any individual member of it."

Zophor finished his cup of tea, then set it deliberately down on the table.

"There have been curious floods, these past few years," he said. "Coming from upstream, rather than the sea. The first were small, starting about five years ago, and they only raised the river a finger-width or less. Of late, they've been raising it several feet, and have been coming closer and closer together. They've been occurring almost daily of late. They appear to be originating from Lake Nelu. Do you know it? It's a vast shallow lake a few days travel upstream from here. No one lives up there, and few venture that far. It's supposedly cursed."

Sabae's pulse sped up, but she tried to keep her expression calm. Lake Nelu was the fourth site, and this was far, far too big a coincidence. Sabae was, abruptly, certain that they'd found Imperial Ithos.

"I have to say, to my embarrassment," Zophor said, "that I didn't connect the floods with the hunt for Ithos until both agents of Kanderon and Havath arrived in force in my demesne. While the floods awoke quite a lot of curiosity among the citizens of my city, they caused relatively little damage, and scrying into Lake Nelu has seldom had much luck— which, I had assumed until recently, had to do with its thin aether."

"You didn't send an expedition to look?" Talia asked.

Zophor raised an eyebrow as he poured himself more tea.

"My dear barbarian child, the farther north you travel in this forest, the more dangerous it gets. And I am not the only great power on the Ylosa. Lake Nelu is the Mage-Eater's territory, and none live or venture there save the foolish and the foolhardy. I am far more than her match, for the Mage-Eater is one of the weakest great powers in direct combat, but she never ventures this far downstream, and I am loath to waste lives by sending my servants after her," Zophor said.

Sabae knew of a lot of great powers, but she'd never heard of one called the Mage-Eater before.

Another great branch arm descended from above and dropped a small package on the table.

"I believe that today is your belated birthday celebration, is it not, Talia?" Zophor said. "It isn't much, but I simply can't allow you to leave without some Tsarnassan fermented tea of your own. I do hope you enjoy the rest of your belated birthday celebrations."

Sabae, recognizing the dismissal, rose and gave Zophor a little bow. Talia quickly followed suit, thanking the lich for the tea.

Sabae's own cup was still two-thirds full, while Talia's was already empty.

As they turned to go, Sabae paused and looked back at Zophor.

"I can't help but imagine a scenario," she said, "where, perhaps, after you separated our two groups, another of your avatars might have shown up to speak to the Havathi?"

Zophor smiled at her. "You know, Sabae, you remind me of myself when I was young in some ways. Tricky beyond your years, and with little interest in toadying up to the powerful. There was even something of a physical similarity— we might have reasonably been mistaken as cousins."

"I've heard rumors you threw away your old body when you were done with it," Sabae said, cautiously.

Zophor frowned pensively. "I did, yes, but I somewhat

regret not giving it a more dignified funeral. I don't regret becoming a lich, and I might have despised my old body, but it served me well enough, and deserved better. And I mean no insult to you by comparing us— it was not hideous, nor malformed, it merely… didn't fit me. Others found it appealing enough, I suppose."

He took another sip of his tea.

"If we were to contemplate a scenario like the one you postulated," Zophor continued, "then it would only be sensible if I offered the Havathi the same information. I may be powerful, but the Havathi Dominion is mighty enough to give me pause in the way few other nations would, and to do otherwise would be to court deep offense. Which, hypothetically speaking, I would seek to avoid."

Sabae nodded. "Thank you for indulging in my little game of hypotheticals."

"I feel tempted to extend it even further," Zophor said. "Perhaps the Havathi, when approached, might be less polite than you two. And perhaps I might well recognize the borders they plan for their Dominion in the future include my demesne in it. And though I would, in this hypothetical, be averse to opposing them directly, well… hypothetically, it's quite easy for guides to get cold feet, for rot to be found in boats, and for supplies to be misplaced. Hypothetically, it could cause a delay of, oh, at least a day, while hypothetically you might be able to get started as soon as tomorrow."

Sabae smiled and gave the lich another, deeper bow.

Talia followed suit, once she'd finished Sabae's tea.

"Oh, and Sabae?" Zophor said. "Next time you speak to your grandmother, pass my regards, and thank her for steering her storms clear of my demesne. It was quite thoughtful of her."

CHAPTER TWENTY-SIX

The Fallen Moon

"I don't care what anyone says," Captain Grepha said, "the Mage-Eater is *not* a great power. She's not even a mage! Or intelligent, for that matter!"
Talia exchanged a slightly baffled look with her friends at the argument between Alustin and Grepha.
Hugh and Godrick had outdone themselves— they'd found a restaurant at the very top of one of the city-trees. It had individual dining platforms that jutted above the canopy, giving a view of the entire Ylosa River delta around them. To the south, you could see all the way to the open ocean.
There were at least three of the strange storms visible in the distance. The revelation that Sabae's grandmother had created them, or at least was guiding them, wasn't a huge surprise, but it was intimidating, to say the least. The differences between a great power and even a powerful archmage were terrifying.
"The Sleeper Beneath the Sands is neither a mage nor intelligent," Alustin said, "but it's unquestionably one of the mightiest of the great powers."
"Or a named power, if yeh go by that classification scheme," Artur interjected.
"I don't," Alustin said, "though I also don't consider the category of named powers entirely useless. Just unnecessary. There are hardly enough of them on the continent to warrant their own category— it's debatable whether any great powers on the continent even deserve being in it other than the Sleeper in the Sands or the Listener in the Silent Straits."
Talia honestly would have been fine with a quiet little event, but Hugh and Godrick had rented out the largest of the platforms and had invited over a dozen of the Radhan from the *Cormorant*, which was still docked below. It was all paid for on Alustin's nearly bottomless operations budget, apparently.
They wouldn't have been able to snag the tables, but there'd been an unexpected cancellation. Talia suspected it hadn't been coincidental. Zophor might be acting for his own political reasons, but Talia certainly didn't mind benefitting from that.

"What about the Wanderer?" Hugh asked from his seat next to Talia.

"She's been dead fer centuries," Artur said.

Alustin gave Hugh a strange look, though.

So did Talia, for that matter— why was Hugh bringing up a children's tale?

"The Sleeper is an ageless unkillable sunmaw capable of devouring the populations of entire cities," Grepha said. "The Mage-Eater has killed, what, maybe a hundred mages?"

"Ninety-three, over the last decade, from what the guides I hired tell me," Alustin said. "Plus around another fifty non-mages. The latter number would be higher, but few non-mages venture that far upriver, and no-one has lived there in, well, living memory."

"How many mages have you defeated in battle?" Talia asked.

"And how many have you defeated outside battle?" Sabae asked.

Alustin ignored them both.

"Oh, and by the way— the leader of that Hand of Swordsmen you just met was Qirsad Vain, wielder of Ashspine. She's one of the most dangerous members of the Sacred Swordsmen— you should fear her nearly as much as the Mage-Eater, to my mind."

"What is the Mage-Eater, exactly? Ah'm not quite clear on that bit," Godrick said.

"It's a storming tigress," Grepha said.

There was a moment of silence at that.

"Someone explain how a tiger can kill nearly a hundred mages," Sabae said.

"Same way a tiger kills anything else," Alustin said. "Attacks from behind, crushes your neck in a single bite. They can kill bears and gryphons, so humans are just small game in comparison. The Mage-Eater's not even the only man-eater in this jungle, just the only one that specifically targets mages."

"Ah thought tigers usually avoid people," Godrick said. "And how can the Mage-Eater even tell the difference between mages and non-mages?"

"Most tigers do avoid people, outside the Ylosa River delta," Alustin said. "The only time that normal tigers attack people is when they've been injured and can't hunt more dangerous prey. It's different in this delta, though. I have no idea why they attack humans more often here. Maybe it's something to do with the brackish water of the delta, or maybe it's just learned behavior?"

Talia started to speak up at that, but Alustin interrupted her. "And no, humans are nowhere near the most dangerous game. We're much more dangerous as hunters than as prey. And to answer your question, Godrick, all cats can see into the aether to some degree, so they can actually see your mana reservoirs and such. Most just don't care."

"How do we even know that?" Hugh asked. "And will I…?"

Alustin speared another bite of fish from his plate. "The answer is, as with so many things, grossly unethical and disturbing experiments by the Ithonian Empire. And no, Hugh, you won't."

Talia assumed Hugh was asking about his sphinx eyes there.

"So the Mage-Eater…" Talia said.

"Was badly injured when she was younger by a mage," Alustin said. "The few confirmed sightings of her report a massive burn scar running from the left side of her mouth down across one shoulder. Tigers may not be fully sapient, but they're certainly intelligent enough to hold a grudge. She's hunted mages ever since. And while your average tiger eats the prey in its entirety— often including the bones— she sometimes just eats the liver and then abandons the corpse near where she killed it, as if to taunt people."

"Still, that's a ridiculous number of kills," Sabae said. "Especially of mages."

"Magic doesn't do you any good if you don't have a chance to use it," Talia pointed out. That was basic combat doctrine for the non-mage members of Clan Castis.

"It's not even that many for a man-eating tiger," Alustin

said. "Man-eaters usually kill a person a week to feed, which over the course of years can often add up to far, far more victims than the Mage-Eater's known kills. I suspect she's killed many more than we know about, as well. Tigers are among the smartest non-speaking creatures, and they're capable of learning and adapting their hunting strategies remarkably quickly."

"I still refuse to call a tiger, no matter how dangerous it is, a great power," Grepha said.

Alustin shrugged. "You don't need to. Zophor did, and honestly, the only real qualification you need to be a great power is to have other great powers acknowledge you as such."

Grepha just glowered at that.

The rest of the evening went by quickly. The Radhan stayed for a little dancing. Talia monopolized Hugh for most of the evening, otherwise only dancing with Artur and Godrick once each. Sabae, meanwhile, danced mostly with Dell, but to Talia's surprise, she also took turns with Tollin and Yarra. They seemed to have gotten over the ridiculous drama, at least for the evening.

The musicians played somewhere down near the kitchens, but the music was somehow magically carried up to them. Talia wasn't sure if they were using some sort of enchantment or if they had a mage among their number doing it.

Probably the latter, but she didn't care enough to find out.

The Radhan cleared out just after sunset, leaving just the six of them. Seven, if you counted Hugh's spellbook, which Talia most certainly didn't.

The sailors probably would have stayed longer, but Captain Grepha herded them all away, which Talia was grateful for— she liked them well enough, but it was good to have some quiet time with her friends.

After the Radhan had all descended, her friends gave Talia her belated birthday presents.

Alustin hadn't gotten her anything, but then, he never got any of them birthday presents. Talia didn't mind, though—

he'd done more than enough for them over the years.

Artur gave her a book filled with biographies of different singular battle mages— those who either had unique affinities or affinities that had been warped somehow, like her own. She'd heard of a few of them, like the Wanderer, but others, like the Kettle, were completely new to her.

Sabae gave her a set of sturdy gloves. They were fashioned out of the hide of some heat-resistant creature or other— the seller wasn't quite sure, but you could stick your gloved hand into a candle flame indefinitely and not feel the heat. Across the knuckles was sewn a thick band of bone, which would deliver a nasty punch, or serve as ammunition for Talia.

When it was Godrick's turn, he handed her a trio of novels that Talia was immediately excited to read— almost all of her reading lately had been from those dry philosophy texts Alustin was forcing on her. They were more interesting than she'd expected, but still, they weren't exactly thrilling.

"Ah've got ta' admit, ah actually picked those up today," Godrick said. "Ah originally was gonna give yeh some more lockpickin' hairpins, because yeh went through 'em so fast, but ah felt awful about yer hair, and partially responsible."

Talia hugged him. "I don't blame you at all, Godrick. You're a good friend, and you've got nothing to feel bad about."

"Actually," Hugh said, "I've been meaning to bring up something about that. Alustin, warlock-awakened enchantments contribute more to resonance cascades, don't they?"

Alustin nodded at that. "Hence why your spellbook probably triggered the cascade in the first place."

Hugh nodded at that. "I noticed something weird about the *Rising Cormorant*'s enchantments while I was fueling them— I think they're in the process of being awakened by a warlock. I'm pretty sure one of the Radhan is pacted to the *Cormorant.* It's not aware at all yet, so it's pretty recent."

Everyone took a moment to let that sink in.

"That could definitely have contributed to Talia's

resonance cascade," Alustin said. "And, uh… give it a few decades, and that is going to turn into a seriously impressive ship."

"That also explains why Yarra and Tollin's families aren't competing over its captaincy," Sabae said. "The warlock pacted to the ship must be the one being groomed to be the next captain! Unless Captain Grepha is the warlock?"

Alustin shook his head. "According to what we know, Captain Grepha helped build the enchantments— at least to the extent of providing her pressure affinity for use, like Godrick did with his scent affinity for Hugh's stink-eating marble."

Talia turned to Godrick. "See, now you definitely can't blame yourself for me getting hurt."

Godrick shrugged, then gave her another hug.

"Pressure affinities are a thing?" Talia asked.

Before anyone could answer, Hugh's spellbook fluttered above the table, and dumped around ten pounds of mixed salt and crushed insects in front of her. Not for the first time, Talia refused to imagine what else the book was keeping in its extradimensional storage space. The salt and insects looked fairly fresh, though— several of the insects were still twitching a bit.

"How… thoughtful," Sabae said, struggling not to laugh.

Talia just glared at the spellbook, which was giving her a hopeful look. It finally wilted and slowly flapped away.

"It's really trying to figure out the whole apology gift thing," Hugh said. "It's, uh… not quite there yet."

Talia just snorted at that.

Finally, it was Hugh's turn to give Talia her present.

"I got this for you even before Midsummer," Hugh said. "Kanderon helped me pick it out for you. I thought about getting you something else today, because I was pretty sure it was a good present for you as a friend, but I wasn't sure if this was a good present for you as a girlfriend, but Godrick told me I was being an idiot, and I'm rambling and I'm going to shut up now."

Talia gave him an affectionate look, then opened her present. It was an old, battered book with a cover made entirely of laminated bone. Faded letters on the cover read simply *Raultha's Ossuary*.

Talia flipped it open to find page after page of intricate drawings of skeletons of a dozen different species, cross-sections of specific bones, and long discussions of different uses for bones by bone mages.

"This is amazing, Hugh!" Talia said, and kissed him on the cheek.

"It's also banned in at least a dozen city-states and the Havathi Empire," Alustin said. "Raultha was a peerless scholar and mage, but he was also an absolute madman. He believed that you could calculate moral outcomes mathematically, which among other things, led him to decide that it was more ethical to remove bones from animals via vivisection than killing them for their bones. He was said to have kept a boneless drake alive in his lab for nearly two years at one point, in constant agony."

"Ah guess ah'm not sleepin' tonight after hearin' that," Godrick muttered.

"I should also note that he tried to become the first bone lich," Alustin said.

"Did it work?" Talia asked.

"Thankfully, no," Alustin said. "Especially considering that it would have taken the bones of literally tens of millions of humans and animals to finish his blueprints. Heliothrax caught wind of his plans and ended him, destroying most copies of the Ossuary. That last was probably unnecessary— there's nothing too insane in there. It's mostly just banned for Raultha's monstrous reputation."

Talia flipped through the pages, tons of new ideas for bones to add to her necklace already running through her head.

"How did his whole calculating morality thing work?" Sabae asked.

"It didn't," Alustin said. "I have no idea how many different thinkers have attempted it over the years, but it almost always leads to monstrous conclusions, like the idea that parents should be allowed to abandon or kill crippled children to make their own lives happier, or that suffering is the greatest enemy and should be defeated by killing all life."

"I'd much rather calculate the yield of explosions than calculate morality, so you don't need to worry about me turning into a monster," Talia said.

Alustin just sighed at that.

Soon after, Alustin began covering the nearby glow-crystals with sheets of paper he pulled from his tattoo to block out their light.

When he was done, he frowned, apparently dissatisfied with how much light was still coming up from below, and started constructing what looked like a tower made of paper.

"I'm going to go talk to Sabae really quick," Hugh said.

Talia nodded, and joined Godrick and Artur to watch Alustin build his weird paper tower.

"Do either of you know what he's up to?" Talia asked.

Godrick shook his head. Artur smiled, but refused to say anything.

Talia glanced over at Hugh and Sabae. Hugh's spellbook was hovering next to them, and Sabae was listening intently as Hugh gestured repeatedly at it. Talia suspected that Hugh was using the spellbook's ability to block scrying— he hadn't told her what he wanted to talk to Sabae about, but it was probably serious.

After Alustin's paper tower had grown to around fifteen feet or so, Sabae and Hugh returned to the group. Sabae looked thoughtful, but just shook her head when Talia started to inquire.

Within a few minutes, the paper tower grew twenty feet up from the platform. It was around ten feet to a side, and a series of flying buttresses connected to each of them. Between the walls of the tower and the buttresses, a narrow staircase wrapped its way around the tower to the top.

"Well, are you coming?" Alustin asked, and began walking up the stairs.

The group hesitated, except for Artur, who started up the stairs immediately. Talia expected the stairs to buckle beneath the huge mage immediately, but they hardly even moved.

The rest of the group followed behind a bit more cautiously.

"Why not just lift us all up on a big platform, if you wanted more altitude?" Talia asked.

"I'm not actually lifting you with my magic," Alustin said. "The tower is structurally sound on its own."

Everyone except Artur gave him skeptical looks, and the paper mage chuckled. "You'd be shocked at how strong paper can be if you fold it right."

More paper began flooding out of his tattoo, and it spread outward from the tower, just below the platform at the top, eventually creating a wide shield to block the light from below.

"Don't step on that part, it's not structurally sound," Alustin noted.

"So… what are we waiting for?" Sabae asked.

Alustin just smiled and pointed to the north.

Talia was waiting patiently for her eyes to adjust when Hugh gasped. She looked over at him, but he didn't even notice, he was looking so intently northward.

"Starting already, is it?" Alustin said.

Finally, after what felt like an eternity of staring into the dark, with the only light coming dimly from below and from the lightning flashes of the distant storms, Talia began to see it too.

Glimmers of golden light were escaping from the forest to the north of them. As Talia watched, it slowly began to grow brighter and brighter, until the trees to the north were illuminated from below nearly as brightly as the city below them. The delta channels were outlined brilliantly, and Talia could see how they slowly converged, and where dry land started to appear in larger quantities to the north.

Hugh stepped over and wrapped his arm around her, and Talia leaned her head against him.

No one spoke for what felt like an eternity, they just watched the gentle shifting of the glowing river to the north.

Finally, to Talia's irritation, Alustin spoke up— the paper mage wasn't exactly good at handling quiet.

"It's some sort of freshwater algae that lives only in the Lower Ylosa River and in Lake Nelu," he said. "On nights with particularly low tides and strong currents from upstream, it can sometimes reach all the way to the city itself. On those nights, the inhabitants dim all the glow-crystals of the city, to let it be illuminated from below."

No one bothered to respond to him.

Talia didn't know how long it had been after that when Hugh stiffened beside her.

"Uh… there's something to the east," he said. "Something big."

Everyone turned to the east.

Talia didn't understand what she was seeing. It looked at first as though the moon had started to rise, but it looked disorientating and wrong, somehow. She realized, with a start, that it was hovering just above the land and was in the midst of tearing through the east-bound storm.

"Ephyrus," Alustin said.

Talia blinked and realized that what she'd thought was the moon was a jellyfish of truly immense scale. It had to be a third the size of the city below them. Its flesh was slightly translucent, and she could see flashes of lightning through it. Its hundreds of tentacles reached nearly down to the treetops, and lightning occasionally crackled between them.

The great jellyfish lunged halfway out of the thunderstorm but then seemed to stall. Even from this distance, Talia could see a great wind spring up, one that tore entire branches off the trees below it, and slowly forced the immense creature back into the storm.

"What was that thing?" Talia asked.

"Ephyrus, the Fallen Moon," Alustin asked. "It showed up in southeastern Ithos three hundred years ago and has roamed its storms ever since. It's always been one of the most inscrutable great powers, but I've never heard of it coming this far west before."

"My grandmother was never up to… whatever she's up to, before," Sabae said.

The storm slowly closed over Ephyrus again, and it was lost to sight.

Talia leaned in a little closer to Hugh, and his arm tightened around her.

The six of them returned to their inn soon after that, the mood of the evening a little overwhelmed by what they'd seen. Talia would normally be impressed by watching the paper tower dissolve and be sucked into Alustin's tattoo in far less time than it had taken to assemble it, but she just kept glancing south, in case Ephyrus might reappear.

The sight of Zophor at night did shake her out of the pensive mood a bit— the streets of the city were well-lit, and descending down from the canopy was a truly spectacular sight. The trees seemed even more immense than they had been during the day, somehow, and the bridges and markets of the city took on something of a festival air, with musicians and illusionists entertaining the crowds.

As they descended the stairs, Talia looked behind her. At the back of the group, she spotted Artur and Sabae whispering about something, Hugh's spellbook hovering just behind them. Talia somehow knew that it was blocking scrying again.

Talia pushed it out of her mind, and tried to focus on walking hand in hand with Hugh.

CHAPTER TWENTY-SEVEN

Upriver

Their expedition upriver set out just before dawn.

Their boat, the *Despondent Toad,* was a far cry from the *Rising Cormorant.* It reminded Hugh of nothing so much as a runty barge, with a wide, flat bottom. Its lower deck was cramped and dark, too short for even Talia to stand up straight. There wasn't anything approaching actual rooms below— just a couple of thin canvas walls dividing the sleeping area from the galley and storage areas. There weren't even proper bunks, just haphazardly strung hammocks.

The deck of the *Despondent Toad* wasn't much better. Much of it was crowded with gear, and there were several weak spots and even a couple holes in the deck. The one sail was dingy and threadbare, and the canvas awning above the back half of the deck sagged, and had more than its share of holes.

The captain of the *Toad* was equally as battered and worn as the ship. Captain Narsa, or simply Old Narsa, as everyone referred to her, was a wiry old woman with a huge shock of white hair and more wrinkles than should possibly fit on a single face. She was constantly spitting, making horrible noises in the back of her throat, and glaring at everyone near her.

Other than Narsa, the ship's crew consisted of only four others. Her husband— a toothless old fellow who never spoke, but always had a smile for everyone— served as the cook. The remaining three were water mages that she'd hired— apparently on the condition that they never tell her their names, because she fully anticipated young idiots like them dying in the jungle. The only reason they'd come along was that they were being paid enough to not have to work for a full year afterward.

And, apparently, because they were idiots.

It somehow didn't surprise Hugh that Talia was immediately fascinated with Narsa.

Strapped to the sides of the battered, splintery railing were a number of long poles. When Hugh asked what they were for, Narsa cackled at him.

"When the aether gets all thin like bad soup, lad, how do you think we were going to keep moving upstream, eh? Not afraid of a little work, are we?"

This was, to Hugh's regret, the only ship Alustin had been able to arrange on such short notice. There was only a handful that went as far north as Lake Nelu.

It took most of an hour for them to pass all the way through Zophor. There were dozens of the mind-bogglingly huge mangroves that comprised the city, and Hugh's respect for the lich grew even more. He was somewhat glad he hadn't met and spoken to the lich like Sabae and Talia.

The *Despondent Toad* put on a surprising pace once it got moving at full speed outside of the city, propelled by the ship's water mages. Captain Narsa seemed rooted to the ship, as though she never intended to move from the tiller.

When they finally exited Zophor, Hugh could see at least a dozen of the great tree faces tracking their movement.

They slowed down a bit as they entered one of the countless channels upstream, between two thick stands of mangroves of a more modest size. It was high tide, so the waves lapped at the base of the branches. Somewhat counterintuitively, this was the most dangerous time to sail upstream on the Ylosa— the currents were more treacherous during high tide, and there were numerous submerged branches eager to puncture the hull of an unwary riverboat.

Alustin, of course, promptly had the four of them training again. Hugh and Godrick worked on controlling ice produced by Hailstrike, while Sabae continued her training with using both armor types at once. Alustin didn't want to risk damaging the battered riverboat with bonefire explosions, so Talia was restricted to practicing with her swarm of dreamwasps.

It started drizzling an hour upstream, and didn't stop the rest of the day. The rain was warm and fell in unpleasantly large droplets. Much of the abundant life of the jungle seemed to simply vanish, though Hugh spotted a few soggy looking flocks of parrots huddled together miserably. The river drakes were the only creatures that seemed to ignore the unseasonal rain, save for the crocodiles.

Training became a wet, miserable business.

A little after lunch— which was a sorry affair compared to Radhan cooking— they entered one of the storms that Sabae's grandmother had apparently sent throughout the region. Hugh could hardly tell where the rain ended and the river began, it was coming down so hard.

Captain Narsa had her crew take down the sail— too much risk of a strong gust driving them into the trees alongside the channel.

The canvas awning was little use against the rain, it had so many holes in it. The rain battered so loudly against it that you had to shout to be heard. Everyone but the two on-duty water mages and Captain Narsa hunkered down in the cramped belowdecks. Even there, the rain struck loudly enough against the ship that it was a struggle to be heard, so most of them curled up with books. Or, in Alustin's case, diagramming dozens of sheets of paper with elaborate spellforms and glyphs.

Talia somehow managed to struggle into the same hammock as Hugh. She was cutting off the circulation to his arm, but he didn't complain or try to free it.

He did try not to glance too often at the contents of *Raultha's Ossuary* as she perused it. There were a lot of profoundly disturbing illustrations and diagrams in it. Likewise, Talia pointedly didn't look at Hugh's spellbook, where he was rereading one of Kanderon's lessons on stellar affinities. There was a shocking amount of math involved, and Kanderon was insistent that Hugh needed to master it. Their spatial affinity took even more math still. He wasn't bad at math by any means, but he really wished he was as good with it as Godrick was.

The storm passed just as suddenly as all the rest, its trailing edge cut as though by a knife.

Within half an hour, the unpleasant drizzle from earlier had returned, and they started making slightly better time as the tide dropped. This far upstream, low tide was only about ten feet below the first branches of the mangroves— which didn't grow any higher than they had to, apparently.

By the time the *Toad* arrived at its camp in the evening, everyone on board was cramped, tired, and grumpy. Camp didn't make them feel particularly better. Spots of exposed land were still few and far between in the delta, so camp was just an old, sagging waystation built suspended between several large trees. It didn't look like anyone else had been there in ages, and the whole thing smelled strongly of mold. A determined enough child could probably batter its way through the walls of the wayhouse.

It was, apparently, the last time they'd get to sleep off the *Toad* for this trip. There were no other waystations farther upstream, and sleeping on land was considered too dangerous in the Mage-Eater's territory.

As they were docking, one of the mysterious floods raced through.

It only raised the water level by a foot or so, but that was enough to tear the ship loose from the waystation. One of Narsa's water mages almost fell into the river before Hugh caught him with a levitation spell. It took nearly twenty minutes to maneuver the *Toad* back into position and rig up a new docking tie to replace the one that had broken off the waystation.

It was after the ship was tied back up that Artur and Sabae chose to confront Alustin.

"Captain," Artur said. "Could yeh and yer crew wait on the *Toad* fer a bit? We need ta' have somethin' of a private conversation."

Captain Narsa didn't bother responding. She just spat on the floor of the wayhouse and led her crew onto the ship.

"Hugh, could you make sure this conversation is private?" Sabae asked him. "I'd appreciate it if you could have your spellbook do its thing and put up a ward as well."

Hugh's spellbook flew down from the rafters at his call, and quickly threw up its weird anti-scrying ability. As Hugh pulled out a stick of chalk to draw a ward, Alustin waved him off. "I can take care of the privacy ward, Hugh."

His arm tattoo lit up, and a swarm of paper began flying out of thin air near Alustin's hand. The papers assembled themselves in a ring filling most of the room, segments of a privacy ward drawn on each vertical sheet.

It was decent work, though a bit less elaborate than Hugh usually preferred. Alustin's prior claims about his wards were obviously correct— Hugh could see how easy it would be to have them function modularly, and achieve different ward types by switching out the relevant sheets of paper.

Hugh wasn't often impressed with others' ward-work these days, but Alustin's was excellent. Nowhere near Hugh's own, but excellent nonetheless.

"I take it there's something you'd like to discuss with me?" Alustin said. "I'm imagining it's nothing to do with Sica's ingenious food preservation methods or the like. No one ever seems to share my interest in comparative agricultural magic."

For all of Alustin's jokes, his gaze was sharp as it passed over them, and Hugh shuffled nervously as it passed him. Sabae had been alarmingly interested in what he'd told her about the intercepted messages his spellbook had been showing him.

She'd also told him that it was highly unlikely he was receiving them accidentally.

Hugh couldn't imagine why Kanderon would possibly be leaking sensitive messages to him, even if he was pacted with her. This was one of the few times he'd ever disagreed with one of Sabae's political assessments.

No one spoke for a long, drawn out pause, and Alustin calmly pulled out a wineskin from his tattoo to take a sip.

Hugh, Talia, and Godrick all exchanged confused glances. Hugh knew that Sabae had been suspicious of Alustin for some time now, but he still didn't exactly understand why.

"What are the Cold Minds, Alustin?" Sabae asked.

Alustin literally spat the wine out of his mouth.

He coughed a few times, stared at Sabae, then took another drink.

A deep one.

Finally, Alustin sighed and adjusted his glasses. "Where in the name of every single fallen mage did you hear of the Cold Minds?"

Sabae just crossed her arms.
"Ah don't appreciate yeh keepin' things like this from me," Artur said. "Ah've got no illusions about coddlin' mah son, not in times like these, but this is clearly important."
"They're the reason you're so worried about the return of Imperial Ithos, aren't they?" Sabae asked.
Alustin took another drink while everyone stared at him.
"Fine," he snapped. "Yes, they are. I'm warning you now, though, once you learn this, you won't be able to unlearn it, and your sleep won't thank you."
"Isn't all knowledge the sort you can't unlearn?" Talia asked.
Despite the tense situation, both Artur and Alustin chuckled at that.
"Ah think every teacher ever wishes that were true," Artur said.
Alustin's face quickly turned serious again, though. "If you really want to hear, I'll tell you about the Cold Minds. But I genuinely want you all to consider if you want to hear it. I've had nightmares about them for several years since I first found out about them."
No one moved, though Hugh was certainly tempted.
Alustin sighed again, then sat cross-legged on the floor. "Well, don't make me crane my neck up at you all."
Once they were all seated, Alustin ran his gaze across them all. "Artur, much of this is probably review for you, but bear with me. Do any of the rest of you know exactly what an aether construct is or how mana reservoirs work?"
Everyone but Artur shook their heads, though Talia was a bit hesitant about it.
"There are certain magical structures that bridge the gap between the aether and the physical world," Alustin said. "The most common of these are mana reservoirs, whether artificial or natural. Your mana reservoirs all exist primarily in the aether, though they're anchored to your mind in the physical world."
"The mind is physical?" Hugh asked.
Alustin nodded. "It's… a little complicated, but yes,

essentially. The mind doesn't normally have any existence outside of the brain. And before you ask how we know, the answer is, of course, disgusting, unethical, and terrifying experiments by the Ithonian Empire in its last days. That's nearly always the answer with questions like this. Anyhow, when you absorb mana from the aether and convert it into attuned mana, you then transfer it back into the aether into your mana reservoirs. I mentioned cats being able to see into the aether? They're seeing your mana reservoirs floating there, along with some other magical structures that connect with your brain that allow you to do magic. They're not there when you're born, but they form over the course of your life as you exercise your mind's eye, and then they fully congeal at a certain point in puberty. On an interesting side note, the—"

Artur coughed, and Alustin caught himself before he could go down a tangent. "Right. Artificial mana reservoirs are aetheric constructs that are anchored inside an enchantment. There are a few other unusual types of aetheric constructs, and there are certain magical materials that exist to some small degree inside the aether as well. Magical tattoos, like Talia's, also exist partially inside the aether."

"What about yours?" Sabae asked. "Are you storing things inside the aether, or…?"

Alustin shook his head. "Magic can't significantly affect the aether in any way except drawing mana from it. It purely acts upon the physical world. Magical tattoos are a whole complex topic, but there's really just an extra-dimensional space anchored to my arm."

Hugh had actually known that part, though Kanderon hadn't started him seriously studying their planar affinity yet, beyond a few texts covering some necessary background material.

"That's all a vastly shortened introduction to the topic," Alustin said. "But it about covers what you need to know to start on the Cold Minds."

Alustin lightly drummed on the floor, then took another sip of wine. Then, to Hugh's surprise, he passed it to him.

"There are two main ways universes die," Alustin said.

"The first, and more spectacular, is by going aether critical. I believe I told you about that last year. Growing numbers of mana wells lead to rapidly escalating levels of aether density, which leads to faster decay of the universe in question, in a never ending and rapidly accelerating cycle. Also produces demons as a side-effect— they're simply organisms adapted to hyper-dense aether."

Everyone nodded. Hugh took a sip of wine, then passed the skin to Talia.

"The other main way universes die is slower and more miserable," Alustin said. "Instead of happening over the course of millennia, it happens over the course of countless aeons. The universe grows colder and drifts apart, and one by one, the stars all go out, leaving only a frigid void filled with orphan worlds. These universes are where the Cold Minds are born."

Alustin shifted uncomfortably on the wooden floor. "Everything from here on I've learned from Kanderon and a few other sources with greater knowledge of other worlds than I possess. The Cold Minds are… similar to liches, in a sense. The process of becoming a lich moves considerable portions of your mind into the aether as an intermediary step to moving it into the substrate of your demesne, but not all at once. Cold Minds, on the other hand, have moved their existence entirely into the aether. It's… a traumatic process, from what I gather, and individuals who attempt it alone invariably perish. All known successful Cold Minds are birthed in universes dying of age and in darkness, and they're composite minds of entire civilizations attempting to escape extinction. Their only goal is survival, at any cost. It warps them, though. Minds aren't meant to exist without bodies, and Cold Minds are mad in a way we can't quite grasp. They must have been profoundly alien creatures to start with— all known Cold Minds predate humanity itself."

The wineskin finished its circuit, and Alustin took another drink before continuing. "Cold Minds drift in a sort of hibernation for aeons in their dead universes, growing ever madder over time, until they're presented with an opportunity to migrate to a new universe."

He drank again, then passed the wineskin to Hugh once more.

"When they're given that opportunity, not much changes at first. The initial incursion of a Cold Mind is just a simple disturbance in the aether— an irregular sphere around half the size of a person has been reported for several incursions. At first, it has little effect on the world around it, but within weeks it begins growing. A few inches in the first month, a few feet in the next. After about a year, they've grown to at most a league in size. So far as anyone knows, this is the stage in which they're attuning themselves to the aether of their new universe."

Alustin took a deep breath.

"Then they begin properly migrating into their new universe. The first sign is usually ice forming in the core of their incursion, as they begin draining away the heat and energy of their new universe. Second, magic begins to behave unpredictably or to fail. Third, within a month of the migration beginning, nearly every sapient being in their new home goes irreparably mad as the incursion swells at an astonishing rate. Perhaps one in ten thousand avoid this fate, if even that much. Most are dead within days. Dragon, human, demon, lich— it doesn't matter. It's not purposeful on the part of the Cold Minds— it's simply them leaking out of the aether into sapient minds. They don't really care about ephemeral creatures like us— and, to be clear, even liches and sphinxes are ephemeral compared to them. By the end of the second year of an incursion, the stars begin going out. Galvachren and other experts on the matter claim that the Cold Minds awaken for a brief spring during this period— that a simulated version of the civilization that they once were awakens in a twisted parody of all its former glory, and its inhabitants live out a few months or years of life unconcerned with and unaware of the costs. Then they finish draining the life and energy from their new universe, and they leave it as dead as their old universe, while they hibernate within it, patiently waiting for an opportunity to migrate again."

There was a long silence before Sabae spoke. “So that’s what you’re afraid of coming back with Imperial Ithos.”

Alustin nodded. “Kanderon and the other Skyhold founders built the Exile Splinter to cast Ithos out of our universe to die a slow, miserable death. They lacked the power to cut it free entirely— they knew it would return someday— but they never intended it to intersect with another universe. None of the Skyhold founders had any deep knowledge of the multiverse. They didn’t even know the Cold Minds existed. They’re hardly common, after all, or the multiverse would be a dead, lifeless place. It was simply an absurd, unlucky twist of chance that Ithos was sent hurtling straight towards a universe where Cold Minds hibernated.”

Hugh reached out to wrap his arm around Talia, feeling cold even in the jungle heat.

“So… what do we do?” Talia asked. “How do we fight them?”

Alustin laughed bitterly. “Fight them? You can’t fight the Cold Minds. They exist within the aether itself. It would be easier to fight the planet beneath our feet or challenge the sun. There is no stopping them, there is no slowing them, and there is no resisting them. Their desperate need to survive, and their crippling fear of death, has turned them into an engine of inevitable extinction. All we can do is hope desperately that they didn’t notice Imperial Ithos, and that they’re not following it to our world. And if they have, all we can do is flee, to seek another world through the depths of the labyrinths. If you can’t flee, kill everyone you love and then commit suicide. If there’s a small blessing, it’s that the Cold Minds cannot travel through the labyrinths. Whoever the Labyrinth Builders were, they were the only ones to have ever found any means of resisting the Cold Minds. They’ve been dead and gone for eons, though.”

Alustin dismissed his ward, calling the sheets of paper back into his tattoo.

No one had anything else to say.

The orange-gold glow of the river algae was far brighter this far upstream of Zophor. Mushrooms grew faintly green on the trunks of trees as well, though Hugh doubted anyone with normal eyes could have seen their light.

Hugh could have easily read in the light from the river, maybe even before his eyes started changing, but he didn't even bother trying. Instead, he just sat on the edge of the waystation's platform and watched the bats and nightbirds hunt moths and other night insects in the river's light. He could see the shadows of fish moving through the water, and occasionally something larger passed below the waystation.

He must have been watching the river for at least an hour when Talia joined him. She didn't say anything, just sat next to him and leaned against him.

He wrapped his arm around her, and tried not to think about Imperial Ithos.

CHAPTER TWENTY-EIGHT

Mage-Eater

On their third day traveling upstream they finally started to encounter land.

It wasn't much at first, just a few low-lying mudbars jutting inches above the water. The tides never reached this far upstream, so the salt-tolerant mangroves were quickly out-competed by less specialized trees. Likewise, the animals present changed drastically. There were no seabirds in sight, and the only tentacled creatures Hugh spotted were a few freshwater octopuses, none of which grew much larger than his hand. They frequently climbed up to the deck to hunt for insects. Godrick had slept in later than the rest of them, and he'd been awakened by a freshwater octopus climbing onto his face.

The rest of them, especially Artur, had gotten a lot of laughs out of the lingering sucker marks on Godrick's face. It had been the first real bit of cheer since Alustin had told them of the Cold Minds.

They got another laugh a short time later, when Hugh's spellbook attempted to give Talia another apology gift.

It was a massive flower, almost a foot across, and it had deep red petals that were as thick as a finger. It also absolutely reeked of rotten meat, and Talia almost vomited when the spellbook dropped it in her lap.

Hugh's spellbook apparently didn't have a sense of smell.

Captain Narsa laughed and told them that they smelled like that to attract carrion flies.

Talia just tried to throw Hugh's spellbook in the river after the flower.

One of the most unusual sights they'd seen had been the fisher spiders. Fisher spiders had bodies the size of a fist and legs that stretched the width of a dinner plate. They were a brilliant metallic green-gold and were unusually elegant for spiders that large.

They got their name from their webs, which actually draped down into the water below. They lived in colonies of dozens of individuals, and maintained huge webs between submerged trees. Fisher spiders ate primarily minnows, tadpoles, and baby octopuses. Anything bigger could easily escape their nets, but when something small enough got caught, the spiders worked together to pull it up out of the water.

Captain Narsa avoided steering the ship through the webs, mainly because they were a huge hassle to clean up.

They spotted their first tiger halfway through the day. It lounged on a thick tree branch a few feet above the water, and appeared to be dining on the remains of a river drake. It spared them only a single curious look, then dismissed them entirely.

It was only about half an hour afterward that they were

forced to take a detour.

At first, they just looked like low-lying, rounded islands in the main channel, each covered in moss and small flowering plants. Three of them were the size of oxen, while the fourth was the size of a large wagon. The largest rested right in the middle of the channel, and actually had a small tree growing at its peak.

"Mossbacks," Captain Narsa hissed, and the crew froze. The ship came to an abrupt halt, then slowly began backing away.

Hugh started to ask what was going on, and what a mossback was, when Alustin shushed him.

Then one of the little islands moved, and a head rose out of the water, water plants dangling from its mouth.

They weren't islands at all, they were turtles.

The creature stared nearsightedly at the ship for a time as it chewed, then began to shift and turn away. Then the largest turtle shifted, and its own head rose out of the water. It had a crocodile larger than Hugh in its mouth, dripping blood into the river.

Everyone stayed remarkably quiet until they'd backtracked to another river channel going upstream.

"Yeh get mossbacks all over the place east a' the Skyreach Range," Artur said. "Yeh don't tangle with them if yeh're sane. They can sprint faster than yeh can run over short distances, can bite through bone, and have tempers worse than any gryphon. They're damn near impossible ta' kill, if yeh were crazy enough ta' tangle with one. If yeh have to, yeh come with a lot a' mages, and yeh stay in the air ta do it, where they can't reach yeh. Ah've never seen one that big before."

"I've seen larger," Narsa said. "They only get hungrier and nastier as they get older and bigger."

It was nearly evening when they crossed into the Mage-Eater's territory. Narsa quickly outlined her rules for them.

No one was allowed to be on deck alone, and you had to stay several feet away from the railings whenever you could. Tigers preferred solitary victims, and you'd never hear or see them coming.

You were never more vulnerable than when you were relieving yourself, so no one was allowed to go off the side of the ship— they needed to use the chamber pot in the little canvas-walled chamber belowdecks, which quickly began to stink horribly until Hugh tucked his scent-eating glass marble into a pocket in the canvas wall.

There had to be at least three people on watch on the deck at all times while in motion, and anyone on deck had to wear a ridiculous party mask on the back of their heads. The masks could sometimes fool a tiger into thinking their target was watching them, and even the most daring man-eaters preferred to attack from behind.

Hugh drew a ward all around the decking, but Narsa seemed doubtful about how well it would work.

On the morning of the fourth day, there were muddy paw-prints on the deck of the ship, as though the tiger that had left it had passed straight through the wards. It was easy to see where the tiger— whether it was the Mage-Eater or not— had investigated the secondary ward leading belowdecks, before it had exited the ward the same mysterious way it had gotten in.

"Tree branch," Artur said, pointing up.

Hugh cursed at that— he'd made a rookie mistake with his ward, and the tiger could easily have crossed through his ward atop the massive branch that stretched over the *Despondent Toad.*

"She wasn't hungry last night," Captain Narsa said, seemingly unfazed. "Else she would have just torn up the decking to get around your ward."

"If that was the Mage-Eater and not another tiger," Alustin said.

Captain Narsa just spat over the side.

Hugh tried not to think about what could have happened if the tigress had been hungry.

By midmorning, the aether had grown too thin for the water mages to continually propel the ship upstream, so

Captain Narsa ordered the poles broken out. Each person poling had to be guarded by someone else while they were working— tiger territories were massive, and they were traveling deeper and deeper into the Mage-Eater's.

Even trading off their use in shifts, Hugh quickly formed blisters on his hands. Sabae's limited healing abilities were having trouble keeping up— though, to Talia's vocal irritation, no one other than the apprentices developed blisters. At the very least, it would have made sense for Alustin to develop blisters, but the paper mage had well developed calluses from training with the sword. They weren't exactly the same as calluses from poling, but they were close enough for short shifts.

At noon, another flood hit the boat. This one was considerably larger, and slammed the *Toad* into a tree jutting out of the river channel. Sabae was knocked entirely off the boat, but launched herself back onto it from the water before any crocodiles could take notice.

The tree-trunk put a crack in the side of the *Toad,* and it took nearly an hour of work before it was ready to go again.

Alustin spent the whole time they were delayed anxiously staring off into space, in the manner Hugh had learned to recognize as Alustin using his scrying abilities. After a time, Alustin started laughing.

"What happened?" Hugh asked.

"The Havathi expedition following us decided they preferred speed to safety, and just sailed right into our mossback friends. Didn't spot them nearly in time. They lost one of their ships, and at least five people, including two Swordsmen," Alustin said quietly.

"Anything from Lake Nelu?" Artur asked.

Alustin shook his head. "Nothing. I can still barely make it out with my scrying."

When the repairs were done, another problem reared its head.

One of the water mages was missing. After a short search, they discovered a set of muddy pawprints, and a few drops of blood on the deck trailing off into the water. None of them had seen or heard a thing.

Captain Narsa didn't say a word, just ordered them upstream.

CHAPTER TWENTY-NINE

Lake Nelu

There wasn't a main channel of the Lower Ylosa River. There was a main channel of the Upper Ylosa, north of Lake Nelu, but the lower Ylosa's countless braided channels simply connected and split seemingly at random, and there were literally dozens of them connecting to Lake Nelu.

According to Alustin, there had been plans to develop Lake Nelu, about sixty years before— a wealthy dragon had dreamt up a scheme to build massive farm barges, and turn the vast shallow lake into productive and profitable farmland. To ship the crops downstream, the dragon had planned a massive dredging project to create a wide main channel to Zophor. Everyone had predicted that would be the doom of the project.

Ironically, it had been the only part of the project that hadn't failed miserably. It had proven surprisingly easy to dredge a large channel starting at Zophor heading north.

The low aether density of the lake had made construction and agriculture highly challenging, and most of the more northerly crops the dragon had shipped in had failed in the humid climate. Huge numbers of workers had been lost to disease and predator attacks, and the whole project had finally been abandoned when the dragon was killed in one of Havath's early wars of expansion.

The dredged channel had filled in within a couple years of no maintenance.

The *Toad* was poling upstream, everyone tense and miserable, when they arrived at Lake Nelu. They poled around a bend, and abruptly found themselves on the edge of a vast, flat lake. The distance was obscured by mists floating above the water, but even if the air had been clear, it would have stretched almost to the horizon. The water lay perfectly flat and still, with countless thousands of lotus flowers in bloom floating atop it near the shores. Only the occasional dead tree or mossy hummock broke the surface of the water.

To get out onto the lake, however, required them to pass through an inexplicable column of midges. It spanned the mouth of the channel entirely, and loomed at least a hundred feet into the air. The tiny insects didn't bite, but they got in your eyes and nose, and everyone was thoroughly irritated by them by the time they broke through to the lake.

"Mating flight," Narsa muttered, then spat into the water.

Hugh decided, then and there, that he absolutely hated the jungle. It had been nothing but misery, bugs, and horrific predators.

"I hate the jungle," Talia muttered.

Hugh couldn't help but laugh at that.

They slowly poled out into the lake. The lake, despite its size, was incredibly shallow. There were many parts, even close to the center, where Godrick and Artur would have been able to stand with their heads above water, though the mud at the bottom was dangerously easy to sink in.

It was far easier to make headway here than it had been in the river— the current in the lake was nearly nonexistent. It wasn't too long before they cleared the lotuses around the edges of the lake and were out into open water.

"What happens if Imperial Ithos really is here?" Hugh asked.

"If what's here?" Captain Narsa asked. "Why would the lost capital of the Ithonians be in a place like this?"

The entire group from Skyhold turned to stare at Narsa in shock.

"Why are you all looking at me like that?" Narsa demanded.

Alustin shook his head and turned back to Hugh. "Two

things. First, I alert Kanderon, and she and as many Librarians Errant as are available immediately head this way. Second, we're probably going to start seeing the city begin to manifest. Bringing enough people who know about the Exile Splinter to the site where it was activated is going to cause its effects to collapse rapidly. Then we just need to hold out against the Havathi until Kanderon arrives."

"Hold out against who now?" Narsa demanded. "You never said anything about no Havathi."

"How are we supposed to do that?" Talia demanded. "They outnumber us, and once we drain our mana reservoirs, they win. Not to mention, the only platform we have to fight on is this old hunk of junk."

"Don't you be badmouthing the *Toad*, girlie," Narsa said. "And you still haven't answered my question."

Alustin turned to the old woman. "You help us finish this job, you'll be set to retire in comfort for life. And not the modest sort of comfort— the ridiculous ostentation sort of comfort."

"Looks like we're fighting the Havathi," Captain Narsa said.

Alustin rolled his eyes and turned back to them. "I'm guessing the Havathi will get here by tomorrow afternoon at the latest. We'll have to think of some way to defend ourselves from them in the meantime. And, if the city arrives, we'll need to figure out a way to defend the Exile Splinter as well. It's the highest priority target."

"And if the Cold Minds arrive with Imperial Ithos?" Sabae asked.

"Then there's no point to any of this, and we flee," Alustin said. "The Havathi Dominion won't have time to figure out the Exile Splinter in enough time to matter."

"There's really no way ta' stop them?" Godrick asked.

"None," Alustin said. "There's no amount of brilliant magecraft or brave heroics that will matter in the least against the Cold Minds. You run or you commit suicide."

"What in the name of Zophor's splintery arse are the Cold Minds?" Narsa demanded.

Alustin shook his head, and started setting up his magical instruments on-deck to take readings.

"In case you all are getting complacent, tigers can easily make it out to the boat. They're better swimmers than any human," Narsa said.

Hugh quickly turned his attention away from Alustin to watch the water.

It was about an hour later when Alustin finished with his readings. "This is it. This was the location of Imperial Ithos."

They were far out into the lake, now. Land was long-since obscured by the ever-present mists, and the only things to be seen were occasional drifting lotuses. Not that Hugh particularly missed the land— it wasn't much more than great heaps of mud sticking up out of the water with trees jutting out of it.

"Did the Exile Splinter just tear it out of the ground and leave this lake?" Hugh asked. "Are we going to get crushed when it returns?"

"I don't think so," Alustin said, pulling his communications diary out of his tattoo. "I think the lake must predate Ithos. The floods would be a lot bigger if enough land to fill the lake was phasing in and out."

"What happens if part of it phases into the same location we're occupying?" Talia asked. "Will we die horribly as our flesh merges with the ruins of Ithos?"

Alustin gave her a puzzled look. "What? No, why would it… that's a disgusting image. No, it'll just shove us out of the way."

"What's yer plan if the ancient Ithonians are still alive?" Godrick asked.

Alustin shrugged. "I highly doubt it, but if they are, uh… try and convince them we come in peace until Kanderon arrives to rescue us?"

"What kind of city do you think Imperial Ithos was?" Sabae asked. "Was it a tree city, or?…"

Alustin sighed. "I have no idea, and I need to alert Kanderon."

Artur cleared his throat, and Alustin leveled a glare at the stone mage.
Artur chuckled at that. "Sorry, ah just didn't want ta' get left out a' the annoy Alustin with questions game."

The day seemed to drag on interminably. The lake around them was beautiful but unchanging, save for the drifting mists. Every now and then, a fish would leap and make a splash, but for the most part, the only noises were the distant calls of birds and drakes around the edges of the lake. The sunlight was muted by the thick mist.
It was beautiful, and a relief from the jungle, but it was hard to enjoy the peaceful lake with everything hanging over their heads. Between the Havathi, the Cold Minds, and the Mage-Eater, Hugh was constantly on edge.
Part of Hugh found it ridiculous that out of all the threats, the Mage-Eater was the one that bothered him most. Havath was the single most powerful nation on the continent, and the Cold Minds were… he didn't even know what to think of the Cold Minds. He simply couldn't wrap his mind around them. The Mage-Eater was just an oversized cat. The other two should be the far greater weights on his mind.
Neither of them, however, had murdered someone on the same boat as Hugh without anyone even noticing.
No one talked much, because on top of the stress, their voices carried oddly over the water of Lake Nelu.
Well, aside from plenty of complaining and muttering from Narsa's hired mages. Hugh still hadn't caught their names. The captain was apparently entirely serious about her "no names" rule.
It was approaching twilight when Kanderon wrote to him through his spellbook.

I am on my way, Hugh. Endeavor not to waste my investment in you.

Kanderon didn't answer any of his responses.
Hugh frowned, and went to go see what the others were

doing.

"Do yeh know what sort a' labyrinth Ithos had?" Artur asked Alustin. "It wasn't a mistform labyrinth, was it?"

Alustin shook his head. "It was a standard tunnel labyrinth. These mists are natural, I believe."

"Yeh believe?" Artur asked.

"I mean, it is somewhat unusual that they don't seem to burn off during the day," Alustin said.

Hugh wandered over to Talia, who was firing dreamwasps into the water. Hugh still thought they should be called dreamflies, but everyone else preferred Godrick's name for them. Dreamfire's bizarre effects were oddly muted when it struck water— it mostly just resulted in bursts of odd-colored steam.

"Should you be using your mana up like that?" Hugh asked her.

Talia sent a series of dreamwasps at a lotus, then sighed. "My mana reservoirs will refill by the time the Havathi arrive, but I suppose better safe than sorry. I just hate this waiting."

Hugh glanced at the lotus, which was dissolving into liquid. It looked as though someone had painted a lotus using colored oils on the surface of the lake.

He wrapped his arm around her. "It's pretty miserable, isn't it?"

"You can say that again," Talia said, and leaned into him. "I think I understand why dreamfire does all sorts of weird things when it hits, by the way."

"Oh?" Hugh asked.

"It turns out that those boring philosophy books Alustin assigned me aren't entirely useless. Remember that whole bit where affinities are intersections between axes that describe physical properties? And how dream and a handful of other affinities are axes rather than nodes? Well, so far as I can tell, dreamfire acts to unmoor the properties of its target along the dream axis, which intersects anything that, well, shows up in dreams. There's no telling what new node it will land on instead. The whole fire part of dreamfire just serves as a sort of… targeting apparatus for the unmooring effect, I guess? It governs how the unmooring travels through solid objects, at least. If I had learned to manifest a separate dream sort of attack, it would cause the unmooring in an entirely different way. No one's ever manifested dream lightning before, to my knowledge, but if they did, the unmooring effect would travel in the way lightning travels, rather than traveling the way fire travels," Talia said.

"That kind of makes sense, in a really weird way," Hugh said.

Twilight in the mists of Lake Nelu almost made up for the miseries of the jungle.

The sun was barely visible through the mists, but they were far enough east that sunset wasn't blocked by the Skyreach Range. It lit up the mists to their west in a stunning array of oranges, pinks, and yellows. And as the light of sunset began to fade, the lake began to take on an unreal, dreamlike appearance.

Once it was fully dark, the algae of the Ylosa River began to glow, lighting the mists from below in brilliant gold. It was like the sun had changed its mind about setting, and was rising straight up through the lake. Hugh could see surprising numbers of fish swimming about in the depths of the water, lit by the algae.

"How bright is the water for you, now that you have weird sphinx eyes?" Talia asked.

"About as bright as the full moon," Hugh said. "I could definitely read by it. What about for you?"

"About as bright as the crescent moon," Talia said. "I can find my way around by it, but I couldn't read by it."

Hugh wanted to come up with something romantic to say, but that part of his brain felt like it was worn out at the moment, so he just leaned in to kiss Talia, because it seemed appropriate at the moment.

Or, he started to lean in, then stopped.

There was a building out in the fog.

Or at least the shadow of one, jutting out of the lake.

Then another, followed by a third, and within moments, dozens.

"Do you see those buildings?" Hugh asked.

"No, where?" Talia asked.

Hugh shaped a spellform in his mind's eye— the one for the starfire beacon spell that he'd used to light their way through the storm. While for the most part he wasn't supposed to alter starfire spellforms, this one had a fairly simple series of lines that determined the distance Hugh could ignite the beacon at. If Hugh tried igniting it near them, it would just reflect off the mists and blind them, but at a distance, it should work.

The starfire beacon ignited out past the closest of the buildings, at the outer limit of Hugh's range. It took considerably more mana than usual to project it out so far, but Hugh had mana to spare.

"What are you doing?" Alustin shouted. "Why are you?"

He trailed off as he arrived by Hugh and Talia, and the others quickly followed, attracted by the yelling and the starfire beacon.

"Imperial Ithos," Alustin finally said. "There it is."

The shadow buildings stretched around them as far as the light could reach. Hugh could see dozens in the relatively small area lit by the starfire beacon. Each of them jutted up out of the water on a veritable forest of columns. They were all sturdy, impressively built structures, but they weren't blocky or monolithic— there were countless windows, arches, and balconies decorating them. Graceful arching bridges connected the buildings to one another. There were few proper streets, but docks ran down to the water, making it clear that transportation had all been by boat.

The shadow buildings, curiously, didn't seem to cast shadows of their own, and Hugh started feeling disoriented as he looked for them. Not a horrible, intrusive sort of disorientation like the Listener in the Silent Straits had given him. This was a more natural disorientation brought on by looking at something that didn't make sense to your eyes.

When the shadows of the buildings started to appear, Hugh was relieved for a moment. It was as though they were draining from the buildings into the water.

Then patches of stone in shades of orange and pink started appearing in the air as the buildings of Imperial Ithos began phasing into their world.

"Ah," Alustin said. "We, uh... might have an unanticipated problem."

Everyone turned to look at him.

"It's not the Cold Minds, is it?" Hugh asked.

Alustin shook his head. "Nothing so lofty. More, uh... there's going to be a rather large flood here in a moment from the water displaced by an entire city phasing into existence, and we're right in the middle of a rather crowded neighborhood. Also, there's a building in the middle of our ship."

CHAPTER THIRTY

Shadow Architecture

Almost immediately after Alustin spoke, the whole ship lurched to the side, hard. Everyone save Alustin was thrown to the deck.

Hugh picked himself up and spotted great patches of stone seemingly growing in midair where their ship had been. He could feel the crystal structure of their minerals, and he could feel where they simply... not ended, but protruded off into some other space that he couldn't reach with his affinity sense.

The ship kept accelerating until it was no longer intersecting the shadow buildings anywhere. As Hugh looked around, he could see that holes were starting to open up in the water where columns stretched down.

Massive ripples began racing through the water as more

and more of it was forced aside by the city phasing into existence.

"Everyone find something to hold onto!" Alustin yelled. "Captain Narsa, get to the tiller!"

"Don't order me around on my own boat!" Narsa shouted, but she was already moving towards the tiller.

"I just scryed, and the buildings towards the center of the lake are massive!" Alustin said. "There's a major surge of water heading our way right now!"

Narsa started shouting orders at the two surviving water mages, and they quickly summoned up currents of water to turn the *Despondent Toad* about.

A particularly large ripple rushed through the phasing columns and battered against the *Toad*, almost making Hugh lose his balance again.

"Hurry up, you idiots!" Narsa shouted. "You get us out of this alive, I'll double your pay and actually bother learning your stupid names!"

The mages had mostly gotten the ship turned around when Hugh spotted the wave in the distance. It loomed up at least fifteen feet into the air, and as the glowing wave rushed towards them, Hugh could spot it breaking over the silhouettes of the buildings, empty except for the steadily growing patches of stone inside them.

"The mast is too tall!" Sabae yelled. "It's going to catch on the bridges!"

"I've got it!" Alustin yelled.

Sheets of paper poured out of his tattoo in great numbers. Most immediately plastered themselves to the mast, but four of them had their glyphs begin to glow brightly, and Hugh recognized the designs of the paper that Alustin had used to shave Talia's hair with.

The four sheets shot forwards, and began slicing through the cables attaching the mast to the deck, then spiraled in towards the mast itself. They sliced through it close to the base almost without slowing down, then all went flying off into the water.

Hugh expected the mast itself to collapse, but instead it actually lifted up into the air. As it drifted off to the side of the ship, he spotted visible strain on Alustin's face, and Hugh realized that his teacher was lifting the mast using the sheets of paper attached to it.

"You'll be paying for that, you daft mop!" Narsa shouted at Alustin.

"That won't be a problem," Alustin said. "I can assure you of that."

Behind them, the light of the starfire beacon vanished as the wave engulfed it in an explosion of steam, leaving them only the light of the lake below.

The mast went crashing into the water off to the starboard side of the ship moments before the wave hit them.

Hugh's last thought before the ship surged forwards was, inanely, that the floods must be the reason why the lotuses had mostly been shoved to the edges of the lake.

Hugh was thrown off his feet again, but caught himself with a levitation cantrip.

Which was a terrible idea.

The ship rushed out from underneath him, and he would have crashed into the water if Artur hadn't grabbed him in midair and pulled him back down to the deck.

The *Toad* was rushing forwards faster than it had ever been intended to go, and it was shaking as though it were about to fall apart. The water mages were trying to keep it steady and lined up with the canal they were rushing into, but it was hardly much wider than the ship, and slightly misaligned from the direction of the surge. Within moments of the *Toad* entering the canal, it slammed against the shadow building on their port side, and the railing on that side of the ship shattered into splinters.

"You're paying for that too, you great idiot stork!" Narsa yelled.

"Fine, just steer!" Alustin yelled.

Despite everything, Hugh was genuinely shocked to see Alustin so stressed.

The ship scraped against the side of another building again as it rushed forwards, tearing apart what remained of the port railing.

"Bridge!" Sabae shouted from the front of the vessel. "Artur, Godrick, duck!"

The ship rushed underneath a bridge that was two-thirds shadow, one-third veins of stone. It would definitely have taken off Artur and Godrick's heads if they hadn't listened, and it did tear off the canvas covering for the back of the deck entirely. If Alustin hadn't cut off the mast, who knew how much damage it might have done to the ship?

"Three-way intersection up ahead!" Alustin shouted. "Get ready to turn hard to port!"

Hugh looked ahead, seeing the intersection Alustin was talking about illuminated in the glow of the lake. They were heading straight at an especially large building with one corner protruding straight towards them like a sword. Said corner was already mostly phased in, with only a few patches of shadow breaking up the stone. It actually looked like the starboard-side canal was a shallower turn, but the port side canal was better aligned with the wave.

"Now!" Alustin bellowed, and the whole ship protested and threatened to shake itself apart as Narsa forced the tiller and the water mages pushed the ship to port.

Hugh held his breath, convinced they were going to break apart on the corner of the building.

They barely made the turn. The starboard side of the *Toad* slammed into the side of the building and was dragged along it for half a ship-length. Great chunks of the decking and the upper starboard hull tore loose, and Hugh felt a brief burst of pain in his cheek as splinters flew across the deck.

Then they were aligned with the new canal, and hurtling forwards again.

Around them, Hugh watched as the patches of stone in the air grew larger and larger, veins of stone racing together to connect them. His crystal affinity sense felt as though it were on fire as countless tons of stone phased into reality in every direction.

The ship gradually started to slow, and Hugh realized that the surge of water had largely passed ahead of them.

Finally, the *Toad* drew to a halt, looking even more

despondent than ever before.

There was a clattering, and Narsa's husband poked his head out from belowdecks. He gave their surroundings a slow, suspicious stare, then slowly retreated back below. A moment later, he reappeared just for long enough to throw Hugh's grumpy spellbook out from belowdecks.

Hugh really didn't want to know what that was about.

He climbed fully to his feet and walked over to the port side, carefully stepping over splinters of the railing. The *Toad* was floating only a foot or so away from one of Ithos' buildings.

Hugh reached out with his affinity sense towards the stone of the building. At the same time, he reached out with his hand, placing it half on stone and half on shadow.

The stone just felt like stone. Cooler than he'd expected, but not strange in any particular way. It appeared to be granite, but with an absurdly high feldspar content, causing its unusual pink shade. The orange stones he could see were similar, just with a slightly different mineral composition. If Hugh had to guess, all the stone around them must have come from the same quarry.

The shadow, meanwhile, didn't feel like… anything, really. It was almost precisely the same temperature as the air, maybe a little cooler, and it didn't really have a texture. It just felt like a force mage was pushing against his hand there.

Hugh could feel the stone spreading beneath his hand, the textureless force of the shadow being replaced with cool stone.

"Imperial Ithos was called the 'City of Endless Sunset' in some of the oldest recovered texts," Alustin said from behind him. "We had lots of guesses why, but this wasn't what I was expecting. Buildings the colors of sunset, softened and blurred by the mists. Nights lit from below by the glowing water. It must have been gorgeous in its prime. It may have been built on the back of conquest and exploitation, but I think there's still something a little sad about Kanderon taking something this beautiful from the world."

Narsa snorted at that. "No matter how pretty it is, this city will smash us to bits if we try to weather another flood in it. I don't care how much you're paying me, we need to get off the lake."

Alustin just kept staring at the building in front of Hugh, and a slow smile spread across his face. "You're absolutely correct, Captain, and I shan't keep you here a moment longer than you need to be. You'll want to exit the lake by a different channel than the Havathi are entering it when you leave, of course."

Alustin summoned a sealed envelope from his tattoo, then sent it floating through the air over to Narsa. Hugh was pretty sure the paper mage threw an extra loop in there just to try and impress her.

"This is a promissory note for an amount that I believe you should find more than sufficient to cover my promises to you. It's quite heavily enchanted, so I wouldn't meddle with it or try to alter it," Alustin said. "Any respectable banking institution should be able to cover it, though I'd chose a large one, because a smaller one might not have that sum on hand."

"You're speaking as though you're not coming with us," Narsa said.

"We're not," Alustin said. "We're staying right here."

His smile grew even wider as he stared at the building.

CHAPTER THIRTY-ONE

The City of Sunset Without Light

"Yeh're insane," Artur said. "This plan is insane."

"Ah'm not sure we ever have a plan that isn't, Da," Godrick said, hauling his pack out from belowdecks.

"And you're all wasting time!" Alustin replied. "Ithos is already fading back into the Exile Splinter's pocket dimension, we need to hurry and get into one of the buildings if we want to go with it!"

"What if the Cold Minds are there?" Hugh demanded.

"Hold still," Sabae said, as she healed the deep scratch the flying splinter left on Hugh's cheek. "Do you want this to scar?"

"Oooh, yes!" Talia called. "I'd quite like Hugh to have a few more scars!"

"It won't matter if the Cold Minds are there," Alustin said. "They're not dangerous in the initial stages of an incursion while they're still attuning to the aether of a new world. We're in much more danger from the Havathi and the Mage-Eater at the moment."

"Get packing, people!" Alustin continued. "If you leave anything onboard the ship, you're not getting it back!"

It took them less than five minutes to gather their things—no one had been particularly eager to spread their belongings about in the dingy belowdecks of the *Toad.* Hugh almost forgot his stink-eating marble, but Godrick remembered to grab it for him at the last moment.

"Yeh're sure this is goin' ta' work?" Artur said.

"Mostly!" Alustin said.

"How comfortin'," Artur muttered.

"Ah mean, worst case scenario, we all get dumped in the water," Godrick said.

Alustin made a face at that.

"Ah saw that look, Alustin," Artur said. "Yeh're thinkin' a' worse outcomes right now. Let's hear 'em."

"Well…" Alustin said. "It could turn out that this is just a fluke, and the city isn't actually coming back to the world, and we get trapped in the pocket dimension for the rest of our lives. Or maybe the Cold Minds dominate the pocket dimension entirely, and we're immediately screwed. Or maybe we get stranded in the non-space between universes, each of us condemned to become a universe consisting solely of our own corpses. Or…"

"Ah've changed mah mind," Artur said. "Ah don't want ta' hear any more a' them."

Godrick laughed at that. It was, admittedly, a bit of a nervous laugh, but it was also just bizarre for him to be less stressed about a plan than his father was. Artur was just so used to being in control and prepared for any situation these days, and Godrick was simply more experienced with feeling like events were out of his control.

Godrick and Artur took turns helping the others and their luggage up onto the balcony next to the ship, then climbed up themselves, shaping footholds into the stone almost in sync with one another.

Captain Narsa shouted up at them as the *Despondent Toad* awkwardly lurched into motion. "I'll make sure to tell everyone you died just like you lived— as complete idiots!"

"I like her," Talia said. "I really do."

"Ah worry about yer role models sometimes," Godrick said.

Talia just smirked at that.

Alustin led their group deep inside the Ithonian building, which was curiously empty. If Godrick had to guess, it had been a minor palace of some sort. There were a few broken ceramic pots, a silver chandelier, and other goods, but there were no tapestries, rugs, or wooden furniture.

Nothing flammable, in fact.

Godrick tried not to think of the implications of that.

"Have you noticed how much denser the aether is right now?" Alustin said.

Now that Alustin mentioned it, Godrick did notice. It was

nowhere near as dense as it was in Skyhold, or even Zophor or Theras Tel, but it was still a massive improvement from the aether desert it had been.

"Either Ithos' labyrinth is phasing back as well, or the pocket dimension's stored up aether is leaking out along with the buildings," Alustin said.

Finally, Alustin settled on a small room on the fourth floor of the palace. It had likely been a solar or a study or something of the sort, and only had a single small balcony leading out. There were some miscellaneous bits of metal and glass in the corners of the room, but it was otherwise empty save for dust, of which there was far less than there should have been. It was as if the room had only been abandoned for a few weeks, rather than half a millennium.

"Pile everything up in the center of the room," Alustin said. "Hugh, craft a ward around us all inside the stone. And hurry, the city's already starting to phase back to its pocket dimension."

Godrick glanced at the nearest wall, and he could see new holes in the walls, where the building was starting to retake its shadowy form.

"What sort of ward?" Hugh asked.

"It literally doesn't matter," Alustin said. "Based on what I know of how the Exile Splinter works, including us in a ward like that should be more likely to make it consider us a part of Imperial Ithos, and take us with it back into the pocket dimension. It would probably work without the ward, it just increases our odds."

Hugh nodded, and Godrick immediately felt the minerals of the stone floor begin to shift and realign themselves. It was always a strange process to feel through his affinity senses— stone magic could reshape the stone itself easily enough, but Hugh fundamentally altered the character and structure of stone. Hugh most commonly worked with quartz, but this time he was reworking the feldspar in the stone— it was absurdly abundant in this granite. Godrick noticed that the resultant ward lines were harsher and more angular done in feldspar, and wondered how it would affect

Hugh's ward.

One of Godrick's feet shifted uncomfortably, and he looked down to spot a patch of shadow underneath his foot. He could still stand on it, but it felt bizarre and unnatural. He quickly moved his foot.

"Faster, Hugh," Alustin said as he set several glow crystals on the ground and activated them. "Everyone, get on the ground, make as much contact with the stone as you can."

Godrick frowned as he lay down. "Ah don't understand exactly how the Exile Splinter's decidin' what is and isn't a part a' the city. Wouldn't it just make the most sense if it targeted a certain geographic radius?"

Alustin shook his head. "It's part and parcel with the Splinter eating the memory of the city as well. It targets both the city and the memory of the city via an idea or description of what the city is. We're trying to fit ourselves into that description."

"Kinda like the description space nodes you have me learning about?" Talia asked.

"Exactly like those," Alustin said.

"Do you think there are actually any ancient Ithonian superweapons left inside the city?" Sabae asked. "The Tongue Eater ritual, maybe?"

Alustin shook his head, then paused. "The ritual spellforms, maybe, but they'd be useless on their own. The Tongue Eater required some sort of artifact, a repository for the languages it stole. The Tongue Eater repository wasn't in the city when Ithos was destroyed, and the last record anyone has of it was when the Last Emperor of Ithos tried to open it and release all its contained languages at once to plunge the continent into chaos as vengeance against the first Skyhold Council. Kanderon and the others stopped him, but the repository was lost in the battle."

"Ah heard the Last Emperor had a dozen affinities," Godrick said. Tales of the Last Emperor had been some of his favorites as a child. There were countless stories of the warlord trying to rebuild Imperial Ithos or get revenge for its destruction. Though, now he supposed that the Last Emperor had been trying to retrieve Ithos from its exile, not trying to rebuild it.

Funny how he'd never questioned Imperial Ithos' fate while under the Exile Splinter's influence. It had never even seemed strange to him that he didn't know where the Empire's heart had been.

"Only nine affinities, according to Kanderon," Alustin said.

"That's still absurd," Sabae said. "Has anyone ever had more than that?"

"Not many, but a few," Artur said. "There was the Two-Legged Army on the Gelid continent. At least a dozen different minds all trapped in a single body, each with their own affinities. Not much is known about them, but they're thought ta' have had at least thirty affinities."

"There was the Stone Arborist," Alustin said. "Had around twenty affinities, all for different types of stone. She wasn't a battle mage, though— she used her magic for art, crafted an entire forest of stone trees deep in the Skyhold Mountains. Most of them are still there, but it's nearly inaccessible. It's about as north as you can go without hitting the sea."

"How does developing new affinities even work?" Godrick asked. "Ah've never been entirely clear on that. Hugh's planar affinity is artificial, right?"

"Kanderon's planar affinity is artificial," Alustin said. "Hugh just got it from her. And there are three ways to do it, though each is terrifyingly complex and time-consuming, and involves countless failed castings of spellforms from your target affinity in an attempt to bud a new mana reservoir. First you can split an affinity, which is to develop a second affinity that's a more specific version of the first. That's what the Stone Arborist did from her original stone affinity. Developing an ice affinity from a water affinity would be another example. Then there's a conceptual jump, where you develop a closely related affinity to your own, like developing a dirt affinity from a stone affinity, or a copper affinity from an iron affinity. The last… well, that involves attempting to bud a new affinity that's nowhere near your own. That's what Kanderon did with her spatial affinity, and it's one of the most impressive achievements a mage can pull off. It requires a deep understanding both of the subject of the affinity and of the theory-craft of the affinity itself."

"What's the easiest artificial affinity to develop?" Hugh asked.

Godrick could feel Hugh's ward activate as his friend spoke.

"Cheese affinity," Alustin said.

Godrick couldn't help but laugh at that, as did everyone else.

"What?" Alustin asked. "I'm not joking, it really is. It's time consuming, sure, but otherwise it's a straightforward process. Takes about three years, but it's almost a guarantee."

"What do you even use a cheese affinity for?" Sabae asked.

"Aside from making cheese?" Alustin asked. "Well…"

Talia interrupted him. "Uh, Godrick? Your arm is gone."

Godrick glanced over and noticed, to his alarm, that his left hand and forearm had faded into shadow. He could still feel it, and when he moved his hand, the shadows shifted where his arm should be.

Gingerly, he touched his left hand with his right. He could feel the weird shadow sensation with his right hand, but the left didn't feel the right hand touching it at all.

"This is really weird," Godrick said.

The shadow started slowly creeping up his arm.

"Your dad doesn't have a mouth anymore," Talia said.

Godrick glanced over to see that the lower half of his father's head had turned to shadow, save for the tips of his beard. Artur glanced over at him and shrugged.

"Weird," Godrick said— or tried to. The sound came out mangled and garbled, and he poked around in his mouth with his tongue, only to not be able to feel half of the inside of his own mouth.

Godrick felt around with his fully shadowed left hand, and

where there was shadow on this side, he could feel stone on the other, and vice versa.

Then one of Godrick's eyes went dark. He blinked, and suddenly he was seeing double.

Out of his left eye, he still saw the room in the normal world. But out of his right eye, he could see the room in the pocket dimension. Everything that was shadow in the real world was visible in the pocket dimension, and everything that was visible in the pocket dimension was shadow in the real world. His mind could barely cope with what he was seeing for a moment, and he felt momentarily nauseous. He struggled not to vomit, though, because he really didn't want to deal with trying to figure out how that worked in his split state.

Everyone else was transferring over in the same bizarre piecemeal manner as well. The worst were Alustin's arm, Hugh's spellbook, and his da's iron ring. Alustin's tattoo seemed to have expanded and twisted, reaching out in directions that Godrick was fairly sure didn't exist at all. Hugh's spellbook seemed simultaneously normal and a great cloud of crystal sheets of paper the size of a house, with sheets drifting in directions simultaneously perpendicular to every axis of motion Godrick had ever seen before.

His da's ring just loomed the size of a small mountain.

Then, all at once, his vision snapped back together, and everything that was shadow became fully visible. The ring, the book, and the tattoo all looked normal again.

"Did it work? Are we through? Ah don't feel any different," Godrick said.

"Listen," his da said.

Godrick listened and heard… nothing. No lapping of water against the building's support columns, no frogs calling for mates or distant growls of predators.

It was quieter than anything Godrick had ever heard before outside of a silencing enchantment.

"We made it," Alustin said. "We've just left Anastis."

Godrick heaved himself to his feet, feeling a bit wobbly.

He glanced down at his hands, and noticed that the smallest finger on his right hand was still shadow. Then, as he watched, it popped into full visibility.

So weird.

He started to walk towards the balcony, only to pause. "Hugh, is it safe to cross the ward?"

Hugh nodded, looking disoriented and a little sick. "It's only a mosquito ward, it's fine."

"Are yeh alright?" Godrick asked.

Hugh nodded. "I'm fine, I just should not have watched my spellbook transfer over for as long as I did. I'm pretty sure I saw into its extradimensional space. Also, my link to Kanderon feels weird. Actually, it feeling like anything is weird, I don't usually feel much of anything from it. Just give me a minute."

Godrick nodded and stepped out onto the balcony, where he saw…

Nothing.

It was pitch-black outside of the light of the glow-crystals.

"Well, that's not ominous," Artur said, stepping beside him and leaning against the stone railing.

"Yeh know," Godrick said, "ah always thought ah'd never match yer adventures. Ah always planned ta' have plenty a' my own, but ah never seriously thought ah'd do anythin' like what yeh had by mah age. But ah guess this isn't half bad in comparison."

Artur gave him a long look. "Ah often wish ah had somethin' ta teach yeh other than magic and war, Son. Ah suppose there's sailin', but yeh get why ah was less than eager ta' take yeh ta' sea, right?"

Godrick nodded. There was a lot Artur had never told him about his years conscripted at sea, but what few stories Godrick's mother had been willing to share had been horrific. Part of Godrick didn't want to know more.

"Ah honestly woulda' loved it if ah could have taught yeh ta… ah dunno, brew ale or somethin'. Did ah ever tell yeh ah fantasize about that sometimes? Settlin' down, openin' an inn somewhere. Highvale, maybe? Always liked it there."

Godrick shook his head. He'd never heard this before.

"It's a pipe dream, and ah know it," Artur said. "That's the thing about power, son. Once yeh step on that path, the only way off is ta' step over the cliff. Archmages don't get ta' retire simply, son. They're always a' threat ta' someone, or someone thinks they can use them. Ah never had a choice about becomin' powerful, because it was either that or never escape the sea. And ah hate the fact that yeh aren't goin' ta' ever get that choice either. As mah son, yeh get ta' inherit all mah old enemies, and yeh have ta' prove yerself against mah image in everyone else's eyes. Yeh never just get ta' live yeh're own life."

"Trust me, ah know," Godrick said. "Ah've thought about it often enough. Ah've never resented yeh for an instant, though. At least, not that ah wasn't immediately ashamed a' myself fer. Yeh did yer best fer me, even after mum got sick. And yeh taught me better'n anyone else coulda'."

Artur wrapped one arm around Godrick's shoulders. "She'd be proud a yeh, yeh know. As proud as ah am."

Godrick just nodded, a little embarrassed.

It felt good to hear, though.

"Ah think ah can see somethin'," Artur said.

Godrick squinted his eyes, then he saw it too.

Patches of gold. They were faint, almost impossible to make out, but they were there.

"Ah think it's some a' the glowin' algae, got splashed up on the walls," Godrick said.

"Ah can't see an end ta' it. How big is this city?" Artur asked.

"We're about to find out," Alustin said, from behind them.

CHAPTER THIRTY-TWO

Movement in the Dark

To his own surprise, Hugh was actually wishing he were back in the jungle right now.

The others kept telling him that they were envious of his night vision, but Hugh wished he didn't have it at the moment.

There was no light in the pocket dimension whatsoever, save for their own and the occasional splashes of gold on the buildings that had been left there by the wave. It was rapidly fading and dying out of the water, and in the relative cool of the air in this place, but every time Hugh turned his head, they tricked his eyes into seeing motion. Every time he focused, it always proved to be nothing, but it was disorienting, and left him constantly on edge.

It didn't help how uncomfortably cool it was in the pocket dimension. Not cold, but cool.

"What would happen if you fell in the canal?" Talia asked, leaning against the bridge railing. "Would you just fall forever, or?…"

"Let's find out," Alustin said, then tossed his glow crystal off the bridge.

It fell about fifteen feet, bounced a couple times, then stopped.

"That's about where the lakebed would be," Sabae said.

"If I had to guess, anytime you tried to exit the edge of the pocket dimension, it would just feel like the way the shadows did," Alustin said. "They would just push you away."

Alustin levitated the glow-crystal back up to his hand.

"I suppose a claustrophobic extra-dimensional cave is better than an endless void," Talia said.

"Can we keep moving?" Hugh said. He really, really didn't like being out in the open like this.

Talia gave him a concerned look as they started back up,

but Hugh just shook his head, then resumed watching the shadows around them.

They trudged on and on through the empty city. It was disorienting seeing how undamaged most of it was— there had been no battle, no siege. The Exile Splinter had struck the city, and in a moment, it was gone, cast out from Anastis.

Hugh wondered what it must have been like. Had it struck in the day, turning the sky black? Had the population of the city panicked all at once? Or had it struck at night, and the realization of what had happened been a slower, more insidious thing?

Had the Ithonian Empire kept control of the city, or had it descended into chaos at once?

How long had it taken the last inhabitants of the city to die?

"It feels bizarre being able to read the street signs," Sabae said.

"The Ithonian language has changed very little in the past five hundred years," Alustin said. "We don't know what they did to it, but they somehow… stabilized it. Made it more resistant to change. Whatever they did, though, it's started breaking down over the years. A couple centuries ago, you wouldn't even find regional accents, and now you have accents as thick as the Lothalan one."

"We speak just fine, yeh're the ones who can't talk proper," Artur said.

Godrick chuckled at that.

Hugh didn't laugh at the emerging squabble, he just kept a watch on the dim lights of the dying algae.

They must have traveled a couple of miles when Sabae gasped. Not miles as the drake flew, of course— the bridges and canal walkways of Ithos were in no neat grid, but instead they went every which way. They'd probably only made it less than half that distance towards the center of the city.

"Anyone else really getting creeped out by this place?" Talia said, a moment after Sabae gasped.

Hugh gave one more look around them, then turned to see what they were looking at.

The wall of the nearby building— a concert hall, perhaps— was covered in carved graffiti. Half of it was illegible, but what Hugh could read was filled with mad rantings about darkness, the cold, and vows of revenge against whoever had banished the city.

Over all of it, written in letters gouged a full hand's length into the stone wall by some mage, was a single word.

Hungry.

Hugh shuddered and looked away.

They stumbled across the first ash pile not long after that. It sat dead center in a great courtyard. There were a few pits where the courtyard had collapsed downward into what should have been water, but none of them were close to the ash pile. It was huge, and filled with scraps of metal and deformed glass. There must have been countless fires ignited there, and Hugh understood exactly why they hadn't found anything even vaguely flammable in the city so far.

Hugh glanced over to Talia and saw that she was staring at the ash pile as though stricken.

"Is it just me, or is it getting colder in here?" Sabae asked.

"It's definitely getting colder," Alustin said. "It was probably only as warm here as it was because of the influx of warm air from phasing into Anastis. I imagine that it drops well below freezing pretty quickly in here. Hence the need to burn everything."

"Talia? Are you alright?" Hugh asked.

Godrick crouched down to pick up something out of the ash. He appeared puzzled for a moment, then gasped and dropped the object, staggering back.

"It's bone," Talia said. "The ash is filled with bits and shards of bone. I can feel them all with my affinity sense, Hugh. There are so many of them. And if I reach out to feel farther, I can feel more in the distance. And they weren't all burned at the same time, either. Some shards were burned decades later than the oldest ones."

Hugh's eyes widened as he understood what Talia was

saying.

"They're all human," Talia said.

She leaned over and vomited. Hugh stepped towards her, then stopped.

"Alustin," he said.

"This was a mistake," Artur said. "Ah shouldn't a' let yeh convince us ta' come here. Ah coulda' built us, ah dunno, an underwater bunker beneath the lake."

"Artur," Hugh said, his voice rising a little.

"It's too late to change our minds now," Alustin said. "And no matter how horrific this is, we're still alone here. Tactically speaking it's still our best place to wait for Kanderon's return."

"You're wrong," Hugh said.

Alustin turned to him, opening his mouth to reassure or argue with him, but Hugh interrupted him.

"We're not alone here. I just saw something moving out there in the dark."

Everyone reacted immediately. Sabae stuck her shield onto her arm and spun up wind armor, Alustin drew his sabre, and Godrick and Artur started to shape armor around themselves. Even Talia drew her dragonbone dagger and ignited it, despite the fact that she was still dry heaving.

Hugh already had his quartz crystal floating over his shoulder, so he didn't bother with anything else.

"How many? Did you get a good look at them?" Alustin demanded.

Hugh shook his head and pointed. "Just one, and it was a long ways down that canal."

"Ah can't even tell there's a canal that way," Artur muttered.

"Everyone be on your toes," Alustin said. "We need to be prepared to be attacked or ambushed at any moment. If these are actually survivors, after all these centuries, they have the home advantage."

"What if they aren't survivors?" Sabae asked. "What if it's some ancient, mad Ithonian lich or spirit?"

Alustin shook his head. “I’d be able to tell if we were in or near a demesne, and so would Artur. It’s something you pick up when you’ve visited enough of them. As for a spirit… well, I doubt it. Those are even rarer aether constructs than liches, and few are willing to turn themselves into one.”

Sheets of paper rushed out of Alustin’s tattoo, and formed a floating ward circle around the group. Hugh could tell this one was considerably more combat-oriented than the one Alustin had used in the waystation.

“Let’s get moving,” Alustin said. “We still need to find the Exile Splinter. Stay alert. Hugh, we’re counting on you to watch for threats.”

Hugh had no idea how long they walked after that. He honestly didn’t know whether it was minutes or hours. The only way he could tell time was by miles walked, and they had walked too many of those.

So much knowledge had been lost to the Exile Splinter, but they did know that Imperial Ithos had been the greatest city of its time, rivaling any city today. It must have had half again the population of Theras Tel, and sprawled out across leagues.

Even so, they must have gotten close to its center and the probable impact site of the Exile Splinter already, but they kept hitting dead ends. They had to double back several times, and once even had to lower themselves down into the canal. It was hard to keep your balance walking on the shadows, and Hugh was convinced that they’d be ambushed as they climbed out.

And all that time it kept growing colder and colder, and Hugh kept watch over the darkness. As the algae died away in the dry and the cold, the radius that Hugh could see shrank steadily.

More and more, he saw movements at the edge of that radius. Never in more than one spot at a time, and often there would be long gaps between, but sometimes it would be atop a building, sometimes in one of the canals. And always, the moment he focused, it would be gone. It didn’t simply disappear, or flicker. Instead it moved unnaturally fast, or held so still that Hugh lost track of it.

None of their affinity senses were picking up anything from their pursuer.

They avoided the ash pits, using Talia's affinity sense to keep track of them. It helped the others stay a little calmer, but Hugh could see the toll it was taking on her.

As they grew closer and closer to the city center, the buildings grew larger and larger, and the ruined bridges appeared more often. Graffiti became more and more common, until it was rare to see a wall without words gouged into them. Hugh did his best not to read any of it.

The crunching footsteps of Godrick and Artur in their stone armor were oddly comforting for Hugh. Artur hadn't grown it to his full size, and kept it about the height of his son's armor, but that was still massive.

Alustin and Artur began arguing about traveling through buildings, but both ultimately decided it was safer not to pen themselves in for whoever was following them.

Even Hugh's spellbook picked up on the news, and hung quietly around his shoulder.

Hugh's range of vision had grown close indeed when he had an idea. He waited until they reached the center of a huge courtyard, then gestured at everyone to stop.

He quickly reached out to the stone around them and crystallized a sound ward in it, so his voice wouldn't carry past the group.

"We're playing their game," he said. "They know the dark and we don't."

"So what do you propose we do?" Alustin asked. "We don't have the mana to light up the—"

Alustin slapped himself. Hard.

"I'm an idiot. I've still been acting as though we're in a mana desert, but we're not."

Hugh smiled grimly. "Everyone use that anti-glare cantrip I showed you."

"Ah don't need it," Artur said from inside his faceless armor. Everyone else, though, just nodded at Hugh.

He took a deep breath, looked behind them, and fired a starfire flare straight upwards.

It detonated in a great wash of light, briefly revealing the City of Sunset in all of its orange and pink glory. In that moment, the city looked as brilliant and as beautiful as any sunset.

And there, directly behind them, something screamed and fled.

Something a deeper orange than the city, with shadowy markings, and a hideous scar stretching from mouth to shoulder.

"It's the bloody Mage-Eater," Hugh said. "We're in an extradimensional pocket in a ruined city, and we're being stalked by a bloody tiger."

It wasn't funny, but Hugh couldn't help but laugh anyway.

CHAPTER THIRTY-THREE

Exile Splinter

They dispensed with stealth after that. Hugh ignited a starfire beacon as bright as he could manage it, and they marched straight down the widest bridges and broadest courtyards they could find. The Mage-Eater was lethal, but its greatest ally was stealth. Any of them could probably take the Mage-Eater in a straight fight. Even Sabae likely had a decent chance in a straight fight against the big cat. And here, in the ruined city, the Mage-Eater was out of its element. Its black stripes were perfect for breaking up shadows in the jungle, but in the even geometries of Imperial Ithos, they made it stand out even more.

It would be dangerous to get complacent, however. In any other city, the orange of the creature's fur would stand out, but here, it blended in somewhat with the stone of the city.

Still, the mood of the group improved significantly. They

had a known, concrete enemy now, not some mysterious phantom hunting them through the dark.

It was starting to get cold enough that Hugh was wishing for some extra layers, but since there was no wind in the pocket dimension, a brisk walk was enough to keep warm.

They didn't notice the city phasing again at first. What were a few extra bits of shadow in a city entirely filled with darkness?

It was only when Talia slipped and almost fell on a patch of darkness that they realized what was happening.

"Let's try and climb a building," Alustin said. "Try and get a better view of the city, so we can know which way to go."

"Ah don't think we have time," Artur said. "It's goin' a lot faster this time."

They all hunkered down again.

"Use that anti-glare cantrip of Hugh's," Alustin said. "Just in case the sun is up."

Phasing back into the world happened far faster than phasing out, and this time Hugh's disorientation wasn't nearly so bad.

To Hugh's surprise, it was still night when they returned to Anastis, and not even that late— maybe a little past midnight. The moon had risen, and though it was just a narrow crescent, it felt brighter than the full moon to them. The city that had seemed so ominous in the dark of the pocket dimension seemed more sad than anything else in the light.

Glowing water dripped down many of the buildings farther out from the wave that had already passed by, before they'd phased in fully. There was a clear gradient, however— the closer towards the center of the city, the less water there was to be found on the buildings.

"I'm going to get some scrying done," Alustin said. "See how our Havathi friends are doing."

While Alustin was doing that, Hugh took a deep breath of fresh jungle air, and enjoyed the sounds of frogs and birds, and of the water lapping at the city's columns.

Then movement caught his eye in the distance.

The Mage-Eater.

She stood atop a bridge, watching their group. The tigress was motionless, except for her tail, which slashed back and forth angrily through the air.

Hugh doubted he could hit the creature with a starbolt at this range, so he just watched cautiously.

The cat snarled once, then turned away. It leapt over the edge of the bridge, plunging into the glowing water of Lake Nelu. Hugh caught one glimpse of her swimming away, and then she was gone.

He guessed she didn't have any more interest in returning to the pocket dimension than he did. Only the Mage-Eater was smart enough to avoid it, whereas Hugh would be returning to it soon.

The city phased back even faster this time. Hugh didn't know if that was a good or bad sign, but he was careful not to watch his spellbook or Alustin's arm as they phased, which helped a lot.

"There's good news and there's bad news," Alustin said. "The good news is—"

"Nope," Talia interrupted. "Bad news first."

Alustin gave her an odd look at that. "Really? The point of giving good news first is to soften the blow of the bad news, like putting a pillow under someone falling."

Talia shrugged. "Yeah, that's the way they always do it in books, too. I'm feeling more ornery than usual. Bad news first."

Alustin shrugged at that. "The Havathi are closer than I'd hoped. They'll be here by early to mid-afternoon at the latest."

"And the good news?" Sabae asked.

"We're maybe a fifteen-minute walk from the Exile Splinter," Alustin said.

"Can we maybe get some sleep, then?" Talia asked.

"We'll set up camp close to the Splinter," Alustin said.

"How many days are we going to have to hold off the Havathi for until Kanderon gets here?" Sabae asked.

Alustin smiled at her. “Hours, I think you mean. Kanderon should be here by tomorrow night at the latest.”

Sabae stopped walking for a moment, then hurried to catch up. “There’s no way Kanderon can fly that fast. Nothing could travel all the way across the Skyreach Range that fast.”

“Thunderbringers can,” Alustin said.

Artur rolled his eyes at that. “And, what, there’ve been all a’ three people in history with large enough mana reservoirs and the necessary combination a’ gravity, force, and wind affinities ta’ fly fast enough ta’ be a Thunderbringer?”

“Why are they called Thunderbringers?” Hugh asked.

“They fly so fast it sounds like thunder, and they can actually shake houses and break windows by passing overhead,” Alustin said. “And there have been at least seven that I know of. None living today, though.”

Hugh whistled at that.

“Kanderon doesn’t need to go that fast to get here on time, not by a long shot. She is one of the fastest fliers on the continent, however, and she can fly for days on end, even sleep on the wing. Not something a normal sphinx can do, but it should be obvious by now that she’s no normal sphinx,” Alustin said.

“The giant crystal wings don’t give it away?” Talia asked.

They were still arguing about Kanderon’s powers when they rounded a corner and saw the Exile Splinter for the first time.

Hugh’s first reaction was disappointment that it didn’t glow. Ancient enchanted superweapons should glow. The Exile Splinter just hung there in the dark of Imperial Ithos, resting in the middle of a great plaza in front of a truly immense palace. The Ithonian Emperor’s palace, Hugh would imagine.

His disappointment rapidly faded as they approached it, however.

The Exile Splinter was a jagged, crooked, and

asymmetrical spike of blue crystal, three times the height of Godrick or Artur, hovering point down above the ground. Obscenely complex spellforms covered its surface and could be made out within its crystal structure.

And deep within the Splinter, at its highest point near the top, was a great beating heart of shadow.

Hugh tried reaching out to it with his crystal affinity sense, but it felt as though it were an inordinate distance away. The pattern of the crystal was irregular and twisted in a way that a crystal shouldn't be, as though the spellforms visible in the outer layers of the weapon were replicated at a level too small to see with the eyes.

"Look at what it's hovering over," Sabae said.

Hugh looked down to see what looked like a pair of massive bronze doors set flush in the ground, as though there was a great cellar below the plaza. Only, there would be nothing but sodden lakebed and sunken stone foundations down below, so…

"Ithos' labyrinth," Alustin said. "Sealed off by the Exile Splinter and used as its power source."

"Why is there a heart in the Splinter?" Hugh asked.

"I have no idea," Alustin said. "Kanderon has told me absolutely nothing about how she and the other Skyhold founders made the Exile Splinter. I don't think that's an actual heart, though— it looks like some sort of construct."

"Why didn't the Ithonians just destroy it?" Talia asked.

"Give it a try," Alustin said.

"Fine, I will," Talia said, turning towards the Exile Splinter.

Then she just stood there, staring at it blankly.

"Talia?" Hugh asked.

"What?"

"Weren't you going to try and destroy the Splinter?" Hugh asked.

"Was I?" Talia said. She seemed genuinely perplexed at that.

"Defense mechanism," Alustin said. "It can erase the memory of Imperial Ithos' location from the entire world, after all, so erasing someone's memory of planning to attack or damage it is nothing. And even if it was managed by accident, according to Kanderon it'd take a great power to even scratch it."

"So why do we need to defend it?" Sabae asked.

"Because while it can't easily be destroyed, it can be stolen," Alustin said. "At least, it can be moved once the pocket dimension collapses entirely, which won't be long now. Given that we're in it now with knowledge of the Exile Splinter, and the Havathi are going to be looking for it, I doubt it will even last out the next day."

"So why didn't the Ithonians cause the Exile Splinter to decay?" Talia asked.

Alustin held up his hands. "I presume because they were in the city when the Exile Splinter struck, but I honestly don't know, Talia. There's only so much Kanderon has told me about it, and I'm sure there's a lot she's held back. So, for now, can we please just set up camp? We need to all get some sleep, and then we're going to need to set up defenses."

Talia must have been as tired as Hugh felt, because she didn't even argue.

When Hugh woke in the palace room they'd claimed and fortified, it was already midmorning. Or, at least, it would be midmorning if they were outside of the pocket dimension. Talia greeted him with a cup of… truly unique tasting tea. Hugh didn't necessarily hate it, but it certainly wouldn't be his first choice to drink.

Most of the others, Hugh noticed, wouldn't touch the stuff.

Alustin was missing when he woke up, but he burst into the room with a huge smile on his face halfway through breakfast.

Then he frowned.

"What are yeh so worked up about?" Artur asked.

Alustin sighed. "Usually when I have a grand

announcement I have an attractive assistant or a mysterious but dashing ally to kiss in excitement. Becoming a teacher has really put a crimp in my style in some ways."

Artur rolled his eyes. "Just tell us yer news."

"Ah, right! There's no Cold Mind incursion in the pocket dimension. Our world isn't going to die horribly to sustain the illusory afterlife of some dead civilization for a few short years!"

"Well, that's just anti-climactic," Talia said.

Alustin gave her an incredulous look. "How is the world not dying anti-climactic?"

Talia started to answer, but Alustin just cut her off.

"On second thought, I don't need to know, and I'll just chalk it up to you reading too many ridiculous novels. We've still got an ancient magical weapon to defend from a ruthless expansionist empire, recall? And the phasing events are happening closer and closer together. They're almost hourly now. We've got maybe six hours until the Havathi arrive, if we're lucky. Probably sooner. We need to set up defenses, and we need to hope that we can hold out long enough for Kanderon to get here— and that she gets here before the Havathi are able to summon reinforcements of their own."

"Yeh're absolutely sure about the Cold Minds?" Artur asked.

Alustin nodded. "If there were an incursion, there would be signs my equipment could read in the aether. Moreover, if the Cold Minds were intruding, Ithos' labyrinth would have closed itself off. The labyrinths exist as much to stop the Cold Minds from migrating as they do to stop universes from going aether-critical."

"Well then," Sabae said, "since that's all settled, let's get to work."

CHAPTER THIRTY-FOUR

Playing Defense

When the first of the Havathi boats hit the outer edges of their defenses, Sabae couldn't help but laugh. It was more to release frustration than out of actual amusement. She'd felt entirely useless during the construction of their defenses, her only duty watching others' backs in case the Mage-Eater had slipped back into the pocket dimension at some point.

That wasn't going to be changing just yet, unfortunately. Setting an ambush was, frankly, boring from the other side.

The six remaining Havathi boats all sped straight out into the lake at top speed, propelled by far more water mages than the *Despondent Toad* had been. On top of that, the aether density in the area was steadily climbing, as more and more leaked out of the pocket dimension.

They hadn't, Sabae was sure, expected to encounter icebergs in a tropical lake.

Admittedly, they weren't very large icebergs, the largest only about half the size of the ships. Godrick had used Hailstrike to grow dozens and dozens of them in the canals whenever the city was phased into Lake Nelu. He likely could have grown them even larger with Hugh's help, but Hugh had been needed on his own projects.

Every time the city phased back in, the icebergs had been sent hurtling and crashing around the lake, and they were surprisingly hard to spot in the ever-present mists.

The leading Havathi boat didn't hit the iceberg directly, nor hard enough to smash itself to bits, but several mages and soldiers on the decks were sent tumbling into the water, and the ship was quite obviously not going to stay afloat much longer.

From her position atop a particularly tall Ithonian palace, Sabae enjoyed watching the chaos, at least until the city phased back into the pocket dimension.

Over the next two hours, the Havathi lost a quarter of their force without ever coming into contact with the party from Skyhold. Several mages and at least one Swordsman drowned as they abandoned their ships for the city— the canals were lethally dangerous with all the ice trapped in them. Much of it had already been forced out to the shores of Lake Nelu, but enough remained that it made the waves produced by the phasing events deadly to ships.

The city itself wasn't much better for the Havathi.

Talia and Godrick, working in concert, had hidden bones in pockets Godrick had grown inside the cobblestones. Alustin, using his farseeing affinity, let Talia know which ones the Havathi were passing near. The Havathi eventually learned the trick of it, and scouted their way with stone mages to avoid the bonefire traps, but not before Talia had killed quite a few of them with explosions from below.

Alustin's paper traps weren't as deadly, but they were far, far more common. The Havathi healers were kept busy taking care of countless burns and cuts from exploding paper glyphs.

It was Hugh, though, who really proved his worth.

Sabae had seen Hugh use his wards in battle before, but he'd always been rushed while completing them. They'd been spur of the moment acts of desperation.

These wards, though…

These wards were terrifying.

Like all their defenses, Hugh had started in at the Exile Splinter, leaving some of his most impressive work there. By necessity, the wards grew hastier and less terrifying the farther out they went, as Hugh had needed to construct them larger and more expansive.

Sabae had thought that Hugh's wards would just be a series of expanding concentric rings, but the city's design hadn't allowed for that, nor, apparently, was that actually optimal ward construction technique. An enemy wardbreaker only had to break circle wards in one spot to pass. Hugh had still used concentric circle wards around the

Exile Splinter, but nowhere else.

Hugh's wards, instead, were scattered strategically around the city, buried in the stone of bridges, narrow walkways, and the entrances of buildings that offered effective cover.

The sheer diversity of Hugh's wards was kind of astonishing. Attention wards shepherded the Havathi away from less defended and more open areas without them even realizing. Flame wards ignited anyone who stepped over them. Simple force wards sent them tumbling into the canals. Glass wards shattered bottles of who-knows-what carried by various mages as the wards blocked the passage of glass and only glass. Gold and silver wards blocked the passage of jewelry, gruesomely tearing out earrings and breaking the fingers of people wearing rings.

Wearing jewelry to battle was, of course, ridiculous, but Sabae knew that most battle-mages thought themselves above a lot of the common rules for soldiers.

The Havathi took the worst damage from the defenses the first time they phased into the pocket dimension with the city. Their positions became even more obvious to the Skyhold party, who were entirely hidden behind wards and shaped stone defenses. Hugh's wards became especially frustrating for them in the dark, because many of them were attention wards specifically built to split apart the Havathi war party, forcing them to spend valuable time reuniting.

Sabae couldn't help but notice how close together the phases were coming now. They were barely a quarter-hour apart on average, and the city was spending nearly as much time in Anastis as in the pocket dimension.

Sabae, meanwhile, just lurked inside the ward Hugh had built for her. It was a powerful attention ward that let her observe everything from atop the Emperor's palace tower without being noticed herself. It also had one secondary function she was even more excited about— it was a momentum magnifier. Just once, when she windjumped out of the ward, it would amplify the jump to speeds and distances far beyond what she normally would have been able to reach.

She just had to pick her moment correctly.

The fundamental principle behind nearly all their defenses remained the same— they were trying to delay the Havathi, not defeat them. Time was more important to them than killed enemies. They quite deliberately included obvious but time-consuming ways to evade or defeat their defenses, like the stone mages searching for Hugh's wards or Talia's bonefire traps. Thanks to Hugh's will-imbuing, his wards and traps were completely harmless to the Skyhold party, meaning they could move around far more freely if they needed to.

They only needed to wait until Kanderon arrived.

The Havathi, of course, decided not to cooperate.

They'd expected the Havathi to eventually come up with the plan of escaping the city into the canals while it was phased into Anastis and positioning themselves closer to the Exile Splinter unopposed in Lake Nelu. Given how much fiercer the defenses were towards the Splinter, they'd likely lose a lot of mages doing it, but it was the logical move.

They hadn't expected the Havathi to try it after only a single phase into the pocket dimension.

The time spent phased into the pocket dimension without the Havathi stretched longer and longer, until most of an hour must have gone by. With fewer Splinter-aware minds inside the pocket dimension, she assumed that the Exile Splinter's power must be less strained.

When it finally started to phase back, Sabae was fully expecting the Havathi to launch themselves from some sort of improvised magical platform onto the stones of the city, and for them to resume their slow, grueling advance.

What Sabae wasn't expecting, however, was a massive tower of vines and intertwined trees, stretching almost as tall as the Emperor's palace, and standing only a short walk away. The trees appeared to be the skeleton of the tower, while the vines lashed them together.

Several parts of the tower's base had been ripped and torn apart by the city's phasing, but it stretched across a fairly massive area, and there was more than enough to keep the slender living tower intact.

Sabae stared at the tower, aghast. Even for an elite magical force like the Sacred Swordsmen, this was ridiculous. The only way this could have been done was if…

Grovebringer. Grovebringer had somehow followed them from Lothal in time to face them. She suspected the vines weaving the trees together had been grown by the brash Swordsman with the vine whip they'd encountered in Zophor.

Sabae's initial panic at spotting the tower started to ebb as she thought through its implications. If they had built themselves a fortification, it seemed probable that they were planning a slow, cautious conquest of the city, with the tower there as a safe base to rest and heal in.

Sensible under any other circumstances, or if the Skyhold party's goal had been actually winning, rather than just delaying.

Later, Sabae would reflect that Talia would have probably been very angry if she'd heard what Sabae had to say then. She'd probably have a long-winded lecture about things you didn't say because they were asking for trouble, all of which she'd drawn from the novels she read.

"They're playing right into our hands."

That, of course, was when the tower started bombarding everything around them with spells.

Not least, what appeared to be a massive boulder of congealed volcanic ash hurtling straight towards Sabae's tower.

CHAPTER THIRTY-FIVE

Living Siege Tower

Sabae didn't wait around for the spell to land. Nor did she wait around to figure out how, exactly, the Havathi had seen through the attention ward around her. Instead, she pulled together wind-armor faster than she ever had before, and detonated all of it at once.

Straight down against the tower.

As Sabae passed up out of Hugh's momentum magnifier ward, she accelerated so hard she actually felt her eyes pressing back against her sockets, and her vision started to spot over. Below her, she could hear an eruption of sound as the lava bomb hammered into the tower. She barely kept herself from falling into a tumble in midair and losing control. Instead, she somehow managed to spin up a new set of wind armor.

As she slowed and reached the top of her ascent, Sabae found herself higher in the air than she'd ever been on her own. She could see the spire she'd just escaped crumbling down to the plaza containing the Exile Splinter. She could see a truly stunning array of Havathi spells tearing apart huge chunks of the city around it. She could see the entirety of Imperial Ithos spread out below her, on a scale that dwarfed even Ras Andis and Theras Tel. Something seemed odd about the layout of the canals to her, but she couldn't tell what. She could see the edges of Lake Nelu, which made the city itself seem small.

Then, as she reached the top of her arc and began to fall, she said something that, in retrospect, she was fairly sure Talia would also be angry about.

"How can this day get any worse?"

Then she looked up, and in the distance, rapidly bearing down on Lake Nelu from the west, she saw something that, unfortunately, was *not* Kanderon. Something she hadn't noticed at first, from the sheer shock of the living tower.

It was one of her grandmother's storms.

Hugh crashed into the hard cobblestones of the walkway, almost rolling all the way into the canal from how hard Godrick had thrown him. Hugh's floating quartz crystal somehow managed to impact his shoulder hard enough to leave a bruise, as did his spellbook as he rolled over it. He frantically turned over to look for Godrick, only to spot him staggering out of the collapsing palace, his magic the only thing still holding up the doorway. The instant Godrick was out, it collapsed in a cloud of dust and debris.

"Ah think the plan might a' gone a bit sideways," Godrick said, then started coughing.

"I think you're right," Hugh said, looking around. He couldn't see Alustin and Talia's position from where they were at, but Sabae's tower was simply… gone. He hoped she'd made it out safely.

Almost reflexively, Hugh started building a protective ward around the two of them. Godrick, meanwhile, was already constructing his stone armor, and putting the quartz faceplate into place.

"Which way should we go?" Hugh asked.

"Ah think we need ta' get ta' cover and regroup," Godrick said. "Then figure out some way ta' take down that tower."

"Works for me," Hugh said. "I…"

He was interrupted by a crack against his ward from something striking it. Seconds later, a tree was rearing up from the canal next to them, its branches reaching for his ward.

"We should run now," Hugh said.

Another arrow impacted the ward, this one already sprouting roots. The first tree was already pressing its branches against his ward, and Hugh could feel it wavering.

"Where?" Godrick asked. "We'll have trees growin' out

a' us no matter which direction we go."

"Not quite," Hugh said, then glanced down.

"I hate this plan already," Godrick said. "On three?"

Hugh's ward started to flicker.

"Nope," Hugh said. "Now!"

The walkway beneath them crumbled apart between the combined power of their spells, plunging the two of them into the lake below them.

Hugh would just be exposing them to arrows if he hit them with a levitation spell, so instead Hugh improvised a crystal spellform that pushed the falling rocks away from them so they wouldn't be injured by them. Godrick, apparently, had the same thought, because they went firing away with astonishing speed. One tore through the trunk of one of the new trees, while several more tore through nearby walls and columns.

They plunged into the water of Lake Nelu, and Hugh immediately dove down and swam away from the canal. When his breath was about to give out, he surfaced, finding himself in the dim space beneath one of the palaces of Imperial Ithos, floating between the columns supporting it. Fairly close by, he could see where the collapsing palace had punched through the foundation and down into the lake.

Godrick didn't surface at first, and Hugh started to panic, thinking that Godrick hadn't gotten his stone armor off in time.

Then Godrick bobbed to the surface a few feet away, armor still on him. The fact that it was floating probably had to do with the fact that most of the armor was ice, with a few patches of stone mixed in. Godrick held Hailstrike in one hand.

The whole palace above them shuddered. Hugh reached up with his crystal affinity sense, but the stone above them still seemed intact enough.

"Ah've got an idea," Godrick said through his faceplate, and touched the striking face of Hailstrike against the water. A floe of ice immediately began to grow around it.

"Are we making a boat?" Hugh asked.

"Not exactly," Godrick said, then explained his plan.

"Well, that's insane," Hugh said. "I'm all in."

Talia shielded her head with her hands, not that it would do anything to protect her from the toppling monolith.

Only it never struck.

She looked up cautiously, only to see the massive stone monument suspended no more than ten feet above her head. A series of white columns stretched between the cobblestones and the monolith.

Talia blinked in shock when she realized that they were made of paper.

"When it comes to paper," Alustin said, "It really is all about how you fold it."

She just glowered at her teacher's obnoxious smirk, until she felt the cobblestones shifting under her feet.

"Though, on second thought, we should probably move," Alustin said.

They'd sprinted out twenty feet from underneath the monolith by the time the cobblestones buckled and the monolith collapsed. It punched through the courtyard entirely, plummeting down into the lake below. The impact threw both Alustin and Talia off their feet. Alustin fell into a graceful roll and sprang right back to his feet.

Talia, meanwhile, crashed hard against the stone, leaving her with a lot of cuts and soon-to-be bruises.

She was still climbing back to her feet when a fireball detonated a short distance away. She looked up to see at least a half dozen more heading straight towards them from the living Havathi tower, as well as several arrows, a slow-flying snake made out of fiery ash, some sort of web of wires, and several more magical attacks she couldn't identify.

Not a one of them hit. They all were simply deflected in midair by a ward. Not one of Hugh's wards, but a great floating circle of paper nearly fifty feet across. Fireballs bounced off to crash into canals in an explosion of steam, the wire net simply fell harmlessly to the ground, and the arrow deflected to start growing into a full tree on a nearby bridge.

Grovebringer.

And then Alustin counterattacked. Hundreds of glyph-marked sheets of paper arced towards the tower. Most were deflected by other attacks or by magical defenses. The living tower appeared to have wards of its own woven out of vines, but they were taking a serious pounding from Alustin's exploding sheets of paper. At the same time, Alustin was covering himself in what looked like spellform-encrusted full plate made entirely of paper.

Talia had never seen another mage channel so many spells at once. It was absolutely absurd.

"You could be helping, you know," Alustin said. "That ward's one-way, it's not blocking your shots."

"My dreamfire bolts can't travel that far," Talia said. "I'm not exactly the longest-range battle mage out there. I'm definitely more of a middle-distance attacker. Unless, of course, you'd like me to use a siege spell right now."

"Dreamfire bolts, no, but did you really think your fine magical control was the only reason I helped you develop dreamwasps?" Alustin said.

Talia gave him a hesitant look, then manifested a dreamwasp. The green-purple spark hovered over her hand for a moment, then she launched it towards the living tower.

She was convinced it would go out before it made it a third of the way there, but it took almost no mental effort at all to maintain it all the way to the living tower, where it splattered harmlessly against the wards.

Or, perhaps not harmlessly. She could swear she detected an odd crunching feeling as the dreamwasp impacted the wards, as though it had taken a tiny bite out of them.

"And how many dreamwasps were you successfully manifesting at once before?" Alustin asked.

A wicked smile crept across Talia's face as dozens of dreamwasps began manifesting in front of her.

Then they exploded forwards.

The swarm of dreamwasps impacted a fireball first, which simply… froze. It tumbled to the ground, and shattered like ice across one of Ithos' bridges.

The swarm was diminished but hardly quenched by that, and slammed through another of Grovebringer's arrows. It sprouted into a tree in midair, but the tree was visibly rotting, and tore apart into sawdust when it impacted Alustin's ward.
Finally, they impacted the slow-flying ash-snake, burning away a large amount of its mass, though it reformed itself and kept flying towards them.

Talia began manifesting another swarm.

"You really don't need gaps in between manifesting dreamwasps," Alustin said. "You should be more than capable of manifesting them continuously."

Talia frowned at him, then tried it. Most of the dreamwasps flew off course or extinguished at first, but within a few breaths, Talia had a thin but continuous stream of dreamwasps flying forwards. Most impacted enemy spells, but a few started consistently making it through to the enemy wards.

And it was hardly using any of her mana.

"Not bad, Talia," Alustin said. "Dreamfire even in small amounts should wear down their wards quickly— it's hard to ward against something so erratic."

She glanced at the hundreds of sheets of paper intercepting enemy spells or detonating against the living tower, then scowled.

"Screw small amounts," Talia said.

The stream of dreamwasps began to swell, the numbers of the dreamwasps doubling, then tripling.

Talia began to laugh.

Though, if you asked anyone else, they'd probably describe it as a maniacal cackle.

Sabae was, to say the least, in an awkward position.

She couldn't actually fly, after all, so she couldn't stay up in the air. And considering the massive bombardment of spells coming from the tower, she didn't want to try to land somewhere near it, nor did she think she could successfully make it outside the range of the bombardment.

So she had, well, decided to land on top of the roof of the living tower.

She'd expected the vines and trees of the tower to immediately grab at her, but to her shock, she seemed to have landed unnoticed.

She didn't try to take immediate advantage of that fact, however. Instead, she took a long moment to look around.

The bombardment was focusing especially hard on areas Sabae knew Hugh had built attention wards in. She didn't know how the Havathi were spotting them, but they hadn't actually seen through them, or they would have just targeted the ones protecting the Skyhold party. Instead, they were indiscriminately firing spells at any attention ward in range.

There were already a shocking number of new trees sprouting across the city from Grovebringer's arrows, and great chunks of the city were being obliterated. The Havathi might claim to be the rightful inheritors of the Ithonian mantle, but they were clearly unconcerned with damage to the ruins— Sabae doubted they had any interest in anything but the Exile Splinter.

Sabae smirked. Or maybe Heartburner.

The whole tower shuddered, and Sabae almost overbalanced, but she caught herself by sticking her shield to the nearest protruding tree branch. When she'd recovered, she let the shield's magical grip on the branch dissolve, and crouch-walked over towards the edge.

Crouch-walking in wind-armor was *hard.*

The source of the explosions was, unsurprisingly, Talia and Alustin. The two of them were somehow going spell for spell against an entire bombardment from the tower.

Sabae swore she could hear Talia laughing, even from this distance.

Not wanting to get accidentally hit by a stray spell, Sabae stepped back from the edge— in perfect time to avoid getting crushed beneath a massive flailing vine.

Rather than dodge back, Sabae lunged forwards, affixing her shield to the massive vine, then letting it hurl her up into the air.

"Well, well, well," a voice said. "I thought I felt someone up here. Look who it is. Little miss…"

Sabae looked up from trying not to be thrown from the thrashing vine and spotted the vine whip-wielding Sacred Swordsman. She promptly ignored his obnoxious taunting, released her shield from the vine, and windjumped straight for him.

He instinctively lurched backward, tripping on one of his own vines, but he also sent quite a few others grasping up from the roof to block her path. Sabae detonated the wind armor around her right arm, sending her shooting away from a particularly thorny vine, then latched onto another with her shield for just a moment, long enough to change her direction.

She skidded to a halt on a tilted protruding tree trunk, then launched herself immediately up into the air to dodge another vine sweeping at her from the side.

Sabae needed to end this, and fast. Plant mages were definitely not a particularly good matchup for her, and she doubted she'd seen everything this particular Swordsman could do.

She detonated her wind armor again, but rather than looking for a more open path, she blasted straight towards the base of several vines. Based on the way they were moving, she suspected the mage had a lot more control of the tips of the vines than their bases.

They slammed together just inches behind her feet as she shot between them and tumbled across the ground. More were already rising between her and the enemy Swordsman, but rather than try to launch herself again, she set a windstrike towards the enemy mage.

It struck him full-on in the chest, sending him tumbling backwards.

Straight off the edge of the tower roof.

Sabae smiled grimly as most of the writhing vines either

collapsed or flailed wildly, but her smile almost immediately vanished as the Swordsman rose above the edge of the roof again, borne aloft by two of his own vines.

"You really didn't think that was going to work, did you?" the Swordsman asked. "Little flea, jumping around and thinking it can kill the dog on its own. You really have to—"

The Swordsman was interrupted by a mid-sized palace exploding behind him. The Havathi whirled to look at it, and Sabae immediately windjumped straight at him. He only had a moment to gape at the colossal figure of Artur with his battle-armor at full size before Sabae's shield adhered to his back, and both of them went hurtling off into the air.

Sabae couldn't help but think that Artur's armor looked rather strange when constructed from pink and orange granite.

The man's vine-whip flailed wildly at Sabae, dripping fluids that she was certain were caustic, but it couldn't manage to break through her wind armor before the two of them slammed into the roof of a nearby palace.

Sabae's wind armor absorbed most of the force of the impact for her, but the Havathi struck the stone face-first, with all her weight on top of him.

He didn't so much crash as smear.

Sabae staggered to her feet in time to see the fifty-foot armored form of Artur slam his enormous hammer into the side of the living tower. It tore through vines and trees like a shark through minnows, and the whole tower began to creak and shake ominously.

He wasn't known as Artur Wallbreaker for nothing, after all.

As Artur reared back for another strike, ignoring the bombardment of spells striking him, Sabae felt the wind begin to rise, and the first raindrops began to fall.

CHAPTER THIRTY-SIX

Perfect Storm

Growing ice thick enough for Hugh and Godrick to walk on was easy enough.

Growing ice thick enough and fast enough for them to run on it was rather more difficult.

Growing ice thick enough and fast enough for them to run on it while also being bombarded with spells from the living siege tower was, frankly, insane.

Hugh had run short on ways to describe escalating difficulty, if he was honest. The two of them only pulled it off working together.

They slid to a halt amidst the foundations of what looked like an Ithonian bank or something of the sort. Behind them, the ice bridge they'd crossed the canal on crumbled beneath the weight of a brand new tree, as well as what had looked like a lava bomb.

Hugh had no idea how the Havathi were still managing to target them while Artur was tearing apart their tower.

They'd expected this to be an easy way to work their way back towards the rest of their group, but the Havathi had been on them the whole time.

"That wasn't a lava bomb," Godrick said.

"It sure looked like one," Hugh said, catching his breath. Not so much from the run— Alustin's training easily had him in the best shape of his life— more from the stress of trying to hold so many spellforms in his mind's eye at the same time.

"It was congealed volcanic ash from an andesitic volcano, ah think."

Hugh gave him a blank look.

"Basically, there are two types a' volcanoes," Godrick said. "The kind that erupt liquid lava, and the kind that explodes. Abyla was a liquid magma mage, and if we'd been fightin' on basalt, she would have been even more dangerous. Andesite is a kind a' stone that yeh find in explodin' volcanoes."

"So more or less dangerous than Abyla?" Hugh asked.

"Differently dangerous," Godrick said.

"Lovely."

In the distance, there was another immense crash as Artur struck his hammer against the tower. This time, however, the tearing, ripping noises kept going.

"Hey, Hugh," Godrick said. "The tower's probably going ta' make fer a lot a' rubble when it falls, right?"

"Yes?" Hugh said.

"And a lot a' it is going ta' fall in the water, right?" Godrick asked.

"I guess so," Hugh said.

"Probably making a rather large splash, and some rather large waves?" Godrick said.

Hugh looked hesitantly at Godrick.

"Ah think we should maybe get out a' the water an up into the city now," Godrick said.

In the distance, the tearing and crumbling noises grew even louder.

"I think you might be right," Hugh agreed.

Talia had to admit, her celebration when Artur started tearing apart the tower was rather diminished when it started falling towards them. She even paused firing dreamwasps for a moment.

It wasn't an abrupt, complete collapse— it was a slow, halting fall as the vines and trees tore and shattered.

It would still crush her just as flat, however.

Then, before she could react, she was flying up into the air, lifted up by one arm.

She was already a good twenty feet into the air, moving rapidly sideways out from the direction of the tower's fall, when she thought to look back.

It was, of course, Alustin carrying her, his armor having sprouted great buzzing dragonfly wings, fashioned out of paper.

"Cover us!" Alustin shouted.

Talia smirked, then turned back to face the tower, in case any Havathi mages were escaping.

There were, unfortunately, quite a lot of them escaping, largely by air.

"Of course they have fliers," she yelled, as she started haphazardly blasting dreamwasps their way. "Why didn't they use them before?"

"It doesn't make much sense," Alustin agreed, as he landed them on a nearby roof. The wings and his armor looked like they were losing their integrity from flying in the light rain.

The tower impacted the city, crushing at least a dozen Ithonian buildings. Lake water and broken masonry were sent hurtling into the air.

Artur's massive armored form lumbered towards the fallen tower and the escaping Havathi.

"I still don't get how Artur's not a great power," Talia said.

"He's probably powerful enough to fit into their lower ranks, he's just never challenged another great power for recognition or territory," Alustin said. "He doesn't want the stress, though. You've got to be a little bit insane to want to be a great power."

Alustin sounded distracted as he spoke, however, and Talia knew he was scrying.

"I believe I've figured out why the Havathi didn't use their fliers until now," Alustin said.

"Why's that?" Talia asked.

"Because they were trying to delay us too. There's a small wing of Havathi dragons on their way now, ferrying more mages this way," Alustin said. "Also, there appears to be a strike force that hid outside the tower, and is currently cutting their ways through Hugh's wards protecting the Exile Splinter."

"Let's go, then!" Talia said.

Alustin shook his head. "I won't be able to fly there

carrying you in this rain— I'll barely be able to make it myself. Can I trust you not to get yourself killed, and to try and reunite with the others?"

Talia drew her enchanted daggers and smiled.

Alustin made it to the Emperor's plaza just as the full force of the storm hit.

He barely landed next to the Exile Splinter in time to keep his wings from collapsing, and rapidly covered his paper armor in sheets of waxed paper to protect it from the rain. He didn't worry about being attacked directly— he'd landed in the middle of Hugh's wards.

He hated having to do that— waxed paper was a hassle and a half to control. Of all the paper he kept in his tattoo, it was easily his least favorite to use.

"Alustin Haber," a voice said.

Alustin idly looked up at the Hand of Sacred Swordsmen facing him.

Unfortunately, he recognized them.

The average Swordsman only lasted a year or two in the line of duty. Any Swordsman was dangerous, but the veterans were by far the worst. The younger ones were often, well, idiots. Warlocks weren't common enough that you could be overly choosy when constructing a force out of them, and most weren't temperamentally suited for membership in an elite force of battle mages, simply because most people in general weren't.

Those that were temperamentally suited, however, were usually the ones that survived more than a few years.

And, unfortunately, every member of the Hand currently facing him was a veteran. Worse, he suspected all their weapons were fully sapient.

Amberglow. The Marrowstaff. Olstes's Hyphal. The Springcloak. Forgeheart.

The Havathi warlocks had names of their own, of course, but Alustin only ever bothered referring to most Swordsmen by the names of their weapons.

Amberglow and Forgeheart were the only two actual

swords among them, and the back of his head insisted that the Swordsmen really needed to change their name to something that acknowledged their wide range of weapons.

"Springcloak," Alustin acknowledged.

"This doesn't look particularly good for you, Alustin," Springcloak said.

"You know, one of you always says that to me. I think I might have some doubts in regards to the quality of Havathi judgment about that," Alustin said.

Olstes' Hyphal had already broken through four of Hugh's primary wards around the Splinter, leaving only two between Alustin and the Swordsmen. The living fungal armor wasn't the most effective direct combat tool, but it was terrifyingly effective for wardbreaking and siegecraft—the armor could sprout a fibrous mycelial network of astonishing size in short order, perfect for tearing apart just about anything, given a little time.

Unfortunately, magical fungal growths were also particularly effective against paper.

"It's usually traditional for us to attempt to persuade our foes to join us or surrender peacefully," Forgeheart said. "Even with all your crimes against Havath, I still feel compelled to offer you the opportunity. It would be a genuine shame to kill one of the only two remaining Helicotan sabre-wielders."

A couple of the others gave Forgeheart irritable looks at his offer. Alustin was widely hated by many Swordsmen for the sheer number of their ranks he'd killed, and many hated the standing offer of amnesty the Havathi Duarchs had on offer for him if he would join them.

"You already know what my answer is," Alustin said, drawing his own sword from his tattoo. "And while there may be two of us who still wield the Lord of Bells' enchantments, only one of us still counts as Helicotan."

Alustin could feel water dripping down the back of his neck from where it was leaking through the wax paper somewhere.

"Even in normal conditions, you'd be hard-pressed to

escape a Hand of veterans," Forgeheart said. "In a rainstorm where you need to defend a fixed position? You don't stand a chance. Please, Alustin, don't simply dismiss this offer. Valia holds out hope for you still, you know."

There was a flash as the Hyphal's burrowing mycelium broke through another of Hugh's wards, leaving only one left.

"Very well," Alustin said. "A moment, please."

Amberglow snorted in disdain, while Marrowstaff laughed bitterly. Olstes's Hyphal remained focused on her work.

Springcloak shook his head. "I'm sure this is just another of your tricks, but you have until we break through the last ward to consider."

Well, this was going to be a problem.

Sabae windjumped off another balcony just as one of the pursuing Sacred Swordsman struck it with another spray of metal bits. They weren't molten, but they ignited into flame the instant they came into contact with water, which meant the instant the Swordsman launched them, considering how hard it was raining.

She'd already been hit by a couple of chunks already, and had the burns to show for them on her arm.

Sabae landed on another balcony, and slid into the dark room connecting to it to hide.

Across the canal, the Swordsman slowly glided down to the balcony she'd just vacated, drawing the flaming bits of metal back into her staff, which was apparently made of the stuff, considering that it was burning too.

Gravity affinities plus just about anything else tended to be a nasty combination.

The Havathi spent a few moments looking for Sabae, but thankfully didn't spot her. Eventually, she took off again, and Sabae sighed a breath of relief. This was the first time she'd evaded Havathi pursuit since she'd killed the vine whip wielder.

She took a moment to consider her options as she healed the burns on her arm. Part of her wanted just to huddle up here and rest, but her friends were out there fighting somewhere, and she couldn't abandon them.

The only one whose location she knew at the moment was Artur's, but then, it would be pretty difficult to lose track of Artur at the moment.

Approaching Artur when he was in full battle armor was definitely a bad idea, though. She doubted he'd be able to easily tell her apart from any of the Havathi fliers. Windjumping wasn't too much different from a force mage's leaps— only the most powerful force mages could truly fly, and she'd spotted several force mages leaping about among the Havathi.

No, making for the Exile Splinter made the most sense at the moment. The closer she got to it, the more of their pre-established defenses she'd cross, putting her on a better and better footing. She'd have to take the long way around to do it, though— Artur and the collapsed living tower, as well as the majority of the Havathi, lay between her and it.

And going the long way would take, well, entirely too long.

No, if she were going to do this, she needed to do it underwater.

Godrick and Hugh had just managed to climb up onto a balcony when three of the Havathi attacked them from a neighboring rooftop. All wore the pristine white uniforms of Havath with their bronze decorations, but only two of them wore the insignia of the Sacred Swordsmen. One of those seemed to be carrying an odd looking pair of pliers and a shield filled with different sized holes, along with coils of wire hung all around his body, while the other had what looked like several iron plates floating in the air around him.

The regular battlemage only managed to hit Godrick with a single firebolt before Hugh responded with a starbolt.

Godrick had been maintaining the anti-glare cantrip for just this purpose, but the starbolt still left afterimages.

One part of Godrick wanted to laugh hysterically about Hugh incinerating a fire mage, another part wanted to vomit, a third noted that the Havathi had just been a battlemage and not a Swordsman, while a fourth part somehow kept it together and tossed Hugh through the door leading inside from the balcony.

Godrick, the ice of his armor only partially melted from the firebolt, rolled to his feet in time to block a web of wire with Hailstrike. It sank a solid inch into the ice before stopping.

Then it started cutting down into Hailstrike again.

Hugh ducked back around the doorway long enough to fire another starbolt at the wire mage, but the third mage finally did… *something.* Hugh's starbolt simply detonated in midair.

Godrick clenched down with his armor on Hailstrike, and the handle broke in two. He sent the hammerhead with the wires digging into it flying towards the Swordsman with the iron plates, while the lower part of the handle he sent spearing towards the Swordsman with the pliers.

Godrick tossed the fragments of ice he was still holding—one of them ring-shaped— into the water below the balcony as the second warlock blocked both attacks with his iron plates.

"Did yeh feel how he ripped apart yer starbolt?" Godrick yelled to Hugh, as he tore chunks of the stone railing loose and started bombarding the two Swordsmen. Bits of wire started pelting his armor, sinking into it. They weren't burrowing fast enough for him to need to worry just yet, though.

He just needed to buy Hugh enough time to pull off his spell.

Godrick noticed that the wires seemed to be made of a variety of different metals, not just steel.

"He somehow tore apart the shielding component of the spell around the starfire itself!" Hugh said.

Godrick narrowed his eyes at that, and reached out with

his steel magic towards the floating iron plate. The enemy warlock easily wrested control of them away from Godrick, but Godrick hadn't actually been trying to take control of the plate.

It had been a test.

As Godrick felt the shifts in the stone below the Swordsmen, he kept up the barrage of stone. Not that he thought they would get through— the wire nets and iron plates were blocking his shots easily. He just needed to keep them on the defensive for a moment longer, though.

"You know, I think I'm rather disappointed," the mage with the floating plates called down. "I'd really hoped the son of Artur Wallbreaker would be a more impressive foe. But then, what else but disappointment could you expect from something of Wallbreaker's? He should have been one of humanity's great defenders, and instead he's just a mercenary battlemage, working for monsters like the Crystal Sphinx, who only benefits from our disunity!"

Godrick did his best to ignore the man's taunts. Some of the wires in his armor were getting perilously deep, but he only needed to wait just a moment longer.

With no visible warning at all, the entire roof the Havathi stood on simply collapsed, the crystal grain of the orange granite having been weakened on a massive scale by Hugh.

The Havathi, unfortunately, didn't collapse with it. Both warlocks hurtled off the collapsing roof, and towards the roof of Godrick's own building, hauled by wires.

Godrick immediately activated the spellform to collapse his armor. The mixed ice and stone dropped off him in great chunks, the burrowing wires deep within it.

Godrick summoned the newly formed Hailstrike to his hand from the lake— it thankfully hadn't been crushed by the stone chunks falling into the canal. He dodged inside with Hugh before the Havathi could recover, and immediately started rebuilding his armor out of stone.

"We've got a wire mage and a lodestone mage on our roof," Godrick said. "Lodestone mages are a perfect counter ta' lightnin' mages too, so ah'm bettin' it's similar with starfire."

"Wire mage?" Hugh asked.

"Well, ductility mage. He's carryin' a blacksmith's enchanted wire drawin' tools. Reckon' he probably can't control non-wire metal, but can turn it into wire easily enough."

"That's bizarre," Hugh said.

"Ah can feel them both up on the roof still, or at least the iron they're carryin'."

Hugh was about to say something, then scowled.

"Look outside and tell me what you see," he told Godrick. "I think they've just trapped us in here."

Godrick raised an eyebrow at that, but poked his helmeted head out the door.

Through his quartz faceplate, he could see spellforms made of wire floating in midair, stretching out of sight in either direction.

"There's a wire ward around the buildin'," Godrick said, pulling his head inside. "How'd yeh feel that?"

Hugh shrugged. "I'm getting pretty sensitive to wards these days. If you can cover me for a little bit, I can probably break through the ward."

"Ah've got a better idea," Godrick said.

Hugh's spellbook gave him a nervous look as he smiled at it.

CHAPTER THIRTY-SEVEN

Broken Bridges

Talia killed two members of the Hand of Sacred Swordsmen with her first spell. It was their fault for standing so close to one of the ash piles scattered among Ithos' ruins.

Talia tried not to think about how many of the bones were from children as she flooded them with bone mana, just as she tried to ignore the pain she felt every time she used bonefire.

Neither worked, but nobody else ever needed to know that.

One of the survivors carried some sort of floating orb above one hand, and the flame and bone shrapnel simply struck some sort of spherical misty shield around her. It didn't seem to do any damage, despite the fact that she was standing right next to the ash pile.

Another survivor, carrying a bronze trident and wearing bronze armor, was simply standing too far away for anything more than a few shards of bone to bounce off their armor. Talia didn't understand Havath's obsession with bronze, she really didn't. It might be more resistant to rust magic and other corrosive affinities than steel, but it took far more mana to strengthen it in comparison.

The third carried a proper flaming sword, and the flames from the blast simply curved around him. Quite a few bits of bone shrapnel still cut into him, though, and he collapsed to one knee.

She hadn't even gotten a chance to see what weapons the other two carried, sadly.

Talia wasn't just watching idly, though— she immediately followed up with a series of dreamfire bolts. They sizzled strangely in the rain, as though the raindrops were trying to feed them instead of extinguishing them.

The first bounced off the weird spherical shield and the second deflected around the Havathi with the fire sword..

The third, at least, did some damage. So far as Talia could tell, it appeared to split the bronze of one of the armor wearer's pauldrons apart into its constituent metals.

Talia sent another dreamfire bolt at the bronze-armored figure, then ran for it.

She didn't run far, though. Just back around the corner, where she immediately started climbing the side of the building she'd just dodged around, using the handholds she'd carved with dreamfire.

The bronze-armored Swordsman was the first around the

corner, which was their bad luck. They crossed the ward Talia had carved into the cobblestones with dreamfire at a dead sprint, and it dumped all of its mana as heat into the Swordsman. The bronze trident and armor glowed red, and there was a smell of burnt hair and meat as the Swordsman collapsed to the ground.

It wasn't her usual mode of fighting, but you couldn't expect her to be friends with Hugh for as long as she had and not pick up any wards, after all. Her tattoos, it turned out, affected her wardcrafting ability as well, but if she was trying to create a fire ward, well… for once it worked in her favor. It was probably the closest to being a real fire mage she'd ever be.

She also couldn't help but notice that her short hair didn't get all sodden and difficult in the rain like her hair used to when it was longer. She still missed her hair, but she wasn't going to complain about this part.

Talia was already on the roof by the time the other two Swordsmen approached the corner, not having seen their armored companion's fate. The woman with the floating orb had brought the wounded flame mage inside the weird bubble shield, and was helping to carry him.

Unfortunately, Talia hadn't the slightest idea of what sort of affinity the Swordsman might have gotten from her pact with that weird orb. It wasn't any material she'd seen before, but it was a dull brown approaching black, with spellforms carved deeply into its surface. Or melted, maybe? They were fairly jagged and irregular.

Generally, the best way to defeat a mage was by knowing what their affinity was, and if that failed, simply by overpowering the enemy mage.

And Talia heavily doubted she could overpower whatever that shield was.

She did have one trick that might work, though.

Talia yanked the shard of sunmaw bone off her necklace, charging it with bonefire, and then hurled it at the spherical shield. The weirdly corrugated pattern of the bone grew even more distinct as it grew larger, and was nearly the size of her torso when it hit the shield.

Then bounced off.

Both of the surviving Swordsmen turned to look at her, and the wounded one leveled his sword at her.

Talia threw herself back as the sunmaw bone exploded.

She waited a few seconds, then she poked her head over the edge again.

The misty shield was still intact, and both of the mages were still unharmed, but Talia noted, to her delight, that there were weird ripples in the shield, almost identical to the corrugations in the sunmaw bone.

"You were on the top of the list for those we should attempt to persuade to join us," the wounded flame mage said. "But I think you've just proven yourself too dangerous for that."

The flames around his sword all rushed into a sphere at its tip.

"Danavar, don't!" the woman shouted, but not in time to stop the man.

Rather than shooting towards her, the flame detonated at the tip of his sword, filling the entire shield with flame. It erupted out in a couple places, but largely stayed contained.

Talia's smile grew wide at that. She'd been waiting for ages for a good opportunity to use sunmaw bone in battle. Sunmaws had a curious property— they disturbed the aether around them, making spells near them collapse and fail. Their bones were famously useful for wardbreaking tools and windshield penetrating arrows as well, carrying some small portion of that effect.

When subjected to bonefire, sunmaw bone didn't shut down spells. Rather, it tended to make them fail.

Explosively.

Just like Talia's spells used to.

It would be at least ten minutes before the aether nearby stabilized enough for spells to work again, so Talia quickly moved to find somewhere more secure.

She vaguely considered collecting the Havathi weapons, but her scalp twinged with remembered pain. Carrying one or two of them around probably wouldn't trigger another resonance cascade, but…

The weapons could stay right where they were for now.

She'd just left the affected area when the city phased again.

When she'd lit up the area with the flames from her burning dagger, she glanced behind her, and realized, to her shock, that the area affected by the sunmaw bonefire hadn't phased with them. There was a hole in the city where a great chunk of the city had been left behind, the edges of it torn and crumbled in that same corrugated pattern again.

Talia whistled at that.

She really wished she had more sunmaw bone, but that stuff was hard to find. If only she'd thought to harvest more from that sunmaw she'd killed out in the Endless Erg last summer.

Right now, though, she needed to find her friends.

One of whom was her boyfriend now. Talia had to admit, she was thoroughly enjoying this trip, for the most part.

If she stumbled across a few more Havathi while looking for her friends, well…

That would just be a nice bonus.

In truth, Alustin's situation was rather worse than the Swordsmen knew. He was running low on many of his standard combat glyph papers, and worse, his paper mana reservoir was down to dregs. It was refilling itself from the newly enriched aether around them, but it wasn't going nearly as fast as he'd like. Going toe to toe against the Havathi in the living tower had been an absurdly mana intensive option, but he'd wanted to pull the tower's attention away from Godrick, Hugh, and Sabae, wherever they were in the city.

He really hoped it had been enough. He'd put a lot of work into his students, and had grown quite fond of them. Unfortunately, he hadn't been able to track them down with his scrying. He was pretty sure Hugh's spellbook was doing its anti-scrying thing, and Sabae tended to move around too quickly to track. Not to mention, his farseeing was location based— he could send his vision to places, but it didn't magically track whatever he was looking for.

Still, Alustin had learned better than to underestimate his students.

Alustin ran his eye across the Swordsmen, who were spreading out to attack him when the last ward fell. His face was still behind a paper helmet, but he tried to keep any expression off his face when he saw what was behind them.

The rain began to pick up even more, and several more leaks sprang in Alustin's armor.

He carefully ran his affinity senses through the storage space inside his tattoo, taking stock of what he had available.

Plenty of blank paper, but he didn't have nearly enough mana left to take on an entire Hand just with blank paper. Almost no exploding glyphs left, and only a handful of flash-glyphs left. He could probably take one or two of the Swordsmen if he blinded them with flash-glyph papers, but that would leave him largely defenseless against the rest when they recovered.

If the Hyphal were closer, he could just attack her from inside the ward, but she hadn't moved in closer than the outermost ward had been yet— her mycelial strands just spread across the stone towards the Exile Splinter.

Alustin ignored his library and his personal effects, none of which would help in the slightest at the moment. He had plenty of ward-papers left, but this Hand would easily be able to overpower one of his modular paper wards.

"Halfway there," the Hyphal said.

Alustin's affinity sense briefly passed over a heavily warded section of his storage space. He never accessed it except when he was somewhere he was convinced was proof from scrying— usually his quarters or office back in Skyhold. Even Kanderon didn't have any suspicions about this project, so far as he knew.

Not that it would do him any good. It was a pipe dream at this point, and he doubted it would be ready for a decade, at least.

And he really wasn't sure he'd still be alive ten minutes

from now, let alone ten years.

He briefly considered his half-congealed third mana reservoir, but an attempt to use it now would probably fail, if not collapse it and waste years of effort on his part. Just a few more months and it would have been ready, but…

Alustin's senses raced past a half-dozen other projects in various stages of completion. Most were intended as weapons against Havath eventually, but none were ready yet.

Most people who knew of Alustin's vendetta assumed he had some grand master plan, but there was nothing of the sort. Alustin preferred a far more improvisatory approach—it was best, so far as he was concerned, to have tools to react to any sort of situation, rather than relying on a more fleshed-out plan.

That isn't to say he didn't have plans at all, of course. Plans were fine so long as you remembered that they were just tools, not goals in and of themselves. People tended to get over-attached to plans, to the point where they would fail to achieve their objective rather than abandoning the plan they'd put so much time and effort into.

Alustin couldn't help but smile as his senses finally crossed over the perfect tool for this job.

They grew even wider when he realized that the Hand still hadn't looked behind them.

"I've given your proposition some consideration," Alustin said. "And I've come to the conclusion that there are three flaws with its base assumptions. Well, quite a few, in fact, but three that are most pertinent at the moment."

Springcloak sighed. "Of course you have. Let me guess, you're somehow going to find a way to lecture us on agricultural magic."

Alustin was vaguely offended by that. His interests were diverse and widespread. Agricultural magic was just a sentimental favorite, was all.

"The first flaw," Alustin said, "is assuming that you'll break through that last ward."

Hyphal gave him an irritable look.

"I should rephrase," Alustin said. "It's assuming that I'll

let you break through that last ward."

"Really?" Amberglow said, sounding contemptuous. "Bold words, coming from—"

"When am I anything but bold?" he asked, interrupting Amberglow.

Alustin really would have let her speak, but he really needed to stay on schedule, at least if he wanted his dramatic timing to work.

He really needed to teach his students to get better at being dramatic. They tended to fight in silence, save when coordinating. It was very deadly, efficient, and intimidating, Alustin supposed, but it was also so… boring.

"Second, you should know that the Exile Splinter's phasing effect seems to start from the outer edge of the city and work its way inward," Alustin continued.

Several of them just stared at him blankly, but Springcloak and the Marrowstaff were clever enough to realize what he meant, and whirled around.

The phasing events were happening faster and faster now, and it took only seconds for the wave of darkness to creep across them, and drag the city back into the pocket dimension. Alustin waited until it had passed, and for the Havathi to ignite various light spells and glow crystals. Forgeheart ignited flame from his molten blade, while Amberglow made the heart of their jewel-blade start glowing in a cascade of brilliant gold.

Alustin let his paper armor collapse off him— he needed the rest of his mana for something else. He gave the Havathi a toothy smile.

"Third," Alustin said, "I don't know what rainstorm you're talking about."

He lifted his arm, and pumped all his remaining paper mana into a particular pile of glyph-covered papers, then blasted all of them out of his storage space up into the air above them, activating their glyphs as he did so.

The huge stack of paper expanded into a massive cloud of gently drifting paper, slowly settling towards the ground, their glyphs glowing faintly in the dark above them.

No one spoke for a moment.

"That's it?" Amberglow asked. "Just… going to throw a bunch of paper into the air? Really?"

"He just ran out of paper mana," the Marrowstaff said.

Alustin would give a pretty penny to know how the Marrowstaff could know that. Or at least one of the wooden coins Talia had turned the sea serpent into, he still had a couple of those sitting around. There were only a handful of mages and enchantments Alustin had ever even heard of that could detect mana levels of other mages.

He turned his head up and watched the paper sheets slowly fall, fluttering through the air.

"Almost through," Olstes's Hyphal said.

Alustin thought the sheets of paper looked oddly beautiful, the glyphs at their centers and edges glimmering as they fell.

"He clearly didn't have enough mana left to activate them fully, or they would have done something by now," the Marrowstaff said, and reached up to snag one of the lowest sheets out of midair.

Perhaps she wasn't as clever as he'd imagined.

The sheet of paper sliced through the Marrowstaff's fingers as though they weren't even there.

Everyone but Alustin stared in shock. A bone mage's reinforced bones should be more than enough to block a sword strike, but they hadn't even slowed the sheet of paper down.

The Hyphal threw herself to the side to avoid another sheet of falling paper, tearing loose from her mycelial web before it could puncture the last of Hugh's wards around the Exile Splinter. The other Swordsmen began dodging the slowly falling paper sheets as well.

Alustin lunged out of the ward before the Swordsmen could even react.

Artur was getting thoroughly sick of Grovebringer.

None of the other Swordsmen posed a significant threat to him, if he were going to be honest. The average Havathi

Sacred Swordsman was powerful, yes, but they also tended to lack versatility. Ashspine was nearly as powerful as Grovebringer, but it was poorly suited in combat against him.

Grovebringer, however, was another story. By the time he could yank out an arrow, it was almost always sprouted into a sapling, if not even larger. Some of the trees reached ten or twenty feet in height before he could tear them out of his armor, and ripping out those root systems tended to do a massive amount of damage.

Worse, Grovebringer's wielder never seemed to run out of arrows, and their range was ridiculous. Well outside of the cloud of rock dust that always hung lightly in the air around Artur's armor.

Artur stomped down hard on the ruins of the living siege tower, taking out a lightning mage and what appeared to be a… hair mage? It was hard to tell through his dust cloud.

Artur couldn't help but be amused at how many wind mages were flying around the battlefield, largely just carrying other Havathi mages. If they had cooperated, they could have easily blown away his dust, leaving Artur effectively blind, sealed away inside his armor.

But then, no-one ever thought twice about the dust cloud, and nobody at all had known about the enchantments on his stone ring.

It was, above anything else, his most prized possession, even over his hammer. It enhanced his affinity senses to an absurd degree, letting him do things like use clouds of stone dust to perceive the world around him while sealed away in his armor. It helped him control prodigious amounts of stone— though that wouldn't be possible without his massive mana reservoirs as well. It was what had finally let him escape the *Hydra's Kiss* all those years ago.

It also was what let him utilize his breathless aura.

Artur tore a tree out of his leg, then tore a balcony from a nearby palace to repair the hole. As he did so, he finally activated his breathless aura.

There were lots of stories about Artur. He'd heard most of

them, but in none of them did anyone speculate that the fear that came over mages forced to fight him was anything but natural.

Some of the fear was certainly natural. Most of it, though, was a spell.

Artur reached out with his iron affinity sense, feeling the iron in the blood of all the mages around him. It would take fine control even beyond his own to tear it from their bodies— even iron liches and blood mages seldom had that ability.

It was not, however, beyond his ability to interfere with it a little.

It wouldn't take long for his foes to start feeling a little short of breath, as their blood found it harder and harder to carry air. It wouldn't kill them, or even knock them unconscious, but it would make them fatigue faster.

And, Artur had found, it made people panic. Something about not being able to get a proper breath in triggered fear at a deep level in people. No one fighting him ever made the connection, though— they always seemed to interpret the breathlessness as a product of the fear, not the other way around.

At least, no one who had survived battle against him had made the connection. Perhaps some of his fallen foes had, but it hadn't helped them.

Artur supposed people didn't like being reminded how at the mercy of their own bodies they were, and preferred to think their minds controlled their bodies, not the other way around.

Artur swung his twenty-foot long hammer at a slow-moving gravity mage flying near him. The gravity mage attempted to force the hammer down with a gravity spell, but Artur just willed some of the hammer's insides into its own pocket dimension to counteract the spell.

What remained of the gravity mage went flying over the city.

Artur's hammer wasn't really a hammer anymore than it was a ring. If he had to guess, it had been the storage spell for some absurdly huge iron foundry on whatever world it came from. Artur really wasn't sure how much iron was stored within it, nor did he really understand how its magic worked, but he could manifest iron from within it in whatever shape he needed. It had no spellforms on it, and as he'd found it deep in Skyhold's labyrinth, he had no real clues where it came from. It still used mana, but it was otherwise utterly foreign in construction from Anastan spellform enchantments.

Using it wasn't too complicated, however. He just needed to picture the size and shape of the iron construct he wanted to manifest. The more iron he manifested at once, or the more complex the shape of the iron construct, the more mana it used. Because of that, he couldn't use his hammer and his breathless aura simultaneously for very long.

Artur seldom needed to use both for very long, though. He tended to end battles quickly.

Artur tore a cedar tree from his helmet. He honestly didn't even need a helmet— his cavity was deep within his armor's belly— but for some reason, enemies often targeted his armor's head first, so it made a convenient decoy.

Three of the annoying mages flying around him broke away, heading towards the center of the city and the Exile Splinter.

"No yeh don't," Artur growled.

As he strode down the wide canal he stood in, he didn't bother stepping over the bridges in his path. He just walked straight through them. His affinity senses could feel how much mud he was stirring up from the lakebed with each step.

His armor's steps might look ponderous, but after no more than six steps, he'd caught up with the fliers. None of them even saw the hammer coming before it swatted them out of the air.

The rain and wind picked up even more as the full force of the storm arrived, and Artur scowled as he lost track of half the fliers chasing him. Storms wreaked havoc on his dust clouds.

He gripped his hammer with both hands, then slammed it

with all his armor's strength through the side of a nearby Ithonian palace. He used his magic to stir up the dust even more, and sighed in relief as his dust cloud expanded again.

Artur swatted at a particularly daring flier who was blasting his armor with ball lightning, but they easily dodged his massive fist. He didn't mind, though, since he could feel the city begin phasing back into the pocket dimension with his stone affinity sense, and he smiled. There'd be no storm there to mess with his dust cloud.

When the city did phase, however, Artur realized he had a little bit of a problem.

He hadn't phased with it.

Lightning began to crackle in the clouds above him.

Sabae cautiously stepped back out onto the balcony, her wind armor spinning, and began pulling at the rain around her.

The first two times she tried, her wind armor exploded off her. The third time, her water armor exploded off her.

The fourth time, finally, it worked.

For a moment, at least, then both armors exploded off her.

Sabae paused to think. This could still potentially work with just the water armor, but it would limit the amount of time she could stay below. Even if she preserved a small amount of air inside it, she'd still have to surface within a few minutes.

The problem was, ultimately, that there was no way to keep both armors thin enough to stay within her limited magic range. Trying to stack them inevitably resulted in one of them protruding out, and leaving the whole thing to collapse.

She could probably use the windlode to accelerate to absurd speeds underwater, but she doubted she'd be able to safely dodge the stone columns supporting the city that way.

If only there were a way to weave them together, as if…

Sabae wanted to smack herself. Of course that was what

she was supposed to be doing as the next step in combining her armor. Weave them together, not layer them.

That didn't do her any more good than a rowboat at low tide, though. She'd need likely weeks to master something like that. If there was one thing Alustin had taught her well, it was to not try and master a new spell or skill in an emergency. You needed to rely on the tools you did have, and come up with creative new uses for them.

It looked like she was going to have to take the risk of surfacing every now and then.

A thought floated back up to the top of her mind. She immediately shoved it back down as mad, but it drifted straight back up again.

Creative new uses for old tools, huh?

Maybe she was thinking in the entirely wrong direction.

Sabae smiled, feeling a bit like Talia, and crafted the windlode spellform in her mind's eye. She spun up her wind armor again, took a deep breath, then activated the windlode and began channeling its mana into her wind armor.

The wind armor promptly began growing and deforming as more and more air was sucked into it, but Sabae growled and forced her will against it, slowly compressing it back down again. She hadn't tried repeating this trick since Theras Tel, but she was far more capable with her magic now.

Again and again her armor tried to struggle free of her grip, but Sabae desperately held onto it. Finally, when she was sure she could pull no more wind into it, she made sure her shield was strapped to her back, bent her knees, and windjumped.

She felt the balcony beneath her crumple and collapse under the force of her takeoff, but she couldn't see it— she couldn't see anything. The acceleration pressed against her so hard that her eyes went blind with spots.

For a long, drawn out moment, it was just her, alone and blind in what remained of her armor, shooting up and up and up. For a long, drawn out moment, she could pretend she was a true storm mage, worthy of her family's name.

When her eyes cleared, she was high enough that she felt like she could reach up and touch the stormclouds, if she wanted to. She was even higher up than she'd jumped with the aid of Hugh's momentum magnifier ward. Far below her through the rain, she could see the swarm of Havathi fliers still darting around Artur's massive suit of armor.

What she couldn't see, however, were the ruins of Imperial Ithos.

It had phased back into the pocket dimension.

"Alright, *now* today can't get any worse," Sabae said.

Sabae reached the top of her arc and started to fall. As she did so, she caught a glimpse of something in the distance. Something huge in the sky she couldn't quite make out through the blur of her wind armor.

Hope rose up in her. If that was Kanderon, then…

She dropped her wind armor at the same time she came to a realization.

She was looking to the east, not the west.

Without the haze of the wind armor, Sabae could see no less than five dragons winging their way towards Lake Nelu under cover of the storm.

As she plummeted back down towards the lake, Sabae frantically spun up her wind armor again.

She really, really wasn't going to make fun of Talia's weird obsession with how things worked in her novels anymore. And she wasn't going to say that cursed phrase again. Wasn't even going to think it. Though, really, even if she did, she wasn't sure how today was supposed to get any…

Above her, lightning began to crackle in the clouds.

Longren toyed with his lodestone amulet as he moved charge between two of his iron plates. He made sure to keep them far apart, for as the spell grew more powerful, their attraction to one another grew accordingly. He had to be careful not to let the moving charge express itself as lightning, not in rain like this. And he definitely didn't want to risk his iron plates attracting lightning, so he needed to finish before this unnatural storm built up its charge again.

He could use his magic easily enough to keep Kai's wire structures from attracting the lightning, but not while he was preparing an attack like this.

Once it was high enough, they'd tear through the stone of the palace below to get to one another. And, if Longren positioned them right, those terrifying living weapons as well.

His amulet sent a feeling of excitement through his mind at that thought. Longren was its second pacted wielder, and in the last year or two it had begun growing more and more aware of itself and its surroundings. He didn't let his amulet's excitement make him hasty, however— as long as the two below him were still alive, he and Kai were still in danger.

No one that young should be as dangerous as Alustin's apprentices were.

Longren was just glad that he and Kai hadn't run into the barbarian girl. Her threat assessment rivaled some archmages, and she probably wasn't even at her full potential.

Beside him, Kai snorted as several more stalagmites stabbed up from the roof, but the two of them were a solid fifteen feet above the roof, atop a wire platform Kai had built, suspended on dozens of twisting wire struts.

"How much longer?" Kai asked.

"No more than a minute," Longren replied.

He could still feel Artur's son and Kanderon's warlock moving around down below— they each had more than enough bits of metal on their clothes for his senses to react to, though he didn't want to try and wrestle with Wallbreaker's son for control of them. The two apprentices were sticking incredibly close together, which was foolish of them, to say the least. Longren's spell would be able to easily take out both of them at once.

"Do you smell something?" Kai asked.

Longren gave him a curious look, and then the full force of the stench struck both of them. Both immediately vomited. Longren lost control of his spell almost immediately, and the two iron plates slammed together with a clang.

The last thing Longren saw was a hammer of ice hurtling towards him.

If he'd lived a little longer, he might have seen a starbolt hurtling towards Kai.

Hugh couldn't help vomiting again after hitting the wire mage with a starbolt. Given that he was hanging off the side of the building's roof, it was rather more challenging than it would normally be not to get it on himself.

Given how hard the rain was coming down, though, it probably would have been washed right off his clothes. Hugh was about as wet as he could get without falling in the lake entirely.

Around the building, the floating wire ward sparked and then fell apart entirely.

Hugh called his spellbook through their link.

"Did yeh get some a' the stink spell?" Godrick asked as he climbed onto the roof.

Hugh shook his head, then followed Godrick up. He automatically began crafting a defensive ward around them in the stone of the roof.

When his spellbook arrived, carrying all the metal they'd had on them, Hugh took back his waterskin— which had a steel cap— and rinsed his mouth out.

"I think me puking in battle when I kill someone is just going to be a thing now," Hugh said. "I'm still not really entirely alright with the whole killing thing."

"Ah think ah'd be a little worried if yeh were," Godrick said. "We only need one battle-crazed maniac in our group."

"I feel like I should be offended by that, since she's my girlfriend now?" Hugh said.

"Are yeh offended?" Godrick asked.

Hugh shook his head. "No, because it's completely true."

Godrick chuckled at that, and the two of them took a

moment to rest and look over Imperial Ithos.

Before, Ithos had been shockingly intact. It had been sealed away from the world and anything that might weather it to true ruins for centuries.

In just a few short minutes of battle, that had changed.

The living siege tower had torn up great chunks of the city when it had fallen. Artur had torn up even more of the city in his battle against the bulk of the Havathi forces. Hugh could see the immense shadowy silhouette of Artur's armor crashing around in the distance, as unseen aerial mages bombarded him with lightning bolts, fire, and other spells.

Off in another direction, Hugh spotted a bonefire explosion, and couldn't help but smile.

"Did you say something?" Hugh asked. "I wasn't paying attention."

Godrick shook his head. "Ah've just been watchin' the city."

Hugh's spellbook gave them both a weird look.

"Though, now that yeh mention it, ah don't think ah've seen yeh use that crystal floatin' over yer shoulder in combat at all."

"I haven't really needed to. Starbolts are just so much more effective. I'm holding this and my sling back for when I run out of stellar mana."

"So why are yeh still keepin' it hoverin' over yer shoulder most of the time?" Godrick asked.

Hugh grinned. "Alustin's modular paper wards gave me an idea for a new project. I'm pretty excited for it."

"Can ah get a hint?"

Hugh just shook his head, and the two of them watched the city for a moment longer.

"City's phasin' again," Godrick commented.

"At least it'll get us out of the rain," Hugh muttered.

The phasing event went far more quickly this time. There were quite a few lights this time— he could see Havathi mages scattered across the ruined city, lighting up glow crystals and light cantrips one by one. He could see the lake water splashed across the ruins begin to light up in the darkness. He could see something going on over by the Exile Splinter, but he couldn't tell what it was. Fairly close by, he could see a familiar burning dagger.

"So I have good news and bad news," Hugh said.

"Ah feel like ah should ask about the bad news first, since Talia's not here ta' do it," Godrick said.

"Well, that's actually the good news," Hugh said. "I see Talia, and she's not too far off. Heading this way, too."

"And the bad news?" Godrick asked.

"I don't see your dad," Hugh said. "I don't think he phased with the city."

CHAPTER THIRTY-EIGHT

No Ground to Stand On

Artur lifted his hammer above him just before the lightning struck. He couldn't even count how many bolts the storm struck it with at once, but he felt the impacts even tucked away into the depths of his armor.

When it stopped, his hammer had huge molten scars across its surface, forming branching webs that immediately reminded him of Sabae's scars. Artur imagined it was probably glowing bright enough to light up the lake around him.

Through his dustcloud, Artur could feel what remained of the Havathi fliers darting around as though drunk, blinded by the absurd onslaught of lightning. None of them appeared to have been struck, all the lightning in the area having been attracted to Artur's hammer.

Artur smiled. He could easily knock a few more out of the sky while they were dazed.

Wait. No. He could knock *all* of them out of the sky.

Artur assembled a modified blacksmith's spell in his mind's eye as he reared back to swing his hammer. The spellform barely fit into his mind's eye, considering the sheer size and complexity of his linked armor spellforms, along with his hammer spellform and the breathless aura. His armor at its full size was the single largest and most complex active spellform Artur knew of, and neither of the other two spellforms was particularly simple or compact. The blacksmith's spell, on the other hand, definitely was both simple and compact.

Artur didn't bother to aim his hammer, he just swung it as hard as he could in a great circle. It actually hit one of the fliers out of the sky, but that was just an unintentional bonus.

Artur pumped iron mana into the spellform. It was originally designed to keep semi-molten iron together as blacksmiths pounded on it, but it was a relatively easy modification to reverse that effect.

His hammer left a trail of immense, red hot iron droplets in the air behind it.

Artur dropped the first spellform and formed another, and the molten iron began to spin in a great circle around him, faster and faster. In seconds, the circle shifted into a cyclone, stretching down to the lake and up into the air.

After a few seconds more, Artur released the second spellform, and the cyclone of molten iron exploded outward.

When he formed a new dust cloud, there wasn't a flier left in the sky.

Sabae wasn't exactly sure how she managed to avoid getting hit by any of the lightning. Just like all the rest of her grandmother's storms they'd passed through this summer, this one had saved up all its lightning to unleash all at once, and the entire lake was lit up by the flash. The only reason she wasn't blinded was the anti-glare cantrip Hugh had taught them.

It was rapidly becoming her favorite cantrip.

She wasn't entirely sure how she survived her landing, either. She repeatedly windjumped upwards as she dropped, bringing her speed down to almost nothing, but her wind armor still collapsed entirely when she hit the water.

She also wasn't sure how her shield stayed stuck to her back, but she didn't complain.

While she spun up water armor around herself, she took a moment to simply watch the cyclone of what appeared to be molten iron spinning around Artur. It lit up the lake and the storm for hundreds of feet in every direction in a baleful, angry red.

There was no way he couldn't seize the title of being a great power for himself if he wanted to. It wasn't quite up to the scale of power she'd seen from Indris or her grandmother, but it more than rivaled some minor liches or dragons that lay claim to the title.

Her musings were interrupted rather abruptly when the iron cyclone detonated, and she found herself having to dodge a rain of molten iron. Some of the droplets were bigger than she was, and hit the water in massive explosions of steam.

The instant the rain of iron had stopped, Sabae blasted forwards, launching herself in and out of the water like a dolphin.

It took her less than a minute to reach Artur's motionless armor, but she desperately hoped it was in time to warn him of the dragons.

Alustin's sabre took Forgcheart's wielder in the chest before anyone else even realized he'd left the confines of the ward.

When you were a paper mage, it was generally a good policy to take out fire mages first.

Alustin activated his sabre's echo enchantment as he danced through the falling sheets of glyph paper. He might be out of mana, but his sabre's artificial mana reservoirs were entirely full. Faintly glowing phantasmal copies of his blade lingered in its path, which Alustin was careful not to intersect— they'd cut him just as readily as they would anyone else.

Alustin didn't need to look to dodge the paper— he was keeping track of each and every one with his paper affinity.

Springcloak's vines and flowers shot towards him, then

collapsed to the ground harmlessly as a gently wafting sheet of paper slid through the warlock's neck without resistance.

A screaming Marrowstaff swung her staff of bone one-handed at him. Alustin knew better than to block it directly— Marrowstaff could hit hard enough to break him into pieces. Instead, he only swung his sabre halfway towards the staff, then he dropped and rolled across the ground, careful not to pass through the path of his blade echoes or the falling papers.

Marrowstaff's blow simply bounced of the floating echo, which promptly dissolved, and Alustin's sabre was already passing through her leg just below the knee. He was sure she was running mana through her bones now, but that wouldn't be enough to stop a Helicotan saber, at least this early in the fight.

Of course, a missing leg wouldn't be enough to stop a powerful bone mage, either.

Alustin didn't even look back at her, he just ran straight for the Hyphal, who was frantically grabbing falling papers out of the air with her mycelial tendrils. So long as the tendrils avoided the edges of the paper, they could stop them easily, but the paper storm was growing thicker and thicker.

Alustin wove through the descending cloud of paper gracefully, leaving a trail of blade echoes behind him.

To this day, no mage other than the Lord of Bells had figured out how to create that enchantment. The Lord of Bells had been absolutely brilliant, though, and had been one of the only multi-affinity liches on the Ithonian continent.

Amberglow cursed as she tried to get past the blade trail while dodging paper, but Alustin would only need a moment.

Hyphal barely even had time to look at him before his sabre cut through her fungal armor and straight into her chest. His sabre left an echo as he pulled it down and out, and Olstes's Hyphal went limp, prevented from falling for a moment by the echo it was impaled on.

Alustin ducked under his trail of echo blades as falling papers missed him by inches. Amberglow was already lunging at him, but Alustin dodged back, albeit at the price of taking a cut across his cheek from a sheet of paper. It was shallow, though, and wouldn't even leave much of a scar.

Amberglow was the perfect weapon for fighting other enchanted weapons. It was significantly weaker than a normal sword in terms of material strength, but when Amberglow struck an enchanted item, it would collapse from amber back into tree-sap, engulfing the other enchantment and nullifying its power.

He ignored the illusion of a lunge Amberglow sent forwards— he could feel several sheets of paper passing through that space. He dodged to the side, instead, and swung his sabre at a precise path near a falling sheet of paper, one that caught the page in the wake of the strike.

There were a lot of tricks to spotting illusions, and Alustin knew each and every one of them. He couldn't see Amberglow, but he could see the shadows the invisible sword was casting off the falling paper and off its wielder.

Alustin almost pulled a muscle stopping his strike midswing, drawing it back just far enough to let an echo form. An invisible Amberglow struck the echo, dispersing it.

The sheet of paper that had been caught up in the wind of Alustin's strike kept flying forwards, though, and Amberglow's illusions collapsed as the paper flew straight through the mage's chest.

Alustin dodged past Amberglow's falling corpse, leapt over part of his blade trail, then danced forwards through the falling paper back towards Marrowstaff.

She'd grown hideous bone appendages in place of her missing fingers and foot already, and screamed as she lunged at him again. Alustin blocked her strike with another echo, and then started dancing around her.

He couldn't get in close enough to strike her properly without leaving himself vulnerable to her massive new claws. Several sheets of paper struck her, but they only penetrated her flesh, not her bones this time. The longer a battle went on, the stronger and denser a bone mage's bones would get. Each cut the paper or his sword made rapidly sealed itself with a mass of bone— after a major battle, a bone mage could end up looking like some hideous living pincushion full of strange bone growths. They generally required massive attention from healers to get back to normal afterward. Apart from Artur, bone mages were among the most dangerous close combat mages out there.

Alustin circled her, dodging and lunging through the storm of paper. At this point, most of the light remaining on the battlefield came from their glyphs.

Then, abruptly, he simply stepped back and smiled as a particularly thick flurry of papers descended towards them. He was easily able to dodge through them, but when Marrowstaff threw herself backwards to dodge, she found herself impaled on at least a half dozen blade echoes.

Alustin had completely surrounded her with a cage of echoes as they sparred.

No less than two dozen sheets of paper cut into her, and by the last one, she clearly wasn't channeling mana through her bones anymore.

Alustin deactivated his blade's enchantment, and allowed himself a satisfied smile as he danced off through the cloud of descending paper, and out into the darkness.

Hugh and Godrick were halfway to Talia's position when one of Grovebringer's arrows slammed into Godrick's armor.

Hugh didn't even notice at first— he heard a loud, inexplicable rumbling noise in the distance, then a sharp cracking noise nearby, and then he felt Godrick tackle him off his feet. Something hot passed just feet overhead, and Hugh felt his hair singe from its passage. The instant the two of them rolled to a stop, Hugh crystallized a ward into the cobblestones around them.

When he stood, he could see the chunk of congealed volcanic ash embedded in the nearby cobbles, and a young oak tree was growing out of the ruins of Godrick's armor. Godrick's faceplate and Hailstrike both lay on the cobbles outside the ward, but Hugh used his magic to pull both inside just moments before an arrow struck the ward, then bounced off. It promptly began growing into a yew sapling, lying on its side on the ground.

Beside him, Godrick was already rebuilding a new suit of armor, carefully avoiding pulling stone up that might damage the ward.

Hugh had no idea what the loud rumbling noise might have been, just before the attack by Grovebringer.

One of the Sacred Swordsmen strode out of the darkness. Hugh recognized her from Sabae and Talia's description as the leader of the Hand they'd met in Zophor.

Qirsad Vain, wielder of Ashspine.

Her white uniform was no longer pristine— it was bloodstained and ripped, and half the bronze ornaments were gone. She was carrying a spear of volcanic stone, riddled with deep spellform cracks. A feverish light emitted from the cracks, and Hugh could somehow feel the heat from here. Volcanic ash leaked steadily from inside it, congealing above her head into another ash ball.

Hugh gulped as he remembered a warning from Kanderon about volcanic ash— it was mostly tiny bits of glass. You did not, under any circumstances, want to breathe it.

Godrick and Hugh's spellbook seemed equally nervous.

Qirsad raised her hand towards the darkness around them. "Hold fire," she said.

She stared at them appraisingly before speaking.

"I assume you saw the ash piles and what was in them, yes?"

Hugh frowned, confused by the question, but nodded.

"Your master did that. I won't deny that the Ithonian Empire had lost its way in its final years, but the countless innocents of this city did not deserve to die slowly and fearfully, in darkness and cold. Kanderon Crux didn't even have the mercy to grant them a swift death— and I'm sure she could have found some way to destroy the city quickly and mercifully if she had really tried. Have you ever asked her why she did it, Hugh?"

Hugh just stared, trying not to make it obvious he was setting up more wards below them.

"Maybe she told you it was to bring a swift end to the

civil war tearing apart the Ithonian Empire? Only, their fall plunged the continent into chaos for most of a century. Perhaps she told you it was to end their horrifying experiments? Those experiments weren't nearly so horrifying as what she did here. No, would you like to know why Kanderon Crux did this?"

Hugh opened his mouth to defend Kanderon, then forced himself to focus and not get riled up. Beside him, Godrick was most of the way done with his armor.

"The Ithonian Empire threatened her schemes. No more, no less. Kanderon, more than any other being on this continent, is caught up in the constant feuding of the great game of powers. So long as no one nation grows too powerful, none can threaten Kanderon or her territory. Beyond that, she simply doesn't care. Kanderon has spent centuries sustaining our endless, bloody, useless system, where the residents of a city don't know who will be ruling over them from one year to the next. To lack magic in our world is to lack any form of self-determination, and Kanderon, more than any other being, keeps it that way. And you, Hugh Stormward, chose to pact with her."

Hugh almost lost track of his new wards again, wanting to protest at the way Qirsad was talking about the sphinx.

"There's been so much debate in Havath about what to do with you. Quite a few of us, including the duarchs, would like to try and turn your friends, especially that little barbarian girl. But you, Stormward… you're pacted to the biggest monster on the Ithonian continent. For peace's sake, she literally eats people that displease her! There are dozens of confirmed incidents of her doing so in the past century alone, and we're sure there are many more. For you, there are only three options. Use you as a hostage against Kanderon, try to find a way to turn you into an involuntary weapon against her through your pact, or kill you."

The ash ball floating above her head continued to grow. It was already far larger than the one that had missed them.

Hugh started rapidly making adjustments to his wards.

"You might as well quit crafting those wards below the

ground," the Swordsman said. "I can feel them just fine, and they're not going to cause me much of a problem. Here's the thing about wards— no matter how clever they are, no matter how well constructed they are, your enemies don't have to be clever to defeat them. They just need enough power to break through. And funny thing, that. I not only have enough power, but after how many of my comrades-in-arms your wards killed, Stormward, I think I've joined ranks with the faction that wants you dead."

Around them, Hugh could see the stones of the city start to phase again. It shouldn't interfere with the function of his wards, but now was a really, really bad time for him to be wrong about that.

Qirsad twitched the Ashspine, and the ash ball shot straight towards them.

CHAPTER THIRTY-NINE

The Right Moment to Strike

Roots started sprouting out of Grovebringer's arrow the second it struck her left shoulder. Rather than try to yank it out of her wound, Talia purged it with dreamfire as she dodged into a relatively undamaged palace.

The pain from purging the arrow was indescribable, but not indescribable in the sense that it was just too much to handle. No, it was indescribable in the sense that she literally didn't know how she would be able to describe it to someone else. It was as if childhood memories were boiling inside the wound while feathers took bites out of her flesh, and she could vividly taste the color green.

The arrow poured out of her wound in the shape of what appeared to be dolphins made of olive oil, which splashed apart against the floor. Talia waited until they were done, then pressed her burning dagger against the open wound, hissing against the entirely describable pain.

One nice thing about her tattoos, at least— they might have distorted her magic, but many of their functions still worked as intended. Burns, notably, would eventually heal without even scarring, even without magical healing. All in all, a pretty useful magical tattoo design for a clan of fire mages.

Talia hadn't even caught her breath when the palace began to shudder. Tree roots began sprouting from the ceiling and walls, ripping through the masonry.

Running back out into the open wasn't an option, and staying in the palace was an idiotic idea. And she sure wasn't feeling like running away out of the back.

Talia chose a spot where the ceiling still looked stable enough, and manifested a dreamwasp swarm. Then she began spinning them down in a spiral, cutting a circle as wide as her extended arms into the stone floor.

It took less than a minute before the section of the floor collapsed downward, but rocks were already falling from the ceiling. Talia kept her kinetic anchor dagger suspended in the air above her head just in case, and it proved wise when a block of stone half the size of her torso bounced off it. It drained a huge portion of her bone mana reservoir, but Talia wasn't complaining.

Once the floor had fallen through, Talia dropped down through the hole, using the kinetic anchor a couple times to slow her fall. She was glad she remembered to hold it in her right hand, but even her uninjured shoulder ached from the jarring stops when she landed on the fallen section of the floor.

The underside of the palace was covered in faintly glowing algae, and Talia let her dragonbone dagger extinguish. She couldn't see a thing other than the outlines of the palace's support columns, but then, there wasn't anything else to see down here.

Above her, the palace shook, plumes of dust falling.

Talia strode out onto the shadows that made up the bottom

of the pocket dimension, barely keeping her footing. Slippery was the wrong word for them. They didn't have any texture whatsoever, it just felt like a force mage was pushing her feet upwards.

Not wanting to risk stabbing herself, Talia sheathed both daggers and scrambled across the shadows, occasionally steadying herself with one hand.

She made it halfway under the next palace when the one she'd been in collapsed completely, in a great tangle of broken masonry and tree trunks.

Talia sipped from her waterskin to make sure she didn't cough from the dustcloud and give her position away, then started moving in the direction she thought the shots came from.

After passing through several canals, Talia climbed up to the balcony of another palace. She had to move slowly— she couldn't rest any real weight on her left arm. Instead, she carefully burned hand-and-footholds into the side of a dripping wet column using dreamfire. In between steps upward, she rested most of her weight on her sheathed kinetic anchor. She'd had a latch added to the dagger's sheath for precisely that purpose, and had a belt made specifically to be able to hold her entire weight.

When she made it up onto the balcony, she collapsed there in the dark to catch her breath. She forced herself back to her feet before long, and staggered off into the palace, only allowing herself the smallest bit of flame from her dragonbone dagger to see by.

She finally made it up to the roof of the palace, and crawled across it to find a good vantage point in the darkness.

Down in a nearby street, she spotted Hugh and Godrick being confronted by the spear-wielding Havathi from Zophor. Qirsad, that was her name. There were a couple of nearby trees growing out of the ground near them, meaning they were in Grovebringer's line of sight.

Talia had to restrain herself from rushing to help them. She needed to trust they could take care of themselves while she took care of Grovebringer.

She did trust them. Both of them.

She just needed to focus on what she had to do so she could help them.

Unfortunately, according to Alustin and Artur, Grovebringer's wielder was supposed to be able to turn invisible.

It seemed like her friends and Qirsad were talking, so Talia started scanning the roofs nearby. She could barely see anything in the distant light supplied by the three down in the street below, however.

To her irritation, Talia realized that she was going to have to do some math. At least it was just geometry— it could definitely be worse.

Talia tried to mentally calculate which roofs around her would have had angles at her friends, on the street where she'd been shot, and the palace she'd fled into. It was hard to focus, however, with her friends fighting for their lives.

Then the city started phasing again, and Qirsad attacked her friends with one of her weird lava bombs.

To her surprise, the attack didn't smash into one of Hugh's wards. Instead, as the lava bomb approached them, it accelerated up and to one side, missing them by a wide margin.

Talia smiled proudly at that. Don't take a hit head-on if you don't need to.

Qirsad didn't launch another lava bomb at Hugh's ward as the rain fully resumed. Instead, what looked like a cloud of burning ash erupted out of her spear, rushing to envelop her friends.

Talia forced her attention away from them again.

It wasn't hard, considering what she saw off in the distance.

Namely, Artur punching a dragon in the face. What was more, Artur's armor was half ablaze with dragonflame, lighting up the storm.

The dragon went tumbling back, crashing through a building. The creature must have been at least a hundred and twenty feet long, dwarfing Artur, but his stone armor still must have outmassed it several times over.

Before Artur could follow up, a second dragon lunged at him from behind, and he went staggering.

Past Artur, three more dragons were landing. She could see what looked like dozens, even hundreds of Havathi debarking from their backs.

Talia's attention was dragged back to Artur as a pair of trees started growing out of his back.

Grovebringer.

She stayed hunkered down, but started scanning the nearby roofs for a spot with lines of sight to her original position, Hugh, and Artur. Grovebringer's range was monstrous, but there weren't many spots with lines of sight to all three, which meant…

There.

Talia didn't fire on the roof right away, she just waited.

And then she saw it.

A patch of rain that wasn't falling quite right, then a blur of motion through the air as Grovebringer fired once more.

Talia began manifesting dreamwasps as fast as she could, not even bothering to aim beyond spraying the general area of the roof where she'd spotted Grovebringer. She kept it up for a count of three, watching tiny plumes of multi-colored smoke and the like rise from the holes she was leaving in the roof, then she dove aside to cover, in case she'd missed.

No return fire arrived, and Talia carefully levered herself up to look.

She didn't see anything at first, and then noticed something lying on the roof.

Grovebringer.

The living bow was massive, with great clumps of leaves at either end.

As she watched, something else faded into view. It had likely been a human body once, but Talia's dreamwasps had mangled it almost beyond recognition.

Talia started to turn towards Hugh and Godrick's battle, until her attention was drawn back to Grovebringer.

Its spellforms were starting to grow brighter and brighter, and several appeared to be… broken. Not to mention sparking.

Talia's eyes grew wide. Destroying powerful enchanted items was generally considered a very, very bad idea. A destructively bad idea. And uhhh…

She may have just damaged Grovebringer irreparably.

And Grovebringer was rather exceptionally powerful.

Hugh's wards flickered again under the pyroclastic assault of Qirsad's volcanic ash. It spun and battered around them like some cruel parody of the sandstorms against the shields of Theras Tel, but this storm was grey, lit an angry red from deep within. Even through his wards, he could feel its blistering heat forcing its way in.

Worse, as his mana reservoirs drained, he could feel the weight and heat of the cloud grow and grow.

"Ah might have a' plan," Godrick said. He nearly had to yell to make himself heard over the roaring ash. "But, uh… yeh're not goin' ta' like it."

"I'll take just about any plan other than being incinerated by volcanic ash!" Hugh shouted back.

Godrick hefted Hailstrike. It was starting to melt in the heat.

Hugh stared blankly for a moment, then groaned.

"Really? Do all of your plans end up involving you breaking your hammers? Enchanted weapons really aren't cheap."

Godrick shrugged.

"Ah'd prefer not ta', especially since it feels a bit murdery, but do yeh have another plan?"

Hugh grimaced. "Hailstrike's about as aware as a snail, if even that, and it doesn't have any sort of conception of self, so I don't think it counts as murder, but yeah, it feels pretty weird. I don't have any better ideas, though.

"Hailstrike's goin' ta' be a lot harder ta' shatter than mah last hammer. Give me as long as yeh can, alright?"

Hugh nodded.

Godrick sighed, then broke the ring of ice out of its hammer shaft. Its spellforms started glowing, and Hugh could feel the stress Godrick was putting the ring under via his affinity sense.

Hugh felt oddly powerless, as though he was just a bystander in a race to see whether Godrick would manage to break Hailstrike or Qirsad would manage to break through his wards first.

As it turned out, it was neither.

Hugh wasn't sure when he started hearing the rumbling noise over the sound of the ash, but it grew steadily louder and louder, until he realized that the ground beneath their feet was shaking.

He exchanged puzzled looks with Godrick, then reached out with his affinity senses in the direction of the noise.

There was something huge tearing through the stone towards them.

Qirsad's pyroclastic assault slackened for a moment, and Hugh got a glimpse of what was rising up nearby.

A tree. Or, rather, a massive, deformed pillar, as though some mad archmage had jammed a thousand different trees into one.

Then the ground beneath the two of them crumpled, and they were hauled skyward by the rising branches of the new tree.

Hugh wasn't paying much attention to that, however. He was paying a lot more attention to the cloud of pyroclastic ash he'd just been hauled through as his ward collapsed.

Alustin was cleaning the blood off his sabre when a new sound reached him.

What he saw when he looked up was surprising even to him, but he took his time wiping off his sabre on the formerly pristine white Havathi tunic.

He was finding it almost impossible to scry his students through the storm, and he was sure at this point that Hugh had activated his spellbook's anti-scrying field, but as he watched the mind-bogglingly huge tree tear its way through the outskirts of the city, he was absolutely convinced his students had something to do with it.

Probably Talia. Blaming Talia for chaos was usually a

safe enough bet.

As Alustin strode off towards the tree, he didn't spare a glance for the Hand of Sacred Swordsmen lying on the ground.

None of them had been veterans, and none of their weapons had earned any sort of real fame yet. Not even the one with the staff that threw chunks of metal that burned on contact with water, and Alustin had only heard rumors of that sort of affinity.

This had probably been their first mission. Most of them weren't much older than his own students.

He almost felt sorry for them.

As sorry as he could feel for any Havathi, at least.

Sabae cursed as Artur almost stepped on her again.

"Ah'm not exactly used ta' carryin' two people in here," Artur said. "And ah'm a little busy fightin' dragons ta' reshape the spells, so yeh're goin' ta have ta' just deal with it fer now."

Sabae climbed to her feet again in the little space inside Artur's armor. It was hot, stuffy, and largely filled by Artur himself. It was also pitch black in here, because Artur wouldn't let her use a light cantrip— he apparently found light distracting while operating the armor.

"Yeh sure yeh can't get yer grandmother ta' end this storm somehow?" Artur asked.

"I have no idea how I'd even contact her. I can almost guarantee she's not paying this particular storm any attention— she's generating them by the dozen. All of her attention is probably on the battle against Ephyrus for control over the winds in this region!"

The armor shook, and Sabae barely kept to her feet. She reached out with her affinity senses, but she only got a garbled impression of storm winds and falling rain.

When she'd windjumped onto Artur, latching herself on with her shield, he'd almost swatted her before somehow realizing it was her. She still had no idea how Artur saw the area around him.

He hadn't, however, seen the approaching dragons, so he clearly had limited range. He'd barely gotten her inside the armor before the dragons arrived.

"Ah've got some good news, some bad news, and some weird news," Artur said. "Which do yeh want ta' hear first?"

"The good news," Sabae said. "I'm not Talia."

"The good news is ah'm not gettin' hit with Grovebringer's arrows anymore," Artur said. "The weird news, which ah reckon is related, is that there's a tree bigger than the ones in Zophor growin' in the outskirts a' the city."

"And the bad news?" Sabae asked.

"Ah've only taken down one dragon sa' far, and ah'm about dry a' mana. Mah suit at full size was never really meant ta' fight fer this long. Which still leaves us with four dragons and a small army a' Havathis."

"That, uh… that definitely counts as bad news," Sabae said.

"Ah don't suppose yeh got any tricks that will help us?" Artur asked.

The armor shook with some massive impact, and Sabae lost her footing again. She barely managed to not hit her head or crash into Artur.

"Actually," Sabae said, "I think I might have a plan. You're going to need to take a fall, though."

Godrick's day went from bad to worse in a shockingly short period of time. And considering that bad had been being trapped inside a pyroclastic cloud bent on their annihilation, that said rather a lot.

When they broke through it Godrick felt the heat of the cloud even through the warded faceplate Hugh had made him for his last birthday. He felt it even though the cloud had already mostly dispersed.

His first thought, to his later shame, was Hailstrike. He almost lost control of its dissolution— destroying it too fast would be even worse than destroying it too slow. Once he'd started the process, he'd rapidly reached a point of no return, but Hailstrike seemed vaguely aware of what was happening to it, and he could feel it fighting back weakly.

His second thought was shock as he looked around. The section of cobblestone they'd stood on had been lifted far into the air by the massive malformed tree growing up through the city. It was suspended halfway out on a branch wider than a hallway. Godrick couldn't even see how big the tree was through the storm. It was a hideous amalgamation of different tree species— he could see pine and oak branches as large on their own as entire trees. The overwhelming majority of its bulk appeared to be yew, however.

Even more alarming, he saw his father, locked in battle with multiple dragons, and what looked to be an entire army of Havathi. His father's armor was burning, half-covered with what had to be dragonflame. The thick, flammable liquid clung to everything, and even submerging it underwater could barely put it out.

There was, at least, one clearly dead dragon sprawled in the ruins of one of the countless Ithonian palaces.

It was only third that his thoughts went to Hugh, and that was only when he heard the cough. It was a nasty, hacking sort of cough, and something in Godrick seized up immediately, knowing there was something wrong.

He almost didn't want to look.

Godrick couldn't see exactly how bad it was, since Hugh was mostly covered in volcanic ash. What he could see was horrible enough, though. Hugh had vicious looking burns across his face and arms, and there were charred spots all over his clothes— some burnt all the way through. His breath rasped and rattled with every movement of his chest. Godrick wasn't even sure if he was conscious or not.

Hugh's spellbook was nuzzling at Hugh's side in confusion, trying to get him up.

Godrick was just about to lean down to check on Hugh when he felt something moving with his stone affinity sense. Something swirling and hot and…

He'd turned and thrown Hailstrike before he even realized what he was doing, propelling it even faster with his magic. Qirsad Vain never even saw him— she was still clambering up onto a lower branch.

The ring exploded just feet away from her, in a massive flare of power. The explosion dwarfed that of his last hammer, only it was cold, not hot, and he could see ice and frost coating the trunk near the blast.

Of Qirsad, or the branch she'd stood on, there was no sign.

Godrick was bending down to tend to Hugh when the day got even worse.

The city was phasing again, but not all at once. Chunks of it were phasing in while some were phasing out, and others seemed to be flickering back and forth uncontrollably. The phasing process was only taking seconds now, not minutes.

The massive tree groaned as several of the buildings holding it up phased out and then phased back in.

The clouds began to flicker, and Godrick knew what was coming. He crouched over Hugh, trying to offer him a little shelter against the rain and any falling debris.

The entire sky exploded with lightning again. It struck his father's armor, it struck building after building, and most of all, it struck the tree. About the only thing it didn't strike were the dragons, who apparently had Havathi mages guiding the bolts away from them.

Or maybe the dragons were lightning mages.

Tree-sized branches tore loose and plummeted burning towards the ground, breaking through countless other branches on the way down. It was only sheer luck and the deformed trunk of the tree that kept any of the debris from striking their own branch.

Then the whole tree shook, and there was a massive groaning sound as it simply began to dissolve. Gouts of sawdust shot out into the air from the trunk as it began to peel apart, though the rain and wind quickly washed most of the sawdust out of the air.

Godrick still had no idea where this tree had come from, or how it had grown so quickly, but it was clearly unstable to start with. Of course, the lightning, the rapid phasing of the city, and Hailstrike's destruction probably hadn't helped anything.

Two more bad things happened as their branch started to shake beneath Godrick's feet. One happened far away and one nearby.

Far away, Godrick saw his father's armor take a heavy blow to the chest from one of the dragons. It wasn't the first time— they'd been circling and battering at Artur this whole time.

The difference was, this time Artur's armor didn't just stagger backward.

This time, it started to crumble as it fell back into a canal.

If Godrick hadn't been watching his father fall, if he hadn't stepped forward, if he hadn't been screaming in denial, maybe the next bad thing, the one nearby, wouldn't have happened.

Their branch gave way completely, and Godrick felt his stomach try to crawl up his throat. He turned and lunged for Hugh desperately, reaching as hard as he could, but his armored fingers closed just inches away from Hugh's leg.

Then a piece of falling debris struck his armor, and when he stopped spinning, Hugh was gone.

CHAPTER FORTY

From the Clouds

Being woken by lightning striking close by was *not* Talia's favorite way to get roused to consciousness.

Dozens of lightning bolts slammed into the tree right above her, so close that Talia could actually feel her short hair stand up straight. The afterimages of the lightning burnt themselves into her eyes even while closed, and they were still there as she opened them, and saw the falling, flaming branches in between the cage the afterimages cast across her vision.

Thankfully, she was well out on a branch that wasn't struck by lightning or falling branches, but she could see the long burnt channels trailing down the trunk, tracing out the paths the lightning had followed down the sides of the tree.

Talia tried to sit up, but her head started pounding. She promptly rolled over on her side and vomited.

She realized she had another concussion, though thankfully not as bad as the one when her hair exploded. Inanely, some part of her mind wished that she wouldn't have to get her hair cut off this time too— it was still far too short to need to brush, but it was just now getting long enough that it didn't just feel like fuzz on her head when she ran her fingers through it.

She knew logically that she wouldn't need to cut her hair again, but she was having trouble focusing.

She managed to shut down that idiot part of her mind before it could start imagining Hugh running his fingers through her hair. Now was not the time.

The back of her head was especially painful, and she gingerly reached back and felt it with her fingers. They came away sticky with blood.

The last thing she remembered clearly was Grovebringer erupting into a massive tree trunk after she'd damaged it, its arrows being eaten and absorbed and sprouting into trees out of what had been Grovebringer's trunk.

Then there were a few flashes of her running across the roof as the freakishly growing tree tore it apart behind her, a flash of pain, and a flash of her legs dangling as she clung to a rising branch, and that was it.

Her stomach lurched, and she tried to vomit again, but nothing came out this time. Then it lurched again, and she realized it wasn't her stomach, but the branch itself.

Then Talia was tumbling through the air. Somehow, she forced mana into her kinetic anchor dagger. Her belt dug hard into her side as it stopped her fall, and the catch holding the dagger in her belt didn't break.

For a long while, she just hung in midair in the rain, dry

heaving and watching the tree collapse in on itself, as though it had never truly been bound together. It just… crumbled into a vast, broken pile, as though the tree had been more dry rot inside than actual wood.

She wasn't sure how long she hung there, just looking.

She couldn't see where Hugh and Godrick had been. That whole section of the city was just gone, vanished beneath the great pile of sawdust and splinters.

She kept looking, kept searching for them. Trying to spot Godrick's armor, or Hugh's annoying green spellbook. But the city below her seemed to be flickering in and out of reality at random, and she turned her eyes away from it, nauseated.

When her stomach was settled a bit, Talia clenched her legs, took a deep breath, and stopped channeling mana into her dagger. Just for a moment, but it was enough time for her to spin about to face the center of the city. She didn't fall nearly so far this time, and her belt didn't dig in nearly as hard.

It still took her a while to regain control of her stomach, and for her vision to stop swimming.

When she finally forced her eyes open again, she wished she hadn't.

Artur's armor was burning rubble in one of the larger canals, two of the remaining dragons and countless Havathi mages were moving in on the Exile Splinter, and another of the dragons was doing a sweeping patrol of the outskirts of the city.

The fourth dragon was flying straight in her direction, accompanied by dozens of mages. More likely, they were coming to examine the collapsed tree, but it seemed almost certain they'd spot her hanging in midair.

Talia choked back a sob. She doubted Artur could have survived the destruction of his armor. If she had to guess, Alustin had probably gone down fighting to protect the Exile Splinter. And Hugh and Godrick…

They had almost certainly been crushed by the aftermath of Grovebringer's destruction, and it was all her fault.

Sabae, at least, might still be alive. Talia hadn't seen or heard anything of her the whole battle, but she was by far the fastest of them, and the best equipped to escape.

She briefly considered trying to fight, or maybe trying to lower herself down in jerks and stops to the ground, but she knew she wasn't up to either. If she tried to lower herself with a levitation cantrip, she'd just set herself on fire.

She briefly considered just letting herself drop entirely, but couldn't make herself do it.

Talia resigned herself to just hanging there.

When the clouds above her started glowing again, she started to laugh.

Maybe she should make a bet on whether the lightning or the Havathi would get her first.

Sabae hauled herself out of the canal and collapsed onto an Ithonian boat dock. Artur followed after, looking even more bedraggled than she did.

Even though Artur had collapsed his armor deliberately to help their escape, they'd nearly been crushed by the collapsing stone. Sabae was pretty sure she was going to have nightmares about dodging burning boulders falling through the water.

On top of that, navigating the canals and foundations of Ithos underwater with Artur stuck to her back with her shield had been absolutely exhausting.

The two of them had spent a couple minutes just catching their breath and staring up at the sky when a familiar face poked its way into Sabae's field of view.

Normally, Alustin would be cracking a joke about them laying down on the job, or something else only funny to himself, but his expression now was grim.

"The Havathi have seized the center of the city, and several of their patrols are heading this way. We need to find the others and get out of here."

"Where are the others?" Sabae demanded.

Alustin just pointed towards where the mysterious tree

had been.

"Are they alright?" Artur asked.

Alustin hesitated, and something inside Sabae seized up.

"Alustin, are they alright? Is mah boy safe?" Artur demanded, climbing to his feet.

"Godrick's fine," Alustin said.

The only reason Sabae didn't grab Alustin and shake him was that Artur did it first.

"What about Hugh and Talia?" Artur demanded.

Alustin shook his head. "Talia's hurt, I'm not sure how bad. She's in a relatively safe, albeit extremely precarious, situation. I still can't track down Hugh. His spellbook must be blocking scrying near him still. He and Godrick got split up, somehow."

"I can go ahead and—" Sabae started, but both Artur and Alustin shook their heads.

"We're not splittin' up again," Artur said.

"And without my help, it'll take you nearly as much time to find the others as it would for you to just go on foot with us," Alustin said. "Besides, how much mana do you even have left in your reservoirs?"

Sabae wanted to argue, but she knew they were right. Even if she knew how to find them, she was running perilously low on mana— not to mention the fact that her mana reservoirs felt… sore, somehow, from repeated use of the windlode.

"Ah'll need days ta' refill mah mana reservoirs at this aether density," Artur said. "Are yeh doin' any better?"

Sabae couldn't help but be a little shocked by that— her reservoirs would probably refill within an hour or two at most.

Alustin shook his head. "Not by much. Every time I start to get a little mana stored up, I get into another fight. We're going to have to depend on stealth and speed if we want to pull this off."

"Lead on, then," Artur said.

Alustin took off at a run, and they stumbled after him.

As the drake flew, it wasn't far to the wreckage of the

giant tree. As they ran, though, parts of Ithos began flickering in and out of the pocket dimension almost at random. They had to turn and detour to avoid many of those areas, but when they had to enter it, they couldn't travel at much more than a brisk walk without tripping on shadows or risking getting separated from the city in either the pocket dimension or the lake.

Even before it had been wrecked by the battle, however, Ithos's layout was hardly designed for traveling in straight lines.

Something clicked for Sabae then. That odd layout the canals had that she'd seen from above…

"Ithos is a spellform!" she gasped out.

Alustin and Artur both glanced back at her as they ran.

"The canals are laid out to form spellforms!" Sabae said.

Alustin just nodded. "That… makes a lot of sense. Mostly defensive spellforms, I'd imagine. I've heard of great powers designing cities like that before, but only a couple have ever been built. It's hardly a city plan that works alongside the actual needs of citizens, so you could only really do it in a city built from the ground up, and liches are usually the only ones who do that. And defensive spellforms on that scale would almost certainly interfere with the functioning of a lich's demesne."

"Less talkin', more runnin'!" Artur barked out.

Godrick couldn't find Hugh in the rubble.

He'd barely made it down to the ground safely. He'd had to shed his armor and use a levitation spell to land, but his mana reservoirs weren't as absurdly massive as Hugh's—getting to the ground safely had just about drained him, and he'd still hit hard. He didn't know if his ankle was broken or badly strained, but he'd needed to encase it in stone to walk on it. He'd also sprained his wrist, but not badly.

"Hugh!" Godrick yelled.

His voice was almost immediately swallowed up by the storm.

He only stopped searching when he saw the dragon approaching from the city center.

At which point Godrick simply sighed and sat down on a nearby branch, itself the size of a tree trunk, and waited.

He could barely even tell the difference between the rain and his tears.

When the clouds started glowing again, Godrick considered finding someplace to shelter from the lightning, but he couldn't even muster the energy to care, let alone stand up and get moving.

He just sat there, watching the dragon approach and the light build in the clouds.

Most of all, he watched the rubble of his father's armor burn in the canals.

Godrick only noticed there was something off about the glow in the clouds a moment before his vision was blinded by a blast of light brighter than any he'd ever seen before in his life. Brighter than the lightning strikes, brighter than Hugh's starbolts or flare spells.

But that wasn't what startled him the most.

It was the glow in the clouds just before the flash of light that really caught his attention.

It had been clearly, unmistakably blue.

CHAPTER FORTY-ONE

The Scene of the Crime

When Sabae finally cleared the glare from her eyes after the explosion of light, it was just in time to see Kanderon descend from the clouds.

The sphinx's great crystal wings glowed far brighter than the moon or stars, bright enough to tint the whole city a vivid, electric blue. They didn't flap at all, simply spread out to either side of the massive sphinx like some vast geometric pattern that held some deeper meaning that Sabae wasn't meant to understand.

The meaning of the expression on Kanderon's face, however, she could understand with ease. It wasn't a complex emotion revealed by it, nor a subtle one.

It was wrath.

Then Sabae realized something else.

She couldn't see the dragon that had been approaching.

Sabae spun up her wind armor with some of the little mana she had left, and windjumped up onto a nearby roof, against the protests of Artur and Alustin.

It only took her a moment to see what she was looking for.

Or, the remains of what she was looking for.

The remains of the dragon had crashed into the city far short of the collapsed tree. If Sabae hadn't known what it was already, she never would have identified it as a dragon. It barely even resembled meat. It was, for the most part, just ash and char.

There was absolutely no sign of the Havathi fliers that had been accompanying it.

Kanderon came to a halt, hovering a few hundred feet above the city. Sabae could make out a small number of figures hovering beside her and standing on her back, but she couldn't make out any details.

The sphinx's tail twitched back and forth as she surveyed the city, almost like a housecat about to pounce. Coming from Kanderon, however, the gesture was far more ominous.

The three remaining dragons and the Havathi were frantically preparing for battle, but none moved to attack.

Sabae couldn't help but notice that the city had ceased its flickering into and out of the pocket dimension entirely at this point.

The standoff continued for several minutes, during which time Artur and Alustin made it onto the roof as well.

Finally, three Havathi fliers approached Kanderon, stopping a few hundred feet away. Sabae could almost swear the woman in the center appeared to be leaving ghostly afterimages behind her.

"Valia," snarled Alustin.

Sabae glanced at the paper mage, and just for an instant, glimpsed an expression of pure rage on his face. It was gone in the blink of an eye, however, and he just stared woodenly up at the fliers.

"You shouldn't be here, Kanderon," the woman— Valia, apparently— called out. Her voice was magically amplified, loud enough that Sabae could hear it even over the storm.

"And yet, I am," Kanderon said.

"This is a violation of the agreement, Kanderon. You were to keep to the west of the Skyreach Range, and our great powers to its east."

Kanderon said nothing, she simply stared at Valia.

Sabae heard a growl and she turned to see that Alustin's look of rage had returned. If she didn't know better, she would swear that this time, however, it was aimed at Kanderon. It vanished again, however, once Valia resumed speaking.

"Do you really think that anyone trusts you enough to let you reclaim the Exile Splinter, Kanderon? Do you think *anyone* trusts you not to use it again, simply to further your own ends? Would you really have the audacity to do so, right here at the scene of your ancient crime?"

"Yes," Kanderon said.

There was a long, drawn-out silence at that.

"If you go through with this, Kanderon, this will be the end of our treaty with you. Do you really think the great powers will unite against us if we move against you now?" Valia asked.

Kanderon started to laugh. It was a cruel laugh, one that raised the hairs on the back of Sabae's neck, but the sphinx seemed genuinely, truly amused.

"Little one, nothing would please me more than if your masters were to end the treaty. It would solve so many problems for me. Moreover, you've done me quite the service, and shown me how little your masters trust even

their most loyal servants with full knowledge of the treaty's contents."

"This will have consequences, Kanderon! You can't simply…"

Valia trailed off as Kanderon snarled. Then, to Sabae's shock, Kanderon's wings began to *grow*. Dozens of new crystals seemed to simply begin phasing into existence, much like Ithos itself had done earlier. The crystals grew larger and larger as the wings extended farther out, some the size of houses. Many of the crystals left Sabae with the uncomfortable impression that she was only seeing the tip of an iceberg, and that far, far more of the crystal rested just out of sight.

Within moments, Kanderon's wings had expanded in size until they dwarfed her massive body several times over. They slowly curled in towards the tips, and some of the outermost hovering crystals had the appearance of great spines, filled with a light that was almost painful to look at.

"Leave," Kanderon said.

She didn't say it in an angry tone. Kanderon didn't make any threats, didn't move at all. Nor did the mages hovering around her. Her facial expression was almost bland, the snarl having vanished off her face.

She didn't say anything else. She didn't need to.

Without saying another word, Valia and her escorts turned and flew back to the Havathi lines.

Sabae thought Godrick was going to crush her with his embrace. Not in the metaphoric sense, but in the sense that her ribs were actually hurting, and she was pretty sure she'd have to use her healing or suffer bruises from it sort of way.

She made a mental note to check with Artur later to see if he needed any healing— Godrick had given him an even larger hug, apparently having been convinced that his father had died when his armor was destroyed.

Not long after that, several of the mages that had arrived with Kanderon landed beside them. Sabae only recognized one of them— Emmenson Drees, Hugh's terrifying spellform construction teacher.

Another, a little old woman, shorter than Talia, looked vaguely familiar, but Sabae couldn't place her.

"Meet the Librarians Errant," Alustin said, waving generally at the arriving mages. "Not all of them, of course, but it is a rather small order."

Sabae couldn't care less about that at the moment. One of the Librarians Errant was carrying Talia, who looked shockingly tiny and frail. She had, apparently, been injured and dangling from her dagger in midair for some time.

While a Librarian Errant tended to Talia's injuries— another concussion and a horrifying shoulder wound— the others organized a search party for Hugh.

When Godrick told them about the last time he'd seen Hugh, and the condition he was in, Sabae's heart felt like it was going to rip out of her chest.

Talia didn't deny it, or rage, or insist on going to search for Hugh. To Sabae's dismay, Talia just seemed to… fold in on herself.

Kanderon, meanwhile, hovered in the air high above them, staring at the retreating Havathi, not moving a muscle. Hardly even blinking.

When the healer had moved on to Godrick's injuries, Sabae sat down next to Talia and wrapped her arm around her. Talia leaned in, but didn't say anything.

It took the searching Librarians Errant over an hour to find Hugh. Sabae spent every minute of it worrying about him and comforting Talia.

When they finally found Hugh, there was another problem— Hugh's spellbook wasn't just blocking scrying, but was also snapping at anyone who got too close to him, and wouldn't let them anywhere near Hugh. It had bit one Librarian Errant hard enough to break a finger.

The instant Talia heard that they'd found Hugh, she was on her feet and demanding to be taken to him.

Hugh was deep inside one of the Ithonian palaces, well outside the debris radius from the collapsed tree that had arisen from Grovebringer's destruction. His spellbook had apparently managed to carry him down through the air, then haul him into one of the palace's inner rooms.

When they arrived at the room, Hugh's spellbook lurked in front of the door, its pages opened menacingly in their directions. If it could make noise, Sabae was sure it would be hissing at them.

The leather strap Hugh used to hang it over his shoulder had broken in half, and hung loosely to either side of the spellbook.

Talia strode forward without even hesitating, then crouched in front of the spellbook.

It raised its cover menacingly at her.

"You finally got the whole apology gift idea right," Talia said. "You brought Hugh back to me."

The book slowly closed its cover, and seemed to shudder.

"You did good," she said, and gently stroked its spine. "You did good. Everyone here is Hugh's friend. No one's going to hurt him."

She picked it up, and stepped into the room. Sabae heard a gasp, and when she followed Talia in, she understood exactly why.

Godrick had said it was bad, but Sabae had never imagined it was *this* bad. For a moment, she was convinced that Hugh was dead, until he took a slow, rattling, painful breath.

Sabae was fighting back tears when the healer set to work on Hugh. Talia, Godrick, and Artur didn't even try to hold their tears back.

Alustin just stared, quietly.

Eventually, the healer ordered them out of the room. As they filed out, Sabae found herself filled with rage. Not at Qirsad, or at Havath.

Rage at Alustin, and at Kanderon. For putting them into another situation like this. For getting them caught up in their games. For using them as pawns.

She turned on Alustin, ready to yell, to rage, to tell him exactly what she thought of him.

And then she stopped.

Alustin wore a look of deep guilt on his face, and he

flinched when Sabae glared at him.

Sabae deflated a bit, but the anger didn't all vanish. She stalked towards a nearby doorway, gesturing for him to follow.

She didn't say anything, she just watched him and considered. Alustin kept eye contact with her, but it looked like a genuine struggle on his part.

"This is my fault," Alustin said.

"Yes," Sabae said. "It is."

"I… I shouldn't have split up the group. I should have kept you all with me. I should have taken Ithos' phasing into account. I should have used Ithos' labyrinth as our line of retreat. I shouldn't have brought you all on an expedition this dangerous in the first place. It's frankly astonishing that you all survived."

"*If* Hugh survives."

Part of Alustin seemed to crumple at that, but he didn't look away.

"Grennan is one of the best healers in Skyhold, I'm sure he'll be able to help Hugh," Alustin said.

Sabae was relieved to hear that, but she didn't let her glare waver.

Finally, Alustin looked away.

"When we get back to Skyhold, if you want to be apprenticed to a new master, I'll step aside without protest. I'll even help you find one, if you still trust my judgment there."

"I haven't told the others," Sabae said.

Alustin gave her a confused look.

"I haven't told the others that you used us as bait. Artur knows, but the others haven't even figured out that Midsummer was a coup yet."

"I don't understand," Alustin said.

Sabae sighed heavily. "The others idolize you, Alustin. Especially Hugh and Talia. Godrick, at least, has his father to look up to instead. They trust you, they rely on you, and I… I don't want to take that away from them, because I think you do care."

"I do," Alustin said, quietly.

"I also think that you value your goals more highly than anything, and if it comes down to it, I genuinely wonder what you'd be willing to sacrifice to reach them. To get your revenge on Havath."

Alustin didn't respond to that, but some of the guilt crept back on his face.

"I'm going to give you another chance, but I'll be watching you," Sabae said. "Try not to waste it."

She turned to leave the room and rejoin the others.

"Why?" Alustin asked.

Sabae gave him a long, considering look.

"Because even if you've made mistakes, even if you and Kanderon have used us as pawns in your games, you've also done a lot of good for us. You saw something in us when no-one else did. And you may have put us in danger, but I don't expect you to keep us perfectly safe. We're training to be battle mages, not mage-craftsmen or something of the sort. It's excessive, foolish risk I have a problem with. And considering the stakes, and the risk that the Cold Minds might have arrived in our world, I don't even know if I can say the risk was excessive. If there was any decision you should have made differently, it was bringing us on this expedition in the first place— and I'm pretty sure even I would have fought against that decision before all of this."

She hesitated, then continued. "And I also realized something recently— my anger at you and Kanderon using us as pawns wasn't because of your games, wasn't because of some moral standard I hold. It was simply because you chose us specifically to be your pawns. It was selfishness on my part, not principle. I was offended that you didn't use someone else. I think, if I'm going to condemn you, it should be for better reasons than that."

Sabae didn't wait to see how Alustin reacted before walking out.

Nor did she say the rest of what she had been thinking.

For all the sheer madness of Alustin's vendetta against Havath, at least he *had* a purpose. What did Sabae have? She'd never be a proper Kaen Das storm mage, but she'd never truly sought out a goal after that. She'd just gone with the tide, rather than try to swim her own direction. No matter how much power she earned, that on its own wouldn't free her or her friends from being used as pawns by others. It was having a purpose that turned you from a pawn into a player, and she didn't have one.

Maybe it was time for that to change.

After hearing the full accounting of Hugh's injuries, Talia was, frankly, amazed that he was still alive.

He'd suffered severe burns across something like a quarter of his body— not to mention minor to moderate burns across much of the rest. His lungs had been severely damaged by the volcanic ash, and Grennan, the healer, fully expected him to have some lasting damage, even with magical healing.

The spellbook hadn't had an easy time carrying Hugh to the ground, which had resulted in even more injuries. None of them could understand the spellbook as well as Hugh could, but they managed to figure out the story eventually. The strap had apparently broken while the spellbook tried to slow Hugh's fall. The spellbook had managed to catch him, but had broken several bones in Hugh's hand and wrist grabbing onto him, as well as dislocating his shoulder. Even with the spellbook slowing his fall, he'd still hit hard enough to break three ribs, nearly puncturing a lung with one and cracking two more, as well as developing a minor concussion. Not to mention plentiful bruises. Lake water had gotten into his burns somehow, and within hours of finding him, he was already running a fever from the infections.

Even with magical healing, recovery was going to be a long process for Hugh. The healer was especially concerned with the lung damage and infections.

The instant the healer was done with Hugh, Talia spent as much time by his side as she could stand, but she wasn't made for sitting and pining. She found herself climbing to the top of an intact palace to brood in the rain.

Once the Havathi had all left, the Librarians Errant had spent several hours scouring the city, mainly recovering some of the Sacred Swordsmen's weapons the Havathi hadn't managed to recover, as well as a handful of Ithonian artifacts.

During that time, the storm finished passing over Ithos, its trailing edge just as razor sharp as any of the other storms.

Kanderon spent the entire time crouched in the central plaza, staring at the Exile Splinter as if entranced. When she finally retrieved it, she simply pulled it from its spot with her paw, then tucked it away into some extra-spatial pocket dimension of her own.

The whole of Ithos seemed to shudder and settle as she did so.

There were only two other things Kanderon paid attention to in Ithos. The first was one of the ash piles scattered about the ruins, filled with shattered human bones. She didn't say anything, or make any expression, she just stared for a few minutes.

The second was Hugh himself. When Kanderon finally saw him, a look of rage crossed her face, and a horrifying growl erupted out of her chest. For a moment, Talia was convinced that Kanderon was about to launch herself after the retreating Havathi forces to take vengeance, but the sphinx managed to contain her fury with visible effort.

It was twilight when they finally took off. Everyone easily fit onto Kanderon's immense back. Her fur was shockingly soft and luxurious, and Talia had to struggle not to fall asleep instantly, especially since Kanderon's motionless wings made for an incredibly smooth flight.

Talia forced herself to stay awake, and watch Imperial Ithos shrink behind them.

The first glimmers of gold were lighting the ruins from beneath as it passed from sight.

Talia turned and went to speak with Godrick.

"This is my fault," Godrick and Talia said simultaneously.

Godrick gave Talia an exasperated look, which she returned. It somehow didn't surprise him that Talia wanted to take the blame on herself, but it definitely irritated him.

Hugh's spellbook, which was happily nestled in Talia's arms, seemed, for some inexplicable reason, amazed at their ability to say the same thing at the same time.

The two of them had moved farther down Kanderon's back from the others to get a little privacy.

"If I hadn't destroyed Grovebringer, Hugh never would have gotten hurt," Talia insisted.

"If yeh hadn't destroyed Grovebringer, it probably woulda' destroyed us, even if we'd managed ta' take out Qirsad on our own," Godrick said. "Ah shoulda' been more use in takin' out Qirsad, though— if ah'd destroyed Hailstrike sooner, ah coulda' defeated her without Hugh gettin' hurt."

"Yer both idiots," Artur said from behind them.

Both Talia and Godrick whirled to face Godrick's father.

"You're too big to be allowed to sneak up on people," Talia said.

Artur just raised an eyebrow at that. "Yeh're all lucky ta' be alive, goin' against Grovebringer and Ashspine at the same time. Ah never shoulda' agreed ta' that plan. Splittin' up against greater numbers was a mistake. Yeh both did fine. Yeh're only mistakes are misunderstandin' yer roles in the group."

"Our roles?" Godrick asked.

"It's obvious yeh aren't goin' ta be fightin' solo like Alustin or mahself," Artur said. "Yeh're going ta' be workin' as a team. What are yer roles in yer team?"

"I'm our heavy hitter," Talia said.

"And ah'm there ta' protect everyone," Godrick said.

Artur snorted, then pointed at Talia. "If yeh're the heavy hitter, then why do yeh keep talkin' as though it's yer job ta' defend the group? Yeh take out the threats facin' yer friends, and yeh count on yer friends to protect yeh."

His finger moved to Godrick. "And no, yeh're not the one protectin' the group. That's Hugh's job. Yeh're a lightnin' rod, Son. Yeh attract the attention a' enemy mages, and yeh hold that attention."

Godrick frowned at that. "Isn't that what Sabae does, too?"

Artur nodded. "Ta' an extent, sure. There's some role overlap fer all a' yeh. Mainly, she's yer flanker, and she's yer leader. So the two a' yeh need ta' stop beatin' yerself up fer not playin' roles that aren't even yers, and start figurin' out how ta' better fit yer own."

"Still, there's got to be something we could have done different to keep Hugh from getting hurt," Talia said.

Artur nodded. "Ah would imagine yeh're right about that, and ah also imagine there's plenty Hugh coulda' done different as well. He tends ta' over-rely on wards, fer one thing, even though he's got plenty a' other options ta' use."

The three of them spent an hour sitting around and talking over the fight with the wielders of Grovebringer and Ashspine, and how they might have gone about it differently. By the time Talia excused herself to go check on Hugh again, it was fully night, though well-lit by the moon. The Skyreach Range, meanwhile, was rising above the western horizon.

Godrick waited for Talia to get out of earshot, then he broached a question he'd been meaning to ask for a while now.

"Ah'm never goin' ta' be as powerful as yeh are, am ah?"

Artur gave him a long, searching look, then sighed. "Not by the same path ah followed, no. Yer mana reservoirs aren't near as large as mine were at yer age, and that's a' pretty reliable indicator a' their later size. On top a' that, several a' mah most powerful tricks are ta' do with my iron affinity an' mah enchanted gear. But yeh were never supposed ta' follow exactly in mah path, Godrick. It can only take yeh so far, and then yeh need ta' figure out yer own path from there. That's true a' anyone that gets powerful. No two archmages worth their salt follow the same path ta' power, and if yeh intend ta' get there, well… yeh'll have ta' figure out yer own way ta' get there."

Artur climbed to his feet. "If yeh're goin' ta' try and get

more powerful, just make sure yeh're not doin' it ta' please me. Ah'm already proud a yeh, Son."

He started to walk off, then turned back. "Oh, and ah think yeh've finally earned a' name fer yerself. Godrick Hammerbreaker."

The smile that had started to form on Godrick's face turned into a scowl at that. As his father walked away, that faded too.

They had a long flight ahead of them, and Godrick would have plenty of time to think about his future.

CHAPTER FORTY-TWO

Warm and Safe

When Hugh woke up, he had no idea where he was. He seemed to be lying in a soft bed with a thick blanket lying atop him. His body was a mass of aches and pains, and his vision was a mass of blurry, incomprehensible shapes.

Eventually, after much blinking, the shapes resolved themselves into mountain peaks, stars shining brightly above them.

Hugh slowly looked around him. He seemed to be on the shoulder of a mountain, or perhaps a ledge of some sort. He couldn't see down into it from this angle, but over the nearby cliff there was probably a river valley of some sort.

Why was there a bed outside on the side of a mountain, and who'd put him there? And why was his bed… furry?

"Ah, Hugh, you're awake," Kanderon said.

Hugh looked up— slowly, and painfully, but he managed it— to see Kanderon's face peering down at him, wearing an odd expression. He realized, with a start, that he seemed to be laying atop Kanderon's front foreleg, which was tucked against her chest as she lay near the cliff edge.

Hugh tried to speak, and promptly started coughing. Each cough was jagged and painful, and seemed like it wanted to tear something out of him. He realized that one of his arms was in a cast, underneath his thick blanket.

A waterskin levitated itself over to him, its lid unscrewing on its own. Hugh drank gratefully as it slowly tilted up for him.

"How are you feeling, Hugh?" Kanderon asked, when he was done drinking.

"Horrible," Hugh finally managed. His throat felt raw and torn, and his voice was raspy and unrecognizable. "Is… is everyone safe?"

He started coughing again, and Kanderon levitated the waterskin to his face once more.

"Everyone will be fine, Hugh. You were by far the worst wounded. You've been unconscious for several days now. Probably for the best— Grennan and Sabae have spent long hours healing your injuries, and you'll need many more healing sessions in the weeks to come."

"Where are we? And where's everyone else?"

"We're in a safe place— a hidden valley, deep within the Skyreach Range. I didn't want to risk flying you all the way back to Skyhold in your condition, and I needed rest as well. Your friends are all asleep— this is the first time you haven't had at least one of them by your side since you were rescued. Talia has been especially attentive."

Hugh smiled at that.

"We're dating now."

"So I've heard. It is of your own choice, correct? You're not under duress?"

Hugh gave Kanderon a puzzled look. "No, why would I be?"

Kanderon gave him a wry look in return.

"Just due diligence on my part. Oh, and she has, apparently, grown quite close to your spellbook. I admit, I was doubtful of its utility at first, but it saved your life

in Imperial Ithos. I suspect it will grow to be the sort of item stories get written about, so I would suggest you think of a name for it. A… more fitting one than Talia's suggestion, perhaps."

"What did Talia suggest for it?" Hugh asked.

Kanderon gave an exasperated snort, the wind of which ruffled Hugh's hair.

"She's been calling it Mackerel. Worse, the aggravating little creature responds to it. Mackerel is hardly an appropriate name for something that will eventually grow to be a legendary magical artifact."

Hugh started giggling at that, only to break into yet another fit of coughing.

Kanderon gave him an exasperated look, but levitated the waterskin over to him again.

"Did we win?" Hugh finally asked. "Did we get the Exile Splinter?"

"We did, yes, in no small part thanks to you."

"What are you going to do with it?"

Kanderon gave him a long, searching look. It was a bit strange, looking at her from this angle.

"I'm not intending to use it again, if that's what you're asking. The risk of attracting the Cold Minds is too high. At Midwinter, when Skyhold's Vault can next be opened, I will seal it away within."

"Why did you use it in the first place? Surely there were faster, less… cruel ways to destroy Ithos," Hugh said.

Kanderon took a long time to answer, and sounded a bit hesitant when she finally did answer.

"Possibly, yes. Ithos was one of the best defended great cities ever to exist— only Havath today rivals its defenses. We still might have come up with some other solution, but those were desperate times, Hugh."

He chose his next words carefully. "I don't trust her, but Qirsad accused you of just wanting to perpetuate the system of great powers, to keep the chaos going to serve your own power. She said that's why you destroyed Ithos."

Hugh had expected Kanderon to grow angry at that, but

instead, the look that crossed her face was pensive, almost sad. She gave him more water to drink before speaking.

"That was the greatest part of why I first flew to battle against the Ithonian Empire, yes. My foes accused me of being a cruel, power-thirsty monster over the century and a half I stood against the Empire, and they were right to do so. I opposed them because their system threatened my own power, my own territory. I like to think I've changed over the centuries, and that my opposition to imperial aims has transformed from a selfish to a philosophical one. It has, at least, become a genuine belief in the deep and fundamental instability of empires and the disproportionate chaos they leave in the wake of their collapse compared to nations or city-states. Has Alustin told you of my work sponsoring new liches?"

Hugh nodded at that.

"It is part of my effort to bring a little more stability to our world without conquest, without imperial expansion. Liches are far more stable over the long term than most great powers, and they're far more resistant to those with imperial aims. I choose my candidates for lichdom carefully, Hugh. I look for those who will not be tyrannical, and who will tend to the needs of their demesne's inhabitants. I don't always get it right, but, well… I can destroy a lich as easily as I help to create one. Even easier, truly. Liches are stubborn, hidebound, and slow to change in many ways. Immortality removes much of their mental plasticity. It can often result in unrepentant monsters, but it can also result in nigh-incorruptible defenders. Create enough of the latter, and perhaps it will help to change the system of great powers, to alter the balance for the better. It will be centuries yet before my efforts will likely come to fruition."

Part of Hugh marveled at how far into the future Kanderon planned.

"One of my foes could spend hours reciting my misdeeds, and I could spend hours lecturing you on my philosophical opposition to empires, Hugh, but neither lie at the heart of why I destroyed Imperial Ithos."

Kanderon went silent, staring off into space.

"Why did you do it?" Hugh finally asked.

"Revenge, Hugh. Ithos attacked my nest, atop the mountain now known as Skyhold. I lost my original wings in that attack. My mate was blinded. And our nestling… the Ithonians killed our child, Hugh. It wasn't an unprovoked attack by any means— I'd spent so many decades being a thorn in their side, and I committed monstrous wrongs of my own. None of that mattered to me, then. The only thing that mattered at all to me was that my child was dead, and I would see her killers pay. Have you ever seen an illustration of a sphinx nestling, Hugh?"

He shook his head.

"They're gangly, clumsy, ugly creatures, who can't go three steps without tripping over their own wings. If I were to attempt to be objective about it, I might have to admit to my daughter having been even scruffier and awkward than most. But she was the most beautiful thing in the world to me. And the Ithonians took her away from me."

Hugh felt Kanderon's massive frame shudder, but out of rage or grief he didn't know.

"All these centuries, and it still hurts as bad as it did then."

Kanderon was silent for a long time after that. Hugh didn't press her, he just watched the stars patiently.

"My mate and I gathered our allies, and we built the Exile Splinter. I constructed its physical frame, my mate constructed its core, and our allies crafted the spells within it and the spells that would carry it to its target. I attuned my aether crystal during the Exile Splinter's construction, Hugh, as you attuned yours constructing the Stormward around Theras Tel. It took us three long years to build, and cost the lives of five of the thirteen of us. Including my mate. But build it we did, and I don't doubt that those who died would still have gone through with it even had they known it would cost their lives, for

we all hated the Ithonian Empire that much. None of us cared a whit for the consequences. And after Ithos was gone, we found replacements for the five we lost, and we founded Skyhold. Not as a place of learning, but as a fortress, dedicated to hunting down and shattering the remnants of the Ithonian Empire. Our hate, our vengeance… it justified everything to us in those days. Even looking back on all the atrocities we committed, Hugh, do you know what my greatest regret is?”

Hugh just shook his head.

“Building the Exile Splinter cost us more than just some of our lives. It cost us many of our memories, Hugh. I don’t remember much of my life before the Exile Splinter. So much of it is just… gone. Friends and enemies, wonders and horrors, all simply gone. Worst of all though? I can’t remember their names, Hugh. My mate, my child. I can’t remember their names. I see their faces in my dreams still. I still remember the long, silent flights I would take with my mate. I still remember how messy my daughter would get when I fed her, and how she would struggle to get away when I cleaned her. But I don’t remember their names. That’s why I wanted the Exile Splinter back. Not to keep it out of the hands of those who would abuse it, or to use it again, or for any higher purpose. I wanted it back out of hope that it might restore my lost memories.”

Kanderon was wearing an expression that he couldn’t place at first, simply because it was so foreign to his image of her.

She was sad, yes, but she was also nervous.

Kanderon Crux, the Crystal Sphinx, the last living founder of Skyhold, the killer of the Ithonian Empire, was afraid of how he would judge her for her actions.

“Did it work?” Hugh asked.

Slowly, haltingly, Kanderon shook her head.

“I’m sorry, Kanderon,” Hugh said. “I wish there was something I could do.”

Kanderon smiled at him sadly, but also with visible relief.

“Thank you, Hugh. In truth, this is no great shock to

me. I don't think I ever really expected to get those memories back. Some prices cannot be unpaid. In some ways, I think it might be a relief, to not have to mourn any longer."

Kanderon seemed like she wanted to say more, then sighed. **"I have kept you up too long, Hugh. You should sleep. You're far from healed yet."**

Hugh had a thousand more questions he wanted to ask, but Kanderon simply adjusted his blanket with her magic and tucked her foreleg in a little closer to her. The warmth quickly had Hugh's eyelids drooping.

"Kanderon?" Hugh asked, struggling to stay awake.

"Yes?"

"Thank you."

"For what, Hugh?"

"For taking care of me."

There was a long pause, and Hugh's eyes drifted shut. The last thing he heard before he fell asleep was Kanderon's voice.

"Always, little one."

There were very few beings on the continent that could sneak up on Kanderon Crux. Vanishingly few who had ever lived who might do so, in fact. But if one of them had done so that night, if one of them had crept up on the great sphinx— crept past the vigilant watch of her Librarians Errant, crept past the defensive wards of the camp, crept past a ward circling the sphinx that kept others from hearing any sensitive words spoken within from escaping, they might have heard something odd. Something that tickled their ears, just at the very edge of their hearing.

If they had been brave or mad enough to sneak even closer, they might have been able to start making out the sound. Even more perilously close, close enough that they might reach out and touch the sphinx with their fingers, and the sound would finally resolve itself into a low, deep, rhythmic rumble. A sound that would be familiar to any farmer or sailor, royal chef or scribe.

Sphinxes are not cats, any more than they are birds or humans. But they share traits of all three.

And that noise— that low, gentle rumble— was most certainly one of the traits sphinxes share with cats.

Kanderon Crux, the Crystal Sphinx, the Doom of Ithos, once known as the Calamity and as the Mad Sphinx, was purring.

CHAPTER FORTY-THREE

Setting the Stage

Duarch Icola was in a truly vile mood as she entered the Conclave's chambers. She didn't show it on her face, of course— she never showed any emotion she didn't want to.

The wiser of the palace servants, however, had learned to read the tone of her footsteps as she strode the halls. Today the bronze fittings on her white-leather boots struck against the marble floors like hammer blows. None of the senior servants were to be seen anywhere near her. Not that Icola would abuse her power against her underlings just to vent her anger, of course— but one could hardly blame them for fearing running afoul of the tempers of the mighty.

When Icola entered the Conclave chambers, she found, unsurprisingly, that she was one of the only members to restrain their anger at all. Her counterpart in ruling Havath, Duarch Locke, was furious, snapping at everyone who approached him. The avatars of the Intertwined, the seven liches whose demesnes wove together to form the bulk of Havath City, were visibly perturbed— which was astonishing in and of itself, for liches were far more capable of restraining their expressions than those made of flesh and blood. Those of the great powers of Havath who could fit into the Conclave chamber were arguing with each other, and with the representatives of those great powers at the borders or those simply too large to fit within the conclave chambers.

Thankfully, it wasn't a full Conclave. The generals, provincial representatives, and archmages would have turned the chamber into a full-scale riot, but they were seldom invited to meetings this important.

Icola took a moment to contemplate the marble and bronze chamber, with its fluted columns, great windows overlooking the city, and its spellform defenses cunningly concealed amongst the decorative bronze inlays.

Quite a few of the occupants of the chamber were eying her, waiting for her to be seated beside Locke so the meeting could begin, but she strode along the outside of the great round chamber, until she came across one of the westward facing windows.

Havath City stretched out for miles below her. It was not only the greatest city on the continent, but also the wealthiest, most peaceful, and even the cleanest. Great marble palaces lined its wide boulevards, mixed with immense, perfectly groomed parks and gardens, none of which had a single blade of grass out of place. Even the slums on the edge of the city were clean, orderly, and well tended. No one went hungry in Havath City. It never rained when the Duarchs and the Conclave decreed it wouldn't, and it never failed to rain when they decreed it would.

Ringing the edge of the city were seven great bronze-armored statues, towering above the palaces of the city, save for the Conclave itself.

Far in the distance, past the great walls of the city, Icola could see the grain-covered plains extend to the horizon in orderly, neat squares, laid out sensibly, laid out rationally, with no quarter given to the chaotic whims of nature.

It was all orderly, it was all neat. The Havathi Dominion existed to bring prosperity, to end the reign of fear and uncertainty that the selfish, feuding great powers brought to Anastis.

Kanderon would not be allowed to challenge that vision. Kanderon would not be allowed to end Havath, just to preserve her own power. Kanderon and her backers were a blight on the Council, and she had finally given them an excuse to move against her without violating the compact the Council had forced on their factions.

She could not be trusted with the Exile Splinter. She could not be given a chance to crush the dream of a better future for the Ithonian continent, for Anastis itself.

She could not be allowed to ruin yet another proving ground for the multiverse.

Icola sighed and gathered her temper. She would need every ounce of self-control she had to deal with the fractious Conclave.

It was time for the Havath Dominion to go to war once more.

On the banks of Lake Nelu, in the first hours of dawn, just as the light of the lake was being replaced with the light of the dawn, the Heir of Ithos crept from the water.

The light still burnt their eyes even while closed. The heat was overwhelming, though not so hateful as the light. After all, heat is what they had been promised by the Wise Ones on the other side of the dark. They had promised that once they themselves were warm again, they would share that warmth with the Heir. They would make sure the Heir had all the food they could eat, all the clean water they could drink.

And all of that with no one there to steal it. No one to fight them for scraps in the dark. No one that you had to huddle with to stay warm, but whom you could not fall asleep near lest they decide you were better used for meat than for warmth.

Of course, they could not fall asleep against you either, for much the same reasons.

And then the Heir had been the last one scrabbling in the

dark. They had been alone. It had been good, until the last of the food began running out. The last of the old ones had filled the heir's belly, but then they had not been there to make bad water good or make warmth out of nothing for the Heir.

As much as the Heir could regret anything, it was eating the last old one. They missed the way it was safe to sleep against the old one for warmth without fearing becoming food. They missed the strange lights the old one could summon, and the mysterious warmth. They had tried to teach the Heir these things, but the children born in the dark could not learn the old ones' magic. All those miraculous things were not what the Heir regretted most about eating the last old one, though.

No, what the Heir regretted most is that they couldn't remember the soft nonsense word the last old one had whispered as they brushed the Heir's stringy, greasy hair with their fingers. It was a word that had described the Heir and only the Heir, and only the last old one had used it, and now the Heir could no longer remember that word.

When the Heir was alone in the dark, they grew colder and hungrier until they were ready to give up.

And then the Wise Ones on the other side of the dark had found them. Had spoken to them. Had taught them how to survive the cold. Had taught them so, so many things. So many tricks, so many strengths. They taught the Heir how to become like the dark itself, that none might remember the Heir after they looked away.

They taught the Heir how to sleep the sleep that was not sleep, that lasted forever and no time at all, so that the Heir could be ready when the time came.

And most of all, they taught the Heir how to call them.

They had warned the Heir how bright this place that was not the dark was. How warm it was. How much food there was.

But they had also warned them how many others there were. How many others to fight for food and to make you not trust where you slept.

The Wise Ones' warning had proven right. The instant the dark had intruded upon the other place for more than mere moments, had grown close enough to that place of light for the Heir to finally awaken fully from the sleep that wasn't sleep, the others had arrived, swarmed everywhere, and destroyed all of the hiding places and not-shadows of the dark.

Three of them had seen the Heir. Two of them that were meat and a third that was not meat but still moved, who was small hung over the shoulder of the meat not wearing a shell of stone.

The Heir had fled then, and they had forgotten the heir, save for the other that was not meat but still moved.

The Wise Ones had promised the Heir that once they were called, they would take care of all the others that might steal the Heir's food.

And the Heir would be alone again, but they would be warm, and they would be full, and they would not need to fear thieves and hungry mouths in the dark anymore. They would not need to fear sleep when it was warm, would not need to fear light as a trap.

The Wise Ones from the other side of the dark promised that when they were done, they would help the Heir forget the last old one, who somehow hurt them by not being there.

And the Heir trusted the Wise Ones' promises, because they had no bodies to betray the Heir with. And if there was only one thing the Heir knew about being human, it was sharing warmth. And the Wise Ones were so cold, and just wanted to be warm again.

On the banks of Lake Nelu, the Heir of Ithos, a creature that might have been human once, turned to face the ruined city that they had once known as the dark, known as their home. And insomuch as the Heir was capable of feeling anything but hunger and fear, they felt nostalgia twined with hate twined with fear of leaving, all aimed at the ruins of Imperial Ithos.

And it was there, as the Heir spent a few moments gazing out into the mists and the ruins that filled them, that the Heir readied itself to call the Wise Ones to this light place so they could be warm again.

And it was there, as the Heir began to look away from its former home, that it would never enter again, that they felt a sudden flare of pain that ended as quickly as their tragic life did.

And it was there, on the banks of Lake Nelu at dawn, as the light of the sun usurped the light of the lake entirely, that the Mage-Eater became the first being since the long-extinct Labyrinth Builders to thwart the plans of the Cold Minds. It was there that the Mage-Eater became the single greatest hero in the history of the Ithonian continent, of Anastis itself.

No one would ever know, of course. And even if someone managed to ask the Mage-Eater about it, it was doubtful that the tigress had any thoughts on the matter, save perhaps irritation at the Heir being so stringy.

John Bierce

Murder at Ras Andis

This story takes place concurrent with the events of Into the Labyrinth, *Book 1 of Mage Errant.*

Ilinia Kaen Das- Stormguard of the South, Protector of Ras Andis, Kraken's Bane, and Hammer of the Sky- glared at her archrival across the table. Without taking her eyes off the cursed woman, she dropped her tile into place, then loudly sipped her tea.

Anicia Fil Dai- annoying old gossipy busybody, general nuisance, widow of a former guard captain, and owner of her family's prosperous bakery- cackled, then dropped her tile onto the board carelessly. "You'll have to try harder than that, you old hussy," Anicia said.

Ilinia glared at the board in frustration. She could already tell that Anicia had this game. If they kept playing, Ilinia might drag it out for another ten or fifteen turns, but there was no coming back from Anicia's advantage.

Ilinia dropped her next tile anyways. Anicia might win two out of every three of their games, but Ilinia had never forfeited a single game before, and she wasn't about to start now.

"Lady Protector," an annoying, nasally voice said. "The Prince..."

Ilinia sighed. Loudly.

The voice continued undeterred. "The Prince would like your support on the matter. We can't simply have our merchants imprisoned on such flimsy charges. If..."

Ilinia sighed even louder, trying to tune out the Prince of Ras Andis' messenger. The Prince and his family held title to the city entirely for the purpose of keeping this sort of aggravating day to day diplomacy and administration from bothering the Kaen Das family. Somehow, though, some sort of supposedly urgent crisis found its way to her door on a distressingly regular basis.

Well, less her door than her favorite run-down little tea shop. If someone didn't know better, they might mistake Ilinia for just another of the old women in this quiet little neighborhood that gathered at the tea shop to gossip and play tiles.

Ilinia would greatly prefer it if many more people made that mistake.

Anicia smiled charmingly at Ilinia as she dropped her tile. "You should play my great-granddaughter sometime, Ilinia. She'd be rather more your speed as an opponent."

Ilinia glowered at her. The little girl was six.

"Lady Protector," the messenger started again.

"Tell them that if they don't release the merchant, I'll sink their city into the sea," Ilinia snapped.

"My lady, Rue Granis is more than a hundred leagues from the sea," the messenger said hesitantly.

Ilinia dropped her next tile, not sparing a glance at the messenger.

"I really couldn't care less," she said. "I'll sink it into the sea anyhow."

Anicia just chuckled. "Your diplomacy is as brutish and crude as your tile game," she said.

The messenger hesitated for a moment, then bowed and rushed out, obviously terrified that Ilinia was about to destroy the tea shop or something.

Ilinia didn't even notice him leave, as focused on the tiles board as she was.

By their fifth game of the morning, Ilinia was feeling considerably less grumpy. She'd won two games against Anicia, leaving them tied, and this game was still anyone's business.

"Shouldn't Enthis be in by now?" Ilinia asked.

"Why?" Anicia asked. "Feeling a little motherly concern?"

"Not quite," Ilinia said dryly.

A couple of old biddies at the next table cackled at that.

Enthis was a large part of the reason the tea shop was always packed- half the women in the neighborhood were in love with him, and the other half were either blind or crazy. For that matter, a great many of the men were too. They didn't make them much prettier than Enthis.

If Ilinia were forty years younger, well...

No, strike that. If she thought Enthis was interested, who gave a storm about forty years. Or fifty.

By the end of the game, however, Ilinia was starting to grow curious. She couldn't remember the last time Enthis had missed his afternoon shift.

Ilinia cast her senses to the winds looking for him, and... found nothing. She frowned. That wasn't entirely unexpected, of course- her wind scrying was far better attuned towards operating at great distances, and tended to fail as often as not if she were using it within a few leagues. There was no such thing as a one-size-fits-all approach towards scrying- or anything in magic, really. Everything had trade-offs, and even the Great Powers couldn't escape that.

"Nassae!" Ilinia called to the shop attendant. "Would you run to Enthis' tenement to check on him, please?"

The girl looked like she was about to say something, but thought better of it and took off at a run.

Ilinia noticed with amusement that the girl hadn't needed to ask where Enthis lived.

Her amusement vanished when Nassae returned terrified and weeping.

Ilinia kicked one guardsman in the ankle, whacked another upside the head with her cane, and bodily lifted a third out of the way with a spell. Anicia followed right behind her.

The guardsmen quickly stepped back without a word of protest, save for the one she'd hit with her cane, who stared at her cane in terror. Or, rather, at the clouds and lightning flowing through her cane.

Ilinia stepped over a pool of blood and stared down at Enthis' body. He'd been stabbed. Not just once or twice, but at least a dozen times, mostly in the chest and stomach.

She moved one of Enthis' arms with her cane, noting the wounds all over his hands and forearms. He'd tried to protect himself, at least.

Anicia chewed on a bit of areca as she eyed the corpse-nasty habit, that, Ilinia was quite fine sticking to her pipe, thank you very much.

"Care to wager on who can solve this one first?" Anicia asked.

"What odds were you thinking?" Ilinia asked, as her eyes roamed the room.

"Loser has to drink that awful Alikean tea for a month?" Anicia said.

"That's just cruel," Ilinia said. "You've got an evil mind."

A ship full of a particularly nasty batch of Alikean tea had arrived a few weeks ago. It was thin, bitter, acrid stuff, and there were a number of running bets on when the supply at their tea shop would get thrown out.

Ilinia had her money on two more months.

"And no honey or milk, either," Anicia said.

"Lady Protector," the guard captain on the scene said, "the city guard is capable of handling this, there's no reason for you to waste your time on it."

"Done," Ilinia said to Anicia. "I look forwards to watching you pucker up when you try and drink it."

Ilinia and Anicia spent a short time poking around Enthis' room for further clues, but there was little to be found. Enthis, by all accounts, had never spent too much time in his room.

He'd spent plenty of time in other peoples rooms, of course.

They split up after that, each with their own ideas of how to proceed. Ilinia strode out into the sweltering Ras Andis sun, not bothering with any sort of spell to keep her cool.

If you couldn't handle the heat, you shouldn't be living in the sun.

Or, at least, you shouldn't use any sort of cooling spell where someone might see. Especially where someone might share the gossip with Anicia.

She did, however, wrap her eseln-cloth around her eyes. The thin, gauzy cloth didn't significantly obscure her vision, but it did cut down on the glare. Most of the passerby wore them as well, in a brilliant array of colors, patterns, and fashions. They were, by and large, the most significant fashion accessory for most people in the city, and some of the more absurd ones Ilinia saw were lined with jeweled beads or laced through with silver and gold thread in intricate patterns.

Ilinia's eseln-cloth was ratty, brown, and heavily stained, mostly by tea.

Once Ilinia had gotten away from the crowd in front of the tenement, she hailed an ostrich cart.

Well, she tossed the passengers out from the first one that went by with a gust of wind, then boarded it herself, but close enough.

She at least muffled their landing so they wouldn't get hurt.

"Stormseat," Ilinia told the driver, who wisely chose not to say anything.

The ostrich gave her a dirty look, though. Ilinia made a rude gesture at it, then turned to watch the city slowly go by.

She'd never get tired of looking at Ras Andis. It was one of the most beautiful cities on the continent of Ithos- for that matter, on all of Anastis.

The coastline of Ras Andis rose straight out of the water in a series of towering, sheer white cliffs- not chalk or marble, as visitors often assumed, but welded volcanic ash compressed into stone over eons. If you were to sail eastwards along the cliffs, you'd see nothing for half a hundred leagues until you reached the edge of the harbor itself. There, the cliffs would abruptly open up, and you'd find yourself in front of the entrance to Ras Andis harbor without warning. (Well, without warning apart from the dozens of fishing boats, merchant vessels, and warships inevitably sailing in and out.)

The massive Ras Andis cove had started as a faultline running out to sea, and had been gradually carved out by the combination of waves and a moderate sized river over the years. It hadn't been used as a harbor very often before the city's construction, of course. It made decent shelter from storms, and the bottom was soft sand that ships could rest on without worrying about damage during low tides, but the cliffs were nearly six hundred feet tall- there was no good way to get people or cargo up and down.

At least, not until the Ithonian Empire built Ras Andis.

It had been the last of their truly great works, and one of the most expensive-- it nearly bankrupted the Empire at the time it could least afford it. Ash-stone was far from the most difficult stone to work, but there had been just so much of it. Their legions of stone mages had carved massive, switchbacking tiers running all the way up the cliff wall. It was, to Ilinia's knowledge, the single longest, widest ramp ever built. The top of the cliffs in the back were carved inwards well over a mile. The harbor was extended sideways as well, almost tripling the volume of the cove, while leaving the entrance alone. The entrance was half a mile across, but it looked far, far smaller in proportion to the cove it guarded.

The Ithonian Empire had collapsed soon after. Half their provinces had already been in rebellion even before Imperial Ithos was lost in a single, fateful day. The bulk of the construction on Ras Andis had been completed, but no one lived there yet. The massive switchbacking ramp and its branches were left abandoned for most of a century.

It had taken surprisingly little time for trade to recover and civilization to stabilize, and it was inevitable that someone would settle in Ras Andis. That someone had just happened to include some of Ilinia's ancestors, who had named it after some long-forgotten mythical figure.

There had been immense amounts of work left to do still,

of course-- the Ithonians hadn't even bothered to measure how high storm surges got in the harbor during storm season, and the entire lowest tier was rendered worthless by it. They'd only built it fifty feet above the bed of the cove, giving them what they thought was a solid ten feet of clearance above the highest tides, but storm surges regularly topped eighty feet or more.

And Ras Andis had mild tides compared to many harbors. You couldn't really accuse the Ithonians of respecting nature, though- they'd tried to build cities in coastal lowlands.

It remained an immutable fact of nature that unless your village was made of boats, you don't build anywhere near the sea, except atop a cliff.

Every tier above the lowest, however, quickly filled up with tenements, shops, warehouses, and cafes. There were entire warrens of streets running here and there across the great ramp, all fashioned of the same white stone as the cliffs. Great brass domes and spires topped many of the wealthier abodes and businesses. Aqueducts carried the tamed river that had once run into the cove throughout the city.

It got bright enough to hurt your eyes during the day, hence the popularity of eseln-cloths.

The only laws that had remained consistent in governing construction? There was always to be left an open space on each side of the ramp. On the outer edge looking out onto the harbor, a wide walkway for people to wander and children to play. Between the buildings and the cliff, a road for the wagons traveling to and from the harbor.

As the Kaen Das family grew in magical power, the storm surges stopped being a concern, and now the lowest tier was as crowded as any of the others.

In the water of the cove, massive floating docks had been built, anchored to massive poles sunk into the seabed. As the water drained entirely out of the cove at low tide, the docks sunk to the sandy seafloor, carefully nestling ships in their recesses, so that they wouldn't tip on the seafloor. There were even specially constructed docking bays for the great keeled ships that traveled to other continents.

The city had grown and grown over the centuries. There wasn't an exact census of its population now, but it was well over a million. The city had overflowed the great ramp and started sprawling out along the clifftops, into the barren, narrow, and rocky waste that separated Ras Andis from the sands of the Endless Erg.

This made a lot more work for Ilinia-- she had to push sandstorms considerably farther out of the way than her ancestors had. You only had to nudge them a bit when everyone lived in the shelter of the cliff walls, but these days she had to push them entirely off course.

It had, in fairness, been like that since her grandmother's day, but Ilinia wasn't going to stop complaining about it for any frivolous reason like facts.

Once they reached the inner road, Ilinia quickly recalled why she so seldom bothered with traveling on foot or by cart. It was slow, and the buildings blocked the view.

Ilinia sighed heavily and slapped a coin on the seat next to her, then hopped out of the moving cart. Before she hit the ground, she reached out and seized the winds, launching herself into the sky.

Anicia always teased her that more men had seen her undergarments than any other woman alive, given how much time she spent in the sky above Ras Andis, but Ilinia couldn't honestly be bothered. There was nothing- nothing- like being in the sky.

Plus, at the speed she liked to take off, she'd be shocked if anyone had ever glimpsed anything. She'd shattered glass a few times taking off when she was younger, though she was a little more cautious in inhabited areas these days. Still, there was usually a blast of dust and grit when she took off that had pedestrians nearby covering their eyes. On top of that, it only took her a handful of seconds to rise above the cliffs in height.

Ilinia took a deep breath as she rose above the cliff walls

and looked out over Ras Andis and the Endless Erg. She dropped her cane, effortlessly snagging it with currents of air and suspending it nearby.

She slowly rotated, taking a moment to look down into the harbor, then looking up to the tops of the barrier cliffs separating the harbor from the sea.

On eastern promontory was the great lighthouse of Ras Andis. Its magical beacon could be seen far out to sea even in the midst of the fiercest typhoons- not that Ilinia was in the habit of letting storms get close to Ras Andis. Sprawled around its base was the enormous palace of the Prince of Ras Andis. (Well, more of an oversize building for clerks than palace- the Prince was mostly a hereditary bureaucratic functionary, as far as the Kaen Das family was concerned.) The beacon was the second largest draw on the aether in Ras Andis, though it would have been by far the largest in many cities. In many other cities, it also would have been by far the tallest structure in the city.

Not in Ras Andis, however, for on the western promontory rested Stormseat.

Stormseat was one of the most notable fortresses on the continent of Ithos, and that was saying a lot. In the chaos after the collapse of the Ithonian Empire, as the resurgent great powers battled the remnant legions for control, the people of the continent had taken fortress building to a new level. Many of the fortresses were built as much for memorability as defensibility, but Skyseat put most of them to shame.

Kanderon Crux, that mangy oversized alleycat, lurked in the depths of her extra-spatial library, itself concealed in the mighty mountain fortress of Skyhold. From it, she wove her centuries-long plots as she manipulated civilization into a form more pleasing to her and her extra-planar... allies. Ilinia had insulted Kanderon to her face on quite a few occasions, but even she'd never been so foolhardy to suggest that they might be Kanderon's masters. Even ignoring them, however, she honestly didn't know how someone could hope to get to Kanderon without luring her out of the mountain.

Intet Slew lurked in the depths of the labyrinth of Louthem, the ruined city filled with her cruel traps and brutal wards. The demonic dragon-thing apparently had no intention of ever giving up the charnel pit she'd fashioned of the city, once a wealthy mining town on the far northwest edge of the Skyreach Range. She had plenty of foes to worry about-- she was one of the biggest threats to stability in the region, and the dragons considered her existence an insult to their dignity. Intet Slew had magically fortified the ruins enough, however, that Ilinia doubted anyone would break through anytime soon-- it would take a truly massive alliance of great powers to do so, and with Havath always ready and waiting for any states or great powers to drop their guard, that wasn't likely anytime soon.

Castle Charax, the capitol seat of Highvale, was large enough and well populated enough that it could easily be considered a small city on its own- even ignoring the huge city surrounding it. For that matter, most of the Highvale wall-forts guarding their mountain passes were larger than the seats of many of the great powers. Highvale might not currently have a great power on their side, but along with their highly disciplined mage corps, those forts and their wards rendered Highvale almost impenetrable, even to the upper echelons of the great powers.

Stormseat wasn't as massive as Skyhold, as intimidating as Castle Charax, or as brutally guarded as the ruins of Louthem, but it was, quite possibly, the most gorgeous fortification in Ithos.

Towering, polished stone spires twisted upwards to points in a chaotic-yet-graceful profusion, reminiscent of twisted horn. Arches and bridges abounded between them, and many of the towers were pierced by great holes, as though they were needles waiting to be threaded. Most of the white ash-stone towers were capped with brass. The base of Stormseat wasn't surrounded by a wall, but instead sprawled out into majestic gardens, hedge mazes, and shallow lakes that migratory flamingos and seadrakes often rested in. Surrounding all of them was a broad, flat ring of polished ash-stone.

Stormseat didn't need a wall around it. No enemy would ever easily cross that ring of polished stone. The entirety of Stormseat was built to funnel winds, and at the slightest threat, the Kaen Das family could raise winds of unparalleled ferocity around the palace. The rounded towers, great arches, and spire holes all helped guide the winds into truly massive spellforms.

Thc citadel was, by any account, one of the most majestic sights in the world.

Ilinia thought it was garish and pompous. She'd lived there her whole life, and she'd seen far too many of her relatives make fools of themselves, thinking it made them better, smarter, mightier, or worthier than anyone else.

A cleaned-up pig in jewelery was much less dignified than a pig in a field, no matter what it thought looking in a mirror.

Ilinia hurtled down towards a landing on the massive central tower of Stormseat. Unlike the rest of the towers, this one didn't come to a point, instead unfurling into a series of great tiered balconies that made it resemble nothing so much as a colossal white rose.

At the very peak rested the Stormseat itself. There were no stairs or lift up to it- it was a great platform, open to the sky, with no railing or furniture of any sort, save for the throne. The only way up to it was either to fly or to be carried up on the winds. The great throne was carved of the same ash-stone as the rest of the city, every inch of it engraved with stylized wind, clouds, and lightning.

She'd delighted in putting the ugliest, rattiest looking cushion she could on it. She'd also managed to find a truly hideous wall-hanging in an awful combination of brown and yellow to drape over the back.

Stormseat had been her family's declaration of power, their crown. The Ithonians might have built the structure of Ras Andis, but Stormseat was entirely built by Kaen Das hands.

Well, paid for by Kaen Das gold. Her ancestors were nothing but full of their own glories, and it had brought them close to ruin time and time again over the centuries.

Stormseat's construction had almost beggared them, and the city had come close to open revolt in protest.

Ilinia barely bothered to slow down as she landed in the throne room, catching herself on a great cushion of air. There wasn't anyone else up here at the moment- most people avoided the throne room in the heat of the day.

As Ilinia shifted a nearby air current to give her a refreshing breeze, part of her winced internally, expecting Anicia to pop out of nowhere and mock her for it.

When Ilinia sat on the throne, her awareness exploded outwards.

Thrones were usually considered to be a symbol of power, but for the Kaen Das family, their throne, the titular Stormseat itself, wasn't a symbol. It was literally the source of a great part of their power. The throne itself was something like an access key to a massive network of enchantments riddling the palace, and reaching deep into the cliffs below. The wards of Stormseat tied into the throne, as did hundreds of concealed enchanted relays stretching across this region of the continent, as well as submerged in the nearby seas and atop nearby islands.

The relays played a oversized role in the power of the Kaen Das family. The family heads had all been great powers in their own right, but the relays strengthened them ever farther, as well as extending their senses across absurd distances. They also drained small amounts of mana from their surroundings, transferring it back to Stormseat.

Ilinia's grandmother had even, for some reason, had a line of relays submerged across the ocean, reaching all the way to the continent of Gelid, where they had a half dozen relays concealed in a small network. Many family members had considered it frivolous at the time, but Ilinia suspected it had been something of a challenge to her descendants- that someday, Kaen Das power would stretch around the world. The relays were hellishly difficult to produce, however, and each relay added to the network increased the difficulty of passing on the Stormseat to the next generation.

The seat had plenty of other tricks as well, of course-- the family had acquired countless enchanted objects over the years, including them or learning from them to improve the seat's power and range of function. Deep in the stone beneath the palace, there were massive artificial mana reservoirs, fed by the relay network. So far as Ilinia was aware, they were the largest mana reservoirs on the planet, far beyond the hypothetical maximum for artificial mana reservoirs. Which was probably because they weren't strictly artificial-- one of her more brilliant family members, long before she was born, had figured out a way for dying Kaen Das members to transplant their mana reservoirs into the Stormseat mana reservoir, though not very efficiently.

Ilinia didn't understand exactly how it was accomplished. Mana reservoirs didn't actually exist materially, but purely as aetheric structures cognitively linked to either minds or pre-cognitive enchantments. She didn't need to understand how it was accomplished, though, just what steps to follow. The mana reservoirs were one of the primary reasons why Kaen Das marriages were so carefully planned-- too much affinity distortion would cause the mana reservoir to decay past maintainable levels.

The other reason Kaen Das marriages were so carefully planned, of course, was the inheritance process. Each new Kaen Das had to go through the painstaking, challenging process of attuning to the throne and the relay network. It grew more difficult as the throne and the network grew in power, leaving a major period of vulnerability during transitions of power that had been steadily growing in length each generation. It had taken Ilinia nearly half a year to attune the throne, and she'd be shocked if it didn't take her heir far longer than that.

Of course, that wouldn't be just due to the growth of the throne and relay network. A big part of the problem had to do with how lackluster the current crop of potential heirs was. Most of them were barely up to the family's traditional standards, whether in power, intelligence, or temperament.

Or magical incompatibility in the case of her granddaughter Sabae, who was otherwise a perfect candidate.

Ilinia was considerably less reliant on Stormseat than many of her ancestors. Her own scrying abilities reached truly massive distances, often rendering the relay network unnecessary, and her mana reservoirs were massive enough that she could often divert storms without needing the Stormseat mana reservoirs.

Still, there were many times when she found herself relying on them. Like now, for instance. Her ancestors hadn't designed the relay network for monitoring Ras Andis itself, but Ilinia found that it served wonderfully as a focusing mechanism for her own scrying abilities, allowing her to examine the city in far greater detail than she would be able to on her own.

Ilinia shifted on the throne as her attention focused itself onto the neighborhood where Enthis had died, looking for anything out of place. They'd already moved his body down to the docks, where it would be loaded onto the funeral ship to be taken out to sea in the early evening. You had to deal with corpses quickly in this heat and humidity, and a city this size produced quite a few every day. The funeral ship took the bodies far out to sea at night, away from the fisheries, where they would be consigned to the seas, then return well before sunrise. The wealthy would often hire their own private funeral ships, but everyone else in the city had their farewell ceremonies before the ship left.

Anicia was only a block away, talking to a crying old woman-- Enthis' mother, if Ilinia had to guess. Ilinia didn't bother to listen in-- she highly doubted Anicia would get any useful evidence from the conversation.

There was an immediate, obvious solution to the murder-- one of Enthis' many admirers, or perhaps a vengeful husband or wife, had stabbed him to death in a fit of jealous rage.

It was, if Ilinia had to guess, entirely too obvious. It just fit too well, made too much sense. It was only messy in the way that people were normally messy. Ilinia couldn't think of a more normal, less suspicious murder.

Thinking there was anything more to it than that would frankly be the height of paranoia, and any sane person would quickly shrug the thought off as useless paranoia.

If there were ever competitive tournaments for paranoia, however, Ilinia was fairly confident she'd take home the victory without having to even strain herself. She'd had to defend Ras Andis for decades now, and there were few comparably attractive targets out there. It was one of the wealthiest, most populous cities on the continent. She even regularly had to deal with Havathan spies, and Havath was almost all the way across the continent.

Maybe Enthis' murder had just been what it seemed, but Ilinia had a strict policy whenever someone she had regular contact with died-- investigate it as though someone was making a move on the city.

It was a policy that had uncovered everything from other great powers making moves on Ras Andis to simple smuggling rings, and Ilinia had never regretted having it, or considered it a waste of her time.

Her breezes had thoroughly canvassed the neighborhood in minutes, so Ilinia expanded her search outwards. It could be for anything-- warehouses full of smuggled foreign troops, barrels of alchemical incendiaries, clandestine councils-- you never knew what new trick someone was going to try.

A particularly powerful, albeit foolish, archmage had once spent weeks smuggling in assorted magical creatures, and even a few mundane bears, lions, and wolves, intending to cause chaos by releasing them in the streets before going after Ilinia. It had taken months to resettle the animals into appropriate homes after they'd been rescued from their cramped holding pens, and Ilinia was confident that some of them still lurked somewhere in the sewers, thanks to the archmage's shoddy containment wards.

From Enthis' neighborhood, Ilinia extended her search outwards. She was well prepared to spend as much time as she needed searching.

Well, as much as her bladder would allow. She wasn't as young anymore, and she'd had quite a lot of tea so far today.

The next dawn had an irritable Ilinia drinking her morning tea atop Stormseat. She'd spent most of the afternoon and evening scrying the city on the winds without any luck. She'd also interviewed her intelligence division, who, of course, were just their usual useless gossipy selves.

Ilinia sighed, ignoring a nearby aide trying to get her attention, and forced herself to acknowledge that the intelligence division hadn't been useless, just that they hadn't had any relevant information on Enthis' murder. They were excellent at monitoring the activities of agents of other great powers, as well as all the fine details her scrying- and her limited time- didn't pick up on.

In her old age, she didn't need as much sleep as she used to, but even so, she'd gotten too little last night, and had already been back up here for hours.

She had never been particularly good at dealing with setbacks of this flavor, where nothing opposed her, where every action failed to hit any resistance and just didn't catch on anything. A seemingly intractable problem she had to wrestle and fight into submission she could handle, but this? This infuriated her.

Ilinia glared out to sea at the funeral ship sailing back into port. It was an unwanted reminder of her failure to make headway.

Anicia was going to win, at this rate.

Maybe it genuinely was just what it looked like- a crime of passion that had nothing to do with Ilinia. Maybe Enthis' murder had nothing to do with him working at Ilinia's preferred teashop. Maybe he hadn't stumbled across something he shouldn't have, or refused to accept a bribe to try and poison Ilinia (not that that would have worked), or had refused blackmail to spy on her, or some other such scenario. Maybe Ilinia was just being egocentric and

overestimating her importance.
No. No, that was entirely too complex of an answer, and relied on far too many unsubstantiated leaps of logic.
Her scrying of the city via the winds had been quite comprehensive. If someone had been smuggling troops into the city, or concealing something in general, she would have caught it if it were at any sort of significant scale. Ras Andis' security forces were far from incompetent, either, and caught onto threats to the city as often as Ilinia did. Well, nearly as often.
Maybe it wasn't something so crude and direct however. Maybe...
Ilinia sighed.
She had to go talk to the clerks again.

Amin Zeth, Prince of Ras Andis, cowered in front of Ilinia.
"Can I at least put my clothes on?" he asked.
"It's already almost an hour past dawn, you should have been dressed already," Ilinia snapped, poking the middle aged man with her cane.
He'd still been in bed when Ilinia arrived at the Lighthouse Palace, to her irritation, so she'd physically plucked him from the bed a gust of wind.
Ilinia scowled, but nodded.
"Sorry," Amin said, hastily grabbing a set of robes to put on.
"You're the Prince of Ras Andis," Ilinia said, "quit apologizing for everything."
Ilinia could see Amin's jaw tense visibly, but it sadly relaxed before he said anything.
One of these days she'd irritate the man enough to make him snap and start cursing her. She was profoundly disappointed he hadn't already. He was far too boring and polite.
As Amin dressed, she filled him in on the investigation so

far.

"Perhaps it really was just a crime of passion?" Amin asked.

Ilinia almost snapped at him, but stopped herself, and replied in a more even tone. "Perhaps, but on the slim chance it is, Anicia or the guards will catch it easily enough. We're a lot better suited towards dealing with it otherwise."

Amin didn't speak for a couple of minutes as he finished dressing. Ilinia waited patiently.

Well, maybe not that patiently, but Amin's cat had decided to investigate the noises in the bedroom, and Ilinia adored Seashell. No one would ever accuse the fluffy little white cat of being particularly intelligent, but she was excessively friendly towards literally everyone, and ridiculously chatty.

"So..." Amin said, pensively fastening the last buckle on his opulent (gaudy, really) robe. "You've found none of the usual signs of a threat or incursion into the city?"

"Of course not, otherwise I wouldn't have asked," Ilinia said, scratching Seashell's chin.

Amin frowned, then gestured at her to follow him, stalking out of the room.

Ilinia smiled at that- once Amin had a problem to solve, he would worry it like a dog chewing a bone.

Within minutes, Amin had collected several dozen clerks. Counting them was nigh impossible, given how often they'd arrive and leave on errands for the Prince. He had them gathering information on everything from tax ledgers to fishing yields to granary purchases to anonymous reports from their informants in the criminal underworld.

The huge table in the middle of the conference room was covered in paperwork before Ilinia had even gotten any tea.

Ilinia moved off to one side of the room, where someone fetched her a small table and chair. She patiently drank her tea-- with a little extra fortification from her flask, as per usual-- and pet Seashell in her lap as Amin and his clerks bustled around.

Well, patiently for her, at least.

She was on her third cup of tea-- in the Lighthouse Palace, at least, her fifth of the day so far-- when Amin started conferring excitedly with a couple of his clerks.

It was only a few minutes after that when Amin bustled over to her.

"We've got something," Amin said. "At first, I assumed that if there was something going on, it would be along the lines of counterfeiting, tax evasion, or something of that sort-- if there were a coup attempt or anything bigger, you would have noticed *something* while scrying."

"Unless it's a rogue archmage who thinks they don't need troops to seize the city and become a great power," Ilinia said.

"True," Amin said, "But that's not what's going on. We've found a whole series of irregularities so far. Grain purchases are up nearly half a percent past reasonable variance this time of year, taking into account population growth and crop yields. Aqueduct water use is..."

Ilinia shushed him. "Skip to the important part."

Amin carefully restrained an irritated look, then started over again. "The population of the city, or at least the city's use of resources, appears to have risen drastically over the past two to three weeks, indicative of hundreds or thousands of new mouths to feed, but we don't have any record of that population increase."

"Someone," Ilinia said, "is sneaking people into the city, for reasons unknown."

"Essentially, yes," Amin said.

"So you're saying my scrying was wrong, that I messed up?" Ilinia said, her voice level.

The clerks all tensed up.

"That," Amin said, almost as tense as the clerks, "is exactly what I'm saying."

The clerks looked like they were about to flee the room. Ilinia only managed to keep a straight face for a few more moments, then chuckled. That never got old.

"Relax," she told them. "Any leader that can't handle being told they're wrong isn't worth a rotten ship's hull."

A few of them chuckled nervously.

"Alert the guard, will you?" Ilinia told Amin. "Have them

start searching. Figure out where these mysterious intruders are and how they got in the city. And make sure the operation is noisy, loud, and has plenty of information leaks. I want them to know we're looking. I want them running scared and sloppy."

Covert operations were all well and good when you intended a root and stem destruction of an enemy force, or you had significant awareness of them, or when they had enough force to be a real threat to you.

Ilinia didn't give a barnacle's ass about any of that. She wanted them running scared, being sloppy, and exposing themselves.

Of course, she'd still have her intelligence division moving on them more stealthily, but Amin didn't need to know that.

By the time the guards began searching the city, Ilinia was already back atop Stormseat, scrying their operations. Her intelligence division had also begun looking, albeit much more quietly.

How had she missed an interloping force so easily? Her scrying should have noticed something like that.

There were, in fairness, quite a few possibilities. A sufficiently trained insertion force could become sleeper agents, posing as normal residents of the city, but that... almost beggared belief. That level of training among that many would be highly improbable, and the rapidity of insertion was even more improbable there.

An elaborate warding scheme was another distinct possibility, but that would require some unusually skilled wardcrafting to evade her notice. It was a much more likely probability than sleeper agents, certainly.

It was also possible that Ilinia had simply missed checking somewhere, but she wasn't that old yet, to have forgotten to search somewhere a small army could hide in.

Interference by another great power with influence over the wind with her scrying was a possibility, but she knew for a fact that Indris wasn't interfering-- Indris and the Kaen Das family had been butting heads for most of two centuries now, and there were specific warning wards for Indris' interference.

Plus, subtlety like this wasn't Indris' style-- if she were making a move, she'd do it far, far more directly, at a moment of vulnerability for Ras Andis.

A nearby aide delivered her another cup of tea, and she accepted it without paying much attention.

Perhaps...

Ilinia cursed, then pulled out her flask, dropping her scrying. She had missed scrying somewhere entirely. She'd even thought about it, but never looked.

The sewers.

Maybe she was getting old. There was no way she would have forgotten about them even a couple of years ago. She...

As she poured from her flask into her tea, the liquid started bubbling and fizzing.

Ilinia tried not to let alarm show on her face as she casually looked around the Stormseat throne platform.

Five assorted servants and aides, no members of the family. She hadn't been paying attention to which had handed her the cup of tea.

She also didn't recognize most of them.

Enjoyment wasn't the only reason she tilted her flask into just about every cup of tea she drank. The alcohol inside- or, as most of her family referred to it, that awful, stomach-corroding rotgut- had a few interesting alchemical additives, which, in combination with some of her flask's enchantments, would cause a vigorous reaction when mixed with most poisons.

Just like what was happening now.

As her eyes scanned around her, she noticed something else, and cursed.

Her cane was missing.

Ilinia sighed, set her cup of tea down, and took a sip directly from her flask. She then carefully tucked it away, and stood with a groan.

The aides and servants all tensed up.
"Well, let's get on with it, then," she said out loud.
Everyone started launching spells at about the same time.

Amin Zeth was having breakfast on a palace balcony when lightning erupted across the bay atop Stormseat. Seashell leapt off his lap with a yowl, scratching his legs through his robes, and the clerks that had been giving him reports of the ongoing operation all froze.

Amin sighed. This day just kept getting better and better.

"Continue," he said to the clerk that had been speaking, then took another bite of his squid-ink noodles.

The clerk coughed, then resumed reading the first reports from the operation.

Lightning and fire billowed up from the top of the tower again, and the clerk's voice wavered.

He stopped talking entirely as an answering explosion rose up below, in one of the middle tiers of Ras Andis.

Amin sighed, and set down his zur sticks, pasta still wrapped around them.

Just... better and better.

Not for the first time, Amin fantasized about abandoning his position and becoming a fisherman. Somewhere else entirely. Lothal, maybe? Seashell would make a decent ship's cat.

Ilinia casually deflected a fireball with a gust of wind, knocking it into the venom mage, who immediately collapsed onto the ground screaming. She had no idea why they'd even brought a venom mage up against her-- even a fairly weak wind mage was more than a match for most venom mages. If she'd been a stone or fire mage, she might have had trouble, but...

Ilinia blocked another lightning bolt from the one aide she did recognize, who was holding her cane. The storm inside

the cane was roiling and erupting. That could be a problem.
She launched a lightning bolt of her own at the silver mage nearby. That normally would be a borderline suicidal idea for a storm mage-- silver mages were ideally suited for deflecting and diverting lightning, even surpassing copper mages-- but Ilinia wasn't most storm mages. She just kept the lightning bolt going, even as the silver mage's floating rods diverted the electricity away.
She blocked another fireball with a gust of wind, then diverted another series of lightning bolts from the aide who'd stolen her cane towards the fire mage, who caught them with some sort of spell, then launched them back at Ilinia.
Ilinia rolled her eyes, and deflected them towards the silver mage. She envisioned a particularly nasty water spellform in her head-- one forbidden in quite a few places.
The fire and lightning mage simply began to dehydrate. Within seconds, she'd shriveled up into a husk and collapsed. Dehydration spells were a nasty piece of work, but thankfully, few water mages could cast them-- they were devilishly complex, and took more mana than most mages had in their entire mana reservoirs.
The venom mage still hadn't stopped screaming.
The gravity mage that she'd thrown off the tower with a burst of wind at the beginning of the fight finally made it back up. Before he could land and start casting anything on her-- gravity based attacks, as ashamed as Ilinia was to admit it, were particularly effective against her old bones-- she began to funnel wind into his mouth and nose. Lots of wind.
Considerably more than his lungs could hold.
She rolled her eyes. What kind of poor excuse for a gravity mage couldn't fly and cast offensive spells at the same time?
She blocked another chain of lightning bolts, then cast a spell to keep the... debris off of her as the gravity mage exploded, the pressure inside him more than his lungs and ribs could handle.
She'd kept the lightning bolt focused on the silver mage this whole time. They'd seemed confident enough at first, but

their swarm of silver rods was starting to glow with heat, even with them magically funneling the heat out of the silver. Several of the rods had begun to melt already.

One last lightning bolt from the mage with her cane got deflected, then Ilinia envisioned a spellform to amplify her voice above the crackling of her lightning bolt and the screams of the venom mage.

"It's traditional here for me to ask you if that's the best you can do, but that's really not necessary-- you'd have to be far, far more impressive than this for me to even work up a sweat," Ilinia said.

The cane thief raised her cane menacingly, then stopped before casting any spells. "You don't even know who I am, do you?" His voice was amplified as well-- if Ilinia had to guess, by the same spell she was using. Sometimes there was just no beating the classics.

"Nope," Ilinia said, just to irritate him. She actually did recognize him-- he'd been working in Stormseat for... five years now, six? His deep but nasally voice was fairly distinctive, and he'd proven an effective, responsible worker.

For the life of her, though, she couldn't remember his name.

The cane thief snarled incoherently.

The silver mage's rods were melting and dripping onto the ground as her lightning bolt kept crackling against them. Honestly, she could have disposed of the mage easily enough with a water or air spell, but Ilinia made a point of showing off that what might be a weakness for other storm mages was nothing of the sort for her. She regularly took down ice mages with water and stone mages with wind.

As far as outsiders need be concerned, Ilinia didn't have any weaknesses.

The silver mage shouted something that was drowned out by the lightning. Probably along the lines of "you can't keep this up forever" or some other such nonsense.

The cane thief recovered his composure and smiled cruelly at her. "Well, that's a problem for you, because I've been studying you for decades, Ilinia. I know all your tricks, all your strengths, and all your weaknesses. I know about the throne, I know about the storm relays, and I know about the mana reservoir beneath Stormseat."

Ilinia raised her eyebrows, honestly surprised for once. "I'm impressed. Not many groups bother to take the time to research me this patiently."

The thief glared at her. "There was no group, this was all me. I spent the time, I took the risks. These buffoons were just the best mages Rue Granis could provide me with. Hopefully their troops down in the city do a little better than this."

A rogue actor with some sort of grudge against her, who sold information to the first resentful buyer he could find? That explained a lot of the oddities of this case. His place inside the bureaucracy of Stormseat explained how they'd caught onto the investigation in time to mobilize in response.

"How did you get the troops in the city?" Ilinia asked.

"Don't you want to know why I'm doing this?" the thief asked, then sent another lightning bolt at her, followed by a scything blast of air that would have cut her in half.

She pulled the lightning bolt into her own, then dispersed the air scythe into a gentle breeze.

"Not really, no," Ilinia said. "At my age, the stories all tend to blur together. My family wronged yours somehow, or the Kaen Das tendency to justify means with ends is evil, or just simple greed. I've heard it all before. No, what I'm interested in is how you smuggled troops into Ras Andis."

"My family is your family," the thief yelled. "I'm rightfully a Kaen Das, but your family cast me aside like trash!"

That... actually was interesting. If it was true, this was the first time Ilinia had faced a rogue family member attacking the family. Not the first time in the family history, but the first time for her.

"That doesn't sound like something we'd do," Ilinia said. In a quite reasonable tone, considering he was attacking her.

"My father promised my mother the world, then discarded her like trash!" the thief yelled. "Ioset Kaen Das!"

Ilinia took a moment to think, batting aside a few more

attacks as she did. Ioset...

Ah, she remembered Ioset! He'd been... a nephew, sort of? The son of a distant cousin, anyhow. He'd died over thirty years ago, if she remembered correctly.

"Ioset died when he was only sixteen or seventeen," she said. "Sounds like he just had an affair, panicked, then didn't know what to do? Our family has a pretty forgiving policy about that sort of thing, we freely accept by-blows into the family proper. Sounds like your mother was just too stupid to actually approach the family and talk about the situation."

The thief bellowed in rage and tried to cast a dehydration spell on her. The instant her affinity senses detected the characteristic water-flow patterns, she immediately pulled more water vapor into her vicinity. It was an incredibly easy counter to dehydration spells-- another reason they weren't more popular.

She was actually starting to buy the thief's story. Lightning, air, and water affinities, mana reservoirs large enough to handle a dehydration spell, and a decent family resemblance?

"Alright, so you resented our family, wanted revenge, because you thought we'd wronged you and your mother. Basically still fits into the first category still. I still want to know how you smuggled troops into the city."

The thief laughed. "Why, so you can close off a hole in your defenses? You're *dead* wrong if you think I'll help you with that. Besides, you won't be alive long enough to stop me."

Her lightning bolt finally tore through the silver rods, sending molten metal exploding outwards as it slammed into the silver mage. The droplets of silver reached her windshield, and were harmlessly thrown away. The thief's eyes widened a little at that-- Ilinia's shield, about four feet out from her body, was entirely invisible. Most windshields started picking up dust and debris immediately.

Most mages weren't Ilinia.

Ilinia considered stopping her lightning bolt, but decided to keep it burning into the silver mage's corpse for the intimidation factor.

"Did you really just put a mocking emphasis on the word dead?" Ilinia said. "You're really doing the ego thing where you give me subtle clues to your genius plan so that I can appreciate it before you try to kill me?"

As the thief spluttered, Ilinia wracked her brain. She loved it when her foes were this egotistical-- it gave her another battleground to triumph on over them. Ilinia could be as egotistical as she wanted, because she'd earned it. They generally hadn't.

An idea occurred to her, and she quickly scryed the harbor-- or, at least a particular ship in it. The thief was good, but not good enough to deserve her full attention.

"The funeral ship!" Ilinia said, snapping her fingers. "You suborned the funeral ship, and you've been loading on troops to smuggle into the city after it drops off its cargo each night. That's why it returned later than usual this morning-- you had to transfer troops onto it!"

The thief snarled and opened his mouth, but she spoke right over him.

"Don't bother with the usual 'It doesn't matter if you've figured it out, I'll still triumph' speech, I hate those. Alright, next question: why'd you kill Enthis?"

The thief gave her a confused look. "Who?"

As she opened her mouth to answer, he tried to condense water vapor out of the air to drown her with. Ilinia easily stole control of it and sent the water towards him. Not in any sort of attack, but simply as a harmless, albeit annoying, splash of water. Meanwhile, she kept part of her attention on the harbor.

"The attendant at my teashop. The cute one. You had him murdered yesterday? I'm presuming he found out about your plans somehow." Ilinia asked.

"I have no idea what you're talking about," the thief snapped. "Why would we do that? That would be moronic of us, and would probably alert you to..."

He stopped, then started laughing. "*That's* what alerted you to our plan? We had nothing to do with that."

He started laughing even harder.

While he was doing that, Ilinia felt her mana reservoirs. Her water reservoir was still essentially full, as was her wind reservoir, but her lightning reservoir was almost half empty. It was her smallest, in fairness, but best not to take any risks, especially with what she was about to do with her wind magic.

She reached out with her affinity senses for the mana reservoir below Stormseat.

Only to find herself blocked.

A ring on the thief's finger started glowing, and his laughing changed in tone as he saw it. "You've finally figured it out, haven't you?" he said. "You finally started running low on mana, only to find that you don't have access to your little stash. I told you I knew about it, didn't I?"

Now that was inconvenient. It wouldn't slow down her plan at all, but...

"Sheer ridiculous bad luck might have alerted you to our presence, but preparation is going to win the day in our favor," the thief said. "I'm hardly arrogant enough to think that I could overwhelm you in a straight fight, but I am more than skilled enough to hold you off until you run out of mana-- especially considering that not only do I have the mana reservoir on my side, I have this as well." He shook the cane in the air.

Ilinia let the lightning bolt ravaging the corpse of the silver mage die away. If he was able to access the Stormseat mana reservoir, then he was definitely a Kaen Das. Pity. She noted that her wind reservoir had dropped precipitously. It wasn't in any danger of emptying, but it was down to about four fifths or so.

"There are so many stories about the storm you have locked in your cane, aren't there? Every time someone discusses your combat abilities, they always remark on your cane. If anyone were ever to defeat you, you'd break the cane and let the storm out all at once," the thief said, wearing a cruel smile. "But I don't think this is a storm. I think that's just an illusion, a cover story. I think this is another artificial mana reservoir of your own. I think this is what lets you operate so much farther away from Stormseat than your predecessors."

Ilinia raised her eyebrow at him. "Are you sure I can't convince you to quit this nonsense and join the family proper? We're always short on capable members these days, and you'd be a welcome addition."

The thief just laughed at her. "Getting desperate, are you? Not a chance, you vile old prune."

She sighed, then pulled out her flask and took a drink. She envisioned a rather specific spellform, then smiled at the thief.

She pumped mana into the spellform, and the cane cracked in the thief's hands. He stared at it in shock as the illusions inside it failed, and the storm vanished.

Ilinia waited until he looked back up at her, smiled, and waved goodbye.

Then she stopped using her wind affinity to hold the funeral ship in the air above them, and instead used it to hurl herself backwards into the wind.

The funeral ship, still filled with enemy troops that hadn't been smuggled into the sewers yet, impacted the platform hard enough to visibly shake Stormseat. Planks and enemy corpses went flying off into the air, and Ilinia could feel the thief's wind spells simply wink out.

She was legitimately shocked he hadn't seen her levitate an entire ship out of the bay. Battle might bring tunnel vision, but still, levitating an entire ship was nothing if not ostentatious.

He'd had a good plan, and he'd actually been right that the cane was just a red herring-- he'd been wrong in assuming that it was anything else, however. People were just as likely to steal it for being a reservoir as being a bottled storm.

She sipped from the flask again, and drew from the massive mana reservoir inside it at the same time. Of course, mana and alcohol weren't the only thing in the flask. If you held the opening of the flask to your ear, you could faintly hear the thunder, wind, and rain inside.

"Storms," cursed Ilinia, coming to a sudden realization. "I never actually got his name."

Ilinia glared across the table.

Everything else to do with this situation was manageable. They'd already discovered the enchantments the thief had used to hijack the mana reservoir. Once Ilinia had turned her attention away from the attempt on her life, she'd easily helped round up and eliminate Rue Granis' mercenaries. They were going to send a simple bill to Rue Granis for the damages-- much more intimidating than any amount of complaining, threats, or bureaucratic posturing. Even the wreckage of the funeral ship was easy enough to clean up. She'd set the rest of her family to that-- they'd hardly been useful at all during the whole crisis.

Though, admittedly, Ilinia probably should have actually mentioned it to them.

This, though, this was less manageable.

Anicia's smile grew even wider as she sipped her own tea. Her perfectly lovely, non-Alikean tea.

She'd solved Enthis' murder within hours, and had simply been waiting for Ilinia to show her face at the teashop. Enthis had been murdered by the jealous admirer of one of his lovers.

No matter how improbable it was that something in Ras Andis wasn't all about Ilinia, in a city of over a million people, it was known to happen occasionally.

Ilinia dropped her tile into play, then sipped at the truly vile cup of Alikean tea, visibly wincing.

At least she wasn't suffering through this alone. The city guard hadn't solved Enthis' murder either. The whole thousands-strong guard was going to be drinking nothing but this swill for the next month too.

With any luck, Ras Andis would run out of the bilge before the month was out.

Appendix: Galvachren's Guide to Anastis *Annotated by [Redacted]*

The world of Anastis should, by any account, be a hub for multiversal travelers. *([Redacted]'s note: Isn't it, though?)* There are more mana wells than nearly any other known inhabited world, with a preponderance of them being junction wells.

For some reason, however, the labyrinths on Anastis have run amok. They're far deeper and more tangled than any others I've encountered, going far beyond the original design of the Weavers. Whether this is a result of the unusual characteristics of this universe's Aether, or a result of how close to going aether critical this world is, is unknown. It's also possible that the labyrinths are evolving over time. I'm curious what the Weavers would think of that, but, alas, we'll never know. *([Redacted]'s note: Galvachren is, so far as we can tell, the only scholar to refer to the Labyrinth Builders as Weavers. We have no idea why. We remain fairly confident that he's not old enough to have encountered the Labyrinth Builders— Galvachren might be ancient, but he's no Cold Mind.)*

Physical Overview: Anastis is disproportionately geologically active, even for a young world. Much of this can be attributed to Anastis' preposterously large moon. Moon is a poor name, really, since Anastis and its moon actually orbit one another— it's not significantly smaller than Anastis itself. This also results in the massive tides of Anastis, which have resulted in the unusual population distribution on the continents— sapients on Anastis only inhabit the coast atop seacliffs or other raised landforms. Atmospheric pressure is also marginally higher than most inhabited worlds— in combination with Anastis' moon, this results in some truly impressive storm systems.

([Redacted]'s note: "impressive storm systems" is understating it.)

Anastis has recently exited an ice age, but it doesn't seem to be thanks to interference by *[redacted]*. *([Redacted]'s note: The ice age is only geologically recent. To anyone else other than Galvachren, recent is a terrible adjective. And of course there's no [redacted] presence— Anastis is one of our strongholds, not theirs.)*

Ecological Overview: Anastis' ecosystems are, to say the least, a mess. Remnants of the original ecosystem can still be found in some parts of the world— Ithos' Endless Erg, Gelid's great mudflats— but for the most part, it has been supplanted by invasive species that have poured out of Anastis' countless labyrinths over the eons. I've personally identified species from dozens of known worlds, and countless more I don't recognize.

There are at least a half dozen tool-using sapient species, and half again as many non-tool using sapients present. None are native to Anastis. This doesn't count the numerous members of the "Great Powers" of Anastis that are the only representative of their species on Anastis. It also doesn't count Aether mutations and [redacted] that can't properly be counted as members of their species any longer. *([Redacted]'s note: Our assessments of the count differ from Galvachren's, but this is, as usual, thanks to differing definitions of what counts as a species. Our official nomenclature also differs with who counts as [redacted]— while many of the Great Powers of Anastis can go toe to toe with [redacted], there's more to becoming [redacted] than mere power. Galvachren, after all, is no [redacted], and, well... Anyhow, by our definition, there are no [redacted] on Anastis. Which is one of the reasons we established this as one of our stronghold worlds.)*

The strangeness of what native life is still present leads me to hypothesize that Anastis originated in a relatively distant habitable reach of the multiverse, and that its connections have shifted over time.

There is a truly splendid diversity of spiders on Anastis. I could fill entire volumes on them. None are native, however.

Aetheric Overview: The Aether of Anastis is singularly unusual. While in many respects its Aether resembles a fairly typical liquid Aether world, there appears to be some process interfering with the free flow of Aether. Aether density is radically variable across Anastis, something usually only found in gaseous Aether environments. Even then, however, it's seldom even close to the Aether density variance of Anastis. There are a few rival hypotheses as to why this occurs.

The most popular hypothesis points to the unusual number, depth, and complexity of Anastis' labyrinths as the cause. While plausible sounding, an actual mechanism for this is seldom put forwards.

Another hypothesis claims that the Anastan Aether is thixotropic— that it responds to shocks by changing its viscosity. Shocks in this sense, of course, being heavy draws upon the Aether. The downside of this analysis, of course, is that no-one has ever felt said viscosity change.

There are a few other minor hypotheses to consider, ranging from the eccentric to the insane, but the last I find worthy of inclusion is that there is some sort of substrate through which the Anastan Aether flows. This is controversial, to say the least— there has never been direct evidence of any such substrate, and solid Aether is, to say the least, quite easy to perceive. Still, there is a marked similarity between the Anastan Aether flows and the movement of liquids in aquifers. *([Redacted]'s note: So far as we can tell, Galvachren was the originator of this hypothesis, but he shows his usual reticence in claiming credit for anything.)*

Regardless, as a consequence of this, Anastans tend to do well as multiversal travelers. They tend to recover from Aether sickness far more quickly when traveling between worlds than natives of worlds with more stable Aether. It seems likely that the variable Anastan Aether density has acclimated their systems to an extent.

As an added benefit, Anastis is far less prone to Aether exhaustion than many other worlds. One city-state overusing its Aether will seldom even affect many of its neighbors.

The magic of Anastis is also unusually versatile in function— not on an individual level, where mages tend to have quite specific portfolios of power, but overall, it's astonishingly diverse.

Political Overview: Thanks to the variable Anastan Aether density, political organization tends to lean towards smaller nation states and city states. While a few empires exist, they're far less common on Anastis than other worlds. The lack of Aether exhaustion as a major threat to civilization also changes political interactions, though in a perhaps less easily definable manner. *([Redacted]'s note: What a polite way to say that Anastan politics are an unstable, constantly shifting mess of coups, civil wars, and assassinations.)*

There is relatively little organized multiversal presence on Anastis. [Redacted] have planted none of their [redacted], [redacted] incursions are unknown, and the [redacted] has built no [redacted]. *([Redacted]'s note: We most certainly have, and Galvachren's visited them. What's he up to? Perhaps he thinks he's doing us a favor by not letting others know we're here? We might be one of the weaker multiversal powers, but we're not that weak],* [Redacted] infections are a non-factor, and there are few [redacted] on Anastis. (*[Redacted]'s note: there are no true [redacted] on Anastis. Again, it's why we made it one of our stronghold worlds. Anastis' Aether is inherently hostile to those belligerent, imbecilic godlings.)* The Radhan are, as with most human worlds, present, though as is often the case, they have little idea how far their own civilization extends. There are a larger than normal number of demons on Anastis, but that's simply a consequence of the numerous labyrinths. (*[Redacted]'s note: It is, as always, exasperating trying to figure out who Galvachren considers to be a multiversal power. His list is considerably shorter than expected, and excludes quite a number of powers that we'd include. Most notably of course, Galvachren himself.)*

Author's Note on Tigers

I spent a long time researching man-eating tigers before I started writing this book, and you know what? Honestly, I had to make the Mage-Eater considerably *less* scary than actual man-eaters.

Take, for instance, the Champawat Tiger. Or, tigress, really. She was the single deadliest man-eater on record, killing and eating at least 436 humans, averaging one a week for over a decade in Nepal and India. (Some of scholars think the number is even higher- 436 is what we can reputably *prove.*)

Most man eaters are wounded tigers, who are no longer capable of hunting the more dangerous large game they prefer, like water buffalo, wild boar, and even occasionally rhino and elephants. The Champawat Tiger lost a number of her fangs to a gunshot wound. (Seriously, whoever labeled humans the most dangerous game was being a bit egotistical— we're actually super easy to hunt, thanks to our relatively weak senses, slow movement, and lack of natural weapons.) The combination of old lingering wounds and expanding human presence is what generally drives most man-eaters to prey upon us.

It's also notable that man-eating tigers, especially the Champawat Tiger, rarely attack at night, favoring the daylight. Though if they are inclined to attack at night, they wouldn't have much trouble tearing through walls or doors to get to people. Tigers are by far the largest big cats, and they're absurdly strong, even for their size. They can easily kill with a single bite or swipe of their paws.

Unsurprisingly, there's a lot of conflicting and unknown information about how tigers hunt. You don't really want to get too close to that sort of thing, unless you want to risk pissing off the tiger. (Pissing off a hunting tiger or a mother tiger is a serious risk to tiger researchers, and often a fatal one.)

There is one major exception to the normal tiger hunting pattern- Sundarbans tigers. The Ylosa River Delta is in great part based off the tidal mangrove delta of the Sundarbans, in India and Bangladesh, where the world's only population of active man-eaters live. For some reason, tigers there (and nowhere else we know of) consider humans a perfectly reasonable part of their diet, and an average of fifty people die to tiger attack in the Sundarbans per year— at least, that are recorded. Sundarbans tigers have been even recorded swimming out into the Bay of Bengal to steal people off of boats— tigers are magnificent swimmers.

There's a lot of theories as to why Sundarbans tigers are the way they are, including from the fact the only water they have is brackish, but it's a bit of a long-winded discussion to have here.

The Mage-Eater is something of a mix of a Sundarbans tiger and a standard man-eater, with a bit of a vindictive streak that I think is quite reasonable to attribute to a cat. I also feel quite comfortable speculating that cats would be able to see magic if it were real.

Man-eating tigers are just too terrifying for me to have included without toning them down a bit— the reality is just too unbelievable.

For how horrifying man-eaters are, it's important to note that most tigers aren't man-eaters, and vastly prefer to avoid humans at all times. We should respect tigers, yes, but right now, they also need our help. Thanks to habitat loss and poaching, tiger numbers in the wild are dangerously low. They've started slowly climbing again after decades and decades of precipitous losses, but there are still less than four thousand alive in the wild worldwide.

Tigers are an essential part of their ecosystems, and, like other apex predators, serve a vital function in regulating herbivore populations. Losing them entirely would cause incalculable environmental damage. And, on a more sentimental level, a world without wild tigers would be a far sadder, less magical place.

I'll be donating a percentage of the proceeds of this book

to wild tiger conservation. (I normally donate 10% of my income to charity anyhow, so this will be on top of that.) If you have a little spare cash, I highly encourage you to do the same— you can, among other routes, adopt a tiger through the World Wildlife Fund.

I never want to see a wild tiger up close, but nor would I ever want to live in a world without any.

Afterword

Thank you so much for reading The Lost City of Ithos, Book 4 of Mage Errant!

We're moving into the endgame now- from here on out things are going to get crazy! Mage Errant is currently planned at 6 books and a short story collection, and with any luck, I'll have book 5, The Siege of Skyhold, out by the end of this year. (It's not like I've got much else to do at the moment but write— COVID-19 is back in Vietnam, so we're all back in lockdown at the moment. And there's only so many videogames I can play.)

If you enjoyed The Lost City of Ithos, please consider leaving a review online! Reviews, especially on Amazon and Goodreads, can make or break an indie author like myself.

If you have any questions or comments, please feel free to contact me at john.g.bierce@gmail.com, on Twitter (@john_bierce), or on Reddit (u/johnbierce). For news about the Mage Errant series, other upcoming works, and random thoughts about fantasy, worldbuilding, and whatever else pops in my mind, check out www.johnbierce.com. The best way to keep updated on new releases is to sign up for my mailing list, which you can find on my website. You can also discuss Mage Errant and my other books on the r/MageErrant subreddit!

I've also have a Patreon, which can be found at patreon.com/johnbierce. There, I post monthly Mage Errant short stories. (Including the story of The Wanderer, who gets briefly mentioned in this book!)

Edited by Paul Martin.

Cover art by Tithi Luadthong.

Cover design by James of GoOnwrite.com

Special thanks to my beta readers Jacob Perkins, Francis James Blair, Travis Riddle, Sarah Lin, Sundeep Agarwal, Eliot Moss, and Adam Skinner.

Additional special thanks to my Patreon backers Otto Schloegl, Diallo Bennett, Josh Fink, Andrew Alves, Andrew Cogan, Jeff Chang, Dylan Alexander, Cortney Railsback, David Kidd, Jacob William Perkins, Robert Rodabaugh, Jeff Petkau, Stephen Neville, Paolo Ruiz, Mikal Hofstad, Andreas F. Sørensen, Jeremy Miller, Kyle Matthews, Anika Howard, Andy Barnett, James Titterton, Ruediger Pakmor, Daniel Williams, Ryan Campbell, Cory Leigh Rahman, Joseph Lee, Scott C. Adams, Zachary Tilson, Nathaniel Ownbey, Marcus Thomas, and Florian Kotnik.

Reading Suggestions

If you enjoyed this book, here are a few others you might enjoy:

- Evan Winter's *The Rage of Dragons*: This book is, well, *intense.* It's a pretty classic vengeance tale setup, with a boy determined to avenge the unjust death of his father, and throwing himself wholesale into training to achieve his goals. Where this book shines is when it comes to execution- Winter does a fantastic job of exploring the emotional depths of vengeance, and the struggles real life can present in staying on that path. Not to mention, the African-inspired Bronze Age setting is one of the coolest settings I've encountered in a long, long time.
- Sarah Lin's *The Brightest Shadow*: Wuxia meets epic fantasy. Absolutely fantastic first volume in a doorstopper epic fantasy series. Fast-paced action, fascinating cultures and races, and, best of all, it's one of the few fantasy books I've encountered set on a prairie!
- Shami Stovall's *Frith Chronicles* series: Follows a gravedigger's son, Volke, as he seeks to become an Arcanist- a magic user whose power comes from bonding to magical creatures. Rather than the phoenix he'd been seeking, however, he finds himself linked to a very different magical creature, as he's put toe to toe against devious foes and a mysterious magical plague.
- F. James Blair's *Bulletproof Witch* series: Fast paced fantasy western series following a pistol witch who's hunting the demon that killed her family. Talking horses, magic duster jackets, demon

possessed outlaws, and magical gunfights galore.

- Blake Charlton's *Spellwright* trilogy: A fascinatingly clever and original setting, where magic is done via magical languages, where misspellings can have disastrous consequences. Which means that few look kindly on the protagonist, who happens to be magically dyslexic.
- John Bierce's *The Wrack*: Hey, look, it's one of mine! *The Wrack* is a depressing standalone epidemiological fantasy novel following a plague across the continent of Teringia. It… was pretty surreal releasing it alongside COVID-19, to say the least. Definitely not my plan there. The Wrack is part of the same multiverse, The Aetheriad, as Mage Errant, and you'll notice some really interesting and unusual crossovers between the two— though you don't need to read one to read the other.

If you'd like to learn more about tigers, I highly recommend:

- Dane Huckelbridge's *No Beast So Fierce*: A history of the Champawat Tiger, the deadliest killer of humans in history.
- Sy Montgomery's *Spell of the Tiger: The Man-Eaters of Sundarbans*: A fascinating exploration of the strange world of the Sundarbans mangrove forests, the man-eating tigers within it, and the beliefs and traditions of the people living alongside them.

Made in the USA
Middletown, DE
25 January 2023

23065192R00262